Acclaim for Ruth Reid

"Reid's second series installment (after *A Miracle of Hope*) works well as a tender romance with a bit of suspense. A solid pick for fans of Beverly Lewis and Melody Carlson."

—*Library Journal* on *A Woodland Miracle*

"Ruth Reid is skillful in portraying the Amish way of life as well as weaving together miracles with the everyday. In this book, she writes a beautiful tale of romance, redemption, and faith."

—Beth Wiseman, bestselling author of the Daughters of the Promise series, on *A Miracle of Hope*

"Ruth Reid pens a touching story of grace, love, and God's mercy in the midst of uncertainty. A must-read for Amish fiction fans!"

—Kathleen Fuller, bestselling author of the Hearts of Middlefield series, on *A Miracle of Hope*

"Reid gives readers the hope to believe that there are angels with every one of us, both good and evil, and that the good angels will always win."

—*RT Book Reviews* on *An Angel by Her Side*

"*An Angel by Her Side* brings together not only a protagonist's inner struggle, but the effect on the character from outside forces. In short, the reader rises, falls, grows, and learns alongside the story's champion."

—*Amish Country News Review*

"Reid has written a fine novel that provides, as its series title claims, a bit of 'heaven on earth.'"

—*Publishers Weekly* on *The Promise of an Angel*

A Woodland Miracle

Other Books by Ruth Reid

THE AMISH WONDERS NOVELS

A Miracle of Hope

A Woodland Miracle

A Dream of Miracles

THE HEAVEN ON EARTH NOVELS

The Promise of an Angel

Brush of Angel's Wings

An Angel by Her Side

NOVELLAS INCLUDED IN

An Amish Second Christmas

An Amish Miracle

An Amish Christmas Gift

A Woodland Miracle

An Amish Wonders Novel

Ruth Reid

Thomas Nelson

Since 1798

Published in Nashville, Tennessee, by Thomas Nelson. Thomas Nelson is a registered
trademark of HarperCollins Christian Publishing, Inc.

Thomas Nelson titles may be purchased in bulk for educational, business, fund-
raising, or sales promotional use. For information, please e-mail SpecialMarkets@
ThomasNelson.com.

Scripture quotations are taken from THE NEW KING JAMES VERSION. © 1982 by
Thomas Nelson, Inc. Used by permission. All rights reserved.

Publisher's Note: This novel is a work of fiction. Names, characters, places,
and incidents are either products of the author's imagination or used fictitiously.
All characters are fictional, and any similarity to people living or dead is purely
coincidental.

ISBN: 978-0-7180-9780-6 (repack)

Library of Congress Cataloging-in-Publication Data

Reid, Ruth, 1963-
  A Woodland miracle / Ruth Reid.
     pages ; cm. -- (The Amish wonders series)
  ISBN 978-1-4016-8830-1 (softcover)
1. Amish--Fiction. 2. Michigan--Fiction. I. Title.
PS3618.E5475W66 2015
813'.6--dc23

                         2014029128

Printed in the United States of America

17 18 19 20 21 LSC 5 4 3 2 1

I couldn't write a book about a man from Florida moving to northern Michigan without dedicating it to my own Florida man, Dan Reid, my husband and best friend. Although in our story, the northern Michigan girl moved to Florida. A move I haven't regretted. Dan, you've brought my life so much happiness and I'm blessed to be your wife. With all my love, Ruth

Glossary

ach: oh

aenti: aunt

Ausbund: Amish hymnal

boppli: baby

bruder: brother

bu, buwes: boy, boys

Budget, the: a weekly newspaper serving Amish and Mennonite
   communities

daed: dad or father

danki: thank you

dochder: daughter

doktah: doctor

dummkopp: dunce

Englischer: non-Amish

fraa: wife

geh: go

grossdaadi: grandfather

gudder mariye: good morning

gut: good

haus: house

hiya: a greeting

icehaus: icehouse

jah: yes

kaffi: coffee

kalt: cold

kapp: prayer cap worn by all Amish women

kinner: children

kumm: come

lieb: love

maedel: girl

mamm: mom or mother

mammi: grandmother

mei: my

nacht: night

narrisch: foolish

nau: now

nay: no

nett: not

onkel: uncle

Ordnung: the written and unwritten rules of the Amish; the understood behavior by which the Amish in the district are expected to live, passed down from generation to generation. Most Amish know the rules by heart.

outhaus: outhouse

Pennsylvania *Deitsch*: the language spoken by the Amish

redd-up: clean up

rumschpringe: running-around period that starts when a teenager turns sixteen years old and lasts until the person is ready to make a commitment to God and the Amish way

Schnell, verschteh?: Quickly, understand?

schul: school

smokehaus: smokehouse

sohn: son

wedder: weather

welkom: welcome

wunderbaar: wonderful

Chapter One

B en Eicher raked his fingers through his damp hair, then pushed his straw hat back into place. He snatched the shovel off the ground and sank it into the dirt. It wasn't even noon and the thermometer on the bank sign read ninety degrees. He glanced over at his buddy Toby, who seemed oblivious to the rising temperature. The first heat wave of the year, according to the DJ on the oldies rock station Ben had been listening to all morning.

Planting shrubs wasn't something he wanted to do the rest of his life. But neither was working for his father in his shoe-repair business. A year ago he worked on a commercial fishing boat. But that was prior to the hurricane. He liked the cool breeze, the scent of salt air, and the endless view of turquoise water. That sure beat digging holes.

Ben gauged the depth of the hole and tossed his shovel. He removed the pink azalea plant from the plastic starter pot and released some of the dirt from around its roots before dropping it into the hole.

Toby covered the plant with loose soil. "When we finish here, we're supposed to go to the deli and check if they have deliveries for us to make."

Ben shook his head. "When I finish here I'm either going to the beach, or I'm going to take a dip in the Tidewater Inn's pool."

"Tidewater's still closed." Toby tapped the mound of dirt around

1

the bush and stood. "Even if the construction was complete, the No Trespassing sign hasn't *kumm* down."

"That might be what the sign says, but they finished working on the pool. There's water in it." Ben lifted his shoulder and caught the roll of sweat trickling down the side of his face. He hoped these soaring temperatures in March didn't indicate a grueling summer ahead. If so, he planned to spend more time swimming.

Toby shook his head. "It's *nett* going to work out well."

"In this roasting heat, I'll take *mei* chances." Ben and Toby had been best friends for a number of years. Twenty-three, if you counted the diaper years when their mothers would get together to quilt and he and Toby shared the same crib during naptime.

"*When* you're caught, don't give the Amish a bad name in the community." Toby brushed the caked dirt off his knees. "Some of us want to stay and raise a family in Pinecraft, or at least have that option," he grumbled under his breath. Toby had changed in the past year. He talked more and more about settling down even though he wasn't courting anyone seriously.

Ben had convinced himself he wanted the same thing at this time last year. Now that Neva was gone, nothing much mattered. Ben pulled a hankie from his pocket and wiped the sweat off his brow. He glanced at the dirty residue on the cloth, then jammed it back into his pocket. Dirty, sticky, and perspiring like the morning's dew, he needed to rinse off. He grabbed the shovel, paced off a few feet, and dug the next hole.

The next time he stopped to look at the sun's position, he figured it was sometime after two. His mouth was parched, his muscles ached, and his sweat-soaked shirt clung to his skin. He couldn't wait to dig the last hole.

A few moments later, Ben tossed his shovel in the small utility cart attached to Toby's bicycle. "I think it's time for that swim. What about you?"

"I'm definitely hot." His friend tipped his beet-red face toward the sun and squinted. "But we should head over to the deli. You got me in trouble the last time we skipped work, remember?"

How could he forget? Ben's father lectured him for days about his lack of responsibility. But that incident paled in comparison to the time he kept Neva out all night. He could still hear the elevation of his father's voice. *What were you thinking? I have no respect for a man who—who places a maedel in a compromising situation.*

Toby backhanded Ben in the chest, leaving his dirty handprint on Ben's shirt. "Let's get a soda."

"*Nay.*" Ben shook his head. "I'm going swimming."

"You're just itching to get in trouble."

Ben peeled his clinging shirt away from his chest. "I'm itching to get out of these sweaty clothes." Toby should understand why Ben still avoided the deli. *Mercy* wasn't part of Neva's parents' vocabulary— toward him anyway. Besides, he'd rather be swimming.

The Tidewater Inn was one of the few remaining resorts along the coast that hadn't reopened since the hurricane. Ben had snuck onto the grounds and swum plenty of times before it closed, but he hadn't had a chance to swim there since it was rebuilt.

"Sure you don't want to cool off?"

Toby picked at the dirt under his fingernails. "I want to, but . . ."

"You're always teetering." Ben wiped the back of his neck with his hankie. He wasn't about to spend all day waiting for Toby to decide. "Don't be so indecisive. Either it's yes or no."

Ben waited a moment, then released the kickstand on his bike. "You know where to find me."

Ben pedaled down the sidewalk until he reached the motel. He laid his bike down in the bushes and climbed over the fence. Minutes later, he shucked all his clothes but his briefs and gingerly eased into the cool water, giving his body time to adjust. Once he was waist deep, he plunged down to the bottom of the shallow end. He swam a few laps, then flipped over and floated on his back. He closed his eyes and relaxed. This was so much better than pedaling his bike in the heat delivering stuff that one of the younger boys could do.

"Cannonball!" Toby's thundering voice called out midair.

Rocked by the wave created when Toby landed in the pool, Ben dipped under the surface of the water and came up sputtering. "You could've given me better warning."

"Feels *gut* to cool off." Toby dipped back under, then resurfaced, shaking his mass of poodle-like curly hair like a wet dog.

Ben cupped his hand and splashed his friend.

Toby returned fire, and neither of them noticed the police officer until he spoke.

"You two climb out of the pool, then put your hands up where I can see them."

Trudging through the water toward the stairs, Ben glanced over his shoulder at Toby. His friend's sobered expression and downcast eyes seared Ben's soul. He shouldn't have teased Toby about being indecisive. Ben climbed out of the pool and stood before the officer as puddles of water collected at his feet. At least Toby had jumped in fully dressed. Ben stood before the man wearing only his briefs. Maybe he could ask to dress before their eviction. He eyed his hat and clothes piled next to a potted ficus tree.

The officer peered over his sunglasses. "What are you two doing here?"

"We wanted to cool off in the pool," Ben said.

"You didn't read the No Trespassing signs? This area is off-limits."

"We were only going to stay a few minutes." Ben shivered when the breeze hit his wet body.

"And I suppose you don't know anything about the rash of break-ins?"

Ben and Toby exchanged glances. "*Nay,*" they replied in unison.

"Are those your clothes over there? Let's see some form of ID."

"We don't have any," Ben said. "We're Amish."

The officer pressed a button near his shoulder and talked into a microphone clipped to his shirt. "Dispatch, this is beach patrol two-nine. I'll need transport for two males found trespassing at the Tidewater Inn."

"Ten-four." A moment later, the woman's voice returned. "Two-nine, be advised there is an officer in the area. ETA five minutes."

Ben wasn't sure what the abbreviations meant, but he was pretty sure he only had five minutes to talk the officer into letting them go. He cleared his throat. "Are we in trouble?"

"You have the right to remain silent. Anything you say can be used against you in a court of law. You have the right to an attorney . . ."

Ben swallowed hard. So many rights. He just wanted the right to put on his clothes. This wouldn't be easy to explain to his parents. Most Amish men at twenty-three were married, starting a family, and well respected in their district. He wasn't any of those things.

Ben waited until the police officer finished reciting the long list of rights, then pointed to his clothes. "Would it be all right if I get dressed?"

The officer crossed the pool deck and grabbed the items. Inspecting Ben's hat, the officer's bushy brows formed a straight line. "What do we have here?" He tipped the hat toward them, exposing the small radio Ben had attached to the inside. "Trying to hide stolen merchandise?"

"*Nay*—sir. I bought that portable radio at a pawn shop." Ben turned to Toby, who looked away. "You were with me. Back me up," he hissed under his breath. He might be guilty of breaking a few Amish rules like owning a radio, but he abided by the government laws. Ben would never steal.

Toby stared at the pool deck, his lips tight.

The officer patted the clump of Ben's clothes. He removed the suspenders, then tossed Ben his trousers. Still dripping wet, Ben shoved his legs into his pants and waited for his shirt.

Soon after Ben finished dressing, another officer arrived and directed them to a waiting squad car. Shuttled to the station and separated from his friend, Ben kept his mouth shut. Goose bumps crawled up his arms as he stood in the air-conditioned building. Ben rubbed his arms and bit down on his bottom lip to keep his teeth from chattering. At least he was dressed.

Once searched, fingerprinted, and questioned, the guard led Ben to the holding cell. The stench of alcohol and vomit assaulted his senses. The guard nudged him forward, and once he was past the gate, it clanged shut. He took a seat on the metal bench beside Toby.

His friend sat with his elbows on his knees and his face buried in his hands.

Ben cleared his throat. "I guess swimming wasn't such a *gut* idea."

Toby lifted his head, shot him a sidelong glare, then covered his face again.

Ben glanced at the others sharing the cell. One man, wearing a sleeveless T-shirt, had a tattooed snake that wrapped around his neck. His arms were canvased in colored ink with something Ben couldn't make out, and he didn't want to risk staring for fear the man might come over to their end of the cell. Another man sat hunched over in the corner, probably asleep, though Ben had no idea how anyone could sleep with the racket another person was making as he paced the floor mumbling gibberish to himself.

Toby had the right idea to hang his head and remain silent. Ben did the same. Now if he could only quiet his mind. Thoughts about what he would tell his parents passed the time, but he had no resolution.

Several hours later, an officer approached the cell. His keys rattled as he unlocked the steel door. "Benjamin Eicher and Toby Graber?"

Ben sucked in a breath and stood.

"The motel owner didn't want to press charges," the officer said. "You two are free to go."

Ben blew out a breath. "Thank you."

"I suggest from now on you stay off private property."

"We will." Ben meant it too. The next time he wanted to cool off, he would do so with a garden hose.

Toby rolled his eyes at Ben, then shoved past him and walked out without a backward glance.

Ben wanted as far away from the police station as possible. Hopefully their parents wouldn't find out where they had spent their afternoon. But once he stepped into the lobby, he realized keeping anything a secret wouldn't be possible. Ben's and Toby's fathers stood up from the bench.

While Toby's father quizzed his son, Ben's *daed* looked him over hard.

"Why are your clothes *nett* wet like Toby's?"

Ben stared at the scuff marks on the floor.

"I asked you a question," his father said.

"I didn't swim in them."

As expected, his father harrumphed at the answer, then headed for the door. Ben had seen his father's shoulders slump a number of times, but never like this. Without uttering a word, Ben and Toby trailed their fathers outside. Streetlights illuminated the sidewalk outside the police station. It was later than he thought. Ben climbed into their neighbor's parked van.

The ride home was silent. Ben's father never spoke about personal matters—or in Ben's case, his son's shortcomings—in front of *Englischers*. Once they were home though, he braced for a long lecture. Instead, his *daed* treated him as though he were poison. When Ben sat down for supper, his father rose from his chair and left the kitchen. Even his *mamm* couldn't convince *Daed* to eat with the family.

The following morning, Ben found his parents seated at the table, his mother blotting a hankie over her eyes and his father stoic. Ben's stomach tightened. "I'm sorry." In most homes, an admission of wrongdoing and an apology would elicit some form of forgiveness, but neither parent responded.

His father pushed back his chair and stood. "You have less than an hour to pack your bags."

Pack? Where was he going? He had two older sisters, both married and living in Indiana. He would only be in the way living with them.

"We're sending you to work in a lumber camp."

Ben swallowed hard. The only lumber camp he'd ever heard about was in northern Michigan, where Toby's uncle lived. It seemed drastic, even for his father, to send him so far away.

"I suggest you pack warm clothes," his father said. "You might be there awhile."

⁂

Badger Creek District, Michigan

Grace Wagler stood inside the station next to the window and studied the passengers as they disembarked from the bus. She had another half hour to wait before her aunt's bus arrived. Grace had planned for more time to do her morning chores so she wouldn't be late, but finished them sooner than she'd expected.

The automatic doors opened and, along with arriving passengers, a gust of wind swept through the building. Grace sidestepped the foot traffic and limped a few feet over to an empty bench. She would move if an elderly person needed to sit, but for the moment, she needed to rest. Days like today she felt older than dirt. The unforgiving concrete floor triggered agony in her joints that no one in their twenties should experience. Grace rubbed the length of her thigh, then massaged her left knee. Swollen. Sometimes she wished she didn't live in such a cold climate. Lately it seemed the winters were longer and her inflamed joints stiffer.

A *beep—beep—beep* from a wall-mounted television caught her attention. A newscaster standing outside of a hospital was speaking, but the low volume on the set made it impossible to hear his report. Normally, if she were anywhere near a television, she would ignore the programming, but a flashing red banner at the bottom of the screen read Breaking News.

Someone close by cleared his throat and she jerked her hand away from her leg. Two men stood before her. Their teeth chattered as they rubbed their hands over their bare arms.

"Excuse me," the taller man with blond hair said.

Her gaze traveled between the two men, landing on the one who spoke. "Me?"

"You're Amish, *jah*?" The man smirked.

Usually only *Englischers* asked that. These two men had on suspenders and wore straw hats, but *if* they were Amish, they were fence-jumpers. She hadn't known any district to allow short-sleeved shirts. The *Ordnung* she followed forbade clothes that showed any skin.

Grace glanced around the depot trying to spot someone from her settlement, then chided herself. The men hadn't returned from the river camp and most of the women had started spring-cleaning. Still, she shouldn't be talking with strangers, especially not backsliders.

Someone turned up the volume on the television. ". . . Again, the man is unstable, has a history of violent outbursts, and is considered extremely dangerous."

The blond man glanced at the television.

Grace pushed off the bench. Shards of needle pricks pierced her leg as she wobbled to the other side of the room. She leaned against the wall next to the window and eased out a breath. The blond-haired man pursued her across the lobby, while the one with curly, dark hair stayed with their duffel bags.

"I'm sorry," the man said. "I didn't mean to sound flip. It's just that we've been traveling three days, so I hope you'll forgive me if I seem rushed to leave the bus station."

Goose bumps crawled up Grace's arms. Now she really wished

someone from her district were in the station. She'd never known an Amish man to be this persistent.

Unstable. The news reporter's words rolled over in her mind. *Just a coincidence.* She should have turned away from the television. Grace glanced out the window. He probably wouldn't follow her outside, not shivering like he was.

The man cleared his throat. "So, where are you parked?"

Chapter Two

W here did you park?" Ben repeated the question slower, and this time in Pennsylvania *Deitsch*. But that didn't elicit a response. The Amish woman's unblinking eyes were as cold as the inside of an ice chest and brown like the color an apple turns when it goes bad.

"So, I take it you're *nett*—"

A scratchy overhead voice broadcasting a bus arrival drowned out Ben's words. He waited, but as the announcement repeated, she turned and scurried out the door.

Skittish pup. She acted as though she had never spoken with a man and she had to be in her twenties. Florida Amish were much more pleasant to strangers than this woman was being to him. He hoped the members of Badger Creek were more welcoming. Ben started to follow her, but stopped when she greeted an older woman who had just stepped off a bus. Obviously, she hadn't been sent to pick up him and Toby. Ben shook his head and walked back into the station.

Toby clapped Ben's shoulder. "Don't worry. If no one comes to get us, I found someone who will give us a ride. He doesn't get off work for an hour, but he said it would take that long to get a cab."

Ben rubbed his arms to warm them. "Let's find a vending machine and get something to drink."

"So, what district is that woman from?"

"I couldn't get her to talk." Ben turned to look out the window. "She's an icy one."

"Or maybe you've lost your charm."

Ben shrugged. Under different circumstances he'd return the jab, but this was the most Toby had talked since they boarded the bus a couple of days ago. Sore at the world—but mostly at Ben— Toby had no sense of adventure. It would take some time to get adapted to the cold weather, but leaving Florida wasn't so bad. Ben just wished the circumstances of their departure had been different. His *daed* drove him to the bus station, but never said good-bye or even wished him well.

Jah, he was ready for a fresh start. Provided his reputation hadn't preceded him.

❧

Grace grabbed the two twine-tied boxes once the bus attendant had removed them from the cargo area. She lugged them a few feet out of the way of the other passengers and set the boxes down, her arms tingling with numbness.

"Let me carry one," *Aenti* Erma said.

"*Nay*. I'm fine." Grace switched the heavier box to her opposite hand, which helped to even out her balance. "Ready?"

Her aunt nodded and they headed toward the parking lot.

Grace scanned the area. After the stranger practically stalked her in the station, she didn't want to linger in the parking lot. The wooden lift her father had attached to the bottom of her shoe had worn down to a nub and hindered her stride. Her legs felt like they were fifty-pound bags of grain, but she pushed herself to increase her pace. Even so, *Aenti* Erma not only kept up, but her breathing wasn't as labored.

"You seem to be limping more," *Aenti* Erma said. "Are you doing all right?"

Grace glanced at the dark clouds directly overhead. "Just want to make it to the buggy before it rains or snows again." Lately the weather had been unpredictable, alternating between sleet and snow. The long season Grace spent nursing her aching joints had made her miserable enough at times to consider her aunt's offer to join her in Ohio. In the past, she had dismissed the notion, but since Philemon shared his upcoming engagement plans prior to leaving for camp, the idea of moving was tempting. Philemon must have known she would need time to adjust to the news.

A mist of frigid rain sprayed her face. But Grace's legs hurt too much to go any faster.

"Are you sure you don't want me to carry one of those boxes?"

Grace shook her head. "I'm fine." The buggy was close by and if she didn't use her muscles she feared they would shrivel like her mother's had. Besides, it wasn't like she had never been caught in a downpour before. It had rained the past five days. Grace motioned ahead. "*Aenti*, please don't wait for me. Get in the buggy where it's dry."

Not watching her feet, Grace stepped into a depression in the pavement. The thin layer of ice broke and the puddle of water splashed on the hem of her dress.

"I'll get the buggy door." At fifty-two, *Aenti* sped past her with ease.

At twenty-two, less than half her aunt's age, Grace's limp made her feel frail and decrepit. *Aenti* was "full of juice," as *Mamm* used to joke about her younger sister's energy. But it wasn't the age difference that separated the sisters' abilities—*Aenti* Erma wasn't plagued with the same illness, which left Grace's mother wheelchair bound and ultimately stole her life.

Grace loaded the crates into the back end of the buggy. By the time she had Jasper untied from the tree branch and she was seated on the bench, Grace was drenched. She looked down at her wet cloak and the bottom of her dress clinging to her legs. "Well, we almost made it."

"I'm surprised you don't have more snow. It's certainly *kalt* enough." Her aunt cupped her hands in front of her mouth and blew on them.

"After five days of sleet, most of the snow has melted." Grace reached behind the seat for the extra pair of gloves and handed them to her aunt.

Aenti Erma slipped her hands into the knitted wool gloves. "I misplaced *mei* gloves somewhere between the first bus stop and here. I had them when I left Middlefield."

"How is your cousin doing?"

"Better *nau* that the cast has been removed. The *doktah* was pleased with how well her leg healed and said she shouldn't have to use the crutches for more than a week or two."

"That is *gut* news."

Aenti smiled. "I didn't expect a two-month delay. How were you able to manage?"

"We did fine." *Aenti* had a big heart for taking care of people in need. She started splitting her months between staying in Ohio and living with them in Badger Creek prior to *Mamm's* passing away and had returned every year since.

Grace used her free hand to rub her leg, trying to relax her knotted muscles.

"Your legs are getting worse."

Grace stopped massaging her leg and grasped the reins with both hands. "This *kalt*, damp weather always gives me more problems." So did carting heavy crates across a parking lot.

Aenti frowned. "Has this last winter been hard?"

"Long." Grace forced a smile. She didn't want to talk about her physical limitations. Those thoughts only reminded her of how her mother's condition started when she was Grace's age and how much she had suffered with muscular dystrophy during her final years. "The maple trees are starting to produce sap."

"You know that's *nett* why I asked."

"*Aenti*, we have this conversation every time you arrive and we'll have it again before you leave. So, before you tell me how much better *mei* joints would be living in a milder climate, I'll just tell you *nau*, I can't move to Ohio. I have responsibilities at home, a job at the lumberyard—I have more orders for dog beds than I can handle. Besides," she said, pausing a moment to calm her rising voice, "I'm taking care of *mei* nephews. Susan's mother took a hard fall on the ice last month and she's still *nett* moving around well."

"You must think of *your* health, *mei* dear child."

"It snows in Middlefield too." A flimsy excuse, but *Aenti* had to know by now that Grace wouldn't change her mind—she couldn't. Who would look out for LeAnn when her father and brothers spent five months out of the year at the timber camp?

Her aunt shivered. "I can't get used to how *kalt* it is up here."

Aenti's teeth chattered much like the man's had at the bus station. If he hadn't talked down to her, speaking slow in Pennsylvania *Deitsch* like she didn't understand English, maybe she would have listened. It was just as well that *Aenti's* bus arrived when it did. Grace wouldn't want her aunt thinking she associated with fence-jumpers.

The low fog hovered over the road and decreased visibility, but Jasper knew the way home. She hoped the dirt road leading to their settlement wasn't flooded. Several days of rain along with the runoff of melting snow had filled the drainage ditch. Her thoughts shifted to her father and brothers at the timber camp. Cutting trees in the rain was more dangerous. The men would be wet and cold . . .

"You're awfully quiet," her aunt said. "Is something wrong?"

"Just wondering how this rain will affect the work at the timber camp."

The men planned the trip according to the thickness of ice on the river. Over the years, Grace had heard plenty of stories of the ice cracking beneath them because they waited too long to begin the journey home. Last year they sent the dogs across first, pulling an empty sled while the men belly-crawled across the frozen water with the supplies tied to their ankles to disperse the weight.

Grace shuddered.

Frozen or not, she hated the river. She hadn't dipped so much as a toe in the water in over five years. And she never would.

"Are you concerned about anyone in particular?" Her aunt let the question linger so Grace would fill in the blank about Philemon.

Aenti probably thought that was the real reason she hadn't wanted to move to Ohio—but just the opposite was true. When her childhood friend made her privy to his intentions to marry Becky Lapp once he returned from camp, Grace battled thoughts of fleeing to Ohio to live with her aunt. At least long enough to mend her broken heart.

"Well?" *Aenti* prompted.

"Of course I'm concerned about *Daed* and Emery and Peter."

"And Philemon?"

"Philemon and *all* the men at camp. We should have seen a signal by *nau.*" Until their settlement devised a way to signal one another, the women had constantly fretted during the months the men were away. At least now when one of the boys spotted the chemically colored smoke, everyone knew the men were closing down the camp and heading back.

"Be anxious for *nothing.*" Aunt Erma often quoted the Bible verse and more so when the ice on the river melted faster than usual.

"I've been praying." Grace's prayers started just after the men had left—for a safe cutting season and that she would have a pure heart when Philemon returned to marry the girl he loved.

"They're in God's hands." Aunt Erma reached across the seat and patted Grace's leg. "Nothing is solved with worry."

Grace nodded. "*Mamm* used to say those exact words."

"And you will one day tell your children that same thing."

If she ever had children, Grace wanted to encourage their faith as her mother had hers. But marriage wasn't likely—not living in a settlement where the women outnumbered the men three to one. Who would want someone in her condition? Philemon didn't. She always wanted their friendship to blossom into more—even prayed for him to see the special connection they shared. But befriending a clumsy little girl out of pity was one thing—seeing her differently when she grew up, wanting to marry her despite a limp, was ludicrous.

Grace slowed Jasper as they neared the road leading to the settlement. The moment she turned, the buggy wheel sank into the soft ground. It didn't seem to matter how many rocks they used to fill the holes, the by-product of winter was thick, slippery, sludge-like goo.

The buggy dipped to the opposite side. *Aenti* Erma jostled on the bench, arms flailing.

"Hold on." Grace veered the horse to one side, the wheel running the ridge of the ditch. She managed to dodge a water-filled hole of questionable depth, but wasn't able to steer them clear of the low-hanging tree limb.

Aenti Erma gasped as the branches scraped the buggy's rooftop.

Grace caught a glimpse of her aunt's wide-eyed stare at the road ahead. "Are you okay?"

"*Jah.*" *Aenti's* face paled. She had never liked going down this narrow road in the buggy.

They still had another bend before they reached the area where the road split. The forked section always flooded first, and judging by the puddles so far, the ride might get bouncier yet.

Jasper picked up his pace rounding the bend. Grace gripped the reins tighter and slowed the horse. A few feet ahead, water encroached from both sides of the road. Unearthed roots webbed the narrow passage. Afraid they'd get stuck if she stopped, Grace clucked her tongue. Rolling over a large root, the wheel thumped. Then something cracked.

❧

The rhythmic swish of the windshield wipers lulled Ben's senses, and he yawned. After traveling three days confined to a cramped seat on a bus, he was exhausted.

The driver, or Clutch, as he said his friends called him, adjusted the wiper speed to match the downpour. "I imagine you've seen plenty of rain like this, living in Florida."

Ben nodded. "But never this cold." Three days ago it was ninety degrees and he would have welcomed rain.

Clutch pressed a button on the dashboard and the vents blasted hot, dry air. "Better?"

"Yes, thanks." Ben repositioned the passenger side vent toward the back, then glanced over his shoulder at Toby. "Can you feel it?"

"I'm fine."

Ben gazed out the window. Trees. He already missed the white, sandy beach, the salty scent of the ocean, the sun. At least Florida wasn't this overcast and gloomy.

"I suppose while you were waiting for a ride, you heard on the news about the crazy man escaping the mental ward." The driver peered into his rearview mirror. "I heard about it right after I said I'd give you a lift."

"We really appreciate the ride," Toby said.

Clutch steered the car with one hand and tapped his leg to the beat of the music blaring out of the speakers with his other. "Wasn't sure if I should trust you or not, you know what I mean?" He snorted. "Wouldn't want to accidentally give a lunatic a ride."

Ben eyed Clutch. The *Englischer* wasn't much older than Ben and Toby, but he wheezed like he had the lungs of an eighty-year-old with pneumonia, and everything he said ended with a nervous laugh or snort.

A moment later, the driver pulled to the shoulder of the road. "Sorry to drop you off in the rain, but this is as far as I can take you. I've gotten stuck on that road before."

Ben looked out of the passenger window at the road. He'd seen bike paths wider—and paved. "How far is it?"

"Half mile."

"We appreciate you taking us this far," Toby said. "How much do we owe you?"

Clutch shook his head. "Just being neighborly. Don't worry about it."

Ben and Toby thanked him and climbed out of the car with their bags.

Ben shivered. At least the rain was warm in Florida. Here it felt more like an ice pelting. "I can't believe we were swimming the other day."

"Don't remind me." Toby tromped down the trail, grumbling under his breath.

"I didn't force you to jump in the pool." Ben's foot sank into the soft ground and made a sucking noise when he pulled his shoe out.

"*Nay*, but you poked fun at me for being indecisive."

"We're here *nau*, and there's nothing we can do about it. Let's make the best of it." Ben's other foot sank, this time past his ankle. Why would anyone choose to live this far into the woods? On a washed-out road? Ben stumbled over an exposed root. No wonder the driver refused to take his car down this path.

The rain turned into a drizzle. Still cold and miserable, Ben and Toby hiked in silence, but the birds chirped like they had something to celebrate.

Reaching a fork in the road, Toby sighed. "*Nau* which way?"

"*Gut* question." The tease of sunlight that poked out from the clouds would fade behind the trees in mere minutes. The wrong direction could mean their sleeping outside. Ben motioned to the right. "Those look like fresh tracks."

His friend inspected the ground, then looked at him. "How can you tell?"

Ben shrugged. He was freezing. Any tracks, fresh or otherwise, meant someone lived around here. They needed to keep walking and hope that the road led to an Amish farm. Doubts formed about Clutch. This wasn't a half-mile hike—it was closer to two.

The wind shifted. Ben sniffed. Smoke. "Do you smell that? Something's burning." He picked up his pace, his foot sliding in the mud. How could anything burn after all this rain?

Finally, nestled between a copse of birch trees, a cabin came into view. Tendrils of smoke curled from a stone chimney. Someone was home. Ben took in the primitive surroundings as they neared the dwelling. An empty clothesline, which stretched between two poles, waved in the wind. A few yards away sat an old barn. A horse poked his head out of the stall door and neighed. Three small shacks took up most of the property. One had wood piled against the side of the building. Another looked like it might house equipment, and the smallest shed had a pipe protruding from the roof. This certainly wasn't anything like Florida where his mother's flowers lined the side of the house and his father repaired shoes inside an aluminum shed. He peered up at the sky. Nothing like Florida. He couldn't even find the sun with so many dark clouds in the sky.

Toby knocked on the door. "I hope this is *mei onkel's haus*. I don't feel like walking anymore."

"Neither do I." Ben spotted a woman leaving the barn and nudged his friend. The woman's head was aimed at the ground and she gingerly carried a steaming pot. Approaching the porch steps, she glanced up and stopped abruptly, sloshing amber liquid over the side of the pot.

"Sorry, we didn't mean to startle"—Ben furrowed his brow—"you."

Chapter Three

Grace suppressed a cry when the hot solution from the steaming pot soaked into her dress and burned her skin. She narrowed her eyes at the men standing before her. "Who are you? And why are you following me?"

"I'm Toby Graber." The curly-haired man motioned to the pot. "Would you like me to carry that?"

She shook her head.

The door opened. "I thought I heard someone knock." *Aenti* Erma waved them inside. "*Kumm* in where it's warm."

"*Ah* . . . they are—" No use trying to object. The men had stomped their feet and were heading inside.

The taller one removed his straw hat, exposing a mop of blond hair that offset his tan skin. He eyed Grace. "You didn't get burned, did you?"

Grace followed his gaze to the oily spot on her waistline where she'd spilled the poultice. "*Nay.*" She crossed the room at an even pace, but once she placed the pot on the counter, her legs trembled such that she needed to lean against the cabinet for support.

"Nice place you have," the one who hadn't introduced himself said, directing the comment to *Aenti* Erma.

"*Danki.*" *Aenti's* gaze dropped to the man's duffel bag. "I, ah . . ." Perhaps she was figuring out that they were not from this district.

"I'm Grace's *Aenti* Erma," she said, finding her voice again. "You can set your things by the door." She turned to Grace. "Why don't you offer your friends a cup of *kaffi*."

Grace shifted so that only her aunt could see her face and mouthed, *No*.

"*Danki*, but we can't stay," Toby said.

The other man set his bag down anyway. His eyes wandered over every nook of the kitchen. "*Mei mamm* used to talk about cooking on a woodstove where she grew up." He cleared his throat. "I'm Ben Eicher."

Toby stepped forward. "We've traveled from Florida to visit *mei onkel*. Alvin Graber. Do you know him?"

"*Jah*," Grace said with reserve. She still wasn't sure about the purpose of their visit. Anyone traveling such a great distance would have made arrangements.

"He's at the timber camp," *Aenti* said.

Why did her aunt offer detailed information? Grace cleared her throat. "That's right. He's *nett* home. And his *haus* is locked."

"Great," Ben muttered under his breath.

Toby cringed. "How far is the camp from here?"

Aenti Erma tapped the ladder-back wooden chair. "A few miles upriver. You two have a seat and I'll bring you a cup of *kaffi*."

"If the camp is a few miles away," Toby said, looking at Ben, "we should get going."

Jah, they should. But Grace couldn't live with herself if she allowed them to wander into danger. Even if they found the area of the river that was still iced over, crossing at night wasn't a good idea. "You won't make it across the river. *Nett* with all the rain we've had."

Aunt Erma motioned to the chairs. "Please, have a seat."

The floor squeaked under Ben's wet shoes as he moved to the table and sat. Toby hesitated a moment longer, but finally left his bag by the door and sat next to Ben.

Aenti Erma filled two mugs with coffee.

Both men sat straighter in their chairs when Grace's younger sister, LeAnn, breezed into the room.

LeAnn greeted them with a cheerful smile. "*Hiya.*"

"Hello," the men said in unison, their attention solely on her. "I'm Ben and this is Toby."

"It's nice to meet you. I'm LeAnn."

Grace pulled a wooden spoon from the drawer and stirred the simmering poultice. The pungent odor caused her eyes to water. Her friend Mattie had given her the ingredients and liniment recipe, something Mattie had developed using dried herbs. Grace wasn't sure wrapping the medicated rags around her legs would help decrease the inflammation in her joints, but the eye-watering scent surely cleared her sinuses.

Overhearing LeAnn sigh when the visitors said they were from Florida grated Grace's nerves. What was her sister thinking flirting with these men? Grace peeked over her shoulder.

LeAnn sat with her elbows propped on the table and her chin resting in her hands. "Have you seen a shark?"

"A few." Ben sipped his coffee.

Six-year-old Jonas shuffled into the room. He took one look at the strangers and sidled up beside Grace. Normally, she didn't mind her nephew using her dress skirt as a safe haven. After all, the extra material she used to add fullness and length enough to reach the floor offered more yardage than a tent. But with strangers here, she didn't want him wrapping around her dress and uncovering her shoes— especially not the homemade shoe on her left foot.

"How blue is the ocean?" LeAnn's questions continued.

Ben smiled. "It ranges. Near the shore it's a bluish green and out in the deep area it's dark blue. About the color of your eyes."

A soft shade of pink colored LeAnn's face. "I would love to see it."

At seventeen, her sister already had a curious, and often wandering, spirit. Sitting forward in her chair, gazing doe-eyed, LeAnn's mannerisms now practically begged them to lead her astray. Grace clanged the spoon against the pot, venting her frustration. "LeAnn, shouldn't you be helping with supper?"

Her sister stood.

"Set two more plates," *Aenti* Erma said. "I'm sure our visitors are hungry."

Grace groaned under her breath. Offering a weary traveler a meal was the right thing to do, but why did this remind her of the time they fed a stray dog and it never left?

The kitchen door opened and her ten-year-old nephew Mitch entered. Since the weather had changed, Mitch and a few other boys spent their after-school hours down by the river watching for when the ice melted and for a signal from the men. He removed his jacket and hung it on the wall peg.

"Anything to report?" Grace asked.

Mitch shook his head as he unlaced his boots.

Grace's heart ached for her nephew. Mitch had asked his father multiple times if he could go to camp this year, but Peter wouldn't allow him to miss the last few months of school.

Aenti Erma placed her hand on Mitch's shoulder. "Will you please show our guests where they can wash for supper?"

Ben and Toby stood and followed Mitch out of the kitchen. A few minutes later, the three of them returned and sat back down, deep in a conversation about fishing. Grace had to hush her nephew so they could bless the meal.

Once Ben and Toby started eating, Grace refrained from bringing attention to how fast they shoveled food into their mouths. They only paused long enough to answer LeAnn and *Aenti* Erma's barrage of questions. Grace could think of a few, too, like how long ago had they jumped the fence? And what drove them so far from home? Hiding from something, or someone, no doubt.

Ben scraped his plate, collecting the last morsel of mashed potatoes on his fork.

LeAnn snatched the bowl off the table and passed it to him. "Would you like more?"

He boldly refilled his plate. "*Danki*, this is really *gut*."

"So, how long do you plan to stay?" LeAnn fluttered her lashes and smiled.

Grace glared at her sister, but she turned away. Her sister's defiant spirit needed caging. At least when Grace pinned Ben with the same stare, he shifted in his chair and redirected his attention to his plate.

Toby finished his milk and set the empty glass on the table. "Our stay depends on how much work *mei onkel* Alvin has for us." He turned to Grace. "Did he say how long he would be camping?"

Grace set her fork on her plate. "It's a lumber camp. They—he left at the first of the year." She stopped short from disclosing that all the men, with the exception of the bishop, were gone. Obviously, Mr. Graber wasn't expecting company.

"I wanted to go." Mitch pushed his peas around on his plate. "But *mei daed* said I was too young."

Grace tapped Mitch's hand. "Stop playing with your food and eat. You have *schul* work to do."

Aenti Erma blotted her mouth with the napkin. "I'm sure the bishop will be able to offer guidance in the morning."

Grace widened her eyes at her aunt. "The morning?"

"Bishop Yoder's place is too difficult for them to find on their own." Her aunt's voice sharpened. "And it's too dark to take the buggy down that road. The poor horse might break a leg."

Her aunt had a point. Unless they knew which path to take through the woods, they would get twisted around on state land and maybe never find the bishop's *haus*. Still, Bishop Yoder should be made aware tonight. After all, they were a household of women. It wouldn't look right. Grace glanced across the table at Ben, then Toby. Their eyes drooped like Rusty's, the coonhound. Sad. Pitiful. "I suppose you can bunk in the loft."

"Or they could take *mei* room," her sister offered.

Before Grace could reject the suggestion, the men chorused, "*Nay.*"

LeAnn blushed. "It was just a thought. I don't mind sharing a room with *mei* sister. Unless"—she crinkled her nose at Grace—"you plan to wear that . . . wretched-smelling balm to bed."

Grace furrowed her brow. LeAnn never missed an opportunity to point out Grace's infirmity. As if these men couldn't detect her limp on their own. Long hours on her feet and cold weather always stiffened her joints.

"*Danki*," Ben said. "But we don't want to inconvenience anyone. You've already done enough."

Ben smiled at Grace, but his eyes mirrored the same pitiful gaze she'd seen from every man in their district. Her chest tightened at the thought of how blinded she had been about her friendship with Philemon. Growing up, he'd protected her from the other boys' teasing, but when she reached courting age, Philemon's attention felt more like pity. Grace chided herself. She should be used to the sympathetic smiles, but it still hurt. She recited the scripture that her mother found comfort in during her infirmity. *My grace is sufficient . . . For My strength is made perfect in weakness.*

"Maybe our guests would like one of your cookies, Grace." *Aenti* Erma motioned to Ben's glass. "Would you like more milk?"

Ben nodded. "Sure."

His easy smile gave the impression that not only was he used to the attention LeAnn and *Aenti* lavished on him, but he enjoyed it. If he discovered that women outnumbered men three to one in their settlement, he might never leave.

Grace pushed away from the table, but LeAnn jumped up and grabbed the cookie jar first. Just as well, her legs throbbed.

LeAnn removed the lid to the cookie jar and held it before Ben, who pretended to grab a fistful, then to Toby, who nodded and took one.

While Ben was playful, Toby's mannerism was more in line with the Amish way. Even so, Grace wouldn't trust either of the fence-jumpers.

A knock sounded on the door, then her sister-in-law, Susan, stepped inside. "The road is washing out," she said, wiping her feet on the braided rug. She moved farther into the room and stopped. "Oh, hello." Her gaze darted between Toby and Ben, then over to Grace. "I didn't know you had company."

Before Grace could introduce Ben and Toby, Jonas eased down from the chair and met his *mamm* with open arms. Mitch, having some of his father's traits, rose slowly. He was more reserved with his emotions and stood back as his little brother and mother hugged.

Grace went to the cabinet and removed a coffee mug. "How is your *mamm* doing?"

"About the same," Susan said, ruffling Mitch's mop of hair. "Were you boys *gut* for *Aenti* Grace?"

"*Jah*," they replied in unison.

"Any news if the men left camp?" Susan's brows lifted.

"Should there be news?" Two days ago, the bishop said he wasn't certain the men would *kumm* back early. "Did Bishop Yoder say something today?"

"*Nay*, but even if the ice hasn't melted completely, it's too thin to—"

"To cross?" Mitch said, his eyes darting from his mother to Grace. "That's what you were about to say, wasn't it?"

Under different circumstances, Susan would have scolded her son for interrupting an adult conversation, but she placed her hand on the boy's shoulder. "Did you finish all your homework?"

Mitch nodded. "I'll get it." His shoulders slumped as he walked out of the room.

Grace caught a glimpse of Toby and Ben exchanging puzzled expressions. She groaned under her breath. Now they knew all the men were away at camp and not just Alvin Graber. She lowered her voice so that only Susan could hear. "I'll let you know if I hear anything."

Susan nodded, then, forcing a cheerful tone, asked, "How was your trip, *Aenti* Erma?"

Grace filled a mug with coffee, then added a teaspoon of sugar and let *Aenti* Erma make the introductions. She introduced Toby and Ben as their guests. And LeAnn was quick to add they were from Florida.

Grace set the mug on the table and motioned to her sister-in-law to take the empty chair at the end.

"Oh, that's for me? I really shouldn't stay. It's late and I have to take *mei mamm* to her *doktah* appointment tomorrow. I hope you don't mind watching the boys after *schul* again."

"You know you don't have to ask. They're always *welkom*." Grace winked at Jonas.

Susan sighed. "I have six sisters and they're all busy tomorrow." She went to the door and grabbed Jonas's jacket off the hook. "Tell *Aenti danki*," she said, helping her youngest son get his arm into the sleeve.

"*Danki*," the six-year-old said as he yawned.

Her sister-in-law and the boys were out the door and gone before the thought occurred to Grace that Susan could have given Toby and Ben a ride to the bishop's house. She supposed it was just as well. Even the bishop wouldn't want strangers showing up on his porch at this late hour.

Chapter Four

Ben hugged the stack of blankets tighter against his chest and trudged alongside Toby and Grace toward the barn. His insides felt bloated like a dead dog lying in the heat. He shouldn't have taken seconds, even though the roast and mashed potatoes were the best he'd eaten.

"It sure is dark." Ben lifted his gaze. Faint light from the cloud-covered moon wasn't enough to see farther than an outstretched hand. Eerie. The ground crawled with fingerlike shadows of nearby branches. Like the old horror movie he'd watched at the downtown theater during his *rumschpringe*. At the time, he mocked the madman who stalked the woods with a machete in search of unsuspecting campers to slaughter. Ben picked up his pace—because he was cold—no other reason.

"It does seem darker here than in Florida," Toby said.

He forgot colder.

"It's even darker in the forest." Grace snickered. "Hope the howling wolves don't keep you awake all *nacht*."

"Wolves?" Toby's voice cracked.

The woman had a sense of humor, even if it was odd. She walked at a snail's pace, a slight teeter in her step. Maybe she'd snuck into a horror movie or two. Ben might have teased Toby about his high-pitched squawk, too, had Ben known for sure he could keep the quiver in the

29

back of his throat from escaping. No sense in them both sounding like *maedels*.

Ben stopped at the cedar-shingled shed with the stovepipe extending from its roof. Small for a *grossdaadi haus*, but he wouldn't complain. His feet ached.

"The barn is this way." Grace continued past him with Toby practically tethered to her hip.

At second glance, he noticed the cabin didn't have any windows. Odd. Why the stovepipe? The lantern light faded as Grace and Toby continued toward the barn. A dog howled close by. Ben rushed to catch up. "Was that a wolf?"

"*Nay*, that was Rusty. He must have heard us coming. His doghouse is behind the barn."

Ben motioned to the shed with the stovepipe. "What's wrong with sleeping in that place?"

"That's the *smokehaus*. You wouldn't get much sleep hanging from a bear hook."

"*Nay*, I suppose *nett*." This night was reminding him more and more of a movie. He vowed never to sneak off to the theater to see horror shows again.

Grace yanked on the barn door. "Sometimes it sticks." She jerked again before Ben shifted the blankets to free his hand. This time the door opened. Grace lifted the lantern higher and entered first.

Something flapped over Ben's head and he jumped.

"That's just a bat," Grace said.

"Are there many of them?" Toby asked in an uneven voice.

"I've never taken time to count. They hang from the roof rafters." She lifted the lantern a little higher and led the way.

Sleeping on a bear hook was starting to sound rather comfortable. Ben sniffed. Not sure about the scent, but decomposing, whatever it was. He burrowed his nose into the blankets.

She guided them through the milking area, past four horse stalls, the goats or maybe they were sheep, and a pen of sleeping pigs. It seemed the only activity tonight was the flapping of the bats, and if he looked near the grain barrels—which he wasn't about to do—he'd probably find that a busy family of mice was the source of the scratchy sounds.

She stopped at a wooden ladder leaning against the wall, grabbed a rung, and climbed the worn slats one-handed while toting the lantern in her free hand.

Ben glanced at Toby. "You can go up next." Even low light didn't hide his friend's grimace. "Or I will." Ben shrugged.

Grace leaned over the opening and swung the lantern, her face spotlighted with a yellow hue. "The loft is up here."

Jah, *where the bats hang from the beams.*

Ben tucked the blankets under his chin, grasped the smooth rung on the ladder, and ascended. Reaching the top, his foot landed on the straw-covered hardwood floor, and a creature flapped somewhere overhead. Suddenly he wasn't so worried how low the temperature would dip tonight—he might just move his bed to the porch.

"Maybe the light's bothering them," Grace said. "I'm sure they'll calm down after I leave."

He willed himself not to panic—or at least not to sound panicky. But his heart refused to steady itself. "You're taking the only light?"

Toby surfaced from the opening as Grace tailored a lecture as if talking to a child about how a tipped-over lantern could cause a barn fire.

"You never know," she continued, shaking her finger like one of his least favorite schoolteachers had when she wanted to make a point. "A critter might knock it over while you're asleep."

Who's going to sleep? he wanted to argue, but instead held his tongue.

"I'll give you a few minutes to find a place to spread out your blankets."

What was she going to do, tuck them in? Follow them to the *out-haus?* His *mamm* wasn't even this hen-ish.

The boards creaked under Ben's feet as he made his way to the loose mound of hay. He tossed the blankets in a heap, then met her at the opening. "Would you like me to walk with you back to the *haus*?"

"Why would I want you to do that? I just walked you out here."

He groaned. "I thought being a *maedel* and all, you'd like . . ."

"Company? *Nay, danki*."

Ben straightened his shoulders. "I was thinking protection."

"Hmm . . ."

Most women appreciated his escort, but she drew out her reply like a song.

Toby chuckled.

"I think I can manage," she finally said, then clambered down the ladder. The loft darkened.

Of course she could manage. She didn't even flinch at the swooping bats.

"Breakfast is at sunrise," Grace called from the bottom of the ladder. A few moments later the barn door rattled closed.

"Fine mess you've gotten us into," Toby said.

"You can't blame me that your *onkel's* gone." Ben crept across the plank floor to the pile of hay. He spread the blanket, then flopped down. His body sank into the prickly hay. "This isn't so bad."

Toby huffed as he arranged his bedding.

Ben intertwined his fingers and cupped the back of his head. Strange how well hay insulated an unheated barn. At the end of March, no less. In Florida, his hankie would be soaked from mopping sweat. Here, his teeth might wear down to the gums from all the chattering he'd done since he arrived. "At least it's sort of warm."

"I suppose."

Ben flipped to his side and propped up on an elbow. "Maybe the bishop will loan us enough money to buy a bus ticket out of here."

"And when we arrive home, we say what? Surprise, your prodigal *sohns* have returned? Something tells me neither one of our *daeds* is standing at the end of the driveway waiting to see us cross the horizon." Toby's voice deepened. "*Fraa*, select the fattest chicken. *Mei sohn* has returned."

Theatrical, but Toby had a point. Ben's father probably had *Mamm* roast a chicken when he left. "I wasn't thinking about going home," he said. "When I leave here I plan to find Neva and set things straight. Although I have no idea where I'll look for her first."

"It's been a year. Give it up."

"There's more to it than you know." How could Toby understand? He hadn't made the mistakes Ben had made. Toby had his father's respect.

"All I'm saying is you've turned this . . . thing with Neva into . . . a conquest. You wrecked her reputation that *nacht* at the beach, and you've been trying to save it ever since by wanting to marry her."

"How do you know about the *nacht* at the beach?" Ben hadn't breathed a word. Neva wouldn't have either. Besides, her parents sent her away almost immediately.

"Ah . . ."

"That's what I thought. You know nothing about that *nacht*." Ben rolled onto his back, folded his hands behind his neck, and closed his eyes. An image rose up of Neva on the beach with her dress hiked to her shins and her toes buried in the sand.

A horse's neigh pulled him back to the sharp reality that they were homeless—sleeping in a barn.

Toby tossed. "I don't know how I'm going to get any sleep between the stench and all the livestock noise."

Ben wished he hadn't run the batteries down on his transistor radio during the bus trip north. Outside of an occasional horse's neigh, the "livestock noise" was mice, maybe rats. "Well, when you do return home, you'll be able to say you slept with the pigs."

"Don't remind me. I almost gagged when we entered the barn."

Ben, too, but he hadn't wanted to give Grace any pleasure of knowing it. Although she'd probably guessed by the way he had covered his nose. Might be why her tour included the entire barn. He closed his eyes again. This time instead of seeing Neva, an image of Grace invaded his mind. Wonder if those bent brows were permanent. She was really too young to have those lines between her eyes.

∞

Grace ambled from the barn to the house at a slower pace and with a more pronounced limp than usual. Fire fed her nerve endings. Her feet burned where her stockings had torn and her tight shoes rubbed against raw skin. Escorting the men out to the barn was foolish when her feet already felt like the size of watermelons and her hip sockets throbbed. Grace rebuked her prideful spirit with every step. Why did it matter so much to appear normal tonight? The strangers would board the next bus headed south and she would never see them again.

Aenti Erma looked up from her steeping tea when Grace entered the kitchen. "I thought a cup of tea would help you relax. Care to join me?"

Grace wanted to relax—in bed with her legs elevated on a stack of pillows—but instead smiled. "*Danki.*" She placed the pot on the stove to reheat the poultice and soak the rags. "This stuff is going to stink once it's reheated."

"Don't worry about that."

"Where's LeAnn?"

"She went to bed." *Aenti* tapped on the chair next to her. "*Kumm* sit down and rest."

Grace sat and let out a long breath.

"Did you get Toby and Ben all settled in the loft?"

"*Jah.*" Her aunt accepted the strangers like the stray dog she'd fed, watered, and made a bed in the barn for last summer. These two strays tonight might not be flea-infested, but they ate like the hound. "I don't like them staying here."

"It's just temporary."

Grace would make sure they were on the bus back to Florida tomorrow. The way LeAnn had gawked at them, she was probably already dreaming up a plan to tag along with them. Grace wasn't about to let that happen.

Aenti Erma sipped her tea. "This is *gut*. I used it from the baggy marked Relaxation."

"That's one of Mattie Diener's new herbal blends." Grace peered inside the cup at the pinkish shade. "But don't ask what's in it. I think she just mixes together whatever she has. Her teas are almost never the same." Grace hadn't had a chance to sample the tea since Mattie brought it over the other day when she dropped off the ingredients for the poultice. Grace inhaled the aroma and smiled. Lavender.

Aenti lifted her cup and wiped a ring of moisture off the table with her hand. "Has LeAnn made comments before about your leg?"

Grace frowned. "It's okay."

"*Nay*, it isn't." *Aenti* Erma reached for Grace's hand and gave it a pat. "While I'm here, there will be no such talk. I'll see to it."

No such talk. Same words her *mamm* used to say. Her mother taught the boys to look out for their little sister and, to this day, her brothers never teased her. LeAnn received the same instruction, but sometime during the five years since their mother's death, she'd forgotten simple kindness. This year, LeAnn waited until the men left for camp before unleashing her pent-up emotions. Grace wasn't sure what fanned her sister's flames, but more and more LeAnn talked about being dissatisfied living such an isolated life.

Jah, Grace had to get the Florida men back on the southbound bus. Tomorrow. Their presence would only entice LeAnn's free spirit to fly the coop. *Daed* would be heartbroken.

Steam rose from the pot. Grace pushed off her chair.

"I can take care of—"

"*Nay*. I'm more than capable." The moment the words left her mouth, she regretted the sharp tone. Grace removed the pot from the stove, placed it on the wire cooling rack, and returned to the table. "I'm sorry for snapping, *Aenti*."

"You're tired. It's been a long day for both of us." *Aenti* Erma took another sip of tea. "*Nau*, tell me about the maple sap you've collected this season. Have you made much syrup?"

"A few gallons. We tapped more trees this year, and on warmer days, the sap runs steady." Grace and her aunt chatted about a new maple syrup recipe, the upcoming berry season, and how much canning they hoped to do. By the time they had finished their tea, the poultice had cooled.

Aenti Erma yawned as she collected the empty cups. "It's so *gut* to be back. This place feels as much like home as *mei* little place in Ohio."

The hundred-acre farm her aunt inherited from her parents wasn't so little. Grace recalled walking every inch of the property the spring she helped her *grossdaadi* plant corn. "Maybe you should extend your stay."

"Oh, I don't know that your father would like that. Reuben is a very private man."

"Even so, you're part of the family." Grace removed a pair of tongs from the drawer and used them to lift the medicated cloths out of the pot and place them on a plate.

"*Jah*, but we both know I remind him of your mother. He isn't ready for me to extend *mei* stay." *Aenti* Erma yawned again. "I think your friend's tea blend is already working. I'll see you in the morning."

Grace hugged her aunt. "*Gut nacht, Aenti*. I'm so glad you're back."

"Me, too, child."

Grace lowered the lamp wick on the kitchen table, extinguishing the flame. She carried the plate of warm cloths into her bedroom and set them on the stand next to her bed. Soothing relief came a few minutes after layering the cloths over her legs. She closed her eyes as rain pattered on the roof. Her thoughts drifted to Toby and Ben in the barn. Would the bats keep them awake?

Chapter Five

B en woke to the ping of raindrops against the tin rooftop. Eyes closed, his brain tricked him into thinking he was in Florida, then a shiver ran down his spine and the scent of hay registered. He opened his eyes and blinked. A hazy film of dust in his eyes made it difficult to focus. Barn living wasn't for him—he was freezing.

Something clanged. Voices murmured. Clanged again. After a moment, he identified the voice in the distance. Toby. Ben flipped to his other side. Toby's blankets lay neatly folded. Ben shuffled to his feet, shoved on his hat, and shimmied down the ladder. The cold cement floor seeped through his socks and sent a chill through his body.

"You might want to put your shoes on." Grace walked past him with a pitchfork of hay.

Ben glanced at his feet. *Dummkopp.*

Toby entered the barn, a bucket of water sloshing over the rim. "Okay, who's next to be watered?"

"Jasper, he's in the second stall," Grace replied.

Ben wasn't about to look like deadweight compared to Toby. But he would heed her advice and put his shoes on first. He scaled the ladder, then kicked around the hay next to his bedding until he located his shoes. Then, without taking time to lace them, he descended the ladder, skipping the last two rungs.

He scanned the dimly lit area, but they were nowhere in sight. It hadn't taken that long to find his shoes. "Grace? Toby?" Ben peeked into a stall. A chestnut horse lifted its head from the water trough and snorted.

Ben called out again. "Toby?"

No response. Grace didn't seem like someone who would play hide-and-seek, but he'd play along with Toby. Ben checked the goat pen, then sucked in a breath and quickly passed by the pigs. Usually he was the one hiding with the *maedel*. Finally, he found Grace in a small tack room in the center of the barn. He snuck up behind her. "Great place to hide. Is Toby in here with you?"

She pivoted around, eyes large. "Excuse me?"

"I, ah . . . I thought you two were playing a joke on me."

She cocked her head and squinted at him as if the idea of playing a joke were something foreign. "There's *nay* time for childish games."

He grimaced. "What would you like me to do?"

Grace reached for the harness on the wall hook, removed it, and slung it over her shoulder. "First, lace your shoes. Then go eat."

Ben followed her to the stall. "Don't you need help?"

She stopped at the stall and turned to face him. "Can you hitch a buggy?"

"I've never tried."

Grace unlatched the gate and slipped inside with the horse. She shut the gate before Ben could enter. "It would be safer if you don't *kumm* in."

Ben bent to one knee and laced his shoes. He glanced up as the horse stuck its head out of the stall opening. The creature knocked Ben's hat off and nuzzled his neck, whiskers tickling his skin. Ben shooed him away so he could finish tying his shoe. "Ouch!" Ben grasped his shoulder. "He just bit me."

The horse jerked back. "Sorry, I should have warned you, Jasper nips." Grace reached out and stroked the animal's neck. "It's okay. Ben didn't mean to frighten you."

"You're taking the horse's side? That was *nay* nip. I think he took a chunk out of *mei* shoulder." He twisted, trying to get a better look.

"Are you bleeding?" The crease between her brows softened. She stepped toward him and stumbled, but her hand caught the stall door, stopping her short of falling.

He leaned closer and when she straightened, they were inches apart. A pink glow covered her cheeks, but when he started to smile, her piercing russet eyes quickened his breath—not in a good way either. Her pin-sized pupils were a bit nervy.

Her lips tightened for a moment. "So, are you bleeding or *nett?*"

"*Nay.*"

She redirected her attention to readying the equipment. Grace placed the bit in the horse's mouth and adjusted the noseband. "*Gut* boy, Jasper." She gave the beast a fond pat on the neck.

A door clanked shut. Toby rounded the corner, his shirt soaked and rain streaming off his hat brim. He carried the bucketful of water to the stall next to them where an even larger horse shifted on his hooves.

Ben sidestepped. He wasn't sure how far the horse could stretch his neck and he wasn't willing to test him.

Toby moved into the stall without hesitation. A moment later, he came out with the empty bucket. He leaned over the stall gate where Grace was harnessing the horse. "Anything else you need?"

"You could feed and water Rusty. His dog food is in the bin next to the oat barrel." She flashed Toby a smile that made Ben feel invisible. "Afterward, you two should eat. *Mei aenti* Erma will have breakfast ready." She guided her hand down the horse's leg as if needing it to steady her squat. Reaching for the dangling strap under the animal's belly, she winced.

"Ah . . ." Ben reached for the gate latch, but stopped when she shot a dagger over her shoulder at him.

"I really don't appreciate people staring at me." She waved her hand dismissively. "Maybe you could offer to help Toby with the dog."

"Gladly." Ben pushed away from the gate. The woman had no sense of humor unless rudeness was a game for her. Ben met Toby at the feed container, bending over and scooping dog food into an empty coffee can. "That woman got up on the wrong side of the bed."

"She's been pleasant to me." Toby handed him the can of dry food, then snatched an empty bucket off the floor. "You can feed him while I pump the water."

Ben walked along the side of the barn under the eave to avoid the steady rain. Even then, water running off the roof troughed at his feet. He heard the dog barking before he rounded the corner and met the hound eye-to-eye, raised up on his muddy hind legs, pawing the air at the end of a heavy chain. "*Gut* boy." What did Grace say his name was—Red? The floppy-eared coon dog was a horse, and a horse had already bitten him once today. "*Gut* boy, Red." He squatted just outside the dog's reach and set the can down, then darted inside the invisible line to fetch the dog dish. The dog jumped on Ben, slinging drool as he barked and leaving his massive footprint on Ben's chest. He grabbed the tin bowl, sloshing rainwater and food residue on his pant leg as he sped back to the safety zone outside the dog's reach.

Toby arrived with the water bucket. "Are you thirsty, boy?" He patted the dog's shoulder, walked past him, and emptied the bucket into the dog's water trough.

Ben pushed the food dish within the dog's parameter while it was sniffing Toby's pant leg.

"You're *nett* afraid of dogs, are you?" Toby asked, giving the hundred-plus-pound dog another pat.

"Only the ones that charge the end of the chain like him."

Toby laughed. "Dogs are *gut* judges of character. Man's best friend."

Another dig. Ben took the blame for them being sent to Michigan, but he wasn't so sure Toby yelling, "Cannonball!" wasn't what alerted the police officer.

"Let's take these back in the barn, then go eat," Toby said.

Ben swept his hand over the muddy paw print on his shirt as he entered the barn, but smearing the mud made it worse. He tossed the coffee can into the feed barrel. "Why didn't you wake me when you got up?"

Toby shrugged. "Grace said farm life takes a little getting used to. She gets up before the rooster every morning." Toby pushed the barn door open and took off running toward the house.

Ben held his hat in place as he sprinted to catch up. "Sounds like you two are chatty ol' pals *nau.*"

"Well, you know what they say about the early bird." Toby smiled and increased his speed.

They clambered up the porch steps, reaching shelter at the same time. Ben bent at the waist and took in a deep breath. "So, you've become a farm boy?" Last night Toby didn't think he would be able to sleep because of the stench, and less than eight hours later he was Grace's right-hand man.

The door opened and LeAnn greeted them with a warm smile. "*Gudder mariye.*"

The scent of bacon caused Ben's stomach to growl. "*Mariye.*" Ben swiped his muddy shoes on the doormat before entering. His and Toby's personal belongings sat just inside the door. Loaded down with blankets last night, he'd forgotten to grab his on the way out to the barn.

"Breakfast is ready." LeAnn ushered them into the kitchen and directed them to the hand pump at the sink to wash up.

Erma flipped the sizzling strips of bacon. "I hope you're hungry."

"Always." Ben dried his hands on a dish towel. He pulled out the same chair he'd sat in last night.

"Sure smells *gut.*" Toby sat beside Ben.

LeAnn placed two cups of coffee on the table, then slid the sugar bowl from the far end of the table over to them.

The heaped mound of bacon Erma set on the table looked thicker than the store-bought bacon his *mamm* cooked. Ben sat up straighter, his mouth watering. A moment later, Erma placed a bowl of oatmeal before him and another before Toby. "Be careful, it's hot." She went to the window and peered outside. "Where is your sister?"

"Grace said to start without her." LeAnn approached the table holding a glass jar between two potholders, then eased the jar down on the table.

The sweet aroma of maple teased Ben's senses.

LeAnn pulled out one of the wooden chairs and joined them at the table. "How did you sleep last *nacht*?"

"*Gut, danki*," Toby replied.

What little rest Ben got after the scratching noises stopped wasn't bad for his first night sleeping in a barn.

Erma folded her hands, and everyone at the table did the same. After the brief blessing, Erma took one of the potholders and slid the jar closer to Ben. "Have you had homemade maple syrup?"

Ben shook his head.

"Tapped from the trees out back," Erma said.

Ben poured some on top of his oatmeal, then passed the jar to Toby. "Is it hard to make?"

LeAnn shrugged, unenthused. "It takes forty gallons of sap to make one gallon of syrup, by the time you boil it down."

Ben sank his spoon into the hot cereal and took a bite. Sweetness melted in his mouth. "This syrup is *gut*. You should think about selling it."

"We do." LeAnn sprinkled sugar over her oatmeal.

Ben lifted his brows. "You don't like syrup?"

"Nope. Too sticky for me." LeAnn sipped her coffee. "So, what do you do in Florida?"

"I work for Toby's *daed*. He owns a landscaping business. We plant trees all day. Mostly shrubs."

"Sounds interesting."

"It gets hot," Ben said, "working in hundred-degree heat."

"Still, it sounds better than working in a lumberyard—or mud camp," she muttered.

"God has richly blessed this district," Erma said. "What started off as a handful of families going together to purchase land has grown into a thriving development. We have over a thousand acres combined, most of which are wooded, and our settlement is surrounded by hundreds of acres of national forest, so even the nearest *Englischer* is several miles away."

"In other words," LeAnn chimed, "we're isolated."

Ben ate as Erma carried the conversation. She told about the lumber mill's products and the different places where shipments were sent. Other than an occasional nod, he just listened.

The door opened and Grace entered. Without removing her wool cloak, she went to a wooden desk at the far side of the kitchen and sifted through a stack of papers.

"There's more oatmeal," Erma said. "Would you like me to fix you a bowl?"

"I'll eat later. I want to go into town for supplies before the weather gets worse."

"If you're looking for the shopping list, it's on the counter." Erma retrieved the paper and handed it to Grace.

LeAnn tapped Ben's hand. "What type of work do the women do in your district?"

"Normal stuff. They cook, clean, do the laundry, garden. Sometimes they get together and sew." Ben's thoughts shifted to his mother. She worked hard both inside the house and outside in the garden.

"That's it? No cows to milk or chickens to feed?"

Ben smiled. "We have a small yard, and it isn't zoned for farm animals."

"I want to live somewhere like that. Somewhere that I—"

"LeAnn," Grace said sternly. "You need to learn to be content. God has you where He wants you." Grace turned to him and Toby. "Are you two about ready to go?" More a summons than a question, she strode to the door, still cranking out orders. "Don't forget your bags." She disappeared outside.

Ben drained his coffee cup and stood. *"Danki* for the meal."

"Jah, danki," Toby echoed, scrambling to his feet.

Bags in hand, they darted outside into the driving rain. Ben climbed onto the bench and slid next to Grace, making room for Toby. Ben's arm bumped hers and rainwater dripped from his hat onto her shoulder. His eyes met and held hers. Something within them tugged at his soul.

She inched closer to the door, leaning awkwardly away from him. "It doesn't take long to reach town, but since it rained all *nacht*, I thought we should get going before the road gets too bad." Grace tapped the reins and the horse lurched forward.

They hadn't traveled far beyond the long driveway before the road disappeared underwater. The horse stopped, lowered his head as far as the reins allowed, and snorted.

"Maybe this isn't a *gut* idea," Ben said. "Your horse seems to know something we don't."

She clucked her tongue. *"Geh* on, Jasper."

"Can you tell the road from the ditch?" Ben couldn't.

"I know to stay in the middle."

Water sprayed the side of the buggy as the horse trudged through the ministream. Maybe she did know what she was doing. The water wasn't as deep as Ben initially thought. He released his breath just as the front wheel on the passenger side dipped into a hole. Ben sprang off the bench like a heated kernel of popcorn, then plopped back down. He pitched forward but grabbed the edge of the bench and pulled himself into an upright position. His stomach rolled more now than the first time he boarded a fishing vessel. It had taken several hours to get his sea legs, but adjusting to being bucked off the bench might be different.

"We can wait," Ben said. Last night he and Toby waded through some muddy areas, but nothing like this.

"*Geh* on, Jasper." She clucked her tongue again and tapped the reins.

Ben tightened his grip on the bench. "Maybe after it stops raining—"

"It's rained six days in a row. This is the best the road will be for a few weeks." Grace slowed the horse as he came to where the road split. She leaned forward and peered out the window at what looked like a mere foot trail.

Ben braced for the turn, silently praying she wasn't crazy enough to take it.

"It's underwater," she said. "Probably shouldn't risk taking the shortcut."

Ben gasped. "I agree."

"*Jah*, me too," Toby said.

She hesitated, then signaled the horse forward.

Ben studied the tree-lined area. In some places, the woods were too dense to see beyond a few feet. "Don't you get scared living this far back in the woods?"

"I find it peaceful."

"I think so too," Toby quickly said. "It's nice to be away from everything."

"Nice? The middle of nowhere?" Ben bit back reminding Toby he had been afraid of the bats last night too. "What if something happens and you need help?"

"We send a message."

Ben snickered. "By pigeon?"

"*Nay*," she said smugly. "By smoke signals."

"You're kidding."

"*Nay* joke. It's true." She kept a straight face but didn't look him in the eye.

In other districts, they alerted one another by clanging a cast-iron bell, so maybe sending a smoke signal wasn't so far-fetched.

They came to the section of the road where the uprooted tree roots made the ride bumpy and impossible to talk. The stretch wasn't more than a few hundred yards, but by the time they reached the main road, Ben's neck, shoulders, and back felt out of whack.

Once on the smooth surface, Grace clucked her tongue, apparently determined to make up for lost time. She kept her eyes on the road and both hands controlled the reins.

"Aren't you afraid the horse will slip on the wet pavement?" Toby asked. He made a good point. In Florida, after a heavy rain, the roads were often slick from oil residue.

"Icy roads are worse," she said, as a matter of fact. A car sped past them and neither she nor the horse flinched.

Ben blew out a breath. Riding a bike in traffic was nothing like this. At least he had the option of riding on the sidewalk or going into the ditch if a vehicle came too close. He wanted to ask what the roads were like in the winter, but didn't dare break her concentration. Toby must have had similar thoughts because he remained silent as well. It wasn't long before the outskirts of town started to look familiar. They were only a block or two from the bus station when Grace pulled into the parking lot of the IGA and stopped the horse.

"I have some supplies I need to buy." She collected her handbag and scooted off the seat.

Ben climbed out behind her. "Looks like it might stop raining."

"It might." She looped the reins around the light post. "You do remember where the bus station is, *jah*?"

Toby got out from the other side and rounded the buggy as Grace was tying the reins. "We really appreciate everything you've done," he said.

Grace stepped toward them. She looked at Ben, then Toby. "If you're *nett* here when I'm finished shopping, I wish you well." She turned toward the store.

Toby's jaw dropped.

"Wait," Ben said, taking hold of her arm. "You're *nett* leaving us here, are you?"

She glanced at his hand on her forearm and narrowed her eyes.

Ben released his hold and folded his arms across his chest. "Your *Aenti* Erma thinks you're taking us to the bishop's *haus*. What are you going to tell her?"

"I'll tell her the truth, unlike you two."

Ben uncrossed his arms. "What's that supposed to mean?"

Grace squared her shoulders. "I think you two have gotten yourselves in trouble and you're fence-jumpers. Go back home where you belong." She motioned to her left. "Take Pine Street one block. The bus station is on the right." She turned and marched toward the store.

"You're *nett* much of a Good Samaritan," Ben called out. "Leaving two weary travelers—and fellow *bruders* in Christ—to fend for themselves in the rain." When she continued walking, Ben turned to Toby. "I told you she was as *kalt* as ice." He shook his head. "The woman has *nay* heart."

Chapter Six

Grace cringed at Ben's remark. True, it wasn't the Amish way to leave someone in need, if they truly were in need. A *bruder* in Christ? Perhaps they hadn't left the church. Still, they didn't deny jumping the fence.

She grabbed a shopping cart and headed down the produce aisle. But even as she collected the items on her list, she couldn't rid her thoughts of them. Guilt clung to her soul like a wet blanket. Finally, standing in the baking section of the store, she closed her eyes and prayed. *Lord, I should have prayed for wisdom before sending them away. They are like foreigners in a strange land and* mei *attitude wasn't Christlike. Please forgive me, Father. I pray if the need arises again,* mei *actions will be acceptable to You and bring You glory. Amen.*

Grace opened her eyes when she heard her name.

Mattie's voice carried from the front of the aisle. As she pushed her empty cart toward her friend, the front wheel thumped against the floor like a piece of gum was stuck to it.

"I'm glad I found you," Mattie said. "I saw a strange man loitering by your buggy only minutes ago."

"Only one?"

Mattie pulled back and cocked her head. "*Jah* . . . You don't seem surprised. Is there something you haven't told me?"

Grace lifted her hand to stop her friend before her mind ran amuck.

"We had some uninvited guests show up last *nacht*. Alvin Graber's nephew, Toby, and his friend Ben came from Florida. They said they came to work, but I find it hard to believe. Why would they arrive four months after the men left for camp? Alvin wouldn't have told them to *kumm* during this time of the year."

"Hopefully with all this rain, the men will *kumm* back early."

"Even so, wouldn't Alvin have told someone they were coming?" Grace caught a glimpse of Mattie's despondent stare. "Oh dear." Grace reached for Mattie's hand and squeezed it. "I didn't mean to sound insensitive. I've been worried about the men, too, and I hope they *kumm* back early."

"Have you accepted Philemon's plan to propose to Becky?"

"Do I have a choice?" Grace shook her head. "The only choice I have is to move to Ohio with *Aenti* Erma."

"I hope you don't do that." Mattie frowned.

"I wouldn't stay away a long time. Just until I come to terms with . . ." She was fooling herself if she thought she could return home anytime soon once Philemon, her childhood friend, was married. Their two families were the first to settle in Badger Creek and she and Philemon had bonded in friendship almost immediately, being near the same age.

"You've always been such *gut* friends. I always thought you two would make a cute couple."

"We both know why it could never be so." Grace shrugged. "God's power is made perfect in *mei* weakness," she said in a rehearsed monotone.

"Be mindful that you don't become resentful."

Don't become . . . ? Grace curled her lip in a strained smile. Her friend had a wonderful husband. It was easy for Mattie to give counsel when her life was perfect. Grace rebuked her jealous thoughts.

"I'm worried all this rain will melt the ice on the river. Andy's usually the first one to cross."

"Your husband also knows the river the best. He knows when it's safe or when they need to take extra precautions. You told me so yourself."

Mattie nodded. "I'll be happy when they finish clear-cutting that side of the river and they can timber on our side again."

"Me too." Grace recalled the long walks she and Philemon would take to check the saplings' progress. She enjoyed watching the trees grow over the years. They planted a few acres of oaks the first year they arrived, spruce the next year. Philemon talked a lot, mostly about the trees, but she never grew tired of listening to him.

"Grace?" Mattie's voice interrupted her thoughts.

"I'm sorry, did you say something?"

"I asked if you were stocking up too." Mattie motioned to the list in Grace's hand.

"*Jah.*" Grace forced a smile, then let it drop the moment she turned toward the shelves. She removed a ten-pound bag of flour from the shelf and lowered it into her cart, then grabbed another one.

Mattie selected a bag of powdered sugar. "I'm replenishing *mei* pantry too. I think we're going to flood early this year."

"Parts of *mei* road already are." They were used to being snow-bound during the winter and blocked from the main road in early spring because of flooding and mud. Everyone planned accordingly and shared as supplies dwindled. Grace glanced at the next items on her list. Sugar, cornstarch, and coffee. Coffee was in the next aisle over.

"How did the poultice work?"

"I was going to stop on *mei* way home and tell you how much better I feel today. A miracle for sure."

"*Nay, nay.*" Mattie held up her hand. "Don't praise me. Give thanks to God."

Grace smiled. "I did when I woke up and wasn't in pain. And then I thanked Him for giving me such a smart friend." Grace lifted the hem of her dress just high enough to show her ankles. "See, they aren't swollen."

"*Gut*. I'm glad you feel better, but you still need new shoes." Mattie fluttered her list. "I better finish *mei* shopping. It's *mei* day to take lunch to the workers at the sawmill, which reminds me, how is Susan's *mamm*? I told her I would work her day at the mill."

Grace shook her head. "*Nett* much better. Please keep her in your prayers."

"I will. Let me know if there is anything I can do," she said, pushing her cart forward.

"I'll be sure to." Grace scanned the list. Coffee was the last item. She pushed her cart forward, the front wheel squeaking under the weight.

Grace selected a can of dark roast, then, remembering Mattie said she saw a man next to her buggy, she headed back to the produce area. Assuming the Florida men liked fresh fruit, maybe they would accept a peace offering. If nothing else, they could eat it on the bus.

Grace inspected a bag of apples for soft spots and placed them in her cart. As she looked at the pears, the bishop's wife, Mary, approached.

"I'm glad to see you're stocking up on supplies. James dropped me off so I could pick up a few things while he went to the feed store and a few other places. He said he had errands to take care of for some of the men."

Their bishop stopped going to camp with the men the year he turned seventy-eight, but he hadn't slowed down around the settlement. Most of the wives and children handled feeding the livestock, but he mended fences and picked up feed when someone ran low. Grace was thankful her father and brothers checked the fences and stocked up on the livestock feed before they left so she didn't have to bother the bishop.

Grace figured Mary would say if she'd heard anything from the men, but she asked anyway. "Any word from camp?"

"Nothing yet." Mary's voice cracked.

"I'm sure they're all fine. Wet, but fine." Grace tried to sound hopeful, but when Mary's sullen expression didn't change, Grace wished she hadn't said anything. Only a year ago, Mary lost one of her grandsons when he got pinned under a tree. The entire settlement mourned his death, as the accident could happen to any one of the men.

Mary dabbed a hankie over her eyes. "They're in God's hands."

"We all are."

The bishop's wife tucked her hankie back into her handbag. "I better finish shopping or James will return from the feed store to pick me up and I won't be ready. Did I tell you he's called a meeting tonight?"

"What time?"

"Six o'clock. I thought I would make a pot of chili. Can you bring a pan of cornbread?"

"Sure," Grace said. "Have you seen Mattie? She's here in the store."

"*Nay*, I haven't." Mary looked around the produce department. "I should go find her and let her know about the meeting. I'll see you tonight."

Grace made her way to the register and paid for her groceries. She hurried through the parking lot in the rain, but when she opened the door of her buggy, Ben and Toby were not waiting on the bench.

❧

Ben slung his duffel bag over his shoulder and caught up with Toby on the sidewalk in front of a women's dress shop. "You think Grace was upset about the pigeon comment?"

"I don't know."

"I thought she was joking about smoke signals."

"Maybe she was."

Ben glanced over his shoulder at the IGA's entrance a half block away. "I still think we should have waited at the buggy."

"For what?" Toby paused at the corner of Pine and First Streets. "She isn't someone easily wooed."

"But surely she would have given us a ride—"

"To the bus station." Toby motioned ahead. "We can walk a block." He stepped off the curb, heading in the station's direction.

The walk seemed pointless. Ben had a few dollars, maybe enough to buy a cheap meal at a fast-food place, but couldn't cover bus fare. He looked up at the gray sky. He'd rather be under shelter when it started raining again.

They reached the cement block building in a matter of minutes. Once they were inside the station, Toby sat on the nearest bench, rummaged through his duffel bag, and pulled out his wallet. "How much money do you have?"

Ben plopped down beside Toby. No need to count his money. He already knew the figure. "Eight dollars and thirty-eight cents." That amount wouldn't take him to the other side of town on a city bus.

Toby stopped counting and looked up. "That's all?"

Ben nodded. "I guess *mei daed* thought if I had more spending money, I might return."

Toby finished counting. "I have eighty and some change."

"That isn't enough to get you out of Michigan, let alone to Florida." They were both stuck.

"I know." Toby shoved the cash back into his bag and stood. "We have to figure out something." He paced across the room and returned. "I guess we should have stayed at the grocery store and begged Grace for mercy."

"We would have a better chance convincing her *aenti* to let us stay. At least Erma seemed to like us."

"*Gut* point." Toby smiled. "Wait with our stuff and I'll see if Clutch is working. Maybe he will give us another ride."

This was yesterday all over again. Even the red banner on the television issued the same breaking news about the unstable mental patient still at large. Ben grabbed their bags and moved to a bench closer to the television as the reporter announced they would cut to a live briefing held by the chief of police.

The police officer opened with a summary of yesterday's event, adding that Jack Harrison, a ward assistant at the county's Behavior Unit, was now listed as a person of interest. Apparently, the worker went missing shortly after the mental patient escaped. The police officer assured the reporters that no charges had been filed, but encouraged anyone knowing Jack Harrison's whereabouts to come forward.

Toby tapped Ben's shoulder. "Clutch said he would give us a ride, but his shift doesn't end for another three hours."

"We'll wait," Ben said. Three hours was still better than walking. He sank into a slouched position—might as well get comfortable. On the television, a reporter asked the officer about the condition of the nurse who was stabbed during the escape.

Toby sat on the bench. "We should probably figure out what we're going to say to Erma."

"We tell her the truth. We have no money and we need a place to stay until your *onkel* returns." Ben shrugged. "Unless you have a better idea?"

Toby shook his head. He leaned down and opened his bag once more, mumbling something about a letter he'd written and wanting to find the post office so he could mail it home. "Have you written a letter to your parents telling them we've made it?"

"When have I had time?"

Toby tapped the envelope on his leg. "I wrote mine on the bus."

"*Jah*, I know." Ben had also seen him mail a letter when they transferred buses in Jacksonville. They hadn't even made it out of the state and he was writing home. Ben turned his attention to the television.

Not that he was interested in worldly news, but he didn't want a lecture about writing home when his father had sent him away.

"Is it true Gordon Wellford hates women?" the reporter asked the police official.

"I'm not able to comment on that at this time." The chief of police pointed to another raised hand.

"I take it they haven't caught him yet," Toby said.

"Doesn't sound like it." Ben missed the next reporter's question, but judging by the officer's comment that he wasn't a physician and couldn't answer questions about the fugitive's medications, Ben figured the inquiry had something to do with the man's state of mind being on the run unmedicated.

The programming returned to the channel reporter. "To recap—"

A white-bearded man stepped in front of Ben and Toby and cleared his throat. "I'm Bishop Yoder."

Ben pushed himself into an upright position while Toby stood.

The bishop glanced over his shoulder at the television set, then turned back to them. "You must be Toby and Ben."

"*Jah.*" Toby stepped forward. "We're from Florida."

"I know. I just received a letter today about your arrival. I hope you haven't had to wait long."

Grace veered Jasper onto the narrow road leading back to the settlement. She had spent more time in town than she wanted, and now she would have to hurry to get home in time to make cornbread for the meeting. The buggy rolled over exposed roots, bouncing the grocery sacks on the bench. She stretched her free arm across the bags to keep them from falling off the seat while holding the reins with her other hand. This road washed out every spring, but never to this extent and never in March. The creek, which ran parallel to the road, had risen since they'd passed through earlier. Keeping Jasper centered between the trees flanking both sides proved difficult.

The buggy wheel dropped into a hole and a groan escaped her mouth. She tapped the reins lightly and heard another groan, louder and deeper than her own. Grace glanced over her shoulder but didn't find anything out of place in the back. Jasper lunged forward, but unable to get traction under his hooves, the horse sidestepped. Perhaps if she lightened the horse's load by getting out of the buggy and coaxing him forward, he could bring the wheel out of the hole.

Grace climbed out of the buggy, her foot landing in a shin-high puddle of water. She waded to the front and took hold of Jasper's reins.

"*Kumm*, boy." She clicked her tongue and, at the same time, tugged the reins. Jasper's nostrils flared as he lurched forward. The buggy didn't budge. She gave the horse a moment to rest, then coaxed him once again to pull. This time, the wheel wrenched forward, but the harness snapped. What little progress Jasper had made moving the buggy ended when the wheel rolled back into the hole. Something thudded. Certain the noise came from inside the buggy, Grace peeked at the groceries. Everything appeared fine. The little bit of rocking the buggy had done hadn't jostled the bags off the bench.

Grace inspected the harness. Nothing she could repair. Thankfully, her father had an extra one in the equipment room. But that wouldn't help her now. Even if she could get the wheel unstuck, Jasper couldn't pull anything with a broken harness. She had no choice but to leave the buggy on the road and walk Jasper home. A chore she dreaded since her shoes were already soaked from standing in the puddle, and water squished out of them with each step.

Grace opened the buggy door and removed the bag of cornmeal from the grocery sack. If she didn't need it to make cornbread for the get-together, she would have left it with the rest of the groceries.

Grace unhitched Jasper. She had led him a few feet away when something creaked behind her. Grace looked over her shoulder. After staring at the stationary buggy a moment, she turned back and took a step toward it, then froze. A chill swept through her body. The buggy had moved.

Chapter Seven

Grace hiked the wooded path leading to the bishop's house with her mind on more than the meeting. Earlier when she'd seen the buggy move, she'd become paralyzed with fear and hadn't had the nerve to investigate. Now she wished she had, just to put her mind at ease.

Her shoes still wet from walking in the rain earlier, Grace slipped on the slick surface of the rocks. It was hard enough to balance multiple pans of cornbread while having her young nephew joined at her hip, clutching a fistful of her dress skirt in his hand, but she managed to keep herself from falling.

"Are you okay?" *Aenti* Erma reached for the pans. "Let me carry those."

"*Nay*, I can manage." Her aunt already had a gallon jar of tea in one arm and the lantern in the other.

LeAnn lifted the plate of fudge-covered peanut-butter bars she was holding. "I'll trade you."

Grace's leg muscles quivered. "I'm fine. We're almost there." Just one more hill—no, mountain—to climb. She took shorter steps until she reached the peak. The bishop's house, nestled between a standing of jack pines, came into view.

Mitch sprinted ahead.

Grace wished she had a fraction of his energy. Walking Jasper to the barn after she got the buggy stuck had worn her out. She hadn't had

58

the strength to go back for the groceries. She planned to send Mitch after them once school ended, but she assigned him the barn chores to do instead. Making it to the meeting on time was more important, and there wasn't anything in the buggy that would spoil. The groceries could wait until morning.

Even as his older brother ran ahead, Jonas remained with Grace.

Mary Yoder opened the door and greeted them with a smile. "It's so *gut* to see you again, Erma."

"It's *gut* to be back." They entered the kitchen and *Aenti* Erma and Mary chatted about mutual friends they had in Ohio.

Grace set the pans of cornbread on the counter with the other food. She reached for Jonas's hand. "Let's get your coat off so you can play with the other children." She tugged his sleeve and he pulled his arm free.

Grace removed her cloak as laughter drifted into the kitchen from the sitting room. In this time of uncertainty about the men's well-being, it didn't seem appropriate . . . unless . . . Grace tossed her cloak on the pile with the others and hurried into the sitting room.

"What am I miss—?" Her smile dropped when Ben looked up from where he was sitting.

"Ben and Toby were telling us about Florida." Delilah Trombly nudged Ben's arm like they were old friends. "Please, continue."

"*Jah,*" Grace said. "Don't let me stop you." Not that it was possible. The man was clearly in his element surrounded by the unmarried women. She wouldn't pamper him with the same attention. Grace turned toward the kitchen. Wasn't it about time for the meeting to start?

❦

Badger Creek was looking better all the time. Ben did a quick *kapp* count of the women. Twenty. "Don't you love the odds?" he said under his breath to Toby.

"It's all in the chase, isn't it?" Toby huffed. "Even Neva."

"Neva chased me. She knew what time I got off the boat and she was waiting at the harbor with an opened bottle of tequila."

Toby's jaw twitched.

"Why do you concern yourself? You're the one who reminded me it's been a year." Ben smiled as the roomful of women surrounded him and Toby.

Grace's sister, LeAnn, had pressed her way through the swarm until she was by his side. The girl had a sweet smile. Ben couldn't help but compare the two sisters. While LeAnn seemed to thrive on competition, Grace retracted as though she had a phobia of crowds—or of him.

Bishop Yoder entered the room. Ben stopped talking midsentence. The unmarried women broke from the tight nest and went to the opposite side of the room as the married women filed out of the kitchen.

Ben glanced sideways at Toby. Did he feel on display too? The men's half of the room was empty.

"I want to start by introducing Alvin Graber's nephew." The bishop motioned to them. "This is Toby Graber and his friend Ben Eicher. For those of you who don't know, they are from Florida."

Ben scanned the women's side of the room, his gaze stopping on Grace. Her eyes connected with his a moment, then flitted away. Snob. All the other women had welcoming smiles. She was pale compared to the women in Florida. Not surprising. He'd been in Michigan two days and hadn't seen the sun once.

"The men have offered to stay for the summer and work," the bishop said.

How kind of the bishop not to mention the letter he'd received concerning the details behind their arrival. Although Bishop Yoder hadn't indicated whether he knew about them illegally swimming at Tidewater Inn and how their fathers had picked them up at the police station, Ben suspected he knew more information than he let on.

Bishop Yoder cleared his throat, stifling the *maedels'* soft chatter. Then he went on to talk about the concern everyone shared about not hearing from the men who were off at lumber camp. "We all know how hard it's been raining—much more than other years. But I'm sure we'll receive news soon."

Grave sighs filled the room. "What if another sinkhole opened? That's what happened the last time we had this much rain at once . . ." The woman's voice broke, and her eyes closed.

A soft murmur erupted. Ben glanced at Toby, then turned to the bishop. "Toby and I can search for them."

The room silenced. Every eye focused on them.

Ben shrugged. "It's only a few miles, right?" Wasn't that what Grace had said? He had walked farther than that to get to the fishing harbor to catch the boat.

"It is," the bishop said. "But it's a very difficult journey."

Ben nodded and glanced across the room at Grace. "Aren't the men loaded down with equipment? We wouldn't need to take that many provisions."

"*Danki*, Ben. We can talk about it more later." The bishop addressed the women. "If you haven't already stocked up on groceries, I suggest you do so. With the roads beginning to flood, we'll be closed off if we can't redirect the water." The bishop asked if anyone had any questions and Erma raised her hand.

"*Mei* niece wasn't able to get down our road," Erma said. "Her buggy is still stuck."

Grace eyed her aunt as if she wanted to say something, but tightened her lips instead.

Ben wasn't sure how they had made it out to the main highway this morning.

"I'm sorry to hear that." Bishop Yoder nodded toward Ben and Toby. "Will you two work on that in the morning?"

"Sure," Ben said. He didn't know an unmarried man who wouldn't want to work for a district filled with so many women—Grace included. It was good to feel needed. Maybe if his father had appreciated him more, things would have worked out in Florida. But any show of affection—be it verbal or a simple pat on the shoulder—wasn't his father's way.

The bishop smiled. "It's *gut* to have volunteers with strong hands. You two will be a big help in our community." The bishop ended the meeting with a reminder to pray for the men and to meditate on the verse in Philippians directing the flock to be anxious for nothing.

Several of the women headed into the kitchen. Grace weaved through the crowd in Ben's direction and stopped before him. "Can I speak with you outside a moment?"

"Sure." He'd listen to her apology. Maybe her heart wasn't pumping venom after all. Ben followed her outside. "*Ach*, it's *kalt* out." He should have grabbed his coat.

"*Jah*, I'll make this brief."

He smiled. She probably thought she could choke down some humble pie with a few words. Ben reached for her arm, her muscles stiffening under his touch. "Let's move somewhere out of the wind."

She glanced at the house, then motioned to a large tree just a few feet from the porch steps.

The tree wasn't large enough to shield them both from the bitter night. He stepped closer. Better. "What did you want to tell me?"

She backed up into the tree. "You and Toby won't need to help tomorrow."

Ben leaned closer still and whispered, "We don't mind."

"*Jah*, well . . ." Her breathing broke into short gasps. "I'd rather you *nett*."

Facing her, he placed his hands on either side of the tree, caging her. "Is there something else you'd like to tell me?" Like an apology for dumping them off at the grocery store?

"*Nay*, I . . . I told you I'd be brief." She ducked under his arm and dashed toward the house.

He jogged up the steps. "Grace, I, um . . . I shouldn't have overstepped *mei* bounds. *Mei* closeness made you . . . uncomfortable and . . ."

"Don't flatter yourself." She opened the door and darted into the house.

Ben hurried in behind her. "I was trying to get behind the tree more—out of the wind," he whispered.

"So you say." She swept her hand over her dress skirt.

His smug smile turned into a grin. "So, you think your closeness was what warmed me up, stopped me from shivering?"

She opened her mouth but clamped it shut when Toby and the bishop approached.

"Grace, I hope you didn't have to walk far from where your buggy broke down." The lines across Bishop Yoder's forehead deepened with fatherlike worry.

"*Nay*, I didn't." She lowered her head and tugged at the fold in her dress skirt.

"Well, these men will get you taken care of."

"Absolutely." Ben nodded when she snapped her head up.

"There's food in the kitchen. *Kumm* get something to eat when you're ready." The bishop walked away.

"So, that settles it," Ben said with a glint of satisfaction. "How far did you have to walk?"

Grace waited until the bishop was out of earshot. "I don't need your assistance or . . . your pity."

Before Ben could respond, Toby bridged the gap between them.

"We want to help," Toby said. "If we're going to be staying in your district, we need things to keep us busy." He moved even closer to her, blocking Ben's view completely. "If anyone's to be pitied, it's us. We're just poor castoffs who don't have enough money to get home."

Next, Toby would be telling her how their fathers were ashamed of them. True, his life was pitiful, but he didn't want to hear Toby talk about it. Ben sidestepped them. "While you two figure it out, I'm going to eat." And maybe mingle with the roomful of *maedels*.

℀

Ben had a better night's rest sleeping at the bishop's house. The air became thick with the welcoming scent of sausage and biscuits instead of hay and manure. Ben tossed the covers aside and bounded out of bed. Toby stirred on the bed next to the window as Ben pulled on his pants.

"I dreamt I was home," Toby said, rubbing his eyes.

"I decided after last *nacht* that I like this settlement," Ben said, shoving his arm into his shirtsleeve.

"You like the attention from the *maedels*."

"And why wouldn't I? We're the only unmarried men here. Get up, it's a *gut* day." Ben pulled his suspender over his shoulder and left the room. The bishop's wife was stirring sausage gravy on the stove as he entered the large farmhouse kitchen.

"How did you sleep?" she asked.

"Perfect."

"The bishop will be in shortly. He's out in the barn doing chores."

"I'll go help him." Ben plucked his hat from the hook. The wind lifted his hat as he stepped off the porch. He held it down and jogged toward the barn. The big red barn, situated on a hill, was massive compared to Grace's. Ben had never known a barn to have a basement, but the bishop's barn had a walkout entry, which led into the milking parlor. His eyes needed a moment to adjust to the dimness.

Ben found Bishop Yoder seated on a stool milking a cow. "*Gudder mariye.*"

"Sleep well?"

"*Jah.* Your *fraa* said you were out here. Do you need help?"

64

"Have you ever milked a cow?"

"*Nay.*" Ben wanted to make a good impression, but sitting so close to a cow looked a little intimidating, not to mention the physical contact required.

Bishop Yoder stood and motioned to the stool. "Have a seat." He went to a shelf and removed a bottle of hand sanitizer, then pumped the spout over Ben's open hands.

Ben rubbed his moist palms on his pant legs. He sat, but with great reservation.

Bishop Yoder chuckled. "Let's have your hands again." He administered another dollop of antiseptic, then set the bottle aside. "I've already milked the back two teats." Bishop Yoder squatted beside Ben. "You hold the teats like this and gently squeeze down." He demonstrated the technique, squirting frothy milk into the bucket, then released the udder and stood. "*Nau* you try."

Ben took a deep breath and positioned his hands. Nothing came out. He glanced up at Bishop Yoder. "I'm doing something wrong."

"Try it again."

This time a light spray splattered against the side of the bucket. "I did it."

Bishop Yoder clapped his shoulder. "*Jah*, you did. Nice work, *sohn*."

Ben continued milking, never getting into a comfortable rhythm like the bishop had, but filling the bucket nonetheless. He milked the cow dry, or so he thought until he and the bishop changed places.

"After some practice, you'll be able to feel when all the milk has come down," the bishop said, getting more milk from the cow. Once he finished, he picked up the bucket and handed it to Ben, then untied the cow from the post and took her to the door that led to the pasture. "I used to milk three solid hours growing up. We had a dairy farm and *mei bruders* and I milked the entire herd by hand."

"Sounds like a lot of work."

Bishop Yoder smiled. "Hard work keeps a man out of trouble."

Ben chewed the inside of his cheek. More than likely the bishop's statement had something to do with the letter he'd received from Ben's father.

The bishop stroked his beard. "We have a lot of young *maedels* in our settlement. Some I'm sure will bid for your attention."

News of Ben's indiscretion in Florida had spread. He lowered his head to avoid the bishop's scrutiny.

"Avoid temptation and walk by the Spirit, so you will *nett* gratify the desires of the flesh."

Ben gulped. "I understand."

"*Gut.*" Bishop Yoder clapped his shoulder. "*Nau* that the boundaries are established, let's go eat."

❧

"You're awfully quiet this morning," Grace said to Mitch as she emptied a bucket of water into the horse trough.

Mitch shrugged.

Grace waited for her nephew to empty his water bucket, then walked with him out to the well pump. "Concerned about your *daed, jah*?" He'd moped since the men left. "Me too." Grace pushed the barn door open. The sun was rising and shades of pink and light blue filled the sky.

Mitch primed the hand pump. "Someone needs to go look for them. A sinkhole could have opened up and swallowed them."

"You were listening to the adults' meeting with the bishop last *nacht*, weren't you?"

He thrust down on the handle. Water gushed out of the spigot and into the bucket.

"I know you're worried. We all are, but sinkholes are *nett* that common. The one that opened up a few years ago was the first in many years."

"Still, someone needs to go look for them." He stopped pumping when the bucket was full and waited until she exchanged it for an empty one. "Those men from Florida said they would go."

"I know. But they're *nett* from here. They might get lost themselves."

"I could show them the way."

"*Ach, nay.*" She shook her head. A ten-year-old and two Florida men were not a good combination to wander in the Michigan wilderness. "We need to trust God. Things will work out according to His will. But we must walk in faith."

"I know." Mitch's somber expression tore at Grace's heart. His faith hadn't materialized into more than someone else's words.

For Grace, words of faith meant realizing she had physical limitations unlike the other children and that she needed to trust in God. She could still hear her mother's voice reciting the verse in Second Corinthians. *My grace is sufficient for you, for My strength is made perfect in weakness.* Grace had learned about Saint Paul's infirmities long before she comprehended her own shortcomings. Yet the words held empty meaning even now. She also recalled in the Bible the crippled man at the pool and how Jesus asked if he wanted to be healed. She'd lost endless hours of sleep contemplating whether her healing was being withheld until she took some steps in faith. Maybe returning with *Aenti* Erma to the city was where healing could happen. She'd find a doctor and with the Lord's help they'd figure out how to restore her body.

"*Mei daed* says you have to exercise faith so that it grows."

"Your *daed* is a wise man." Grace's oldest brother, Peter, was a good role model for his son, much like her father. She placed her hand on his shoulder. "Sometimes the easiest way to take your mind off your troubles is to keep busy. After breakfast, would you please go to where I left the buggy and bring back the groceries?"

"Okay."

Grace picked up the water bucket. "Let's get these animals fed and watered so we can get something to eat." They walked back to the barn.

By the time the morning chores were completed, her nephew's shoulders no longer slumped. He ate so fast *Aenti* Erma had to tell him twice to slow down.

Mitch set his fork on his plate and wiped his sleeve over his mouth. *Aenti* Erma crinkled her brow.

"I'm done. Can I be excused?" He pushed to his feet the moment Grace nodded.

"I asked him to fetch the groceries from the buggy after breakfast," Grace said to *Aenti* Erma, then took a sip of coffee. Perhaps the talk with him had helped.

A few moments later, someone knocked and Grace rose to answer the door.

Toby and Ben stood on the stoop. "*Gudder mariye*," they said in unison.

"Hello." She hesitated a moment, then swung the door open for them to enter. "I thought maybe you had changed your mind." After all, she had asked them not to come.

"Nope." Ben grinned. "Why would you think that?"

"Because I . . ."

Ben tilted his nose in the air and sniffed. "Did *Aenti* Erma cook bacon again?" His question wasn't directed at Grace but the kitchen, as he moved past her.

Aenti Erma rounded the corner, wiping her hands on a dish towel. "*Gudder mariye*. Can I make you two a plate?"

Ben's smile widened. "How could I pass up—?"

"We've already eaten," Toby interjected.

"Oh, but . . ." Ben rested his hand over his midsection.

Grace snatched her coat off the hook. She had other things to do today. Laundry if it didn't rain, and once the buggy was pulled out of the rut, she needed to deliver the dog beds she had ready to sell in the pet store in town.

Toby elbowed Ben. "I think Grace is ready to go."

At least one of them seemed conscientious of something other than eating, although she had no idea how Ben could stay so . . . fit. She shook her head, casting those thoughts aside, and pulled the door open. She shot down the porch steps and walked to the barn as an image of Ben standing before her under the elm tree outside the bishop's house stole her attention. She'd fought half the night with the image of him leaning toward her and the memory of his warm breath brushing against her ear—while the other half of her restless night was spent reminding herself how he'd centered himself in the cluster of unmarried women. Flirts never lasted in their settlement and neither would Ben.

Grace stood for a long moment in the barn, her mind blank. She growled under her breath. The shovels were in the equipment barn. She pivoted around and marched outside, vowing that she wouldn't let Ben Eicher distract her again.

Ever.

Grace glanced at the house and huffed. Ben stayed inside to eat, and no doubt persuaded Toby too. She headed toward the equipment shed. Ben was as transparent as an icicle, only he dripped with phony eagerness.

The screen door snapped. Eager Beaver jogged across the lawn. His sidekick, Toby, was a few lengths behind.

Ben caught up to her. "Sorry, we were detained."

"I wasn't concerned," she said, keeping her eyes fixed on the shed.

"You're walking fast. I didn't realize you were in such a hurry."

"Saturdays are always busy. But please don't let that stop you from eating."

"I was being polite to your *aenti*." He turned so that he was walking backward in her direct path. "And I like bacon that isn't store-bought and buttermilk flapjacks with maple syrup that isn't watered down." He shrugged. "Is that a sin?"

She stopped when Ben blocked the door to the shed. Grace folded her arms. "*Nay*, it isn't a sin. *Nau* will you please step aside so I can get in there?"

"I didn't eat," Ben said, opening the door.

Toby followed her into the building. "He didn't. LeAnn came up from the cellar and had her arms loaded with canning jars. We helped her bring another load up."

"You don't have to explain." She grabbed a shovel and handed it to him. "I wasn't trying to put you on the spot."

"Who's the fisherman?" Ben motioned to the rods hanging on the wall.

"Those two belong to *mei* father and *bruder*." She moved the garden rake and hoe aside to reach another shovel.

"Where do they catch fish around here?"

"The river mostly." She went to hand Ben the other shovel, but he had moved closer to inspect the fishing tackle. He glanced over the leaders and rubber waders, then eyed the bamboo rod off to the side. "And this one?"

"That one's mine."

He lifted one brow at her. "This is a fly reel."

"I know what it is." He didn't believe the pole was hers.

He ran his thumb and index finger down the line. "It needs greasing. It won't float."

"It hasn't been used in a while."

Toby elbowed him. "*Kumm* on. We have a job to do."

At least one of them could stay focused. Grace left the shed. She had more to do than listen to Ben reminisce about fishing. Fishing was for leisure and she had no time to spare. The laundry was piled up because of all the rain, and she needed to tackle the spring-cleaning. The windows had a film of soot on them from burning wood in the woodstove all winter.

"It sure would be nice to go fishing," Ben said as they started down the path. "It probably wouldn't be too hard to find worms after all this rain."

She found simple satisfaction watching him scan the ground. Apparently he didn't know grasshoppers worked best for fly-fishing. Or that peak season for steelhead and brown trout wasn't for another month. A vision of him fighting the icy current in waders and catching nothing but the bushes behind him in his cast made her smile. She might be tempted to wander down to the river and spy on his first fishing attempt.

They came to a large puddle that took up the entire width of the road and stopped. Ben dipped the shovel into the water and the metal part disappeared.

"That's too deep." Grace searched for a shallower section where she could see the bottom. Still, the water would cover her shoes. She hesitated.

"So, Grace, if you no longer go fishing, what do you do for fun?" Ben jumped the puddle, clearing it in one long stride.

Toby landed short and made a splash.

"Thanks a lot." Ben wiped his pant leg where he'd been hit with murky water. "I was going to try and stay dry today."

Grace spun around. "I just remembered. We need the horse. I'll meet you at the buggy."

"Hey," Ben called.

She faced him. *"Jah?"*

"You didn't say what you do for fun."

"Laundry." She started walking again.

"That's it?"

"I wash walls and windows too," Grace answered over her shoulder. "It's a lively frolic that one doesn't want to miss." She chuckled softly. If Ben expected fun and games when he arrived, he would rethink his decision to stay. That suited her fine.

Chapter Eight

Ben stopped shoveling at the sound of a horse's neigh. He spotted Grace riding toward them, a smile on her face. Ben stabbed the metal part of the shovel into the ground and approached the left side of the horse once it stopped. "You should add horseback riding to your list of fun activities."

"I forgot how enjoyable riding is." She leaned down and patted the animal's neck. Her expression stiffened. "But buggy horses are not intended to be ridden for mere pleasure. They provide a service."

The woman had already let her guard down, but he wouldn't mention it. Ben raised his hands toward her waist. "Can I help you down?"

"*Nay*, I'll be fine."

Of course she wouldn't accept his help. The horse turned his head close to Ben's backside and snorted. He jumped away from the animal's reach and gave Grace plenty of space to dismount. He liked bicycles better. They didn't bite.

She swung her leg over the back of the horse, but the horse sidestepped as she slid down. Before he had a chance to react, Grace lost her footing and landed in a puddle of water.

Ben rushed to her side. "Are you okay? Did you get hurt?"

"I'm okay. Please," she said, scrambling to arrange the bottom of her dress skirt. "Turn around."

It wasn't like her legs were showing. She didn't need to fret over covering her shoes. He stretched out his hand. "Let me help you up."

She shooed her hand toward his. "I don't need your help," she snapped. "I just want you to turn around and stop gawking at me."

He crossed his arms. "And just *what* am I gawking at?"

"You know what." Her eyes shifted from her dress hem up to him. She pushed a stray hair away from her face and left a streak of mud across her forehead.

The red tinge spreading over her cheeks made it difficult not to stare. He fought to restrain his laughter, but when his eyes met her icy glare, he turned. She sputtered something under her breath.

Splash.

Water sprayed his backside and rippled at his feet. He peeked over his shoulder. She'd slipped on something and fallen back into the puddle. Ben turned and extended his hand. "Don't you think it's about time to swallow your pride?"

She opened her mouth but then closed it and surrendered her hand.

Ben assisted her to her feet, wrapping his arm around her waist until she was steady. He hadn't held a woman to keep her from falling since Neva, and she'd clung to him drunk.

Toby surfaced from the woods carrying an armload of sticks. His brows bent in puzzlement, but he said nothing.

"You can let go of me *nau*," she said in a hoarse whisper.

Ben released her. He rubbed his mud-covered hands down the sides of his pants.

"Are you . . . ready for the sticks?" Toby lifted his armload.

"Almost." Ben grabbed the shovel. He needed to do something to expel his nervous energy. The simple gesture of helping Grace left him weak-kneed and breathing fast. He wasn't sure why. Ben sank the head of the shovel into the ground and moved the mud from around the wheel. He removed a few more shovelfuls, then used the weight of his body to rock the buggy up far enough for Toby to arrange the sticks in the hole.

Toby rose from his knees. "Should get traction *nau*." He motioned to Grace. "If you wouldn't mind hitching the horse, we can see if this is going to work."

She wheeled the horse in a sharp circle, then backed him into position. A moment later, she announced that Jasper was ready.

"Wait until we give you the signal," Ben said. He and Toby went to the back of the buggy and got in position to push. "Okay, go."

She coaxed the horse.

Pushing hard against the buggy, Ben grunted. The buggy moved an inch or so, then stopped. A moment later, while they were still pushing, Grace appeared.

"Where's *mei* nephew?"

Ben relaxed his arms and stood upright. "What?"

"Mitch. I sent him to get the groceries."

"And you need to know where he is *nau*?" Ben shook his head.

She peered through the buggy window. "He didn't even get them all."

"Grace." Ben motioned to the puddle he was standing in. "Can we talk about that after we get the buggy out?"

She squared her shoulders. "You don't have to use that patronizing tone."

Ben glanced sideways at Toby. "Talk to her, please. We can't move this buggy if she doesn't get the horse to cooperate."

Toby turned to her. "He's right, Grace."

She looked at the remaining groceries once more and then returned to the head of the horse. She clicked her tongue. The buggy jerked forward, then started to roll backward. Ben and Toby thrust their weight against it and kept it from dropping back into the hole. She gave another command and the horse lurched. This time the buggy cleared the area, although it wobbled like a bent wheel on a bicycle.

"Okay, you can stop," Toby called out.

As they inspected the damaged wheel, she rummaged through the inside of the buggy.

Grace held up an apple core. "I would offer you an apple, but it looks like you have already helped yourself to *mei* groceries."

"I didn't eat that," Ben said.

"Me either." Toby pointed into the woods. "I saw an apple core in the woods when I was gathering sticks, but I didn't think anything of it."

"Maybe your nephew got hungry." Ben turned his attention to the cracked wheel. He nudged Toby. "This isn't safe."

"Hopefully, it'll stay on long enough to get back to the barn." Toby wiped more mud from his hands onto his pants. "I'm sorry," he said to Grace. "We'll have to walk. I don't think the wheel can handle the extra weight."

"That's a *gut* idea." She took hold of the horse's reins at the bit and clicked her tongue. "Let's go, Jasper."

The horse lurched forward, and the buggy hobbled on its cracked wheel. The way it wobbled lopsided, Ben wouldn't be surprised if it fell off the axle on the trip back to the house. He caught up to Grace. "You might want to steer the horse away from the potholes."

She glanced over her shoulder at the wheel. "Do you think it'll make it back to the *haus*?"

"I don't know. It's limping pretty badly. Do you have an extra wheel? Toby and I can change it."

"*Nay*, but I'll ask around. I'm sure someone does."

He glanced at the clear blue sky peeking through the bare trees. "Were you going to find out about the wheel today?"

"Why do you ask? Because I wouldn't feel comfortable loaning the buggy if that's why you're eager to change the wheel."

"Wouldn't dream of asking to borrow your buggy." The horse might be a gentle giant in her hands, but Ben wanted nothing to do with trying to control the beast. "I was thinking about going fishing. That is, if you think your *daed* wouldn't mind if Toby and I use his poles."

Grace narrowed her eyes. "Hasn't the bishop assigned you work?"

"*Jah*, to get your buggy back home. Would you like to go fishing with us?"

"I don't have time to waste."

"Fishing is never a waste of time," Ben said. "Maybe if you had some fun, you'd smile more."

She opened her mouth as if she were going to say something but shook her head instead. Except for the sound of wind in the bare trees and the shrill cry of a hawk nearby, all was calm. Too calm. Ben didn't like the awkward silence between them.

He eyed her left leg. "Did you get hurt?" He'd asked her after she'd fallen from the horse, but her puffed-up pride may have prevented her from being honest.

"I'm fine." She tipped her chin higher. "Why do you ask?"

"You're limping. I thought—"

Toby speared him in the ribs with his elbow.

"What?" Ben waited, but Toby merely furrowed his brow and shook his head. Ben turned back to Grace. "I can put you up on the horse if it's too painful to walk."

"I told you I'm fine." Her voice broke.

Ben didn't need another elbowing by Toby to know he'd said something wrong. He changed the subject. "So, do you think we could use the fishing poles?"

❧

A lump had formed in the back of Grace's throat. She wouldn't get the first word out without squeaking. Where was the rain when she needed it to wash her face of tears? She tilted her head back and hoped he didn't see them fall. *My grace is sufficient* . . . Reciting the verse had always helped when someone whispered behind her back about her limp, or in Ben's case, pointed it out. *My grace is sufficient* . . . It wasn't working.

Her wet dress clung to her legs and made it cumbersome to move. *Almost home,* she silently coaxed, catching a glimpse of the barn through the woods.

Fishing. He had an easy life. She couldn't even rest from her responsibilities long enough to apply the poultice to her legs and relieve some of the joint swelling. Once she took care of Jasper, she had clothes to wash. Maple syrup to can. She had enough work to keep her busy the rest of the summer. When did she have time for fun? Not that fishing was fun—she respected but despised the river.

They reached the yard and Toby pointed to the smokehouse. "Would it be out of your way if the buggy sits over there?" he asked Grace. "It would be easier to change the wheel if we leave it out in the open instead of parking it under the lean-to."

"As long as it's away from the clothesline." She led Jasper to the spot and unhitched him. "Make sure the poles are returned to the rightful place. And *nett* with their lines tangled either." She collected the groceries scattered on the floor of the buggy. She called for Mitch the moment she stepped inside the house.

"He isn't here," *Aenti* Erma said, taking one of the bags from Grace's arms.

"Where did he go?"

"I haven't seen him since breakfast." *Aenti* set the grocery bag on the counter and reached for the other one in Grace's arms. "You're all wet, child. Why don't you change into something warm before you catch a *kalt*."

Grace emptied the contents of the grocery bags onto the counter, recalling the apple core she found inside the buggy and the other one in the woods. The bag of apples, the pears . . . the walnuts, all were missing. Things a boy would pack if he were on a mission to find his father. She rushed from the room.

"Grace?" *Aenti* followed her to the door. "What's wrong?"

"I have to find Mitch."

Chapter Nine

Adrenaline fed Grace's veins. It wasn't like Mitch to disappear. She sped through the barn, searched every pen, every stall, even the hayloft, but he was nowhere to be found.

Grace bolted outside. "Mitch!"

Mitch's words echoed in her mind. *Someone needs to go look for them. A sinkhole could have opened up and swallowed them.*

She cut across the pasture and sprinted into the woods. The spongy carpet of pine needles along the path cushioned her feet. The well-traveled footpath led to the fishing hole, the deepest part of the river. She hoped Mitch wasn't foolish enough to try to cross in that area. Faint sounds of rushing water became louder. She ran faster.

She spotted Ben and Toby several yards ahead meandering down the trail, fishing poles propped against their shoulders. Ben glanced over his shoulder and then stopped. "Did you decide to go fishing with us?"

"*Nay*," she said, gasping deep breaths. "I'm looking for Mitch. Have you seen him?"

Voices echoed from the direction of the river. Laughing louder than any adult in their district would. "That's probably him with the other boys." Grace marched toward the river. She had half a mind to load him up with a week's worth of chores for what he'd put her through.

Ben came up beside her. "Maybe you should go light on him. You know . . . if he's with his friends."

"You probably think I should let him go fishing."

The pack of boys raced toward them. "More ice has melted," Owen Schmucker said, slowing his pace as he approached. "The river's almost crested."

She eyed the group of boys but didn't see her nephew. "Have any of you seen Mitch?"

"*Nett* since yesterday." The boys kept running. "We've got to tell the bishop about the river."

The river! She took off running toward the water in an uneven gait that put pressure on her hips.

Ben flanked her side. "Aren't you headed in the same direction where the boys just came from? None of them saw him at the river."

"I know." She slowed her pace as they approached the clearing. The boys were right. The rushing water meant more than just a little ice had melted. She hadn't ventured down the sandy embankment to go near the water since the last time she went fishing. Grace peered at the water. Many of the large boulders that she'd once sat on while dangling her feet in the river were underwater.

"What kind of fish are in here?" Ben peered over the drop-off.

"Steelhead, brown, brookie, and rainbow trout mostly. Salmon sometimes," she mumbled.

Grace stared at the swirls of frothy water and cakes of floating ice. Mitch wasn't a strong swimmer. If he had tried to cross at this point, the current would have swept him downstream. She headed to the footpath, which cut through the wild grass growing along the riverbank.

"Grace?" Ben's raised voice grabbed her attention. "*Nau* where are you going?"

"I have to find him," she said over her shoulder.

Ben sped up beside her on the trail. "If he came to the river, wouldn't he be with his friends?"

"That's what I'm worried about. I think he might have tried to cross." The runoff from the melted snow had softened the ground and the heel of her shoe sank into the spongy earth. She jerked her foot free. The ground was this soft the year the sinkhole opened. Mitch had probably overheard some of the women comparing how similar the wet seasons were.

"Why would he?" Toby asked, trailing behind.

"He overhead the discussion about the men last *nacht* and was upset. He thought someone should search for them." Apparently, the talk she and Mitch had in the barn hadn't helped. She should have recognized her nephew's determination and kept a closer eye on him. Even her brothers, Peter and Emery, the best swimmers she knew, would be hard-pressed to make it across. The high water level and turbulent flow would cast anyone downstream.

Several feet ahead, a grouse rose from the dense brush, flapping its wings wildly. Toby and Ben paused, their eyes following the bird until it landed on a nearby beechnut branch. It wasn't uncommon to kick up game along this path. As the underbrush along the riverbank became thicker, the trail led them farther away from the water and deeper into the woods. She stepped over a fallen limb.

Tree branches snapped in the distance.

More birds jetted up from the bushes.

Grace halted. This time, something—or someone—else had spooked the wildlife. "Mitch?" she yelled.

No answer.

She scanned the wooded area. "Mitch?" she said louder, cupping her hand to her mouth.

Toby and Ben echoed her call.

Silence.

"Why do I get the feeling that someone is watching us?" Toby asked, gripping the fishing rod like a weapon.

Ben guffawed. "How much protection do you think that pole will give you?"

Toby said something about how jumpy Ben was when two

squirrels scurried up a nearby tree, but Grace ignored the banter and focused on her search.

The area had changed since she was here last. Nothing looked familiar. Maybe this wasn't the right direction. But it wasn't long before the trail led them back to the river and they came upon the old watermill. The dilapidated building's cedar-shake exterior was barely visible with the overgrown vines covering it.

Ben lowered the fishing rod to the ground. "Let's check it out," he said to Toby, who was already walking toward the structure.

Toby took a few steps and stopped. He glanced over his shoulder at her. "Are you coming?"

Grace shook her head. She hadn't been to the mill in years and it wasn't a place she wanted to revisit.

Toby and Ben disappeared behind the building on the side facing the river.

Grace planted her hands on her hips and stared at a boarded-up window. "Mitchell Wagler. If you're in there, you better *kumm* out. *Nau.*" She eyed a section of wall where the bottom of a board had rotted. When nothing moved, her hope deflated. Mitch wasn't there or he would have responded.

A moment later, the tall cattail weeds between the building and the river moved. Ben. He climbed up the rocky embankment and removed something he'd tucked behind his suspender.

"I found this." He held up a browning apple core.

Grace gulped a mouthful of air.

Ben turned it over in his hand. "It can't be too old or it would have degraded."

"Or an animal would have eaten it," Toby said, coming up behind Ben.

"He's been here recently." Grace peered up at the sky and closed her eyes. *Lord, please watch over and protect him. Let it be Your will that he's all right.*

Ben cleared his throat. "We checked the building. There's only one door on the lower level *nett* boarded up, but it's stuck. He wouldn't have enough strength to pull it open either."

Grace nodded. "Will you show me where you found the core, please?"

"This way," Ben said, motioning toward the river.

The apple cores they'd found at the buggy and now this one didn't make sense. Mitch had eaten a large breakfast before racing out of the house. She followed Ben around the side of the building and stopped at the edge of the embankment. The rocky slope was steeper than she remembered. She focused on the massive wooden wheel that years ago generated the power to run the equipment. Now many of its paddles were missing. Loose stones cascaded several feet down and plopped into the water. Her mouth dried. Her ears rang. A wave of nausea washed over her as her vision doubled and she stumbled backward.

❧

The only time Ben had seen someone's face turn as white as Grace's was seconds before the seasick crew member leaned over the side of the boat and vomited. She wobbled backward, and he caught her elbow. "Are you okay?"

"*Jah.*"

"Sure? Your eyes are closed," he said.

"I will be." Her shoulders lifted and fell as she breathed. Her dark lashes fluttered and she opened her eyes. Her big, brown—river-colored—eyes.

"I, ah . . . I thought you were about to fall." He released her elbow and motioned to the sandy shore. "I found the apple down there."

Her eyes glazed. She used the corner of her sleeve to wipe at them.

"Maybe the apple wasn't his," Toby said in a soothing tone.

"I bought a bag of apples in town yesterday and they disappeared from the buggy." Her lips trembled. "We need to go back and get help."

Ben didn't need to hear any more. After seeing her eyes water, he couldn't tell her he'd seen footprints in the sand. He started down the embankment, the ground crumbling under his feet. Once he landed on solid ground, he unlaced his shoes and kicked them off.

"Are you going to cross the river?" Toby asked.

"I swim a lot better than you do." Someone needed to go after the boy. He removed his socks. The cold ground should have clued him in on what to expect, but his legs turned numb in the water almost immediately. He gritted his teeth to keep them from chattering and took another step. Only the bottom of the river dropped from under him. The chest-deep current beat against him, bending him like a reed. His foot slipped on a moss-covered rock and the rushing water swept him under. He bobbed up to the surface, sucked in a breath, and was pulled back under.

Kick.

Kick.

His arms and legs were like sandbags. Heavy. Numb.

Shuttled downstream in a spiral, he couldn't be certain which direction he needed to swim. He turned his face in the direction of his name being called just before his head hit something hard.

Chapter Ten

Grace gasped when Ben plunged underwater. Seconds later, he resurfaced a few feet downstream, coughing like he'd taken water into his lungs.

"We have to help him!" Toby shouted. "Bring the fishing pole." He sprinted along the riverbank.

Grace grabbed the pole from where Ben had left it on the ground and raced to catch up with Toby. She hadn't quite reached him when Toby yelled his friend's name.

Ben's body slammed up against a dead tree and he grabbed onto a branch.

"Hang on!" Pole in hand, Toby slid down the sandy embankment, landing at the edge of the water. He scrambled to his feet. "I don't see him. Can you see him from up there?"

"*Nay.*" The limb was missing at the spot where he'd grabbed onto the tree. Had the current pulled him under? Ach, *Lord, keep him from getting snagged on a branch underwater.*

"Do you see him yet?" Toby paced the shoreline.

"*Nay.*" She should have kept her eye on Ben instead of watching to see if Toby had made it down the steep embankment safely. Now they'd lost Ben. *Oh, Lord, please . . . please help him.*

A short distance downstream, she caught a glimpse of Ben's blue shirt. "There," she said, pointing. "I see him." This time she kept her eyes on Ben rather than on Toby scaling the incline.

"Oh *nay*," Toby cried out as he slid on his belly down the slope. He landed with a thump and was showered by falling rocks, but somehow he'd managed to grasp his ankle, then roll to his side.

"Are you okay?"

"*Jah*," he said through gritted teeth. He motioned toward Ben's body, floating downstream. "Follow him. I'll catch up."

She hesitated a half second, then sped off. Ben was heading toward one of the widest and deepest parts of the river. The water turned almost black in some spots. She pushed herself to run faster despite how badly her lungs burned.

Up ahead, Ben slammed into a beaver's dam.

Almost there. Don't let go, Ben.

She tossed the pole over the side of the cliff. Time spent at the river as a child taught her to sit down and scoot to the bottom, but this section was steeper and rockier than any of the areas where she'd played. She eased downward. Her heel snagged on a root midway down. She tried to jerk her foot free, but in doing so, she lost her balance and toppled to the bottom.

※

"Grace?" Ben's faint voice didn't carry past his mouth. She'd taken a hard fall and he couldn't help. He'd lost feeling in his legs, either from injury or hypothermia, but he tried to pull himself up higher on the dam. The network of sticks cracked under his weight.

She didn't move for what seemed like an eternity. "I'm okay," Grace finally answered. She pushed to her feet. Standing at the edge of the water, she stared at him. "Can you get out?"

He sure wasn't soaking in icy water for any health benefits. "*Nay*," he replied, remaining calm.

She bit her bottom lip and looked from side to side.

Maybe she was stunned from the fall and needed prompting, or maybe she was looking for Toby. Where was he?

"Grace, can you find a long stick?" He shouldn't have to say it, but he did anyway. "And preferably not one from the beaver dam."

It took half a second for his request to register, then her eyes widened and she stepped into action. She picked up the fishing pole. "Will this work?"

He hoped so. This dam wouldn't hold him much longer. The mound of twigs snapped under his weight and parts of the habitat floated away.

Grace extended the end of the pole toward him.

Ben stretched out his arm, but the rod was beyond his reach. He made another attempt, his muscles screaming despite the freezing water, which up until now had dulled his senses. Ben fell against the dam, dog tired.

"Where's Toby?" He needed someone who wasn't so timid and would take a step or two into the water.

"He said he would catch up. Do you want to wait?"

No. He didn't want to dangle another minute on a pile of crumbling sticks. He pushed up higher on the mound. If he could get over to the other side, the water was bound to be shallower. He hoisted himself up, had one knee on the structure, when it split in half. Water whooshed by in a swirl, taking the section he was resting on. The rush of water sledded him into a shallow stream, but being tossed over the riverbed of rocks was worse than any body surfing he'd ever done. He found a large boulder to hug and, in doing so, prevented the current from whisking him back into the deep section.

Grace appeared on the shore and stretched the fishing pole out once more. She leaned forward, eyes closed and grimacing. "Here, take it."

Another time he might have pulled her into the river and coaxed her into taking a swim. But not today. The temperature wasn't much above freezing.

He pushed off the rock and stood. The water was only thigh-high, but it frothed around him and the rapid flow was such that his numb legs could buckle at any time. He dragged himself to the shore and collapsed on the cold sand.

Grace knelt next to him, tears budding in her eyes. "Are you okay?"

"Just let . . . me rest . . . a minute." The air wasn't much warmer than the frigid river. He crossed his arms, shaking uncontrollably.

"You have to get back to the *haus* where it's warm."

"We have—to find—" His teeth chattered, making it difficult to talk.

"Your lips are purple," Grace said, taking off her cape. "Can you sit up?"

The moment he pushed himself up, she slung her cape over his shoulders and fastened it under his neck. If he wasn't so cold, he would rebuke the woman's cloak. Wearing any article of women's clothing was mortifying. The scratchy wool material rubbed against his wet skin.

"*Danki*," he said, too exhausted to object. He looked over the water. No more than thirty or forty feet after the shallow rock bed, he could swim that stretch against the current, if his muscles would cooperate and not spasm. Someone still needed to find Mitch. After the fight he had with the current, Toby wouldn't make it across. For that matter, Mitch wouldn't have made it either.

"I wasn't sure you were going to make it out of there," Grace said, a choked sob breaking from her lips.

He brought the cape higher to block his ears from the biting breeze. "I'm surprised you didn't leave me."

She crinkled her face. "Leave you!"

He cracked a smile. "You left me at the grocery store."

"Hey, you two," Toby's voice boomed from the hilltop. "Look who I found."

The ten-year-old standing beside Toby bowed his head.

Grace squealed with delight. She bolted from her kneeling position next to him and made her way to them.

Ben rose to his feet and wobbled in place. His legs tingled as the nerve endings thawed and he regained the feeling in his toes. He reached the top of the hill as Grace pulled her nephew into what looked like a smothering embrace, based on the boy's grimace.

Grace pushed Mitch out to arm's length. "I've been worried sick. Where have you been?"

Keeping his head bowed, he shrugged.

"I found him just before the river bend. He was curled up on a bed of pine needles under some white pine saplings."

"Mitch, you must've heard us calling." Grace's tone sharpened.

Ben shivered. "Maybe we can talk about this somewhere warm."

"*Ach*, how inconsiderate of me." She directed her attention to Toby. "How is your ankle?"

"It's swollen, but I'll be all right."

She hadn't asked Ben what the copper-tinged water tasted like. He must've ingested a gallon or more every time the current sucked him under.

"We'll take the logging road back," Grace said. "It's easier than cutting through the woods."

Pine needles stabbed the bottoms of Ben's feet. He hobbled a few steps.

Grace stopped abruptly. "I know *mei* limping must be entertaining, but you don't have to mock me, Ben."

"Please don't tease her," Toby chimed in. "We've all had a rough day."

Rough day. Who almost drowned? Ben lifted his foot, pulled out a picker, then held it up for them to see. "It's a little difficult walking on a carpet of needles." He tossed the thistle on the ground and lumbered a few more steps. He went barefoot in Florida a lot. The soles of his feet shouldn't be this tender.

"I forgot you're barefoot." Grace tapped her nephew's shoulder. "Run to the watermill and get Ben's shoes. He left them by the river." The boy took off running. "Most people wear their shoes into the water because it's so rocky."

"What about you? Do you swim in your shoes?" He glanced down at her stiff-looking black shoes. At one time they were probably her Sunday best and shined when they were buffed with a soft rag. Now, the leather was cracked.

"I don't swim," she said, adjusting her dress skirt to flap over her shoes.

"Even in the summer?"

"Ever."

Her personality matched her shoes—tough and unforgiving. "You're missing out on a lot of fun."

"*Jah*," Toby huffed. "If sitting in jail sounds like fun," he said under his breath.

His friend held a grudge as deep as the ocean. Then again, Ben had instigated the mess they'd gotten into in Florida.

The boy ran back to meet them. "There aren't any shoes by the river," he said, panting hard.

"They wouldn't have disappeared," Grace said.

Ben agreed. It wasn't like in Florida where if you left your shoes too close to the ocean, the waves would take them out to sea.

"I looked all over."

"Someone from the settlement must have found them. I'm sure they will show up," Grace told Ben.

"I'll be all right." His feet were already starting to adjust to the prickly needles and cold dirt. He couldn't imagine someone taking his shoes. The bishop was short and small-framed and the other men were gone. Who would be interested in a pair of size eleven sneakers?

Chapter Eleven

Grace steeped a pot of her friend Mattie's special tea. She still had enough leaves from last year when her chest had filled with fluid from what the doctor said was walking pneumonia. Ben had changed into her brother Emery's dry clothes, but he hadn't stopped shivering. If he wasn't careful, he would come down with pneumonia from being in the water for so long.

Grace poured Toby a cup too. It probably wouldn't do anything to help his swollen ankle, but the cayenne pepper in the brew would set fire to his insides.

"The river must have been freezing," *Aenti* Erma said, placing a few oatmeal cookies on a plate. She craned her neck toward the sitting room. "Poor Ben is still shivering even wrapped in a wool blanket and sitting in front of the woodstove."

"I know." Grace was glad he hadn't refused to wear her cloak. He looked like he might at first. Most men would rather freeze to death than be caught wearing something meant for a woman. "Ben's shoes and socks went missing and he had to walk barefoot back to the *haus*. I'm hoping a cup of Mattie's tea will help."

"No wonder he can't warm up."

Grace picked up the cups of tea and *Aenti* followed her into the sitting room with the plate of cookies.

"Here's something that should warm you up." Grace handed Ben one of the cups. His hands shook such that the ocher-tinted liquid sloshed over the rim.

"I'm sorry. I spilled some on the blanket."

"It's *nett* your fault. I shouldn't have filled it so full." Grace handed Toby the other cup. "I made you a cup too."

"*Danki*." Toby dunked his cookie into the tea and took a bite.

Aenti offered Ben a cookie, but he shook his head. "I don't think I could eat anything just yet."

"I'll leave the plate on the lamp table for when you're hungry." *Aenti* Erma set the plate down, then returned to the kitchen.

Ben wasn't eager to try his tea either. He looked up at her with a discerning gaze. "You didn't brew river water, did you?"

Grace smiled. "*Nay*. It's an herbal tea that one of *mei* friends concocted. It helped me when I was sick last winter."

"I've never been sick a day in *mei* life," he protested.

Grace motioned to the cup. "Drink it anyway."

"Yes, *Mamm*." He blew over the steaming cup. His eyes held a twinkle as he looked at her over the rim.

Ben wasn't sick. She didn't know why she was fussing over him. Toby was the one needing attention. His injured ankle had swelled to twice the size of his uninjured one. "I'm going to get a pot of salt water for you to soak your foot in," she said to Toby on her way to the kitchen.

Ice was the best thing for reducing swelling, but the large slabs cut from the lake, which kept the *icehaus kalt*, would be too difficult to chip. She removed the mop bucket from the closet and took it outside to the pump. Submerging his foot in the spring-fed water would help. She cranked the iron handle to prime the pump and water gushed out from the spigot and partially filled the bucket.

Once inside, she added the Epsom salt crystals into the water. She doubted he could stand the cold water long, but any amount of time in the footbath would help soothe his sore muscles.

She carried the bucket into the sitting room and placed it next to Toby's foot. "You need to soak your foot in this. It'll help bring the swelling down."

Toby reached down and peeled off his sock. Gingerly easing his foot into the bucket, his eyes widened. "That's *kalt*! I don't know about this."

"Trust me," Grace said. "Your ankle will feel much better."

He shuddered but obliged.

"I'll get you a wool blanket." She went into her bedroom and stole the top quilt from the bed. She also grabbed a bath towel from the linen closet. As she returned to the sitting room, the front door opened and LeAnn and Mitch entered.

"I'm sorry, but no one has seen your shoes," LeAnn said to Ben as she crossed the room.

"We asked everyone," Mitch added.

"That's okay. I'm sure they will show up eventually." Ben drank more of his tea.

Grace estimated his foot to be the size of her brother's. "Emery has a pair of mucking boots out in the barn. They should fit."

Ben's lips formed a tight, straight line. "Like I said, I'm sure they will turn up. But thanks all the same."

She couldn't really blame him. The barn boots stank. The first night neither he nor Toby seemed overly eager to sleep in the barn. She remembered Ben burying his nose in the pillow and blankets he was carrying.

Mitch cleared his throat. "*Danki* for looking for me."

Her nephew directed his thanks to Ben and Toby, but Grace could not have been prouder if Mitch were her own son.

"And *danki* for pulling me out of the water." Mitch's gaze shifted from Ben to Toby, then back to Ben.

"I didn't pull you out." Ben looked sideways at Toby. "Did you?"

"*Nay*." Toby shook his head. "I found you under the tree. Asleep."

Mitch held a blank stare.

If he had gone into the water, he would be like Ben—unable to warm up . . . or worse. Not alive. Grace moved closer to her nephew and placed her hand on his shoulder. "Maybe you were dreaming?"

"*Nay*," he said. "I went to the river to find *mei daed*."

Grace motioned to Ben's clothes draped over a kitchen chair next to the woodstove. "Mitch, your clothes were dry. How did you *nett* get your clothes wet if you had been in the river?"

"I don't know why mine are dry." He touched his shirt. "The last thing I remember was being in the water and sinking to the bottom."

She was going to have a talk with Mitch's *mamm* when she came to pick him up. Nothing good came out of a lie.

"I'm telling you the truth, *Aenti* Grace. A man grabbed me by the shirt and pulled me out of the river."

Grace folded her arms across her chest. She probably should let his mother pump him with questions, but Grace hoped if he were cornered in his lies, he would change his story and admit the truth before Susan came to pick him up. "So, what did this man look like?"

Mitch searched Ben's face, then studied Toby's as if silently expecting one of them to come forward and confess. But both Toby and Ben looked as puzzled as Grace. Her nephew sighed and shrugged his shoulders. "I don't know how to describe him. I never really saw his face."

❧

Ben understood Mitch probably better than anyone else in the room. The boy had gone to the river with intentions to cross, but changed his mind. And not wanting to be viewed as a coward, he made up an elaborate story. Ben had sure told his share of stories at Mitch's age— swimming with alligators was the one he remembered the most clearly.

Grace stood, much like his mother did when she demanded answers, with her hands on her hips and her eyes piercing the boy's soul. "Tell me again what happened."

Ben sat up straighter in the chair. This is where his stories always grew. He hated to be quizzed over and over.

But Mitch repeated the story—without expanding or deleting any of the details—and while maintaining constant eye contact with her.

Ben deemed the boy convincing—but judging by Grace's rigid posture, she didn't think so. Ben coughed into his hand. "Grace, do you think I could have more tea?"

"*Jah*, of course." Grace took his cup and left the room, giving the boy a reprieve. A few moments later, she returned with another steaming brew. She placed the cup on the lamp table, then turned to face Mitch. "I think LeAnn can use your help with checking the sap buckets."

Mitch nodded.

"And, Mitch," she said, halting his step. "What did you do with the groceries you took from the buggy?"

The boy lowered his head. "I never went to the buggy."

Grace's face fumed. She stared hard at her nephew, but instead of accusing him of lying again, she shooed him outside. The door closed behind Mitch and she released a weighted sigh, shook her head, and walked back to them. She peered into the bucket that Toby was soaking his foot in. "How is your ankle?"

"Numb." Toby lifted his foot, splashing water from the pail. "What do you think? Has the swelling gone down?"

"Maybe a little, but I think you should let it soak longer."

Toby grimaced, but he dipped his foot back into the water.

Despite the hot tea and being wrapped in a wool blanket, Ben couldn't get warm. Surely the water wasn't as cold as Toby made it seem. Not as cold as the river. Ben would have called him on it if he could stop his teeth from chattering. His lips were probably still purple and he might never regain the feeling in his toes. So far he didn't have much to like about Michigan. If he ended up with pneumonia, maybe his father would regret sending him away.

Chapter Twelve

Ben's ribs throbbed from coughing and the breathing spasms had left him hoarse. Grace warned him that his cough would move into his chest if he didn't drink more tea, but after four days he couldn't stomach another cup of bitter-bark extract. Even if she offered to spoon-feed him. Not that it was an option. Grace had brought the brewed concoction over to the bishop's house in a gallon jar with special instructions for how often he was to drink it. She didn't stay to keep him company, although he wouldn't have been much company. Whatever was in the tea made him sleepy.

Sitting up in bed, Ben peered inside the cup and cringed. He couldn't drink it and couldn't stay in bed another day. He tossed the covers aside.

Mary, the bishop's wife, was at the stove stirring something in a kettle when he entered the kitchen. "Ben," she said, "are you feeling well enough to be up?"

"I feel okay." Certainly not normal, with his head spinning and his ears ringing. He pulled a ladder-back chair out from the table and sat. He hoped that once he ate something solid, the dizziness would pass.

"You must be hungry. I'll make some eggs." She removed the long wooden spoon from the pot and set it on the counter. "Do you want *kaffi*? Or maybe you'd rather have a cup of tea?"

"*Nay*—I mean . . ." He cleared his throat. "*Kaffi* sounds *gut*, *danki*." He never wanted to see another cup of tea—unless it was plain black tea.

The bishop's wife reminded him of his *mammi*. Only his grandmother was humpbacked from osteoporosis, and because of her stooped posture, she had lost several inches in her height over the years.

Mary set a mug of coffee on the table along with the cream and sugar containers. "This should get you started. I'll have the eggs ready in a few minutes."

"*Kaffi* is enough. You've already done so much."

She smiled. "*Nay, kaffi* is *nett* enough. I won't have any of *mei* guests hungry." She removed a cast-iron fry pan from the lower cabinet and set it on the stove. "We've all been worried about you," she said, cracking an egg into the pan. "This is the wrong time of the year to be in the river."

"*Jah*, I found that out." He took a sip of coffee.

"We're all thankful that you made it out okay."

Even Grace? He dared not ask. Instead, he took another drink.

She placed a few biscuits on a cookie sheet. "I made these earlier. They'll only take a few minutes to reheat," she said, slipping them into the oven.

His stomach growled. Four days without substance had angered his stomach. Anything other than chicken broth would taste good. Within a few moments, the kitchen filled with the smell of cooking food, teasing his senses. His mouth watered as she placed the biscuits and eggs on a plate.

Someone knocked on the door as she set the food on the table. He picked up his fork but paused. His mother never appreciated anyone eating without permission. The moment Mary waved her hand and told him not to wait, he took his first bite. The eggs seemed to dissolve in his mouth. He hadn't realized how hungry he was until he'd practically inhaled the two eggs.

Mary invited the caller inside. Footsteps trailed into the kitchen. He lifted his eyes from the plate as Grace came into his peripheral view.

"I see you're up. Are you feeling better?" Without giving him time to answer, she motioned to the glass jar in her hands. "I brought some more tea. Do you want me to pour you a cup?" She set the container on the counter.

"*Nay*," he said too quickly.

She eyed him over her shoulder but said nothing.

"I-I'm better." He tilted his empty plate her direction. "I'm eating *nau.*"

"See, Ben? I told you we've all been worried." Mary placed her arm around Grace's shoulder and gave her a motherly squeeze. "Grace has stopped by every day to check on you and to bring you tea."

Grace's face turned a rosy shade. "I'm just the delivery person. Mattie made the tea using herbs from her greenhouse."

"Well," Ben said, "you can tell Mattie that the tea stimulated *mei* appetite. So it must have worked."

"*Jah*, I'll be sure to tell her." Grace turned to the bishop's wife. "I should get back to the mill. I received several more orders for dog beds in the mail today."

"That's *wunderbaar*. Oh, that reminds me." Mary's eyes widened, looking at Ben. "You and Toby both received letters in the mail today." She grabbed the envelopes off the counter and handed one to Ben.

Ben recognized his mother's handwriting and decided to read it later. He pushed his chair away from the table and stood. "Did you say you were going to the watermill? If you don't mind, I'll walk down to the river with you. I'd like to look for *mei* shoes."

"I'm *nett* going to the river."

"Oh . . ."

Grace smiled. He must not have masked his disappointment. "The watermill hasn't been in use in over a decade," she said.

Of course it hadn't. The building was boarded up.

"But I'm sure Ben would like to get some fresh air," Mary said. "It's okay if he walks with you, right, Grace?"

"*Jah* . . . if he wants." She retied the string of her winter bonnet.

Not much of an invitation. He should apologize for the inconvenience. Acknowledge how much he would miss her *charming* company, but insist on finding his own shoes. He opened his mouth to speak just as the bishop's wife thrust more envelopes at him from the top of the mail stack on the counter.

"Since you're going to the sawmill, could you take these letters to Toby? He's working there today."

"Sure." Ben glanced at the letters. He assumed the one from Pinecraft was from Toby's *mamm*, but who in Indiana knew he was in Michigan? "*Danki* for breakfast," he said, following Grace out of the kitchen.

"Your boots are next to the door."

They weren't his boots. They belonged to Grace's brother. But Ben slipped them on his feet. "I hope you don't mind if I wear these again."

"Emery won't be home for a few weeks."

Mary rounded the corner. "Here's a warmer coat you can use."

"*Danki*."

"I plan to do laundry today. Are your and Toby's dirty clothes in the basket?"

He shook his head. The wet clothes he'd been wearing when he jumped into the river he tossed on the line to dry, but that was four days ago. He left his other clothes, clean and dirty, piled in the corner of the bedroom.

"Well, I'll figure out what's clean and what's dirty. You run along and have fun." The short, grandmotherly woman returned to the kitchen.

Grace waited for him to shove his feet into the boots, then pushed open the screen door.

Ben shoved his arms into the coat sleeves and hurried outside. He took in a sharp breath of cold air and coughed. The clear blue sky meant nothing in Michigan. The temperature hadn't risen above forty all day. He rubbed his arms. "When does it warm up around here?"

She peered up at the sky. "This *is* warm."

"Warm, you say?" He laughed.

"Yup." She drew in a long breath much like he often did of the salty air at the beach, then blew it out—a white puff of cloudy breath.

"Did it get colder over the last few days, or am I imagining that I can see our breath?"

"It's colder. But there shouldn't be too many more cold snaps."

He exhaled again just to watch his cloudy breath linger in the air.

"This is nothing. In the winter, ice will form on your eyebrows."

"Can't wait." He kicked at a clump of mud that didn't move, and Grace pretended not to notice. She unlatched the gate of the horse corral and closed it once he had entered. The horses loitered around a water trough and didn't seem to mind their presence. The ground was hard, at least the layer of muck he was most concerned about stepping in.

Grace took a cow path across the pasture, which led them up a hilly incline. At the top, he paused for a moment and gazed across what looked like miles of rolling meadows. "You're right. This is nice."

"*Jah*, it sure is." Her eyes held a sparkle as she looked at the scenery. "You should have seen it this morning. The frost-covered fields practically glittered at dawn."

"You make it sound poetic."

She studied the ground a moment and when her eyes met his again, they had lost their sparkle.

"You don't see much pastureland where I'm from in Florida." He waited for her to go down the hillside. "It's overly populated. Lots of tourists. Nothing . . . poetic."

She paused at the bottom of the hill. "That's *nett* how you made it sound to LeAnn. You painted a vivid vision in her head about the ocean."

"Maybe yours too?" He smiled, but she didn't return it.

She turned away, limping a little after coming down the hill. "That's why I left you in town. So you could return to Florida."

"Because I made you visualize the ocean?"

"Because you made LeAnn want to leave. She's talked about jumping the fence before. She certainly didn't need two fence-jumpers from Florida encouraging her to go."

"I'm *nett* a fence-jumper—I haven't left the church fold."

She lifted her brows as if wanting to challenge the statement.

"I haven't been baptized yet—but I love God—and the church." It wasn't like him to testify so boldly about his beliefs, especially since he was still trying to sort out some of his ill feelings toward his home district, mostly toward his father and Neva's parents.

"So short-sleeve shirts are allowable in your district?"

"Ah, *jah*. It gets hot in Florida."

"They're viewed as immodest here."

"That's nice to know." Neither the bishop nor his wife had mentioned anything to him. He only owned one long-sleeved shirt.

"I'm sure you won't want to stand out," she said.

"Your *Ordnung* must state something similar about vanity."

"It does."

He eyed the bottom of her dress. Although plain in material and in a bland, dark-green shade, it fanned out at the bottom and its hem dragged on the ground. It seemed more showy than practical. "I didn't notice any of the other women wearing long gowns." He lifted one brow. "Kinda sets you apart from the rest, *jah*?"

Grace went silent over several minutes and Ben didn't press her for a response, nor did he apologize even though he didn't truly believe she was vain at all. She was, however, different. More so than anyone he had ever known. Different from Neva in so many ways. Neva laughed more—a lot more. She loved the beach, the call of the gulls, the ocean. Her eyes used to light up much like Grace's did when she gazed over the pastures.

"So," he said, breaking the silence. "You never said when it really warms up."

"August."

His jaw went slack. "*Nay*." He couldn't wait for August to feel his toes again.

She chuckled quietly to herself.

"August. Really?"

"Sometimes it gets hot by July."

They came to a split-rail fence that separated the pasture from the woods. Grace crawled between the rails. "When does it get warm in Florida?"

"I thought you weren't interested in Florida." Ben winked.

She furrowed her brow.

Ben bounded over the fence and nearly tripped. The borrowed mucking boots slowed him down and made for a clumsy stride. He ducked under a low-hanging oak branch and spotted Grace near a cluster of birch trees.

"Florida is warm year-round, or at least you don't need a coat. Well, some days I suppose it's *kalt* enough to wear one. But I—" A thick pine branch she'd pushed out of her way snapped back and hit him in the chest. He dodged multiple other prickly branches as they trekked deeper into the woods.

They didn't seem to be on any trail. For all he knew, she was leading him deep into the forest to leave him to fend for himself. He looked around, trying to get some sense of direction. Trees blocked the sun and the splotches of light made erratic patterns on the ground. Some of these fallen logs looked familiar—if that was possible. He had a sneaky feeling she was leading them in a large circle. "Do you know where you're going?"

"The sawmill."

"Mmm . . . I can't imagine Bishop Yoder taking this route."

"I thought you'd enjoy the scenic route. You're *nett* still afraid of wolves, are you?"

He underestimated her wry sense of humor. "I'm flattered you would want to spend this much time with me." His comment caused a bright cherry-red tint to spread over her face and neck like a bad rash. Ben winked. "I see I've gotten under your skin."

"Like a festering splinter." She tromped between a stand of jack pines, leaving a wave of prickly limbs floundering in her wake.

After he was slapped in the chest a few times with pine needles, Ben hung back a few feet. A careful observation of the side of the tree the moss was growing on explained why they didn't seem to be going anywhere. She'd taken them in a circle. He jogged up to her on the trail. "So, how much farther?" Not that his endurance was waning. He just didn't like the idea of wandering in the woods at night.

"Oh . . . probably another . . ." Her lips twisted and she lifted her face toward the sun and squinted.

He would let her ponder their course. They still had plenty of daylight and he rather enjoyed her company. "So, did you really *kumm* by the bishop's *haus* every day to check on me?"

Her face flamed.

"All joking aside," he said. "That was very nice. *Danki*."

"Well, I did feel responsible for you getting sick. This harsh environment is different than what you're used to and the river current was just too strong."

"I am a *gut* swimmer." He squared his shoulders, his muscles flexing involuntarily.

She turned and started walking.

"I am."

Glancing over her shoulder, she barbed him with a patronizing smirk. "I'm sure you are."

"I swim better than you hike . . . At least I don't swim in circles," he muttered under his breath.

"Did you say something?"

"I'm *nett* opposed to walking in circles with you, but you could have just said you wanted to spend time with me."

She stopped midstep. Her back stiffened.

"I'm *nett* complaining. I think it's rather creative of you to lure me into the woods."

She gasped. Her hands fisted at her sides. "I did no such thing."

"You do know you've taken us in a circle."

She shook her head.

"*Jah*, since we rounded that last bend you've been veering off." He pointed to the left. "I think you want to head that way." He shrugged. "But it's up to you. You feel up to walking more, I'll stay the course with you."

Her jaw twitched. She continued in the same direction several feet, then stopped. Lifting her finger to her mouth, she pointed to the right.

He scanned the area. Trees. Ferns. A fallen log. And then he saw the spotted fawn a few feet away. The sight of it wobbling on spindly legs nearly stole his breath. He leaned closer to Grace. "Where's its *mamm?*"

"I think she's lying down in the ferns," she whispered.

Standing perfectly still, their shoulders touched. Grace was too interested with the fawn to move, and he wasn't complaining. He wasn't as concerned with the fawn's well-being as he was with shoring up his friendship with Grace. She wasn't as coarse as she pretended and that sparked his curiosity. A few moments later, another freckled fawn, not much larger than a dog, stood up.

"Twins," he said.

Her eyes glazed and she nodded.

What was it with women and newborns? She reacted to the wild creatures as though they were human *bopplis*. Another time he might have snickered at her overtly sentimental reaction, but something quickened within him and he didn't wish to disturb this moment. He stared at her as she gazed at the fawns. Everything about her had softened.

Grace sighed. "I've only seen—" She stepped back as if she realized how close they stood to each other. Branches crunched underfoot and her attention snapped to the deer. Standing up from the bed of ferns, the doe sniffed at the air. She flicked her tail, and a moment later the doe and the fawns were deep into the underbrush.

"We shouldn't waste any more time." Grace broke a new trail.

Ben traipsed behind her. "You're always concerned about wasting time. Don't you do anything spontaneous?" A pine-needled branch slapped him in the chest. He pushed it aside.

"You're an adventurous soul, Ben Eicher," she said in a condescending tone. "You'll never be satisfied with anything mundane, will you?"

"Why should I? And more importantly, why are you?"

She shot him a glare. "It's our way. Simple. Plain."

"It doesn't have to be mundane."

The deer trail they'd been on ended at the bottom of a ravine. He knew by the way she chewed her bottom lip while studying the area that they were lost. Ben smiled. "None of this looks familiar?"

She narrowed her eyes, then proceeded forward.

He followed even though the winding, upward track didn't seem like the wisest choice. At one point in the climb, his ears popped and he became light-headed. Maybe he hadn't completely recovered from the flu. The passage narrowed and his foot slipped. Ben grabbed hold of a tree root and pulled himself back up. Was she testing his skills? This wouldn't be so difficult if he had boots that fit. As it was, his feet slipped inside the boots as much as on the wet hillside. Ben crawled to the top on his knees. He pushed himself up, then extended his hand to her. She surprised him by accepting his help and even thanked him once she was standing.

He peered over the edge at the steep drop. There must be an easier way. He wasn't about to blindly follow her lead any longer. He scanned the surroundings. The sun, directly overhead, wasn't much help in determining the direction. He turned his face upward to receive some of its warmth. Despite the cool breeze, this was nice. He breathed in the scent of pine, closed his eyes, and smiled.

"I suppose you have the right idea. I should be praying too."

He looked over at her. "So you admit that you've gotten us lost."

She snapped open her eyes. "I'm *nett* lost—just twisted around . . . I think." She turned in a complete circle, searching the area.

"Admit it." He grinned. "We're lost."

She shook her head, but as she moved in another circle, her confidence seemed to waver. "I suppose *mei* sense of direction is a little off."

"A little?"

Her face contorted.

"Does someone in your district even own this land?"

She shrugged.

"We're trespassing?" This wouldn't look good on his record. He'd promised his mother he wouldn't get into trouble in Michigan. He patted his coat pocket for the letters—still there.

"I haven't seen a No Trespassing sign, have you?"

"So that makes it okay?" Now he was sounding like Toby.

"Well . . ."

He smiled, captivated by the glimmer of sunlight in her eyes. She could make him forget about warm weather and sandy beaches. Standing here with Grace, he thought the scent of pine trees was suddenly more enticing than the salt air of the ocean. Ben shook his head. He must be still loopy from all the tea he drank over the past few days. This piney scent could never replace the ocean.

"Isn't this view beautiful?" Her gaze canvassed the massive timber landscape.

He stared at her, feeling a foreboding warmth that drained his confidence and suddenly made him small in her presence. "*Jah*, the view is . . . overpowering. I'm glad you brought me here."

She whirled his way, aiming her pointed finger. "I didn't lure you."

"Lighten up," he said, lowering her hand. "I was joking." But the shot of electrical current that went through him as he touched her hand was no joke.

Grace smiled as if she'd cornered him in a game of cat and mouse. "So you're *nett* missing Florida?"

"*Jah*, well . . ." His throat went dry. He was the mouse. He swallowed hard. "It's . . . different here." Now his palms were moist. He must still be sick. Girls didn't typically affect him like this. He wasn't sure he liked this weakened state of mind, nor did he trust a cat. "*Kumm* on," he said. "Let's try this direction." He headed to the right for no other reason than the ridge was wider. "Watch your step." He didn't want her tripping on the rocks, and he wasn't sure he trusted the sandy soil either. It felt loose under his feet.

After they had been hiking awhile, Ben glanced over his shoulder. "You're awfully quiet. Do you want to stop and rest?"

"*Nay*, I'm fine."

He stopped anyway. Across the ravine, what looked like a large opening in the side of the hill caught his eye. "What do you think that is?"

"This must be the area *mei bruders* talked about exploring when they were younger. The boys used to tell stories about a cave entrance at the bottom of a sinkhole."

"Sinkhole?" He peered down at the rocky hillside. It had to be over a hundred feet straight down.

"According to the rumors, the cave is over a mile long and comes out at an old prospector's cabin, or I should say a stone chimney, because that's all that remained after the cabin caught fire." She raised her brows and wiggled them. "People say the place is cursed. The prospector's partner killed him with a shovel and the last family to own the cabin died in the fire set by their deranged son."

He'd heard plenty of rumors about cursed ships when he worked on the fishing boat, but he refused to believe them. Grace seemed too smart to believe such nonsense. Still, he had to ask, "You believe in curses?"

"Is greed a curse? Supposedly, there's either copper or silver underground." She shrugged. "It might just be a bear den."

"Let's get out of here. We're not going down into that sinkhole to find out if that's a cave at the bottom."

"*Gut.* This time of year it wouldn't be wise. I'm sure there are a few bears that haven't come out of hibernation yet."

Ben was thinking more about getting off the rim of a sinkhole and onto safer ground. He hadn't given any thought to bears. Hungry bears. Another reason—a good reason—they needed to focus on finding their way out of the woods.

Chapter Thirteen

B en found a remnant of an old timber-cut road that wasn't too far from the sinkhole. Although downed poplar trees and pines prevented vehicles from having access to the road, Ben managed to follow the old trail. It went on for miles and led them through a swampy section. Cutting through the dense underbrush left him wet, cold, and scratched up.

Ben paused and lifted his hand to his ear. "Cars. We must be close to the main road."

"Finally."

They maneuvered their way through another stand of pines before reaching the road. A car zoomed by as Ben climbed out of the ditch. He reached for Grace's hand and helped her up the drainage embankment.

Relief washed over her face and she smiled. "I know where we are *nau*."

"Oh *gut*. I was hoping we wouldn't have to backtrack." He coughed into his fisted hand. The cool air on his ears and the long hike had worn him down. He hoped he wasn't getting sick again.

Grace pointed to the south. "The sawmill isn't too far from here."

They walked along the gravel shoulder of the road, which made it faster than stumbling through the woods. Ben didn't care if he ever saw another tree. He wanted to get off his feet, and judging by the grimace on Grace's face, she did too.

He walked slower, noticing her struggle to keep his pace. She was a trooper, but by the time they reached the mill, even his steps were dragging.

A horse whinnied as they neared the barn. Smoke billowed from a stovepipe that protruded from the roof. He looked over at Grace and smiled. At least it would be warm inside and they shouldn't have to walk back.

A blast of warm air and the scent of cedar welcomed him into the pole barn. The room hummed with saws and hammers. It took a few moments for Ben's eyes to adjust to the dim lighting, but eventually a long table in the center of the building came into view. Several women and a group of young boys guided a piece of lumber down the table and through the large blade of the table saw. Sawdust sprayed the air as Toby and the bishop stood at the opposite end of the saw and received the cut lumber.

Grace tapped his arm and said something Ben couldn't decipher over the buzz of the saw. He cupped his ear and bent toward her. "What did you say?"

Grace wiggled her index finger and motioned with a nod for him to follow her over to a couple of wooden chairs along the wall. On this side of the barn, a few feet from the generator, a mixture of gasoline and exhaust overpowered the scent of fresh-cut lumber. In the wall behind the machine was a small opening that held a fan, but it wasn't enough to vent the fumes. He sat.

"You'll get used to the noise," she shouted.

Ben wasn't sure his ears would ever stop ringing, but noise wasn't the major concern. She should worry about the toxic smoke the old machine was pumping into the room—a stench no one should get used to.

He tapped the empty chair beside him. "Are you going to rest? You must be tired."

Grace looked around the room as if to see if anyone would object, then sat.

Ben leaned closer. "Feels *gut* to sit, doesn't it?"

She nodded.

Taking a deep breath, his chest tightened. He turned and coughed into his fisted hand.

Toby tossed a plank onto a pile at the far end of the pole barn and walked toward them, wiping sawdust from his gloved hands. "I wasn't sure if you were going to get up today or *nett*," he said to Ben. "Are you feeling better?"

"I was." Thankfully the barn was heated and it wouldn't be long before he thawed. Ben caught a glimpse of Grace's downcast expression. "The fresh air did me *gut*," he said with an upbeat tone. "I'm feeling like myself again." He wasn't, but he didn't want Grace feeling guilty for getting them lost.

"*Gut*." Toby pointed to the stack of lumber. "Those need cutting and there's more outside. We're working on an order that will be shipped to Cedar Creek, another Amish settlement about one hundred miles from here."

"I think Ben needs a hot cup of *kaffi* first." Grace rose. "Would you like a cup, Toby?"

"*Danki*, but I have some." He pointed across the room to a mug sitting on a knee-high stack of lumber.

As Grace ambled away, Ben reached into his pocket and pulled out the crumpled letters. "These came for you today," he said.

Toby glanced at the first envelope, then flipped to the next and smiled. He muttered his thanks without looking up and walked over to where his coffee mug sat.

Ben opened his letter. A five-dollar bill fluttered to the floor. Now he could buy batteries for his transistor radio. He picked it up and blew the flecks of sawdust off it before shoving it into his pocket.

Dear Ben,

I pray your trip was good and that you are adjusting all right. I thought I would have received a letter from you by now. Toby sent a letter home, so I know you both made it to Michigan. How is the *wedder?* Here, we've had rain over the past few days. The azalea bushes are in full bloom, even the ones you and Toby planted by the bank are blossoming.

Your father is busy in his shop. He sends his hello.

Ben paused. Even with thousands of miles between them, his mother was still trying to keep the peace between his father and him. Impossible. His father had lost respect for Ben and he was a man who rarely changed his mind. *Daed* probably didn't know anything about the money *Mamm* sent. She would have snuck it out of her seed fund. He continued reading. She wrote about the large garden she hoped to put in, gave him a quick update on many of the members—nothing he didn't already know—and ended the letter with her hope to see him soon.

"A letter from home?" Grace stood, coffee mug in hand. She lifted her brows.

"Ah . . . *Jah.*" He cleared his throat.

"I'm sorry, did I interrupt you? Should I wait over—?"

"*Nay.*" He folded the letter. "I'm finished."

She handed him a mug, sat in the chair beside him, then bounded to her feet. "Are you sure I'm *nett*"—her eyes flitted to the letter in his hand—"interrupting?"

"*Nay,* you're *nett.*" He jammed the letter into his pocket. "Please, sit."

She hesitated a moment, then sat.

He took a sip, then glanced into his cup. Specks of coffee grounds floated on the surface of the dark roast.

"It's strong," she said after taking a sip.

"*Jah,* it'll grow hair on your chest."

Her eyes widened and she touched the front of her dress where the apron met her neckline.

"Sorry." He needed to watch his words. He wasn't talking to Toby. He took another drink.

"So, how is everything in Florida?"

"Rainy." He glanced over to where Toby was reading his letter. He flipped pages. His mother must have found more to write about than just the weather.

Several minutes later, Ben drank the last of his coffee. Toby was still reading the letter, or maybe he had started it over. Whichever it was, his friend sported a wide smile. At least Toby was missed. Ben exhaled a deep breath.

Grace leaned toward him. "How's your *kaffi*?"

He tipped his mug.

"Do you want me to refill it?"

"*Nay, danki.*" The coffee grounds hadn't settled in his stomach yet.

"Is everything all right?" Her tone was serious—heartwarming.

"*Jah*, why do you ask?"

She shrugged. "You seem . . . different since we got here."

He thought a moment. "You think it has something to do with the letter?"

"Or . . . the *kaffi*." She glanced into her mug and frowned. "It's old." She popped off the chair and reached for his mug. "I'll be right back."

His gaze followed her across the room. Did she sense something strained, or had Toby said something about his *daed* sending him away?

She returned and handed him a fresh cup.

"*Danki.*" He didn't need more caffeine, but he took a sip anyway. Not as many grounds, but it would still grow a crop of chest hair.

"Better?" She lifted her brows.

How could he dash the hope in her eyes? He nodded.

The generator hiccupped a puff of black smoke and stopped. The fumes choked Ben and he turned and coughed into his fist.

"It's out of gas," Grace explained.

If it weren't for the smoke burning his eyes, he might have forgotten the generator was in the room. Grace was right about getting used to the noise. And his sense of smell had deadened.

When the generator stopped, so did the large band saw. He heard pinging sounds and looked up at the tin roof.

"It's raining just like in Florida," she said.

The temperature in Florida would be in the eighties or nineties. Here, he doubted it was much above forty. He glanced sideways at her and smiled. "*Nett* exactly. It would be warm and humid in Florida. *Nett* raining ice."

Ben recalled the time, just prior to the hurricane, when hail had pelted him and Neva. They sought shelter in a storage shed, and as golf-ball-sized chunks of ice drummed the rooftop, Neva trembled in his arms. The hailstorm lasted only minutes, but the intimate moment he shared with her had been burned in his heart.

Ben shook his head. He had to cast those thoughts out of his mind. Reminiscing about the past was only beneficial if there was someone to reminisce with.

A woman carrying a wicker basket entered the shop and looked around.

"That's Mattie." Grace sprang off the chair and went to greet the woman.

It took half a second to register that Mattie was the woman who made the special tea. Ben hoped she hadn't brought more tea. But as the woman unloaded what appeared to be lunch from the basket, Grace and her chatted, leaning close together. The women both smiled, then Grace bowed her head. Mattie glanced in his direction and grinned. He looked down at the sawdust-covered floor. Now his neck and face were heating.

"What did your letter say?" Toby plopped on the chair next to Ben.

Ben shrugged. "The Mullets had family visiting from Lancaster. Sunday service was held at the Knepp family's *haus*. Nothing that couldn't be read in the *Budget*. What did your letter say?"

"Same stuff."

Ben took another drink of his coffee. Toby's letter was multiple pages, more than the same stuff. But for some reason Toby didn't want to share, nor had he offered any information about who had written to him from Indiana.

His friend leaned with his elbows on his knees and twiddled his thumbs. Something was on his mind. "Who sent a letter from Indiana?"

Toby's face turned an ashen shade. "I, ah—*mei mamm* sent me money."

Ben studied him a moment. Did he really think he was being sly changing the subject? He and Toby had been friends for years—but something had changed. Ben sighed. "*Jah, mei mamm* sent money too."

Toby unfolded his hands and glanced up from his hunched position. "She did?"

"You don't have to look so shocked."

"*Nay*, I think it's great," he said with rising excitement. "We can leave Monday."

※

Grace scooped a shovelful of cedar shavings off the shop floor. "I wouldn't care if he left tomorrow," she said as she emptied them into the empty grain sack Mattie was holding.

Mattie smiled.

Grace had already told Mattie what had happened at the river, but it bore repeating. "I asked you to mix one of your special teas so Ben wouldn't catch pneumonia because he was carried downstream by the river current. I was concerned about him, but don't mistake concern for infatuation."

Mattie's smile remained. "I was glad to help."

"And I appreciate it." Grace filled the shovel with another load of shavings. "I learned that lesson from Philemon. I mistakenly believed his friendship meant more."

"I'm sorry how that worked out. I thought you two would get married." Mattie pressed the cedar shavings down in the bag to make room for more.

"Me too." Grace recalled when Philemon shared his engagement plans. She could hardly congratulate him without her voice breaking. It was best not to think about those things.

Grace tied the grain sack. "This should stuff several dog beds. Did I tell you the pet store in town wants to sell them?"

"That's *wunderbaar*."

"I have orders for over three dozen. Everyone seems to like that I fill my pet beds with cedar shavings instead of foam. The cedar helps control fleas. That and I sprinkle the wood with boric acid powder like you told me."

"*Gut*, I'm glad it's working."

"It works to eliminate wet-dog odor too." Grace pinched her nose. "Why anyone would want an indoor dog is beyond me." Her dog slept outside on a mound of hay.

"Just be thankful they do, or you might *nett* sell many pet beds."

"True." Grace gathered the last of the wood shavings off the floor. This would keep her busy for a while. As it was, after prewashing the quilted outer coverings this morning and hanging them on the line to dry, she counted ten more she still needed to make in order to fill the current orders, and she wanted to satisfy the orders before she moved to Ohio.

"I have some news to share." Mattie's smile grew larger. "I'm expecting a *boppli*."

"That's *wunderbaar*!" Her friend had been praying for a baby since she got married three years ago.

Mattie leaned closer and lowered her voice so that only Grace could hear. "I just found out yesterday. Please don't say anything yet.

I want to wait until Andy returns from camp before I share the news with anyone else."

"I won't breathe a word." Grace motioned to Mattie's hand resting on her belly. "But everyone's bound to figure it out. I don't think you'll fool anyone that you have indigestion. They'll see your face glowing and know."

Mattie touched her face and giggled. "I have the glow?"

"I was going to ask you what kind of tea you were drinking. I wanted some."

"Your day will *kumm*."

Grace opened her mouth to rebuff the comment but stopped when Becky Lapp, the woman who stole Philemon's heart and Grace's future, approached.

"I thought I would come over and say hello while the generator was down," Becky said.

A barking cough from across the room gave Grace a reason to look away. Ben still sat, shoulders slumped and hugging himself like he was cold. He was miserable and it was her fault. If she had not gone through the cow pasture and cut their own trail through the woods, she wouldn't have gotten them lost. She couldn't tell north from south once they were deep into the woods. Trying to prove the Florida man wasn't a woodsman had opened her eyes to her own deficient skills.

Chapter Fourteen

I s everything all right at home?" Ben studied Toby's expression. Calm. Toby wasn't worried or he'd be pacing.

"*Jah*, why do you ask?" Toby removed his hat and a mop of dark curls sprang to life. He brushed his forehead with his shirtsleeve, pushing the curls to one side, then slapped his hat back in place.

"We haven't been here a week and your parents want you to come home already?"

"I asked if I could *kumm* home in *mei* letter. You said you were sent money too."

"Spending money." Ben turned and coughed into his fisted hand. The exhaust from the generator had turned his throat to sandpaper. "Five dollars doesn't buy much."

"Oh, I guess I assumed . . ." Toby batted a wood shim between his boots.

"*Mei* father isn't as forgiving as yours." Ben doubted his father knew that his *mamm* had sent him spending money. He would expect Ben to earn his way back—earn his father's respect and love. But could a black sheep ever look clean in his father's eyes?

"I probably have enough for both of our tickets," Toby said. "That is, if you want to go back."

Did Toby really think Ben may want to stay in this tundra with people he didn't know? His gaze trailed across the room until it stopped on Grace. If he stayed . . . well, he wasn't going to stay. Ben rubbed his irritated eyes. "I'd pay you back, if that's what you're worried about."

Toby handed him a bandanna from his coat pocket. "Tie it around your face and it'll stop some of the fumes. Plus it'll stop you from breathing in the fine particles of sawdust floating in the air."

"*Danki.*" Ben held the cloth up to his face, took a few filtered breaths, then pulled it away. "Can you keep the ticket purchase between us? I'd rather *mei* father think I earned *mei* way back." He lowered his head. "Maybe he'd have more respect for me."

"*Jah*, I won't say anything."

Bishop Yoder dropped a piece of lumber on the stack, then came up to Ben and Toby. "You don't sound much better, Ben. I'm surprised Mary let you out of the *haus*." His smile reminded Ben of his grandfather's.

"I thought some fresh air would be *gut*," Ben replied.

"Please don't feel obligated to help if you're *nett* feeling well. This *wedder* is a big change from Florida. It'll take some getting used to, isn't that right, Toby?"

Toby nodded. He made eye contact with Ben a moment, then motioned to the pile of lumber. "I should get back to work." He walked away without any signs of his ankle still hurting from twisting it at the river.

While Toby seemed to be fitting in, Ben couldn't shake the awkwardness of not having anything to do. He wasn't opposed to hard work; his hands weren't soft. But Bishop Yoder must have thought he was a slug. Ben's father would, if he knew about him staying in bed for four days. Even Toby had looked at him curiously when Ben blamed the tea for having knocked him out. When he did wake up, Mary insisted he drink more.

"Is there something you would like me to do, Bishop Yoder?"

The elderly man stroked his beard, then motioned to Grace,

Mattie, and another woman, who were all squatting in a circle next to the wall. "A few of the women are cleaning up the wood shavings from the floor. You could help them."

Cleanup. "Sure, but don't you need help cutting the lumber?" He might not know how to run the table saw, but he could help Toby move the boards. Even sick, he could work faster than many of the women combined. At least he shouldn't be demoted to cleanup duty without having the chance to prove his worth.

The bishop shook his head. "If you could load the grain bags the women are filling, that would help. And when you're finished, I think you should go back and rest."

"You don't have other work? I don't feel that bad."

Bishop Yoder placed his hand on Ben's shoulder. "I'll have plenty of work next week. But you'll need to be rested up for the task." He patted Ben's shoulder. "It sure is *gut* having some strong men to help out."

Ben forced a smile. Telling the bishop they were going back to Florida would be difficult. This was Saturday, Sunday was a day of rest, and the following day, Toby wanted to catch the bus home. Today was the only day Ben could help.

"Isn't there anything I can do today?" The dryness in the building irritated Ben's throat and he coughed.

"*Kumm* with me. I'll make arrangements for someone to give you a ride home." Bishop Yoder took a few steps without Ben and stopped.

Ben eyed Toby near the lumber pile. If he could get Toby's attention and wave him over, they could tell the bishop together that they would be leaving on Monday.

"Do you have a rebellious spirit, *sohn*?"

Ben groaned under his breath. Just the opposite was true. He appreciated everything the bishop and his wife had done. "I'd like to earn *mei* keep. Even the Bible has something to say about a man who doesn't work."

The bishop nodded. "You're right. But God also expects you to mind your elders. *Nau kumm* with me before these women leave you without a ride home."

Ben obeyed.

"I thought that would change your mind." The corners of his mouth lifted slightly. "We have a truck coming at the end of next week to pick up a lumber order for Cedar Creek, but after that I'll teach you how to drive a buggy so you don't have to be dependent on the women."

Not knowing how else to respond, Ben nodded. After Jasper nipped his shoulder, he wasn't sure if he wanted to be that close to another horse. His worries were a moot point. The day after tomorrow, he would be on a bus heading back to Florida. Not soon enough for him. Even though he was wearing another man's winter coat, chills had reached his bones. Springtime in Florida meant green grass and the citrusy scent of orange blossoms in the warm air and not having to wear cumbersome clothes.

"Excuse me," Bishop Yoder said, approaching the women. "Would one of you kindly drive Ben back to the *haus*?"

Ben lowered his head, feeling ten years old again.

"Grace and I will be leaving as soon as we load the wood chips into the buggy. He can ride with us," Mattie said.

"*Danki.*" Bishop Yoder turned to Ben. "I know you would rather stay and help, but I think you would be better off resting another day. If you're feeling too restless, I'm sure the women will find you an indoor task."

Grace said, "That won't be a problem."

For a split second, Ben's heart leaped. He might like spending the afternoon with her.

"Do you know how to sew?" Grace smirked.

This was a strange district. Just because women worked in the lumber barn shouldn't mean he was expected to do women's work. He would be laughed out of Pinecraft. Toby was probably laughing right now.

The bishop turned to Ben. "I need to get back to work, but I'll see you at supper. Mary likes to eat around six."

"Okay." He would make a point to be back from fishing by then. Even if the ice hadn't melted completely, he would rather cast a line than have to worry about keeping stitches in a straight line. And with all the rain, he shouldn't have a problem finding worms.

Once the bishop walked away, another *maedel* in the group stepped forward. "I'm Becky Lapp. I saw you at the bishop's *haus* during the meeting the other *nacht*, but I didn't have a chance to *welkom* you to Badger Creek. I've been working with Toby the past few days. He said you two are from Florida." The round, freckle-faced girl had a sweet smile.

"*Jah.*"

"Are you getting used to the *wedder*? Falling into the river must have been a shock to your system."

Falling into the river? Someone who fell into the river wouldn't have time to remove his shoes. He shouldn't let that concern him, but it did.

"We're a small community, so word gets around fast."

"So you say." He tightened his lips into a smile.

Grace made a knot before looking up. Her forehead wrinkled. "Were you saying something to me?"

He shook his head.

"I was asking Ben how he was adapting to the *wedder.*"

"Oh." She lifted her brows at Ben. "Don't let me interrupt."

"I was just going to ask Becky if she had heard anything about *mei* missing shoes." He faced Becky. "I took them off at the river when I jumped in and *nau* they're missing."

"*Nau* that you mention it, I did hear something about the missing shoes. But they haven't turned up—*nett* that I've heard anyway."

"I'm sure word will get around when they do." Apparently, his sarcasm went over her head because she returned his smile.

The generator roared to life.

"I better get back to work," Becky said above the noise. "I'm sure I'll run into you at Sunday service tomorrow." She joined the other workers.

Ben tapped Grace's arm, then motioned to the grain bags. "Are you taking all of these?"

"*Jah.*"

He grabbed the bags, two in each hand. They weren't heavy. He could carry more if they weren't so bulky. "I'll *kumm* back for those," he told Grace when she bent to pick up the remaining two.

She grabbed the bags anyway and headed to the door with Mattie at her side.

Ben tagged behind the two friends, feeling like a fifth wheel.

"*Mei* buggy is over here," Mattie said, directing them to the corner of the barn.

The temperature had dropped at least ten degrees since they came inside the barn. Now he wasn't so sure fishing was a good idea. But sewing with women? What could he possibly add to the conversation as they stitched whatever it was they stitched?

❧

Grace sat on the buggy bench shoulder to shoulder with Mattie on one side and Ben on the other. A tight fit, but that couldn't be helped as the sacks of wood shavings took up the back section of the buggy. Grace tried not to think about the closeness, but her thoughts circled in a maddening way. Earlier, Ben had accused her of luring him into the woods. She could only imagine what he thought of her suggesting he sew with them. She shouldn't have teased him.

Ben stretched out his legs and ran his hand down his thigh as though he were releasing tension from his muscles. "So, do you use a buggy in the middle of the winter too?"

"We have sleigh runners that *mei* husband, Andy, mounts on the frame when the snow gets too deep," Mattie said.

"Other than Widow Klem, who relies on others to take her places, I think everyone uses the iron runners," Grace added.

"What keeps the horse from slipping on the ice?"

"Borium. It's welded to their shoes for traction." Grace sucked in a breath and braced for the turn onto the dirt road, which led to her house. As her body swayed in the turn, she grasped the edge of the bench. So did Ben. His large hand covered hers, sending fire shooting through her veins. He didn't move his hand after the buggy straightened. Ben's brave attempt to cross the river to search for Mitch had affected her heart. It wasn't until he grinned that she realized her mouth was agape.

"I'm so thankful this road is no longer flooded," Mattie said.

"Filling the holes with rocks made a big difference," Ben said.

"Toby and the boys worked nonstop for two days on it." Grace had prepared a big lunch for them the first day, and the young boys her nephew's age ate as much chicken and dumplings as Toby had.

"*Jah*, Toby mentioned repairing the road and digging new drainage into the creek." Ben stared out the side window and sighed.

Grace marveled at how effective the new drainage was. "Toby said he learned about drainage working in landscaping. He said he could fix—"

"Toby, Toby, Toby," Ben muttered under his breath.

Grace paused. "Did you say something?"

"*Nay*, go on," he said, continuing to look out the window.

"I was just going to add that the bishop was pleased. Our road has never been dry this time of the year." Had she said something wrong? This was the most disengaged she had seen Ben.

Mattie pulled into the driveway and stopped the buggy next to the porch. "Grace, if you don't mind I'd like to skip sewing today." Mattie patted her belly. "I'm *nett* feeling so *gut* all of a sudden. I think I'll go home, fix a cup of tea, and rest."

"I don't mind. I hope you're *nett* coming down with a cold." Grace suspected it was early-pregnancy queasiness, but many of the women had recently come down with the flu from all this wet weather. Their April showers could drown any hope of May flowers.

Ben climbed out of the buggy, waited for Grace to crawl out, then leaned down to peer into the window opening at Mattie. "*Danki* for the ride."

"Anytime." Mattie tapped the reins and the horse lunged forward.

"Wait." Grace waved her hand to stop Mattie, but failed to get her friend's attention. Grace turned to Ben. "Wasn't she going to take you back to the bishop's *haus*?"

"I thought you wanted help sewing." Ben looked up at the sky. "I suppose I could go fishing instead."

"I was teasing about you sewing." She smiled amusedly. Up until now she didn't think his self-confidence could be tampered with.

"Mmm . . ." He looked toward the barn. "Did you ever get a new buggy wheel?"

"Toby already changed it for me."

His jaw tightened.

"*Nau* it makes sense why you were irked on the ride here. You're jealous of Toby."

He huffed.

"You couldn't help that you were sick . . . And, well, I'm sure it didn't help that I teased you about sewing." She hadn't known any man who sewed.

"Are we going to stand outside all day? I thought we had sewing to do—what are we making anyway?"

"Dog beds. But if you don't know how to sew—"

"Then you'll ask Toby?" He smiled. "He doesn't know how." Ben motioned to the house. "Shall we get started?"

"Okay," she said. "But I still think you're jealous." She headed to the clothesline. The quilted coverings for the dog beds should be dry by now. She smiled. Watching him thread a needle would be entertaining.

"You find it funny? I'm *nett* jealous."

"I was thinking about something else." She eyed him suspiciously. "Have you ever threaded a needle?"

"You can show me." His smile turned into a grin.

She stopped at the clothesline. Places on the line were bare and many of her quilts were gone.

℘

Ben wasn't sure what had changed Grace's demeanor, but she stared at the line, dumbfounded by something. Her lips moved without making any sound and her gaze traveled the length of the line. Was she counting them?

"Is something wrong?"

"Some of the quilts are missing."

"Maybe your sister or *aenti* took them inside."

"I don't know why they would only take a few of them." She reached for the first item and removed it from the line, then unclipped the next one.

Ben went to the opposite end of the line and felt for dryness. The material was so cold he wasn't sure if it was damp or not. He took it down anyway and draped it over his arm. Grace worked fast, mumbling to herself as she went. He worked his way toward the middle.

"How many do you have?"

Didn't she already count them? As he handed the ones he'd collected over to her, he counted them one by one. "Eight."

She released a long sigh.

"I'm sure there's a logical explanation for where they are." He smiled. Although his shoes were still missing and that couldn't be explained.

"I hope so." Grace's shoulders slumped.

"I say we get started."

She peered up at him. "Do you really want to sew? I wouldn't want you to feel duty bound."

Ben nodded. As strange as it was, even if the trout were doing belly flops in the stream, he would give up fishing to spend time with her, and that realization made his heart pump harder.

Her lips twitched into a smile, then she turned abruptly and started walking toward the house.

Ben joined her. "Why do you wash them if they're for a dog?"

"It doesn't make much sense to me either. The owner of the shop in town where I sell them suggested I label them prewashed—preshrunk. I suppose it's a marketing gimmick."

"Why doesn't your dog sleep on one?"

"He's *nett* a pampered pet. He's a hound and a stray at that. Besides, he doesn't seem to mind the mound of hay in his dog *haus* or that he gets to sleep in the barn during the winter." Her mouth dropped open and she covered it with her hand.

"What is it?"

"I forgot the cedar shavings in Mattie's buggy."

Ben lifted his brows. "Can I talk you into going fishing then?" A brief image of Grace snuggled next to him on the riverbank flashed across his mind, taking him by surprise.

"I can't." She trudged up the porch steps. As she opened the door, Mattie's buggy pulled into the yard.

They glanced at each other, then met Mattie in the drive.

"I made it all the way home before remembering the wood shavings were still in the back of *mei* buggy."

"I'll get them out." Ben walked around and opened the hatch. A strong cedar aroma filled his senses. He grabbed the grain sacks, then, unsure where Grace wanted them put, he waited for a break in the women's conversation. They chatted as if they hadn't seen each other in a week when it hadn't been more than a few minutes. It was too cold to wait for Grace to finish telling Mattie about the missing quilts. He carried the bags up the porch steps and left them next to the door.

"I hope they show up soon. I have the order to fill for the store in town, plus I just got another order, so I'll be busy sewing to get them all done in time." Grace sighed.

"That's strange that your quilts are missing," Mattie said. "One of the pies I made this morning disappeared from *mei* back porch. I left two of them out to cool and when I got home, one was gone."

Ben set the last bags down. "In Florida, the ants and roaches would have a picnic with anything sweet left outside."

"It's too *kalt* for bugs." Grace shrugged. "But *nett* for bears."

"Bears? But you said—" He paused a half second to calm the anxiety growing in his voice. "Earlier, you said they're still hibernating."

Grace smiled but quickly covered it. "It wasn't a bear."

"Oh?" Ben crossed his arms and stared at Grace.

Mattie stifled a soft giggle. "A bear would have eaten both pies. And it would have left a mess."

Ben forced a smile. Apparently, these northern women were intent on making a fool of him.

Chapter Fifteen

Sitting on the sofa, Grace leaned closer to Ben and studied his stitches. Straight, even. Amazing. "You've done this before, *jah?*"

"I've had plenty of practice." He weaved the needle through the cotton fabric with ease and pulled the thread taut.

"And you made me show you how to thread the needle." She shook her head.

"You can't blame a man for wanting to get close to a woman."

"I should have known."

"You're *nett* going to tell anyone *mei* secret, are you? After all, I might get invited to a sewing frolic." He wiggled his brows at her.

"You're . . . you're—"

"Irresistible."

"That's *nett* what I was going to say."

He shrugged. "It's what your eyes said."

She stiffened, then pinned him with a deadpan expression. He wasn't going to get the best of her.

The playful flicker in his bright-blue eyes sent a chill skittering to her core. As he sat in front of the window, his blond hair shimmered with a halo, but he was no angel. He probably held every *maedel* captive with his smile back in Florida—here in Michigan too. Even Becky Lapp had been taken by his charm, and she was about to be proposed to when Philemon returned.

Grace cast her gaze across the room as warmth spread across her cheeks. *Think of other things* . . . The curtains were starting to look sun-faded. The windows had a thin layer of soot that would require full-strength white vinegar to get them clean.

He shifted on the sofa, glanced in the same direction, then continued to stitch the quilt block. "I know it's tough to deny me."

"You're so full of yourself." She quirked a brow. "I think you believe it too."

He pushed the needle through the material, jabbed his thumb, and yelped. He boyishly shoved his finger in his mouth, then plucked it out and looked at it.

Grace resumed sewing. She wasn't falling for his pretend injury.

After a minute, he picked up the block of navy-blue fabric with the needle hanging from it and continued to sew. "The first day I met you, I told Toby you were an icy one."

"I'll take that as a compliment." She pushed her sewing aside and stood. "I'm going to warm *mei kaffi*. Would you like another cup?"

He bit the end of his thread, then tossed the finished block on the pile. "I'm *gut*, Icy, but *danki* for asking." He grabbed two more pieces of fabric and sandwiched a section of batting between them.

She took her mug and retreated into the kitchen. *Icy one.* She could only imagine what type of women he shared his time with, certainly *nett* someone with strong beliefs.

Aenti Erma looked up from the table. "I'm just finishing a letter to *mei* cousin."

"Tell her I said hello." Grace dumped the cold coffee from the mug into the sink, then put the kettle on the stove to boil.

Aenti folded the letter. "How are the quilt blocks coming along?"

"*Gut.* Ben can actually sew straight stitches. And he's fast." *At more things than just sewing.*

"It doesn't sound like you need *mei* help." *Aenti* smiled as she stuffed the letter into an envelope. "I think I'll get supper started. Maybe you could invite Ben to join us."

"*Nay*. I mean, Bishop Yoder and Mary are expecting him."

Aenti licked the envelope and sealed it. "Maybe another time."

"*Jah*, maybe," she said, hoping to sound indifferent. She stared at the clear top on the percolator. *Brew already*, she silently coaxed.

"Why don't you ask him over tomorrow *nacht*?"

"Tomorrow is Sunday." The entire settlement spent the afternoon together fellowshipping after service, and usually they ate a big meal and heated leftovers at suppertime.

"I know what day it is." *Aenti* lifted her brows. "I'm *nett* so old that I don't remember Sunday singings."

Grace snatched the kettle off the stove even though it hadn't stopped perking. She filled the mug with weak coffee.

"I just thought it would be nice if you invited him—"

"Before someone else does?" Someone who didn't limp. Grace picked up the mug. "We only have singings during the summer and early fall when the men are home. And since when do women ask the men to court?"

"I was only suggesting supper."

Grace left the kitchen before her aunt got any more crazy notions. Even if Ben wanted to share a porch swing one evening, he would have two dozen unmarried women to choose from, so why would he pick her—the icy one?

Ben greeted her with a smile as she entered the sitting room. "I finished another block."

She set the mug on the lamp table and picked up the blocks as she sat on the sofa. She studied his stitches. Some stitches were longer than others, but overall the spacing was good. "Nice work. When did you learn to quilt?"

"These are *mei* first blocks."

She shook her head. Those were no beginner blocks.

"They are, really." He reached for his mug and took a drink. "*Mei* father is a shoemaker, although most of his work consists of repairing old shoes. He taught me basic sewing, which until now, I didn't have much use for."

"You never mentioned working for your father. Only that you worked on a fishing boat and in landscaping. Did something happen?"

He flipped the material over in his hand and examined it as if trying to decipher between the right and wrong sides of the fabric.

Ach, *you do have a weakness.* She was going to draw attention to his avoidance, then chose not to. It took a long time after her mother died to talk about it. A moment of silence fell between them.

"*Mei daed* and I have never seen eye-to-eye," he finally said. "I upset him when I didn't want to be the fifth generation of Eicher shoemakers." The sparkle in his eyes faded.

"Telling him must've been difficult."

He nodded. "So was telling him that shoemaking was a dying trade. But it's true. A person could buy three pairs of shoes for what it cost him to buy supplies for one."

"I'm sure his shoes last longer."

Ben sighed. "*Mei* father argued that point as well."

She made a few stitches. "Is that why you left Florida?" When he didn't answer, she looked up from her sewing and met his gaze. "Oooh . . . You're hiding something, Ben Eicher. Don't you know that every *gut* sewing frolic has juicy gossip to talk about?"

He cracked a smile, but only for a second. "Some things happened that I'm *nett* proud of." He bowed his head. "I disappointed *mei* father—for the last time, as he put it. Then he sent me here."

Grace recalled the disappointment she'd seen in her father's eyes when she brought up the idea of seeing a specialist about her limp. *Isn't God's grace sufficient for you?* her father had asked, creating an abyss of guilt so deep, it swallowed her whole. After that, she avoided the subject of moving to Ohio, and even when her muscles grew weaker, she pretended to believe in God's grace.

"You're awfully quiet," Ben said. *"Nau* that I've told you all that, you *nay* longer like *mei* character?"

"I hate to burst your bubble, but your character was a little sketchy to begin with. But that's coming from an 'icy one.'"

"I only said that because . . . well, you're judgmental."

"Nay, I'm *nett."*

His brows shot up and his eyes widened.

"Okay, so I did judge you in the beginning. I thought you were a fence-jumper . . . And that you might lure LeAnn away with all that talk about the ocean. You don't take anything serious."

"I'm *nett* a fence-jumper, although I have thought about it, but I wouldn't intentionally lure her away."

"Danki," she said with a smile. "LeAnn's been talking about leaving since she turned seventeen last spring, and I find her gazing at the bus station every time we go into town. It's been especially hard on her since our mother died. *Aenti* Erma has *kumm* every year to help while *mei daed* and *bruders* go to camp for the winter, but I think LeAnn's convinced she doesn't want to live in northern Michigan. It's too desolate."

"And you?"

"I don't mind our small settlement. The winters are difficult with the men gone, but we manage. I'm sure Bishop Yoder is grateful that you and Toby are here and are available to help. He's probably already told you about the lumber order that needs to be shipped by the end of next week. And once the men return with the fresh-cut timber, it'll have to be debarked and rough cut. They timber a year in advance since it takes several months for the wood to be seasoned."

"Jah, he mentioned it." His expression sobered.

"Is something wrong?"

"Nay. Nothing." He smiled, though it appeared strained and disappeared quickly.

"Shipments don't always go as planned. The weather has a tendency to interfere." She followed his gaze to the floor. What was he staring at, her shoes? Grace tucked them under her dress, but it was too late. Ben had slipped off the sofa and was bending at her side.

"May I see your shoes?"

"Why?" She slid her feet back against the sofa.

"Please," he said. "I think I know what's wrong with them."

She did too. The wooden lift on her left heel was worn to a nub. But she sure didn't want him inspecting them. And yet, he hadn't moved from his kneeling position. The man was forward speaking, asking for her foot the way he had. Now he stared up at her with coonhound eyes.

"You've teased me enough, Benjamin Eicher."

"I'm a shoe repairman, Grace. I'm *nett* teasing you."

She inched her good foot out from under her dress and gasped when he reached for her ankle.

Cradling her foot in the crutch of his elbow, he pressed the tip of her shoe, pushing first against her big toe, then worked his way across. "*Nett* much room. Do they feel tight?"

Did he really expect her to answer? She could barely breathe.

His hands moved to the back of the shoe, sending a parade of tingles that prevented her from concentrating on anything but the trailing sensations coursing along her nerves. He had unlaced her shoe and slipped it off before she could object.

He lowered her foot to the cold, plank floor and examined the shoe. His forehead crinkled. "No arch support to speak of . . . ," he said, more as a note to himself.

The front door opened as Ben readied the shoe to slip back on her foot.

Humming softly, LeAnn entered the house. She removed her cloak, hung it on the wall hook, then, turning to face them, her jaw dropped.

Grace snatched the shoe from Ben's hand and glared at him until he rose from his squatting position.

"It's her left leg that gives her problems," LeAnn said, stepping farther into the room.

Aenti Erma breezed in and wrapped her arm around LeAnn's shoulder. "I'm glad you're home. I can use some help in the kitchen getting the meal ready. Ben, you're *welkom* to join us for supper."

"*Danki*, but Bishop Yoder and his *fraa* are already expecting me."

"I hope you'll plan on having supper with us another time," *Aenti* Erma said.

"I'd like that." He watched them leave the room, then turned to Grace. "I should probably go so I'm *nett* late." He ran his hands down the sides of his pants as though drying them. "I could help you sew more blocks tomorrow, if you want."

"Sunday service is tomorrow morning, and the meal afterward takes up the entire afternoon."

He shrugged one shoulder. "Do you already have plans for the evening?"

❧

Sunday service was always shorter in the winter and early spring. With the ministers away at camp, there wasn't anyone to read the Scripture. The group sang several hymns from the *Ausbund*, then Bishop Yoder combined the Scripture reading with his main sermon.

Grace shifted on the bench. This service was running longer, or so it seemed. Bishop Yoder tended to direct most of his sermon about living a godly life toward Ben and Toby, who sat attentively on the front row in the bishop's sitting room.

Once the congregation was dismissed, the children went outside to play in the yard, Ben and Toby loitered in the sitting room with the bishop, and Grace followed the women into the kitchen. Everyone looked forward to the Sunday afternoon meal following service. The scent of roast beef made her mouth water. She stood at the counter beside Mattie. "Did you find anything out about your pie?"

"*Nay*, but I see plenty of desserts. I don't think it'll be missed."

Grace removed the cover from a cheesy noodle dish, then handed it to Jenny, one of the teenage girls, to set on the table.

Mattie leaned closer and elbowed Grace. "Did you get much sewing done yesterday?"

"*Jah*, we did." Grace stuck a spoon into the green-bean casserole. "I thought he was bluffing about being able to sew, but he can stitch a straight line." She glanced over her shoulder into the sitting room at Ben. Some of the *maedels* who had finished setting the table were socializing with Toby and him. Her sister was one of them. A spark of jealousy niggled at Grace.

Aenti Erma tapped Grace's shoulder. "Did you remember to bring the bread? I can't seem to find it."

"It must still be in the buggy. I'll go get it." Grace scooted outside without grabbing her cloak. If it wasn't for the gusts of cold air sending a chill down her spine, she would have preferred to eat outdoors. A robin chirped on a nearby beech tree branch, a sure sign that spring wasn't far away. Soon the lilacs would bloom.

Grace opened the buggy door. The bread wasn't on the bench. She searched the floorboard and the back but didn't find the loaves there either. It didn't make sense. Closing the buggy door, she spotted a large set of footprints in the soft ground. Grace followed them. The tracks went from one buggy to the next. Some of the teenage boys had large feet; perhaps one of the boys was looking for a place to hide while playing hide-and-seek. Mitch had better not be one of them—the boys all knew not to play by the horses.

Grace reached the last buggy, but the tracks continued toward the horse corral. She rested her hand on her hip and scanned the area. No sign of anyone. She hiked over to the fence and crawled between the rails. This was foolish. Was chastising the boys so important that she would chance getting manure on her favorite Sunday dress? She had saved up for months to buy the plum-colored material, and she didn't want it soiled. Something blue flashed in her peripheral vision. She turned in that direction and proceeded toward the barn.

The bishop's barn was one of the few with a walk-out basement. She followed the slope of the concrete steps down the side of the barn and entered through the milking parlor. Her eyes needed time to adjust. The small windows near the ceiling were intended more for ventilation than a source of light.

Behind her, the door hinges creaked. Light flooded the area. She held her hand up, shielding her eyes, as a silhouetted form stepped forward.

❧

"Grace?" Ben blinked a few times before his eyes adjusted to the dim light.

"What are you doing here?" Her voice cracked.

"I didn't mean to frighten you. I'm sorry." He crossed the empty parlor. The place looked larger without cows standing in the milking stalls. "So, what are you doing?"

"I was getting the loaves of bread—"

"From the barn?"

"*Nay*," she said sharply. "From the buggy. What tore you away from the swarm of *maedels*?"

A smile tugged at the corners of his mouth. "I saw you leave the *haus*." He stepped closer. "And I'm pretty sure you saw me wave at you from the porch."

She cocked her head and shot him a you've-got-to-be-kidding glare before crossing the milking area and disappearing into the larger section of the barn where the horses were stalled.

He leaned against the barn wall and watched as she peeked stealthily around the half wall of the calf pen. The young calves met her at the fence and she gave them a scratch on their foreheads. They tilted their heads up and bawled when she left. The woman was on some type of mission. She went to the opening, which led to the hayloft, and looked up.

He joined her at the ladder. "You don't think the bread is up there, do you?"

She angled her brow at him. "I thought I saw a man in a blue shirt," she said, her focus fixed on the haymow. "I noticed muddy tracks near the buggies and I followed them here." She placed her hands on the ladder rung.

He caught her wrist. "Are you serious?" He eyed her closely. She was. "Toby and Bishop Yoder are in the *haus*. And I'm *nett* wearing a blue shirt."

"I'm just going to take a peek." She lifted her foot to the first rung.

"Let me."

Grace stepped aside.

Ben climbed the length of the ladder. Rays of sunlight shot through the cracks between the boards and motes of hay dust danced in the air. She hadn't followed him up the ladder. She was a tough one to figure out. He climbed down. "Just a bunch of hay," he said, taking the last step. She was inches from him and energy shot through him like he'd been infused with caffeine. He smelled a hint of laundry soap on her dress. On her *kapp*. "We should go back inside," he said, warding off the voice in his head enticing him to kiss her.

"*Jah*, you're right." She turned.

His heart hammered hard. Fast. Blood whooshed in his ears as adrenaline fed his blood supply. He reached for her arm, swung her around, and lowered his lips to hers. Gentle at first, then unleashing what little reserve remained, he placed his hand on her back, pressed her closer, and deepened his kiss.

For all of a second, the tension drained from her body and she melted into his embrace. Then she broke from the kiss, breathless.

His throat dried and he swallowed. He tried to recall the bishop's sermon. Godly living . . . avoiding temptation . . . Ben's mind went blank.

❧

"I didn't . . . lure you out here." She gasped ragged breaths as she stepped backward, every fiber in her body quivering from his touch.

"I know." His voice was a hoarse whisper.

"Then wh-what was that—all about?" Her lips still tingled where he'd kissed her so completely as only a husband should do. He left her flushed with excitement and her speech muddled. "Answer me."

He scratched the back of his neck.

She fisted her hands at her sides, ready to fatten those lips of his if he made an offhanded remark. "Ben Eicher," she said through gritted teeth.

He shook his head and shrugged.

She spun around, heat blazing in her face, and fled to the door.

"Grace," Ben said, trailing her out of the barn. "Don't leave upset."

He stole her heart and wrung the life from it all at the same time, and he didn't want her leaving upset? She hurried across the yard.

"I didn't mean to get you riled."

She halted at the base of the porch steps and whirled around to face him. "Then you should have asked."

His eyes shined with pride. "Okay," he said with a nod. "Next time I will."

"You shouldn't assume there will be a next time." She shot up the steps and pushed open the door. Considering the stares from some of the women, she should have taken a moment to catch her breath. Grace touched her prayer *kapp*. Thankfully it was still in place.

Grace moved quickly through the sitting room and into the kitchen. She found her aunt in the kitchen talking with Mattie and her sister-in-law, Susan. The way the women were fussing over Mattie, they must have figured out her secret. Grace came up beside *Aenti*. "I couldn't find the bread."

"I must have left it on the counter at home." *Aenti* shrugged. "I don't know what's happened to *mei* memory."

Grace placed her hands on her hips and cocked her head sideways. Her *aenti's* memory was impeccable. She wasn't fooling anyone.

"Here," *Aenti* Erma said, handing Grace two plates. "Give one to Ben. You both must be starved."

"Don't forget these." Mattie handed her two sets of utensils, smiling widely. Had they seen Ben and her leaving the barn together?

Ben entered the kitchen. He ran his hands down the side seams of his pants. "Mary sent me in here to get a plate." He almost sounded apologetic.

"Grace?" *Aenti* said, giving her a gentle nudge. "Give Ben his plate."

Grace handed him the dish and utensils without making eye contact. How could he eat? Her stomach was twisted tighter than a lid on a canning jar.

LeAnn breezed into the room. "I just heard you and Toby are going back to Florida. What time does your bus leave in the morning?"

❧

Ben drew a deep breath and knocked on Grace's back door. He hadn't been this nervous standing on a woman's porch in a long time. But since Grace had avoided him the remainder of the afternoon after their kiss in the barn, he wasn't sure the supper invitation still stood.

"Ben." Grace sounded surprised.

He shuffled his feet awkwardly when she didn't immediately invite him in. "I, ah . . ."

Erma came up behind Grace. "Don't leave Ben standing on the porch. Invite him in."

Grace opened the door wider and stepped aside.

"I'm warming up meatloaf. I hope you're hungry," Erma chirped.

"*Jah*, it smells *wunderbaar*." Ben stole a glimpse at Grace, whose furrowed brow and deep lines between her eyes were anything but inviting.

Erma turned. "Supper will be ready in ten minutes," she said over her shoulder.

He cleared his throat, a noisy rattle rising from his chest. "You avoided me all afternoon."

"*Jah*, I know." Grace removed her cloak from the wall hook.

"Are you leaving?" He'd come to spend time with her, not her *aenti*.

She rushed out the door without giving him another look or taking time to put on her cloak.

He shot out the door behind her. "Grace," he said, following her to the woodshed. "Didn't we have plans this evening?"

"I assumed you had packing to do." She stooped down at the woodpile and collected a few of the smaller pieces of kindling.

Ben squatted next to her and filled his arms with wood. "I was going to tell you tonight about *mei* plans to leave."

"Tonight!" Her jaw tightened. "You kissed me—knowing that you were leaving."

He nodded sheepishly. He'd berated himself over his actions all afternoon, starting the moment he saw the hurt in Grace's eyes when LeAnn had asked what time his bus was leaving.

"Why? To brag to your buddies in Florida?" She shook her head. "Never mind. I don't want to know." She marched toward the house, but stopped prior to entering and turned to face him, eyes glaring. "*Jah*, I do want to know—I deserve to know. Why did you kiss me if you knew you were leaving?"

Hurt flooded her eyes and he wanted nothing more than to tell her the truth. He began with a slight catch in his throat. "I wanted to know if there was a reason to stay."

Her eyes narrowed to slits and she spun around.

Ben jostled the armload of kindling and, reaching for the door-knob, kept her from going inside. "I care about you." His throat dried. Her maddening silence bored through him like acid. "Is there a reason for me to stay?"

She blinked, and for a moment, the lines between her eyes soft-ened. But with renewed vigor, she straightened her shoulders and jutted out her chin. "*Aenti* Erma doesn't like it when supper is delayed."

She should have just kicked him—the air left his lungs as though she had. He opened the door and waited for her to enter. On his way into the kitchen, he tried to come up with an excuse to leave, but couldn't. Perhaps after supper he would have the chance to sit with her on the porch. Beg for her forgiveness.

Erma carried the conversation throughout the meal, with excep-tion to LeAnn asking about the length of the trip. Seated directly across the table from him, Grace refused to look him in the eye. The meatloaf settled in his stomach like a bag of cement.

Ben cleared his throat. "*Danki* for the meal," he said to Erma.

"You're *welkom* to join us anytime."

He wished Grace had extended the same invitation. His hands turned clammy and he rubbed them on his pants. He looked at Grace, but she averted her gaze when he opened his mouth to speak.

Grace scooted her chair back from the table, stood, and started collecting the dirty supper dishes.

"I can get these," Erma said, rising from her chair.

Ben rose, too, and picked up his plate. He followed Grace to the sink. "I'll help."

Erma set a stack of dishes on the counter. "If you two are going to *redd-up* the kitchen, I think I'll sit in the other room and read." She left the room, signaling for LeAnn to also.

"You don't have to stay. I'm sure you have a lot of packing to do." She lowered the dishes into the sink and started to fill it with water.

"I didn't *kumm* with much."

The sink hadn't filled completely before she started washing the plates.

Once the dishes were rinsed, he dried them with a dish towel. "Where do you want these?" He motioned to the stack of plates.

"You can leave them on the counter. I'll put them away later." When she rinsed the last pan and handed it to him, their hands touched. She released the pan immediately and jerked her hand away. She busied herself by the stove, adding more slabs of wood, then placed a large pot of something liquid on the cast-iron surface.

"Do you have a few minutes to go for a walk or sit on the porch?" he asked.

"I don't think that's a *gut* idea." She removed a wooden spoon from the drawer and stirred the concoction.

Ben tried to decipher the scent, but the best he could come up with was a liniment of some sort. Then he recalled the day he arrived and how she'd come out of the barn carrying a similar-sized pot. The kitchen stank that night, too, as she heated the mixture.

"What are you making?" He leaned closer to look into the pot.

"Nothing to eat."

"I figured that. It smells like medicine."

She stiffened briefly. "It is." She resumed stirring and kept her focus on the pot. "I have problems with *mei* joints and this reduces the swelling."

"You need a better pair of shoes."

Her shoulders rose and fell with a deep breath. "It's more than just old shoes. I limp because one of *mei* legs is shorter than the other."

"I know that. I looked at your shoes, remember?"

"Oh yes. The man who snubs his nose at repairing shoes inspected mine. I remember."

Grace lifted the steaming pot from the stove and placed it on the wire rack. She removed a pair of tongs from a drawer and dipped them into the water. She removed the amber-soaked cloths from the pot and placed them on a plate. His eyes watered.

She picked up the plate. "Good-bye, Ben. I hope you have a safe trip."

Chapter Sixteen

Ben jammed another shirt into his duffel bag. Tomorrow morning couldn't come soon enough. How did he let that icy woman get under his skin? He'd stooped to groveling. *Is there a reason for me to stay?*

"These are yours." Toby sent a pair of socks flying across the room.

Ben caught them midflight. *"Danki."* He shoved them into the bag.

"What lit your fire? I've never seen you in this much of a hurry for anything."

"I'm just ready to get out of Badger Creek." But the thought of returning to Florida unsettled his nerves. He wasn't ready to face his father either.

Toby snorted. "This afternoon you made it sound as if you might stay. What changed?"

Ben plopped on the mattress, exhaling a sigh that did nothing to ease the burden weighing on his heart. "I kissed her."

"And you got slapped—*again.*"

"Nay," Ben snapped. "She responded."

"They all do, don't they?" A scowl crossed Toby's face as he rolled his head, as if stretching out his neck muscles.

Ben shot off the bed, a low growl rumbling in his throat. "Graber, I've heard enough of your digs. We were best friends. What happened?"

148

Anger flicked in Toby's eyes. "You tell me."

A knock sounded on the door. "I've got the rest of your clothes," the bishop's wife said through the closed door.

Ben opened the door and forced a smile. "*Danki*, Mrs. Yoder."

She handed Ben the neat stack of laundry. "I'm sorry, but I can't seem to find the clothes I put on the line the other day."

"Don't worry about it. They're old clothes." Ben gently set the items on the bed.

She placed her index finger on her temple and her forehead creased. "I don't remember if I checked the wash *haus*." She looked up at him. "Would you be so kind as to look for me? I'd hate for you to go back to Florida and leave something behind."

He was already leaving his pride behind. A few shirts didn't matter. "Sure." Ben clipped Toby with a challenging glare. "You coming?"

Toby tossed the pants he'd been folding on the bed, smiled stiffly, and headed to the door. "Let's go."

They donned their coats and hats and grabbed a lantern before heading outside. Ben couldn't help but notice Toby clenching and unclenching his hands as they fled the house. The simmering pot was about to boil over, and for the life of him, Ben didn't know why. He waited until they were halfway across the yard before starting the conversation. "What's gotten into you, Graber?"

"They're all a challenge to you, aren't they?" Toby shook his head in disgust.

"You've said that before." Ben shrugged. "I don't get it. You've known me all *mei* life. I haven't changed."

"Exactly. And Grace deserves someone better than you."

Ben nodded. "I was wrong. I misread the look in her eyes and I shouldn't have kissed her."

Toby growled under his breath.

"I—was—wrong. What else do you want me to say?" Ben scowled when Toby merely huffed. "I thought you were *mei* friend." He jerked the door open to the wash *haus* and waited for Toby, who was carrying the lantern, to enter first. "I actually feel rotten for what I did—even without your reprimand—so back off."

Toby stepped into Ben's path. "When you kissed Neva in the storage shed, did you feel rotten about that too?"

Ben's spine stiffened.

"I didn't think so."

For the first time, Ben saw anguish behind the anger in Toby's eyes. "*Jah*," Ben finally admitted. "I felt bad about her too." He touched his face, remembering the sting of her slap. "I wore Neva's handprint on the side of *mei* face for a day. I never thought she would talk to me again."

"But she did."

Ben winced at the condemnation in Toby's hiss. He sounded more and more like his father. He peeked inside the washtub, found it empty, and moved to the door. "I don't see any clothes out here. I'm going back inside." Ben hung his head. He should never have acted on his attraction to Grace. Why did he kiss her when things were still unfinished between him and Neva? Toby had been right to call him a fool.

⁂

Grace closed her eyes as tears trickled down her face and fell onto her pillow. She couldn't erase the image of Ben's expression when he looked into the poultice solution. *It smells like medicine.* What did he think was making his eyes water? The scent was caustic. The fumes of the mixture seeped from the rags and mocked her condition—her lot in life. Her eyes burned.

"God, I've tried to accept my weakness, to understand the meaning of Your Word, 'My grace is sufficient for you, for My strength is made perfect in weakness.' But it doesn't make sense. You are all-powerful.

You laid the foundation of the earth. You tell the mountains to move. You command the thunder and send the rain. So, I don't understand. Why do You need my weakness to make perfect Your power?"

A knock sounded on her bedroom door and Grace swiped her hand over her face to dry her tears. "*Kumm* in."

Aenti Erma entered the room. "Grace, are you okay?"

"*Jah,*" she whispered, thankful she had already turned the lamp wick down. But the lack of light didn't stop *Aenti* from moving farther into the room or from sitting on the chair beside her bed.

"Ben didn't stay long. Is everything all right?"

"He needed to get back to the bishop's in order to pack." Her throat tightened. She didn't want to talk about Ben. "*Aenti,* was I named Grace because *mei* left leg is shorter than my right? *Mamm* recited the verse about God's grace being sufficient ever since I can remember."

"You are your mother's unmerited favor. She hadn't been able to have a *boppli* for six years, then God blessed her with a daughter. But it was your father who named you. He said they were blessed with God's grace and that's what your name needed to be." *Aenti* patted Grace's shoulder. "You're a blessing, child. You've certainly filled this lonely woman's life with joy."

A new crop of tears pooled in Grace's eyes. She wished her aunt would stay year-round. *Aenti* believed *Daed* avoided her because she looked so much like *Mamm,* but Grace wasn't so sure that was the reason. Even so, Grace couldn't help but believe that she was her aunt's favorite niece because they had so much in common. Including that neither would ever marry.

❧

Ben dropped his bag next to the bench in the bus station. It wouldn't be long before Badger Creek was behind him. He pictured himself sitting on the beach with foamy water washing the shore and the *caw—caw—caw* of seagulls in the distance. He loved Florida. So why did the thought of returning home—leaving Badger Creek—feel unsettling?

"I'm sorry you're leaving so soon," Bishop Yoder said. "I know it's tough being away from family. It's *gut* that things worked out for you to go home."

"*Danki* for allowing us to stay with you," Toby said. "Please tell *mei onkel* I'm sorry I missed him."

"Maybe you'll have the opportunity to visit again." Bishop Yoder turned to Ben. "It was *gut* to meet you, and you're always *welkom* back."

"*Danki* for everything."

Toby motioned to the ticket counter. "Looks like it's getting busier. We should probably get in line to purchase our tickets."

Bishop Yoder nodded. "I'll be on *mei* way. I have a few other stops to make while I'm in town. Have a safe journey." He clapped their shoulders. "*Kumm* back anytime."

As the bishop ambled down the corridor, Ben couldn't help but compare this departure with his last. When he left Florida, his father hadn't clapped his back or even invited him back.

Ben and Toby crossed the lobby and joined the throng of people waiting to buy tickets. The automatic door leading to the platform opened and a gust of wind swept through the station.

Toby shivered. "It'll feel *gut* to get out of this *kalt wedder*. Just think, in a few days we'll be planting shrubs again. Trees will have leaves instead of bare branches."

This was the most Toby had talked since their heated conversation last night. His friend was certainly anxious to go home. "On our way here I saw some buds starting." Ben moved forward along with the other people in the line. Badger Creek wasn't so bad. Other than Grace making it clear she didn't want him here. But unlike Toby, Ben didn't miss planting shrubs, and the thought of returning home soured his stomach.

The bishop's words rolled over in Ben's mind. *It's gut that things worked out for you to go home . . .* They'd worked out for Toby. His parents sent him bus fare. Ben's parents weren't expecting him. Nothing had changed between his father and him. He certainly wouldn't have earned his father's respect in this short time away. It took longer than that to destroy it. Recalling the incidents that led to his being sent away, Ben hadn't paid attention that they were next in line until Toby nudged him.

"You coming?" His friend moved toward the vacant window.

Ben followed.

"Two tickets for Sarasota, Florida." Toby opened his wallet.

"Make that one ticket for Florida and one for Shipshewana, Indiana." Ben turned to Toby. "I'll pay you back."

"Indiana?" Toby narrowed his eyes. "Why there?"

"I can't go home. *Nett* yet."

"We're going to need another minute," Toby told the woman. He tugged on Ben's shirtsleeve and they stepped away from the counter. "I thought we were both going home . . . *Daed* will give you back your job."

Having a job hadn't stopped his father from sending him away. "Your situation is different. I can't go back—*nett* yet."

Toby scowled and crossed his arms. "Why Indiana? You've never mentioned going to Shipshewana before."

"My two sisters are there. One of their husbands should be able to find me work."

Toby mumbled something, turned toward the window, and stared outside.

The way their friendship had been strained over the past few weeks, Ben hadn't expected this response. "Hey, maybe if I'm *nett* there to get you into trouble, you'll find a *gut* woman and settle down. You've been saying you want to get married and start a family."

Toby didn't have to say anything, or even turn in Ben's direction. The reflection off the window mirrored Toby's frown.

They had always been like brothers, but Ben had no clue what was irking Toby. "I think I'll walk over to the vending machine. Do you want anything?"

Toby shook his head without turning to face him.

Ben had enough change to select a pack of gum. He headed toward the row of benches and sat.

Toby continued to stare outside several more minutes, then turned and lumbered over to Ben. "I have to tell you something." He drew in a breath. "I should have told you . . . sooner." He looked down at the cement floor.

"What is it?"

"Neva lives in Indiana."

Ben vaulted off the seat. "How do you know?"

Toby stepped backward. "She's living with her second cousin."

"Did your *mamm* write that in her letter? When did you find out?"

"I've known"—Toby bowed his head—"all along," he whispered.

Ben's thoughts whirled. His friend, his best friend, had known her whereabouts? As the news rolled over in Ben's mind, questions began to surface. "Why didn't you tell me? I don't understand—we're best friends."

Toby snorted.

"If you have more to tell me, you'd better spit it out."

Toby released a weighty sigh. "We were secretly seeing each other—long before you kissed her in the shed that day."

Ben's mouth fell agape. "And you think I would have done that had I known?" He shook his head. "Never!" Acid rose to the back of his throat as he recalled the night she met him on the boat pier, stumbling drunk and rambling about a ruined future. "You know about the *nacht*—"

"Yes!" Anger flared in Toby's eyes.

"Was the letter you got from her?"

Toby nodded. "We've been corresponding."

154

Ben glanced at the large clock on the wall. "We should probably get our tickets."

Toby blew out a breath and headed to the line. Neither spoke as they waited, and when they reached the counter, Toby said, "One ticket for Sarasota, Florida, and"—he turned to Ben—"where do you want to go?"

"And one for Shipshewana, Indiana, please."

Toby removed his wallet and paid the fare. He collected the tickets and handed Ben his.

Ben glanced at the ticket. "You gave me the wrong one."

"What are you talking about?"

"It's you that needs to go to Indiana." Ben smiled. "And stop being so indecisive. If you two have been writing back and forth this entire year—"

"Ben, there's more to it than you know."

The overhead speaker crackled and a woman's voice announced that passengers should board on platform D.

"Sounds like your bus is here," Ben said as the woman gave the departing information. "*Nau* exchange tickets with me and get out of here."

Toby glanced at the double doors leading to the loading dock, then back to Ben. "I can't. I told you . . . there's more to it."

A second call rang out for boarding. Ben nudged Toby toward the doors. "I'll walk you out."

Outside on the platform, Toby dropped his duffel bag and, squatting next to it, pawed through the contents. He stood, holding a fistful of twine-tied envelopes. He hesitated a moment, then handed them to Ben. "After you read these . . . you might . . ."

Ben glanced at Neva's fancy handwriting addressed to Toby, then at his best friend's despondent expression. Ben smiled. "Don't let that bus leave without you. It's time to stop being indecisive and seize the day."

"You need to read the letters."

The bus hissed and a puff of exhaust fumes clouded the loading dock.

"You need to catch that bus."

"Ben . . . I hope you can find it in your heart to forgive me."

⊗

Grace stayed busy all morning, washing walls and windows, but thoughts of Ben still besieged her conscience. It was just as well that he returned to Florida. Not many people could tolerate the hard work and bitter weather conditions in Badger Creek. She barely could.

Grace stared out the sitting room window at the land she planned to till this spring. She wanted to put in a larger garden this year, even double the amount of red potatoes and yams. But working in the garden would have to wait. The ground was still too soggy for planting.

She doused the plate glass with pungent vinegar, then pulled apart a few pages of the *Budget* to wipe the window with. She liked using newspaper because it never left streaks like paper towels did.

"There," *Aenti* said, admiring the wooden lamp table. "I think I'm done dusting." She removed the glass chimney on the oil lamp. "I'm going to take this into the kitchen to wash. Should I put the kettle on for tea?"

"Sounds *gut*. I'm almost done with the windows."

Aenti left the room humming, a tune Grace recognized from the *Ausbund*. Humming along, Grace rubbed the glass with the wadded-up newspaper until it squeaked. It always amazed her how much soot built up on the windows over winter. She moved to the next window, wetted it with vinegar, and, through the blurred window, caught a flash of blue movement near the barn. Grace scrubbed the glass clean, but the image was gone. Maybe her eyes had played a trick on her. She hadn't slept well last night and her eyes were droopy. Still, when LeAnn left the house this morning to gather maple sap, she was wearing a forest-green dress and her black cloak. The men weren't back and even though the image was distorted through the blurry glass, it appeared too large to be one of her nephews. Grace set the spray bottle on the windowsill and went into the kitchen.

Aenti stood at the sink, washing the oil lamp's glass chimney in the soapy water. She stopped humming when Grace entered the room. "The kettle should be hot any minute."

Grace removed two cups from the cupboard and set them on the counter. She meandered over to the window and peered outside. Usually, she looked forward to this time of the year, when the trees budded with new growth. It meant Philemon and the other men would be home from camp soon. Anticipation of the men's return always sent a buzz throughout the settlement as the women worked together to prepare a welcoming feast. Grace's chest tightened. What did she have to look forward to? Philemon had made his intentions known prior to leaving that when he returned from camp, he and Becky were going to marry. Grace's vision blurred with tears. *Ach*, foolish old maid. Why hadn't she seen the signs? Philemon hadn't misled her; it was she who had hopelessly believed something more would come from their long-standing friendship. And after Ben's kiss left her utterly speechless and her entire body tingling, she'd have a difficult time looking Philemon in the eye even if he had changed his mind about marrying Becky while he was gone. Not that there was a chance of that occurring.

She blotted the corners of her eyes with the edge of her dress sleeve. She wouldn't ever marry. Not with one leg shorter than the other. A paralyzing thought stiffened her joints. Her mother was Grace's age when her muscles started failing her. Shortly after, she received the news she had muscular dystrophy.

"Is everything all right?" Her *aenti's* voice broke the silence.

Grace turned from the window and forced a smile. She didn't dare speak for fear her voice might crack with the egg-sized lump growing in her throat. Even so, her lips were trembling.

Aenti tossed the dish towel on the counter and patted Grace's shoulder. "What's troubling you, child?"

"Just feeling a little blue. It'll pass." Lord willing, her heart would mend. She went to the stove, picked up the hissing kettle using a potholder, and poured the steaming water into the cups. "Did you want honey in your tea?" Grace loaded a spoonful of the thick, golden sweetener and let it dissolve in her tea.

"Grace, what's wrong? Is this about Ben leaving for Florida?"

"*Nett* really." She forced a smile. "*Mamm* was *mei* age when she was diagnosed, wasn't she? Her legs started to spasm and then her arms, right?"

"*Jah*, child."

"I think I want to move to Ohio. I have to know if I have . . ."

"Grace, you know I'd love for you to *kumm*, but I think you shouldn't make any rash decisions. I know this has to do with Ben. I saw the way you two looked at each other after you went to the buggy for the bread yesterday."

Grace added honey to her aunt's tea and stirred. She hadn't realized how perceptive *Aenti* was. Did the others suspect something as well? Grace recalled Mattie's smile when she handed her the dishes. "I'm *nett* sure *Daed* will like the news, but . . ." Grace bowed her head. Her father wouldn't be pleased, especially after he found out why she wanted to leave. The last time she brought up seeing a specialist, he accused her of being desperate to satisfy a vain desire to be like everyone else.

"What is it?"

Grace shrugged.

Aenti Erma reached for her hand and gave it a gentle squeeze. "If you really want to go, then I'll talk with your father when he returns from camp. He wants the best for you."

Her father's best had never included seeing a specialist in the past, but maybe *Aenti* could change his mind. "Keeping up with the household chores might be too much for LeAnn. She's *nett* that eager as it is." Grace craned her neck to look out the window for her sister. She wasn't boiling maple sap under the lean-to next to the barn. The sap buckets hadn't been collected either. "Have you seen LeAnn lately?"

Chapter Seventeen

Grace pulled her cloak tighter around her neck and stepped off the porch. The weather hadn't warmed up much since this morning when she'd done the barn chores. At least the sky wasn't overcast like it had been earlier. They didn't need more rain.

Grace crossed the yard, walked past the lean-to, which was void of activity, and headed into the woods. The last time she had checked the sap buckets was when LeAnn had the flu. Grace recalled having to wade through a foot of snow to reach the maple trees that were tapped. Some trees had multiple taps and it took several trips to carry heavy buckets back. By the time she made a fire and boiled down the sap in small increments, her arms ached from constantly having to stir the thickening syrup. Later, she discovered the batch she had made wasn't as sweet as LeAnn's, which seemed to please her sister.

Grace spotted a white bucket hanging from one of the tapped red maple trees and cut through a patch of ferns to reach it. She peered inside the bucket. Except for a smidgen of watery sap, the bucket was empty. Perhaps the season had reached its end.

Branches snapped. Grace froze for a half second, then slowly turned around. She hadn't heard of any bear sightings yet, but they were bound to be out of hibernation anytime now. Not that she would know what to do if she saw one. She couldn't outrun a bear and it could climb to the top of a tree faster than she could. Grace scanned the woods. Nothing. A little more at ease, she moved to the next red maple. A much larger tree, it had two taps protruding from its trunk. The lower bucket empty, she rose to her tiptoes and peered over the rim of the second bucket just as a man's voice called out her name.

Grace spun in the direction of the caller. She sucked in a sharp breath as the nearby pine branches moved. Ben emerged from the evergreens, brushing the pine needles off his pale-blue shirtsleeve.

"What are you doing here? I thought you went back to Florida," she said.

He motioned to his boots. "I couldn't leave wearing your *bruder's* boots."

"Really?" Grace shook her head in disbelief. "You missed your bus to return those old boots? I don't think Emery would have missed them. Besides, he has another pair."

"That's okay. I had another reason too." He kicked at a leaf on the ground.

Grace's thoughts whirled in a million directions. "Did you and Toby decide to stay and help Bishop Yoder with the orders?"

"Toby went back." Ben moved past her and over to the tree. He tipped the plastic bucket and looked inside. "That's all the sap the tree puts out?"

"Ah . . . *jah*, this is the end of the season," she said once Ben's question fully registered.

Ben inspected the tree trunk. He touched an area where the tree had healed from a previous tap.

"Those marks are from a couple of years ago," she said.

"How many times can you tap a tree?"

"Several, if it's healthy. The red maples live to be well over a hundred." She looked up at the branches full of new buds. "This one's in *gut* shape. Our *kinner* will tap—I didn't mean *our*—as in yours and mine." She blew out a breath. Could she have sounded any more desperate? "Other generations, I meant to say. *Nett* our—"

A smile tugged at his lips and her thoughts flitted to his lingering kiss. Heat crawled up the back of her neck.

"I know what you're trying to say."

She narrowed her eyes. "Then why did you let me babble on like some fool?"

"You take things too seriously," he said. "Don't call yourself a fool. That's far from the truth." He mumbled something else under his breath. As his gaze traveled up the tree, his expression sobered.

The awkward silence gnawed at Grace. "You could have mailed the boots."

"I suppose." His lighthearted mood was suddenly missing as he continued to study the tree.

Perhaps it had something to do with why he didn't return to Florida with Toby. "How long do you plan on staying in Badger Creek—*nau* that you've had the chance to return the boots?"

He motioned to his feet. "I haven't given them back yet."

Does that mean indefinitely? She stopped herself from asking. It didn't matter. In another week or two, the men would return from camp and she and *Aenti* would leave for Ohio. "I suppose I'll see you around," she said, taking a few steps toward the path.

Ben caught up in a couple of long strides. "Where are you going? The *haus* is that way." He motioned in the opposite direction.

"I thought I would find LeAnn collecting the buckets, but *nau* I'm thinking she went to her friend's *haus* on the other side of the woods."

"She didn't."

Grace stopped midstep and pivoted toward him. "You saw her?"

He nodded. "At the bus station."

Her jaw went slack.

"I had no idea." Ben lifted his arms, palms out. "That's the truth, Grace."

"Where did she go? Did she leave with Toby?"

He shook his head. "His bus had already left. I don't think she was there for us."

"I don't understand."

"I was sitting on the bench at the bus station reading a letter—when I glanced up, I saw her. She looked startled, and . . ."

"And what? Tell me, please, I need to know."

"She was talking with an *Englischer*. His name is Clutch."

"Clutch?"

"He works at the bus station." A squirrel made a *tsk-tsk* sound and Ben paused long enough to look behind him. It flicked its furry tail, then darted along the length of a fallen log and disappeared into the underbrush. Ben turned back to her. "I didn't get the impression she was waiting for a bus. I think she went there to see him."

Grace put her hand over her mouth. Her father would be distraught over the news.

"She's at the *haus* now," he said.

"You made sure she got home safely? Is that why you didn't leave?"

Ben bowed his head and shuffled his feet. The man was humble.

"*Danki*." Grace drew a deep breath and released it. "Did you talk with her? Did she tell you what she was doing at the station—with an *Englischer*?"

He shook his head. "It wasn't *mei* place to ask."

"Well, it is mine." She marched toward the house. Her sister had some explaining to do. Clutch. Who in their right mind would name their child after a piece of machinery?

"Grace," Ben said, coming up beside her. "Everyone makes mistakes. I've sure made plenty of them."

"What are you saying? I should let her ruin her life so she can learn from her mistakes?"

"I don't know what I'm trying to say—except you don't need to be so . . . judgmental. Understanding and forgiveness goes a long way . . ."

Grace stood ramrod straight.

"Condemnation will push her farther away."

When Grace's eyes locked on his, it was as if God removed a veil from her eyes, and she sensed the depth of his pain. *I disappointed* mei *father—for the last time, as he put it. Then he sent me here.* She recalled Ben's words and the same hurt in his eyes.

He looked away. "We should get going. I still need to speak with the bishop."

A deafening silence fell between them as they continued the course. He kept his head down and appeared to be deep in thought. Reaching the house, Grace cleared her throat. "Would you like to *kumm* inside for a cup of *kaffi* before you leave?"

"Just *kaffi*? *Nay* cookies?" He protruded his bottom lip in a pout.

Grace smiled. "I think I can find you a few cookies."

She led the way up the porch steps and opened the door. Voices came from the kitchen. Grace recognized *Aenti's*, but not the man's voice. Clutch? Had he come to visit LeAnn? Anger rose within her. She murmured a short prayer for the right words as she rounded the corner to the kitchen.

Seated at the head of the table, the man jammed a cookie in his mouth. The crumbs spilled onto his whiskered face and down the front of what looked like the same short-sleeved shirt Ben had worn the first day he arrived.

Aenti Erma made a nervous nod toward the man. "We have another visitor from Florida."

A hungry visitor. The cookie jar was full this morning and now it had maybe a half dozen left.

"This is Gordon Wellford." *Aenti* smiled warmly at the man, then turned to Ben. "He's a long way from home. I told him your district was in Florida too."

"Long way," the man said, looking at *Aenti* as if for reassurance. "Long way from home?"

He didn't know? Grace took a step farther into the kitchen, and the stranger snatched the cookie jar from the table and pressed it against his chest. She paused for a half second, and then, feeling his gray, wide-set eyes following her across the room, she moved in front of the sink.

The floor plank creaked when Ben took a step.

Still clutching the jar, the stranger snapped his attention to Ben. His shoe tapped the floor.

"*Hiya*," Ben said.

"*Hiya*," he echoed. He tapped faster.

Ben inched into the room. "You're from Florida?"

"Florida." The man's body rocked back and forth in the chair, while still tapping and still clinging to the cookie jar.

"Those are *gut* cookies, *jah*?"

"*Jah*." Clenching the jar protectively, the tips of his fingers paled.

Ben eyed the man's tapping foot. "How's your *fraa* and *kinner*?"

Why was Ben asking him about his wife and children? Did he know the man? His face had day-old whiskers and the beginnings of a mustache, something all Amish districts forbade.

When the stranger didn't answer, Ben continued questioning him in Pennsylvania *Deitsch*.

"Stop!" The stranger squeezed his eyes shut. "No more voices. No more voices. Tell them to go away."

Grace inched closer to *Aenti*, then took her by the arm and led her over to the sink. "Where's LeAnn?" she whispered.

Aenti leaned closer. "Fetching the bishop."

"No more voices!" The man's warning rang out.

Grace clamped her mouth shut and squeezed *Aenti's* arm. She caught a glimpse of Ben, edging closer to them, his hands fisted at his sides.

"Gordon," *Aenti* said in a soft tone. "Would you like me to make you something to eat? I could fry some eggs."

His expression softened and he smiled almost childlike and nodded, tossing his matted, unkempt hair.

"*Gut.*" *Aenti* turned to Grace. "I'll need some meat from the *icehaus*, and, Ben," she said, turning to him, "I'll need you to fetch more wood."

The hairs on Grace's arms stood on end—she wasn't about to leave her *aenti* alone with the man. Grace widened her eyes at *Aenti* Erma, then nodded at the full woodbox beside the stove.

Aenti Erma nudged Grace's shoulder. "Please run along, and be sure to show Ben where to find the *special* wood inside the shed. We'll need a big armful to get a strong fire going."

"*Jah*... okay." She glanced at the man shoving another cookie into his mouth. At least he hadn't noticed that the woodbox was full—not yet, anyway.

Chapter Eighteen

Once outside, Ben grasped Grace's elbow. "*Kumm* on, we have to hurry." Leaving Erma inside the house alone wasn't wise, but he needed to get Grace as far away as possible. The man might notice the woodbox was full at any moment and go into a rage.

"Why is he trying to dress like us? He's *nett* Amish."

"I know." Ben walked faster. Still guiding her by the elbow, she didn't resist the increased pace. She turned to glance back, but tripped over a rock. "Careful," Ben said, steadying her balance. "He might be watching us. We shouldn't chance drawing attention to ourselves by looking back."

Her eyes widened.

"Everything will be all right. I'll figure something out, but you'll have to trust me."

Lips trembling, she muttered, "Okay," in a hoarse whisper.

Once they reached the *icehaus*, Ben yanked the wooden door open, then, waiting for her to enter, he stole a glimpse of the house. At least the man wasn't standing at the kitchen window watching them. The fact that he let them both go outside unattended puzzled Ben, but he planned to make the most of the opportunity.

Ben squeezed inside next to Grace. "*Nett* much wiggle room in here," he said.

She scooted over a few inches, giving him enough room to close the door. The place looked much larger from the outside, but with floor-to-ceiling shelves lining the plastic-covered walls, and the large slabs of ice stacked end to end, space was limited.

"Usually there isn't enough room for two people in here," she said. "Blocks of ice take up most of the room. The men cut slabs of ice out of the nearby lake, then chop it into blocks for the *icehauses*. Usually by the end of winter, most of the meat has been either eaten or canned and stored in the cellar." Her lips tightened into a straight line. "I'm sorry. I shouldn't be rambling about such nonsense when *Aenti* is alone with that stranger." She rubbed her arms.

"Are you *kalt*?" He'd never stood inside a freezer before. It was cold enough to see his breath. He moved closer to her, wishing he had the nerve to put his arm around her shoulders.

"*Mei* skin is still crawling. Did you see the way he looked at me? He guarded the cookie jar like it was a prized possession."

The stranger was creepy all right, but sharing those thoughts wouldn't help the situation. "I don't think he's eaten in a while." *Other than an apple pie from Mattie's back porch.*

Grace sniffled. "What do you think he wants from us?"

"I'm *nett* sure, but we need to assume he's dangerous." He kept his tone even. "The day I arrived, I heard a news report that the authorities were searching for someone from the county Behavior Unit."

She nodded. "*Jah*, I remember."

"If the man inside is the same person, he's unstable. He attacked a nurse."

Grace's shoulders shook, and she started to sob.

He shouldn't have said anything. Now she was upset and he didn't know how to comfort her. "Grace," he said, placing his hand on her shoulder. "I know this is hard news, but we have to stay focused. We don't have much time."

"I'm sorry," she said, wiping her face dry with the back of her hand. She reached up to one of the shelves and pulled down a white, freezer-paper-wrapped package of meat marked Bacon.

He motioned to a lower shelf that held several tin containers labeled Jerky. "Is there anything in these?"

Grace handed him the package of bacon, then grabbed a tin container. She popped off the lid. Empty. She checked another canister and discovered it was empty as well. "I know this one had venison jerky in it last week." Her face paled. "You think he took it, don't you?"

Ben nodded.

"And Mattie's pie?" She gasped. "Wh-what do we do?" She would hyperventilate if she continued to breathe at this rate. If she passed out, he wouldn't know what to do.

"Take a deep breath." Ben demonstrated. "And blow it out slowly."

Following his instructions, Grace breathed in and out. "Why were you staring at his shoes?"

"They're mine. The ones I left by the side of the river."

"What?" she rasped.

"It'll be all right," he said, calmly repeating the statement until the tension disappeared from her face and her breathing returned to normal. "Are there any more containers to check?"

She wiggled around to his other side, then squatted down next to the shelf to reach a container from the back of the bottom shelf. She shook the can and something thumped inside. "He didn't find the tin of smoked rabbit meat." She removed the lid and gathered a bundle of stiff, dried meat.

"Erma said something about needing special wood. Do you know what she's talking about?"

"We use kindling in the stove for cooking, but the box was full."

"Didn't she stress 'special'?"

"*Ach*, of course. It's in the *smokehaus*." She reached for the door, but he stopped her from opening it.

"Let me go first." He eased the door open and scanned the area. Nothing seemed out of the ordinary. He stepped outside with Grace following closely. They hurried across the yard. The *smokehaus* was even smaller. He couldn't close the door completely behind them. Rows of galvanized pipes made up the drying rack along the wall. Above them, hooks, some the size of his hand, dangled from a metal rod that spanned the width of the building.

"The larger hooks are used for hanging bear or deer meat and the smaller ones are for rabbits, chickens, chipmunks—I'm sorry. I'm rambling again."

If it kept her mind preoccupied, he would listen to her recite the dictionary. He pulled back a canvas tarp, uncovering a wooden crate.

"That's it," she said.

He reached into the crate and grasped the twine-tied bundle of lightweight balsam wood. *Kindling?* Maybe it burned faster. It made sense that Erma would want to feed him fast and hope that he left. The paper-thin wood would certainly catch on fire faster, but it didn't look like it would burn long enough to cook anything. He eased the door open more and poked his head outside long enough to look around. He hadn't wanted to alarm Grace, but the officer who gave the news update had mentioned someone else—a person of interest. Ben wished he could remember enough details to know if there were two men on the run or one.

Ben took the supplies from Grace's arms. "How's your leg?"

Grace squared her shoulders, embarrassed that he'd brought up her infirmity. "Fine."

"One of us needs to notify the authorities. I can't leave you and Erma alone with that man." He rubbed the back of his neck. "Do you think you can make it to the *Englischers'* farm off the main road?"

"*Aenti* Erma sent LeAnn to fetch the bishop."

"That's *gut*, but the police have to be notified. The man is dangerous."

He looked upward. At first, she thought he was eyeing the rafters, then he reached up and removed one of the hooks from the metal rod. He turned it over in his hand. She gulped.

He tucked it under his straw hat, then placed his hand on her back and nudged her toward the door of the *smokehaus*. "Once you reach the *Englischers' haus*, stay there."

"But—"

"Grace, promise me you'll stay where it's safe. I'll find you when it's over."

When it's over. So he was expecting something bad to happen. Her eyes welled with tears.

For a moment, he lowered his head and shifted his feet as though uncomfortable with her crying, then he lifted his head and smiled. "I'll take you fishing when it's over."

"Fishing?"

"And I'll bait your hook." His expression sobered, and he opened the door wider. "Go quickly."

She leaned her head out the opening, glanced at the kitchen window, then, not seeing anyone, darted across the yard. She came to the large willow on the edge of the property and stopped long enough to catch her breath. The shortest route to the main road wasn't the easiest route by any measure. It meant breaking a new trail through the woods. She whispered a prayer for strength before speeding off without looking back.

Chapter Nineteen

Please, God, watch over Grace and keep her safe. Ben stood at the door of the *smokehaus* until Grace was out of sight. He blew out a breath. Sending her to get help was the right thing to do. Now maybe the knot in his stomach would untangle.

Or maybe not.

A silhouette, too tall and broad-shouldered for Erma, shadowed the kitchen window. He should have sent Grace earlier and looked for the supplies himself. It would have given her more time. But stalling too long would put Erma in greater danger.

Ben repositioned the package of bacon, the jerky, and the bundle of balsam wood in his arms. The shadowy figure had moved away from the kitchen window. Did it mean he was no longer standing guard? On his way out of the building, he spotted an axe leaning against the chopping block next to the woodshed. He ventured in that direction while keeping his gaze fixed on the house for any suspicious movement. He grabbed the axe by its handle and hurried to the house.

On the porch, he faltered, axe in hand. It was difficult to assess the situation from outside. He couldn't risk endangering Erma more. He propped it up against the side of the house next to the window in the sitting room and whispered a prayer that it would go unnoticed.

He turned the doorknob slowly and eased open the door to keep it from squeaking, but as he went to close it, the man came up behind him, slammed it closed, then grabbed him by the shirt with one hand while clutching the empty cookie jar with the other. The man shoved him into the other room. Ben held his hat in place, but the package of bacon slipped from his grip.

He thumped Ben's chest, sending him a few steps backward. "What took you so long?"

Ben motioned to the package of meat on the floor. "I wanted to bring you the largest package of bacon. I know you're hungry." He craned his neck toward the kitchen. Where was Erma?

The man combed his fingers through his hair and turned in a wide circle. He repeated the action, only this time in the opposite direction. He stepped closer to Ben, aimed his steely gray eyes at him, and shouted, "Stop looking at me!"

"Sorry." Ben lowered his head and shuffled a few steps backward when the man wasn't looking. He was closer to the kitchen, but he didn't dare turn around.

The man mumbled to himself and paced the room.

Footsteps sounded behind Ben and stopped beside him. He glanced sideways without lifting his head and recognized Erma's dress. She took a few more steps, then stooped down next to the package of bacon and picked it up. "I'll let you know when the meal is ready." She turned around. "Ben, I'll need you to bring the wood into the kitchen."

He stole a glimpse of the man still talking to himself as he paced. He didn't seem to notice Erma enter or leave the room. Ben turned slowly and went into the kitchen.

He rushed to Erma standing beside the stove. "Are you okay?"

"*Jah*, toss the wood pieces into the stove." She unwrapped the bacon.

Ben opened the side compartment of the cast-iron stove. Flames shot out at him and he leaned back. "You have a *gut* fire."

"Do as I say, *sohn*." She layered the strips of bacon in the fry pan.

Ben broke the twine binding on the bundle of wood. Feeling a waxy coating on the wood's surface, he looked at Erma and lifted his brows.

She nodded. "You'll want to open the flue all the way."

"I'm afraid I don't know much about woodstoves."

"Turn the disc to the right. It'll create an updraft so the smoke goes out the chimney better."

He turned the lever and the metal disc inside the stovepipe flipped.

"*Nau* put the wood in."

Ben followed her instructions and loaded all the wood that would fit. He placed the other pieces in the woodbox. "I sent Grace to get help," he whispered.

"*Gut.*" She flipped over the sizzling bacon with a fork. "I think he's eaten too many sweets. He hasn't stopped pacing and he keeps mumbling something about a buried treasure."

"I wondered what he was saying." Ben tiptoed to the kitchen's entrance and peeked around the corner. The man was deep in his own world, still talking to himself, still pacing. Ben went back to the stove. "I think we could sneak out without him noticing."

❧

A surge of adrenaline kept Grace pushing forward when her leg muscles burned and threatened to seize. She stumbled over a rotted log and scuffed the heels of her hands when she fell. She pushed herself back up. Fire shot through her hip. She pressed her hand against her side and limped forward. "Lord, *mei* legs ache. I memorized Your Word about Your grace being sufficient for me. I know Your power is made perfect in *mei* weakness, but Lord, I need strength to finish this journey. I need Your power to dwell in me. *Aenti* Erma and Ben are relying on me."

Thunder rumbled in the distance, louder and longer. God was near. Peace washed over Grace as another scripture came to mind. *Praise the*

Lord, because He heard my prayer for help. The Lord is my strength and shield. I trust Him, and He helps me.

Branches snapped. *A deer,* she told herself. Branches crunched somewhere close. She scanned the surroundings. Nothing. But as the sound grew louder, every fiber in her body charged.

She sprinted.

Her labored breaths filled her ears.

Keep going.

Her side cramped. She doubled over, clutching her side and panting quick breaths. The stabbing sensations didn't ease. She screeched in pain.

A hand smelling of nicotine came from behind, covered her mouth, and slammed her against a man's chest. He tightened his hold over her mouth and jerked her around to face him.

He wasn't the same man—the one who clutched the cookie jar like it was a treasured possession. His breath was a putrid mixture of stale tobacco and poor hygiene, and his clothing smelled sour like a stagnant pond. His unkempt hair had pieces of straw, which led her to believe he'd been sleeping in someone's barn. She assessed his lanky build. Her brothers could wrestle him to the ground and hog-tie him in seconds. But her brothers weren't here. Neither was Ben.

"Help! Hel—" A hard blow to the mouth sent her whirling to the ground. Sprawled out and breathing in the scent of the loamy earth, he planted his knee just under her ribs and pressed hard. At the same time, he clasped his hand over her mouth. Unable to fill her lungs completely, she wheezed for air. Her ears rang with a high-pitched squeal and white spots filled her vision. Was this it? How she would die?

He released the pressure, stood, then jerked her off the ground. "Where were you going?"

"To see"—she cleared her throat—"a neighbor. I-I wanted to borrow something."

He wrenched her arm behind her back and pushed her forward. "Change of plans."

Grace's vision blurred, but prodded toward the house, she managed to stay one step ahead. After a time, her joints were so swollen, she had to slow down. He shoved her, launching her into a pile of brush.

"Get up."

Her leg muscles quivered and refused to cooperate. "Give me a minute. Please." She needed time to think. If she could get away, Emery and Susan's house was close. She would have to cut through the patch of thorny blackberry bushes to go this way, but—but she couldn't risk subjecting her sister-in-law and nephews to the stranger. Why did the nearest *Englischer* farm have to be so far away?

He pulled a cigarette from his shirt pocket and dangled it between his teeth as he struck the match. With his hand cupped to block the wind, he lit the cigarette, then tossed the match over his shoulder. "Get up." Thick smoke escaped his mouth. "Now!"

Lord, where are You? Can't You see that I'm spent?

Thunder clapped and the sky darkened. A strong breeze swept through the woods. She pushed off the ground and continued the course. If she paced herself, maybe God would give her the opportunity to get away. The man was breathing harder, puffing on the cigarette.

She came to the path that ran from Mattie's house to hers and stopped.

"You should know your way home," he growled. Apparently, he did too. He pushed her to the right.

Grace walked several feet before she noticed the faint smoke up ahead. Green. She smiled.

Chapter Twenty

B en stood at the kitchen entrance and peeked into the sitting room. The man still clutched the cookie jar and wore a path between the woodstove and the hallway. This was as good a time as any for Erma and him to sneak out the back door. Even if they could only reach the barn, they had a better chance of hiding there than in the house. Ben moved back into the kitchen. He eased the meat hook out from under his hat, but it slipped from his hand and clanged on the floor in the middle of the entry. Startled, the man turned in jerky movements as if seeing his surroundings for the first time. Ben sucked in a breath and held it. *Don't see it. Look away.* The moment the man turned his back, Ben swooped down and snatched the hook from the floor.

Too close.

Ben blew out a breath.

Gordon stomped across the room. Ben hid the hook under his hat just as the man entered the room.

"Where is she?" Gordon eyed Ben with an icy stare. A tic twitched his cheek and his shoulder jerked up and touched his ear. He narrowed his eyes. "Where"—he repeated the gesture—"is she?"

"I'm right here." Erma finished piling the bacon onto the plate. "Are you ready to eat?"

Quick thinking, Erma. Gordon's demeanor softened, and he licked his lips, almost childlike.

"Are your hands clean?"

Gordon nodded.

"Sit wherever you'd like," she said in a perky voice as she indicated the kitchen table.

Gordon sat at the end of the table. He set the cookie jar in front of him, took one look at Ben, and snatched the container back into his arms.

Ben lifted his hands in surrender and moved to the opposite side of the room near the window. He leaned against the wall.

Erma set the plate of food in front of Gordon. He picked up several slices of bacon, jammed them all in his mouth, and chewed.

Erma cleared her throat, her voice small but firm. "You don't pray before you eat?"

He glared at her, then his expression softened. He folded his hands and bowed his head.

Forgive me, God, if I don't close mei *eyes.* Ben pushed off the wall as Gordon's closed. If he could get Erma's attention, maybe they could slip out the door.

"Bless this food." Gordon rocked back and forth. "And all who partake. Thank You, God, for my baby sister, Marsha, Mommy, and—" His voice broke. He opened tearful eyes and looked at Erma. "They're dead." He shoved his plate across the table, knocking over the salt and pepper shakers, sending them off the table.

Ben lifted his hand to the back of his neck and pretended to scratch it. He could arm himself in less than a second and, if need be, spike the man with the hook.

"Young man." Erma planted her fists on her hips.

Gordon certainly wasn't a young man. He was fifteen, maybe twenty, years older than Ben. But the man stood from his chair and retrieved the salt and pepper shakers off the floor.

"Thank you, Gordon." Erma slid the plate back to its place and pointed at the empty chair. "Now take a seat. I know you're hungry."

Looking at the floor, he shuffled back to the chair and sat. "Are you mad at me?"

"Of course not." Erma smiled with motherly reassurance.

It wouldn't surprise Ben if she reached out and hugged the man. Not a wise move, but neither was ordering him to pick up the stuff he'd knocked off the table. The man seemed to trust her enough that she could probably drive him to town and walk him into the police station. Ben pondered how he could make that plan work. It would require hitching the horse to the buggy. He wasn't confident he could figure out that puzzle in a timely manner. Under the circumstances, the man could flip personalities at any moment. No matter how he was responding to Erma, Ben needed to be mindful of what the news reporters had said about the escapee being off his medicine. Erma wasn't aware he had attacked a nurse either.

A gust of wind rattled the window, and Ben glanced outside. The room dimmed as the sun disappeared behind a cloud. Behind him, a chair screeched across the floor. Ben looked over his shoulder at Erma resting her hand on the man's forearm so he didn't stand.

"Don't be afraid," she told him.

He rocked faster. "Gordon don't like storms."

Erma tried to soothe his fears by telling him how God used the rain to water her garden and provide for His wild creatures.

Ben's thoughts turned to Grace. Had she made it to the *Englischers'* house yet?

Ben caught a glimpse of smoke outside the window. Green smoke? He pushed the curtain back and pressed his face against the window to get a better view. Sure enough, the smoke was green. Growing up in Florida, he knew very little about burning wood. Still, he'd never seen smoke the color of peas.

Erma cleared her throat. "Ben, you're likely to fall straight through that glass leaning against it like that." Her brows lifted and she deliberately widened her eyes. "Close those curtains. Gordon doesn't want to see the rain."

It wasn't raining, but he did as she instructed. Remembering the waxy substance on the balsam wood, Ben glanced at the woodbox. Grace had said their settlement sent smoke signals to alert one another of a crisis. The women were certainly clever. They not only sent the message without the intruder knowing, but Ben had no idea and he helped carry out the plan.

The kitchen door swung open and slammed against the wall. Someone pushed Grace inside with such force she catapulted into Ben's arms. She clung to him, buried her face in his chest, and sobbed.

The newcomer stormed across the room and cuffed Gordon. "You idiot! You let them build a fire."

Gordon cowered like a whipped dog, raising his hands to protect his face. "Gordon's sorry, don't hit me, Jack."

Jack grabbed Erma's arm and jerked her off the chair. "Put it out." Erma scurried over to the sink and filled a pot with water.

"Hurry up!" Jack barked over Erma's shoulder.

Water sloshed over the sides of the pot as she carried it to the stove. Ben didn't want to release Grace, who hadn't stopped trembling, but Erma needed help. He went to the side of the stove and, using a large potholder, opened the firebox. Heat from the roaring flames baked his face. He took the pot from Erma and tossed the water over the fire. The wood hissed and a mixture of green smoke and steam billowed into the room. Ben turned his face away from the opening and coughed.

Erma took the empty pot. "I'll get more water."

Ben reached for the fire poker next to the woodbox, but a swift kick to the ribs doubled him over at the waist as sharp pain tore through his side. Feeling his hat slip, he dropped the iron rod and shoved his hat back in place.

"You'll think next time before you do something stupid." Jack grabbed the fire poker and wheeled it up like he was going to strike Ben.

"Leave him alone!" Grace rushed to his side. "Ben, are you okay?"

"*Jah*," he said, wincing as he spoke. He tried to stand more upright, but a razor-sharp pain stole his breath. He dropped to his knees. Being kicked by Jack's pointed cowboy boots hurt worse than the time he flipped over the handlebars on his bike and bruised his ribs.

"Can you get up? Let me help you." Grace took his hand, but a stronger force fisted his hands around his shirt and reeled him from the floor.

"You're not very smart," Jack said, backhanding him in the face.

Ben stumbled backward, warm blood oozing from his nose. He caught the edge of the counter and hung on.

Grace's eyes brimmed with tears. "I'll get you a wet rag." She opened the drawer, removed a dishcloth, then went to the sink.

Jack stormed across the room. He snatched her wrist. "I didn't give you permission."

"He's bleeding." Grace's voice trembled.

Gordon stood. "Jack, you promised not to hurt anyone else. You promised, Jack."

Jack spun around to face Gordon. "And what are you going to do about it?" His baleful laughter filled the room. He strutted over to Gordon and pushed him back into the chair. "You were supposed to steal food, not get caught! Now I have to take care of them."

Gordon hugged the cookie jar. His eyes blinked with every harsh word Jack barked.

Jack snatched the jar from his grip and stepped back when Gordon bolted up from the chair. Taller by several inches, Jack dangled the jar above Gordon's head.

"My treasure." Gordon flailed his arms.

"It's an old pickle jar."

"No, Jack." Gordon patted his chest. "Gordon's treasure."

Jack flung the jar at the wall. It shattered, sending tiny pieces of glass flying in all directions. "That's what I should do to your head."

Gordon covered his ears and shook his head. Mumbling something in what sounded like a foreign language, he began to pace.

Grace's eyes widened with terror. She looked at Ben as if silently pleading for him to give her instructions on what to do. Ben was just as helpless. He wiped his nose on his shirtsleeve, blotting it with blood.

Jack pressed his hand against Gordon's chest and stopped him midstep. "Stop pacing. You're driving me crazy."

Continuing to mutter, Gordon pivoted around and left the room. A moment later, the door opened.

Jack flew out of the kitchen.

Chapter Twenty-One

"Y our lip is cut open," Grace said, dabbing a cool dishcloth on
Ben's face.

Ben winced.

Grace lifted the cloth. "I'm sorry." His lip started to bleed again
and she blotted it clean. "Do you think they'd leave if we packed up
food and supplies for them?"

Footsteps trumped into the kitchen. "Who said you could talk!"

Startled, Grace dropped the rag and spun to face Jack. His eyes
narrowed as he directed his gaze to each of them. Moving toward
Grace, his glare had an unnerving flicker.

Grace inched backward. *Lord, help us.*

His form towered over her and when he leaned toward her, his
nose practically touched hers. She gulped. Her stomach wrenched at
the stench of his stale tobacco breath. She looked away, but he grabbed
her chin and brought her face back in line with his. The man stroked
his hand down her cheek. Vomit rose to the back of her throat. Grace
backed up until she bumped into Ben.

Jack laughed. He stepped closer, sandwiching her between himself
and Ben.

Ben backed up, giving her room to retreat, but the wall stopped
him. Ben's arm circled around her waist and he pulled her even closer
to him, a comforting gesture.

"If this is your girl," he said to Ben while letting his fingers linger on her neck, "keep her out of my way."

The moment Jack dropped his hand, she spun around and buried her face in Ben's chest. Behind her, the man's footsteps moved away. Ben's hand came up to rest on her back and an odd sense of security rippled through her core. Ben would figure out a way for them to escape. Her muscles relaxed. She took a few deep breaths, breathing in the scent of burnt wood embedded in Ben's shirt.

"Are you okay?" he whispered next to her ear.

She nodded. *Aenti* sniffled behind her. Grace pulled away from Ben and wrapped her arms around *Aenti* Erma. "Ben will figure something out."

"Pray, child," *Aenti* whispered.

A knock sounded on the door. Grace's heart leapt. She looked at Ben, wanting him to give her direction, but it wasn't Ben who instructed her. Jack grabbed her arm and whirled her toward the door.

"Get rid of them," he hissed.

Grace opened the door slowly, and only enough for her to poke her head out. "Mattie," she said, willing her voice to stop shaking. She didn't want to endanger her friend.

"What's wrong? I saw the smoke."

"Ben put the wrong wood in the stove." She nodded.

"I was over at Ann Brennerman's *haus* delivering some herbs and— Aren't you going to invite me in? I have more tea for you too."

"I, um . . ." Grace couldn't think of anything to say.

Mattie frowned. "Grace, what's going on?"

Jack pushed the door open, snatched Mattie's arm, and yanked her inside, slamming the door closed with his boot. Mattie clutched her chest and heaved heavy gasps as if unable to catch her breath. Jack clenched his hands around her arms, lifted her off the floor, and shook her hard. "Shut up!" He dropped her midair.

Mattie hit the floor and lay there trembling, balled up in a fetal position.

Grace fisted her hands at her sides. She didn't believe in fighting, but turning the other cheek wasn't something she wanted to do either. They had to get rid of these men somehow.

"Get up." Jack nudged Mattie's side with the tip of his cowboy boot. "Now!"

Grace reached for Mattie's hand and helped her to stand. Her friend's eyes connected with hers. Grace gave Mattie's arm a gentle squeeze. *Stay strong.*

Jack stomped into the sitting room and bent over Gordon, who was crouched down low with his head tucked between his arms. "Why are you hiding in the corner?"

Gordon whimpered something inaudible.

Grace led Mattie into the kitchen where they joined Ben and *Aenti* Erma.

"I'm going to offer to make them a food package to go," *Aenti* said.

The two men tromped into the kitchen. Jack pointed to one of the kitchen chairs. "Gordon, take a seat."

Gordon did. Folding his hands on his lap, he bowed his head.

Jack patted Gordon's shoulder. "Now, you watch them."

"Okay, Jack."

Jack left the room.

Grace craned her neck and watched Jack walk through the sitting room and disappear down the hallway toward the bedrooms. She had money from her dog bed sales stashed in her stockings drawer. Perhaps they would leave if they had cash.

"Gordon, you must be hungry," *Aenti* Erma said.

It hadn't been more than an hour or so since she made him breakfast, but Gordon licked his lips like he was starved.

Ben edged toward the sitting room.

"I'm watching you," Gordon said, pointing his finger at Ben.

"That's good. That's what Jack told you to do. Watch me go into the other room." Ben slipped into the sitting room.

Gordon stood. "Hey."

"I could make a special batch of cookies," *Aenti* Erma said quickly. "What kind is your favorite?"

Gordon forgot about Ben and redirected his attention to *Aenti*. "Peanut butter."

Grace tiptoed into the sitting room as Ben was prying the window open. Her heartbeat clambered against her chest. *Don't leave, please.* She stretched her neck toward the hallway. Any minute Jack would find where she had hidden her money and be back.

Glass shattered in one of the bedrooms. Her heart pounded. Grace could only think of one thing that could make that sound. Her *daed's* gun cabinet. Grace caught a glimpse of Ben leaning out the window and gasped.

She had to get his attention before Jack returned. "*Psst.* Ben."

Ben scrambled back inside, pulling an axe through the window opening with him. He stashed it behind the chair as Jack tromped down the hall, her father's deer rifle in hand. Jack marched over to the window and slammed it shut, then glared at Ben. He hoisted the gun up to his shoulder and pointed it at Ben.

Grace gulped. "Please don't shoot him. We'll give you anything you want. You want food? I'll make a basket . . ." Jack ignored her and jabbed the gun against Ben. "I have money!" she blurted. "In *mei* stockings drawer."

"Go get it."

Grace glanced at Ben. His complexion was whitewashed as he stood with his hands in the air. She sped down the hall to her room and rummaged through her drawer. She rushed back to the sitting room, toting a canning jar filled with cash and coins.

Jack motioned with the gun. "Move," he told Ben. Once Ben's

back was toward him, he lowered the gun and snatched the money jar. "You two," he said to Grace. "Get back in the kitchen."

That was close. Grace turned and with Ben's hand on her lower back gently nudging her forward, they hurried into the other room. Not hearing Jack's footsteps behind them, she glanced over her shoulder. Jack was standing at the window, staring outside.

Please don't let him find the axe. Please . . . But as Jack turned away from the window, he stopped beside the chair. Grace's breath caught in the back of her throat.

Jack burst into the kitchen, wheeled the butt of the gun at Ben, and struck him in the head. "You're lucky I didn't hit you with the axe. Next time I will."

Ben dropped to his knees, his eyes rolled back, and he fell face-first on the floor. His hat came off and something clanged.

Grace dropped to her knees beside Ben. Eyeing the metal hook, she moved her dress skirt over it.

"What was that?" Jack's eyes roamed the floor.

Grace checked the bottom of her dress for the hook. Concealed.

Jack's gaze stopped on Ben's hat. Just as Jack scooped it off the floor, Grace spotted wires protruding from the inside.

"Why are you hiding this?" Jack shoved the hat toward Ben, who still hadn't opened his eyes. Jack nudged him with the toe of his boot, but Ben didn't respond. He towered over Grace. "Wake him up."

She placed her hand on Ben's shoulder blade and bent down closer to him. "Ben?"

Nothing.

Tears blurred her vision. She glanced up at Jack and shook her head.

Aenti Erma wet a cold rag and handed it to Grace, who placed it on Ben's forehead. *Lord, please help us.*

Jack tore the small radio from inside Ben's hat and tossed the hat on the floor. He turned the radio on. Static.

Under different circumstances, Grace would have reprimanded Ben for listening to worldly music and bringing a radio into their district, but today she could kiss the transistor as Jack assumed it had made the clanging noise.

Ben moaned. He touched the egg-sized lump on his forehead and peered up at Grace, dazed. He lifted his head slightly and squinted.

"Don't move," Grace said. She had to figure out how to get the hook out from under her dress before she stood.

Gordon hung on Jack's arm. His eyes were wide and lit up like a boy given his first horse. "Can I see it? Can I?"

Ben pushed into a sitting position. He glanced somberly at Grace as he put his hat back on.

Grace lifted the hem of her dress skirt enough to show Ben the hook.

Jack handed the radio to Gordon, who showed *Aenti* and Mattie, then turned back to Jack, smiling wide. "My treasure."

"Now everything's your treasure?" Jack scoffed. "It better be gold like you said."

"Gold, yes, like you said." Gordon parroted Jack without taking his eyes off the radio.

Jack rested the rifle against his shoulder, walked the length of the room, and stopped by Mattie. "You're going with us."

Mattie wheezed. She clutched her belly and spewed vomit on the kitchen floor, spraying the man's pant leg.

"I should make you lick it off my pants." He shoved her aside.

Grace vaulted to her feet, the hook clanging to the floor. She bent down again, but Jack shoved her hard, knocking her off balance. He swiped the hook off the floor, then narrowed his eyes at Grace. She scooted backward, but Jack grabbed her by the front of her dress and hoisted her off the floor.

Ben shot up, then staggered once he was upright. "Let her go!"

"Now aren't you the hero," Jack sneered. "She's going to keep me company."

Dread clung like a spiderweb, causing her skin to crawl.

"She's got a bad limp. She'll slow you down. You'll make better time by yourselves."

Jack snickered. "I won't let her slow us down." He pulled a cigarette from his shirt pocket and lit it.

"Then you should let me fix her shoe," Ben said. "It'll only take a few minutes."

That's the best he could come up with? Fix my shoe?

Jack grabbed the bottom of Grace's dress and hiked it up, exposing her calves and causing her to suck in a jagged breath. "Show me the bottom of those shoes," he said, smoke bellowing from his mouth.

Grace coughed, inhaling the toxic smoke. She lifted her shorter leg with the heel worn to the nub, and then the other one to show the difference. "It does slow me down. I've been meaning to have it fixed."

The man grumbled something under his breath. "Well," he snapped at Ben. "Fix it. And make it quick." He peered at *Aenti* and Mattie, who were squatting on the floor wiping up the vomit with wet rags. "Put together some food—and matches."

Ben went to the woodbox near the stove.

Grace steeled her expression and shook her head slightly at Ben as he bent over the woodbox. Kindling was too flimsy. She needed a piece of oak or beech.

Ben selected several pieces of the balsam wood, then glanced at her. "I'll need a hammer and tacks."

Grace headed to the door.

Jack grabbed her arm and jerked her toward him. "Where are you going?"

She lowered her head but couldn't escape the cigarette smoke. "The hammer is in the shed."

"Gordon, go with her." Jack released his grip and she resisted the urge to rub her arm.

"Gordon," Jack said louder. "Put that down and go with her."

189

Gordon set the radio on the table and stood. Once they were out-side, Gordon lifted his face upward and sniffed. "I smell smoke."

It took walking outside for him to smell smoke? Her nose stuffed up the moment Jack lit his cigarette, and now smoke was all she could smell. She hiked to the shed, unlatched the door, and entered. Ropes and tools lined the walls. She made her way to her father's worktable, where he usually kept a box of wooden matches in a glass jar.

"Dark," Gordon said.

She glanced over her shoulder. Gordon had stopped at the threshold. He scratched his head and mumbled something she didn't understand. *Afraid of the dark, are you?* Grace stopped searching for matches. She didn't need light from a lantern to find the hammer and nails. Her father never left for camp without his tools neatly arranged. She located an old grease rag hanging from a hook on the wall and spread it out on the table. She placed a handful of nails on the cloth, rolled it up, then stuffed the bundle between her dress and apron. *Think. What else?* Her mind went blank. Her father had a few hand-saws, but those were too large to hide.

"Come on," he said. "Jack's waiting."

"Okay." She couldn't risk stalling much longer. She removed the hammer from the pegboard and grabbed a few tack-sized nails.

"Jack said to be quick." The man swayed sideways. "Don't want Jack mad."

She didn't want him mad either. Grace stepped out from the build-ing and pulled the door closed. She cupped the nails in one hand and carried the hammer with her other.

Inside the house, *Aenti* Erma and Mattie were busy packing food into the basket Mattie had brought with her herbs.

Ben pulled a chair out from the table. "If you want to sit and take your shoe off, I'll fix the heel."

She handed Ben the hammer and slipped off her shoe.

Ben snapped several pieces of balsam and layered them over the heel area. He tapped a few nails into the soft wood and frowned when the wood splintered.

Normally glue would work better, but in this case, he was using the balsam wood that was saturated in the chemical mixture for making the smoke green. Dipped in wax, the wood burned longer, but it also would prevent glue from adhering to its surface.

He tapped another nail in place. "This probably won't hold. Will you take me instead? She's going to slow you down."

Jack sniggered. "You're not someone I want keeping me warm at night." He jerked the shoe from Ben's hand and tossed it at Grace. "Put it on."

Acid burned the back of Grace's throat. *Save me, Lord. Protect me, please.*

Jack motioned to the basket Mattie and *Aenti* Erma were assembling. "Is that ready?"

"Almost," *Aenti* replied.

Jack opened the door that led down to the dirt cellar. "Gordon, go down there and make sure there isn't another way out."

Gordon craned his neck into the stairwell. "It's dark."

"So what!"

"Gordon don't like dark."

As Jack argued with Gordon, Mattie leaned closer to Grace and whispered, "Don't drink the tea."

Grace crinkled her brows and mouthed, *Don't?*

Mattie nodded, then motioned with her eyes at the men.

Jack shoved Gordon, causing him to stumble at the stairwell. "Look for another way out." Jack slammed the door, muffling Gordon's shrill cry.

Grace glanced out the window. What was taking LeAnn so long to get the bishop?

Gordon tapped on the cellar door. "Let me out. Please, Jack. Gordon looked. No way out."

Grace could have told him there wasn't another way out. Not that he would listen. Jack wasn't even nice to Gordon, his cohort.

Jack opened the door and Gordon came out hugging himself. "Gordon don't like it dark," he muttered repetitively.

Jack eyed Mattie and *Aenti* Erma and motioned to the cellar. "Get down there." He pushed Ben toward the cellar. "You too."

Ben glanced half a second at Grace, a despondent look in his eyes.

"You breathe a word to the cops and I'll kill her." Jack shoved him again, this time hard enough for Ben to lose his balance and tumble down the stairs.

Grace cringed.

Jack bolted the cellar door, then wedged a chair up against it. "Get the basket, Gordon." He motioned to her with a head jerk toward the door. "Move it."

She hesitated a moment, taking a last look at the cellar door.

He jabbed her with the barrel of the gun. "You best do as I say."

She wasn't about to tempt him to pull the trigger. She shuffled to the door behind Gordon.

"Jack, look!" Gordon pointed toward the woods. "Smoke!"

That wasn't just black smoke funneling upward—that was a fire.

Chapter Twenty-Two

A cid crawled up the back of Grace's throat. In the distance, thick clouds of black smoke darkened the horizon, obscuring the origin of the fire.

Jack tossed the match he used to light his cigarette on the ground. "I guess we're not going in that direction." He inhaled the tobacco, red ash lighting up the end. "On second thought," he said, releasing a mouthful of smoke as he spoke, "yes, we are. No one would think we would go this way."

"Gordon doesn't like fire. Fire's bad. Fire is very bad. Don't play with fire." Gordon repeated his words in a panic-driven tone.

"Let's go," Jack said.

Rocking his weight from side to side, Gordon shook his head. "No fire. Fire bad."

Jack cuffed Gordon on the back of his head. "Did you hear me? Let's go."

With them distracted, Grace bolted to the porch. She made it to the top step when Jack lunged at her, grabbing her prayer *kapp* and hair. "We can't leave them trapped in the cellar," she cried, clenching her fists to keep from grabbing his hands away from her head. It wouldn't do to antagonize him further.

His grip tightened. "I said let's go." He reined her by the hair like a horse on a lead.

She dug her heels into the ground, but it didn't slow her ascent. "Please," she said. "Don't leave them trapped." He had her in such a firm hold, her scalp burned. Grace stumbled over a rock. Her feet went out from under her.

Jack jerked her back up, twisting her arms around her back. "I should put a bullet in you."

At the moment, dying seemed like a suitable option.

They stopped at the barn. "Gordon, go in there and get a shovel."

A shovel . . . to dig her grave?

"No dark. No more." Gordon shook his head. "Please, Jack. I don't want to—" Shoved inside by Jack, Gordon disappeared and moments later came out with a shovel.

Tightening his grip on her arms, Jack continued toward the back of the barn. Rusty lunged at the end of his chain and caught Jack off guard. He jerked her in another direction.

Concentrate.

Grace reached into the rag she'd placed between her apron and dress and removed a nail. She managed to drop two before they reached the edge of the woods. Finding the nails would be like finding a morsel of salt in the snow. A desperate attempt to direct someone who might try to follow after them, but she had to make the effort.

"Gordon don't like fire . . . I want to go back," the man whimpered.

"There's no going back," Jack said sharply. "You stick with me and you'll be all right. You hear?"

"But—" Gordon cringed, looking up at the smoke-filled sky.

"Gordon!" he snapped. "We'll get our stuff and find the treasure you told me about. You want to find it, don't you?"

He nodded.

"Then we have to move fast." Jack released his hold on Grace's arm and slapped her shoulder, pushing her forward. "You stay ahead of me."

Prodded and poked, Grace managed to stay ahead of Jack by some miracle. They had walked several miles when the sky turned black and thick smoke settled in her lungs. Between the muscle spasms in her legs from fatigue and respiratory spasms from lack of clean air, Grace couldn't go much farther. Her pace slowed; her left leg dragged, refusing to cooperate.

"Stop," Jack ordered.

She did so gladly, although standing in one position hurt almost as much. Following Jack's sideways gaze at the connecting pathway off to the right, Grace saw a figure emerge from the foggy haze. *Mitch. No, go back!*

Running hard and breathing heavy, her nephew, followed by his friend Owen Schmucker, approached, arms waving. "The watermill's on fire!" Mitch yelled.

"We didn't mean to start it," Owen added.

"Fire!" Gordon said. "No fire. Fire is bad. Oh dear." He turned in a circle. "Gordon don't like fire."

Grace glanced at Jack from the corner of her eye, then addressed her nephew. *"Geh to grossdaadi's haus. Schnell, verschteh?"*

Mitch's brows crinkled.

She made a shooing gesture. *"Geh nau!"*

Jack grabbed Mitch by the throat. "What did she say?"

Owen took off running into the woods.

Mitch's face turned red and he wheezed for air.

"Stop! You're choking him!" Grace kicked Jack as hard as she could in the shin. "Let him go!" She kicked him again. And again. Until he turned his rage toward her and released Mitch.

Jack grasped her by the back of the neck, intertwining his fingers under her *kapp* to get a firm grip on her hair. "I'm going to tame that spirit of yours."

Grace managed to squeak, "Go!" and this time, Mitch took off running in the same direction that Owen had gone.

"You say something, kid, I'll kill her!" Jack yelled.

"Jack." Gordon tapped his arm. "I want to go too. Can I go?"

Jack thrust her forward. "You better hope they don't send help."

Danki, *God, for letting Mitch and Owen get away safely.* Grace tried to reposition her prayer *kapp*, but with so many pins missing, she had a difficult time keeping it in place. Her scalp pulsated like her hair was still being pulled.

Prodded forward, she felt the metal gun barrel dig into her spine. She didn't go far before her legs began to ache, and she staggered. She glanced over her shoulder at Gordon. He lagged a few feet behind, his gaze darting.

"Hurry up." Jack shoved her shoulder.

"I need to rest." She stopped next to an oak tree and leaned against it.

"I didn't give permission to stop," Jack said.

"I have to catch *mei* breath." She wheezed, taking in breaths of smoke-filled air. *Stall.* She took more labored breaths.

Gordon swayed from side to side, his focus up in the trees. "I want to go back. Let's go back."

"That's long enough. Let's go." Jack motioned toward the trail.

"The woods are on fire. I can't breathe." She clutched her throat and coughed while at the same time keeping her eye on Gordon for his reaction.

Gordon ran his hands through his unkempt hair. He turned in a circle. "We need to get out of the woods."

"Gordon's right. We're going to die if we stay in the woods," Grace said, lacing her words with panic.

Gordon tugged on Jack's arm. "We have to go back. Can't we leave?"

"The fire's a long ways away."

Grace looked at Gordon and shook her head. "The last time the woods caught on fire *hundreds* of acres burned. People died."

Jack leveled the gun at her face. "You keep talking, and I'll shoot you."

Grace clamped her mouth closed. *Be strong in the Lord. Vengeance is God's. He will not leave me nor forsake me. He will deliver me from evil.* She took pleasure in Gordon turning circles, mumbling, and fretting over going farther into the woods. He was in the throes of a panic attack and Jack would have his hands full.

"Knock it off." Jack smacked Gordon on the side of his head.

As if Gordon had slipped into his own secluded world—cocooned himself—he ignored Jack.

A harsh *jaay—jaay* call of a blue bird and the echoes of other wildlife sounds sent a chill down Grace's spine.

Gordon dropped the shovel and basket and clapped his hands over his ears. "Tell them to stop."

"Wildlife always knows when there's danger," Grace said.

Jack jammed the gun against her spine. "Shut up."

A pair of pheasants took sudden flight, and Gordon jumped back a foot. His gaze darted in different directions with every sound. Grace could almost read the thoughts bombarding his mind just from his panicked expression. She almost pitied him, but prodded by the gun in her back, she continued up the trail.

She hadn't gone too far when a small fox came out of a dead log, its ears perked. Grace had never seen a fox at midday. Usually they prowled at night, but this one moved stealthlike into the center of the path. Not wanting to startle it, she stopped. The fox did too. It held its bushy red tail perfectly still and stared at her with beady black eyes.

"Rabid varmint." Jack raised the gun and took aim at the fox.

Grace couldn't let him kill an innocent animal and pushed the gun to the side just as it fired.

"Why, you . . ." Jack snarled and lifted the gun again.

Whoosh.

The stock of the gun slammed against the side of her face. She teetered a moment, unable to see anything but black spots as a shudder of pain rippled over her in pulsating throbs. She dropped to her knees as everything around her went dark.

Ben groaned as he lifted his face off the cellar's dirt floor.

Erma leaned closer, dangling a lantern over him. "Are you hurt?"

"I don't think so." He rolled to his side and pushed up, but a ball of fire shot through his shoulder when he put weight on it. He collapsed.

"Don't try to move too fast." Erma covered her mouth with her hand. "This is all *mei* fault."

Mattie wrapped her arm around Erma and led her over to the shelves of canned goods.

Ben sucked in a breath through gritted teeth and pushed himself up. His entire right side ached. His ribs were tender, his shoulder throbbed, and his right knee didn't want to move.

"I recognized one of the men," Mattie said. "He was loitering around Grace's buggy in the IGA's parking lot."

Erma sniffled. "I thought he was another visitor from Florida. He was wearing a short-sleeve shirt similar to yours, Ben."

"Stolen." Ben rubbed the back of his neck. The bishop's wife wasn't senile like he thought when she said his shirts had disappeared from her clothesline. He should have put it together with the other items that disappeared. "I'm sure they stole your pie and Grace's dog bed quilts."

"I don't doubt it," Mattie said.

Ben grasped the handrail and climbed the steps. He pinned his ear to the door. "I don't hear anything." He turned the handle and pushed on the door. Locked. He changed positions and rammed the door using his other shoulder. It didn't budge. He ran his hands over the door's surface and over to the trim. Just as he thought, the hinges were on the other side. Maybe he could take the doorknob off. "Do you have any tools down here?"

"We can look," Erma said. She and Mattie moved some jars around on the shelves and searched the area behind the stairs.

Ben slammed against the door. The force sent a wave of pain vibrating through his body. He couldn't give up. He hated to think what Jack planned to do with Grace. *Lord, I need Your power to work through me.* He thrust his weight against the door, bounced back too far, and stumbled down a few steps.

"I found a putty knife," Erma said. "Do you think it'll work?"

"It's better than nothing." He met Erma on the step and took the knife. It was rounded at the end, so he wasn't sure if it would do any good or not.

Erma sighed. "I don't know what's taking LeAnn so long."

She was probably back at the bus station with Clutch. She didn't look too pleased about going back home.

"I'm sure I'm *nett* the only one who saw the smoke signal," Mattie said. "The others will *kumm.*"

He would like to believe that, too, but the wood hadn't burned long before Jack barged through the door, demanding the fire be put out, and the wind would have carried the signal away.

He pushed against the door. If he kept at it, eventually it would open. It just had to.

❧

Grace blinked a few times but couldn't focus her eyes. Her head throbbed, especially her right cheek. She touched her face. Swollen. Her fingers moved gently over her right eye, which must be the size of a goose egg. No wonder she couldn't see more than a slit of daylight out of it. She looked down at the quilt top covering her and recognized it as her own. *Thieves.*

The scent of mildew wafted from the sandy ground and engulfed her senses. She patted the area around her, touching rocks rather than branches or dead leaves. Grace closed her eyes and listened to the lull of rushing water. She was drifting—feeling at peace. Then a light spray of sand hit her face. She swept the sand away from her mouth, squinting at a hazy figure.

He bent down beside her and reached his hand toward her face.

Grace jerked away. Shards of sharp pain pierced her head and she cried out.

The man placed a sopping wet cloth over the right side of her face. Within seconds, the frigid water numbed the nerve endings and lessened some of the soreness.

"She's awake, Jack." Gordon patted her shoulder. "He said to tell him when you opened your eyes."

Why, so he can hit me again? Grace bit back her thoughts. She didn't want any more trouble.

"It was an accident. He didn't mean to hurt you. Ain't that right, Jack? Tell her you're sorry."

She slid her hand under the quilt and touched the area of her dress where she had stashed the nails. No! They must have fallen out when Jack knocked her unconscious. She touched her head—her matted hair. Her *kapp* was missing too. Grace pulled the wet cloth away from her face, discovered it was her *kapp*, and covered the swollen side of her face with it again.

Gordon rose from his place beside her and went over to where Jack was sitting on a log near a small campfire, digging through the basket Mattie and *Aenti* Erma had packed. A tin cup and empty pie pan were at his feet.

Grace pushed the prayer *kapp* aside to survey her surroundings. The river was on her left and not far from the area where Ben had tried to cross. She repositioned herself to look the opposite direction, but the trees were too tall to see anything beyond them.

Lord, are they out of the cellar yet? What about the fire? Has it spread? She closed her eyes as the verse in Philippians came to mind. *Be anxious for nothing, but in everything by prayer and supplication, with thanksgiving* . . . Grace's throat tightened. Over the years, she had avoided that particular verse. She had never found a reason to be thankful for the infirmity she'd been born with, and she couldn't see a reason to be thankful about her current situation.

But the verse kept coming to mind.

"Lord, I want the peace that surpasses all understanding, like Your Word promises," she prayed in Pennsylvania *Deitsch*. "Show me how I can be thankful—with a clean heart—about two men who forced me to leave my home and family and go with them." She sighed. "I can't."

"Your mumbling is starting to sound like Gordon's." Jack laughed. "Hey, Gordon, maybe you're really Amish."

Gordon crinkled his brows. "I'm Amish?"

"Well, you're dressed like one." Jack chuckled to himself as he tore a chunk of bread off one of the loaves in the basket. He took a bite, chewed with his mouth open, then broke off another piece and handed it to Gordon.

Grace closed her eyes. She'd sent Mitch to her house, but he might have gone home instead to tell his *mamm*. Susan wouldn't know what to do. Her thoughts drifted to Ben. He'd told her to trust him, that he'd figure a way out of this. Maybe he was on his way to her now.

Chapter Twenty-Three

Ben wedged the putty knife under the metal ring on the doorknob, then used the end of the mop handle to hit the knife. A slow process, but the flat part of the knife slipped farther under the metal ring with every hit. At least he hoped it moved and it wasn't just a shadow. Erma and Mattie took turns holding the lantern as high as they could, but with the wick low to conserve lamp oil, it didn't cast much light on the area he needed to work on.

"I'm sure grateful to have you here, Ben," Erma said. "When did you decide to stay in Badger Creek?"

She was just passing the time with small talk, but he didn't want to discuss why he didn't leave. After reading the letters Neva sent to Toby, he wasn't interested in seeing either of them anytime soon. They stole a part of him he would never get back. He jammed the mop handle against the knife, moving it a fraction of an inch.

"Do you smell smoke?" Mattie tilted her head and sniffed.

"*Mei* sense of smell isn't so *gut*." Erma shook her head. "*Nay*, I don't smell anything."

"It's probably coming from the woodstove in the sitting room," Ben said.

"That would mean someone changed the damper," Erma said.

Mattie turned to Erma, who was standing a few steps down from the top landing. "Will you hold the lantern?" The light flickered as she and Erma exchanged places. Mattie went down several more steps, then sat.

"Are you feeling all right, dear?" Erma asked.

"I'm feeling dizzy and nauseated." She peered up at Erma. "I don't want to lose *mei boppli*."

"God has this situation under control."

Ben continued working on the door as the women chatted about Mattie's health concerns. He didn't know much about pregnant women other than they tended to get emotional. Ben blocked out their chatter and focused on removing the door handle before panic ensued. If he'd had the right tools, he could have had it dismantled in minutes. Finally, he hit the putty knife just right and the metal ring attached to the door popped loose. He squatted next to the doorknob, seeing some light from the kitchen for the first time.

"*Aenti* Erma? *Aenti* LeAnn? Anyone?" a faint voice called from the other side.

"Down here!" Ben pounded on the door. "In the cellar."

Erma and Mattie echoed his call for help.

On the other side of the door, Ben heard what sounded like a chair sliding on the wooden floor. A moment later, the latch clicked, the door opened, and Mitch stood in front of them, his face red as a beet and taking deep breaths.

"The old mill is on fire," the boy said, sprinting to the door.

Ben waited for Mattie and Erma to exit the house, then followed them outside. In the distance, a thick, concentrated funnel of black smoke billowed over the trees.

"The old mill is close to the bishop's *haus*!" Erma's face went white. "I sent LeAnn there. We have to warn them."

Ben followed them to Mattie's buggy and untied the horse's reins as the women crawled inside. "I'm going after Grace."

"The man said they would kill her." Mitch's brows crimped. "I wasn't supposed to tell anyone. He has a gun." Tears streamed down the boy's face. "Owen ran home to tell his *mamm* about the fire. Grace told me to come here."

Ben stopped Mitch from climbing into the buggy. "Where did you see her?"

"They'll kill her." He looked at Erma sitting on the bench. "I believe him."

"Mitch." Ben placed his hands on the boy's shoulders and pivoted him to face Ben. "I have to know where you saw her last."

"At the cutoff. With two men. They have a gun, Ben."

"What cutoff? Where is it?"

"I can show you," Mitch said.

Ben shook his head. "*Nay*, it's too dangerous. I've been to the watermill before. How far from the river are they?"

"They weren't really close. It's a trail that splits off from the one that leads to the watermill."

Ben nodded. "Okay, I'll find her. You go with Erma and Mattie."

"He's going to kill *Aenti* Grace. He said if I told anyone . . . he's going to kill her," Mitch repeated as he climbed into the buggy.

"Ben, be careful," Erma said.

He nodded. "I will. Let Bishop Yoder know about Grace. He can decide whether or *nett* to notify the police. I'm going to let the livestock loose in case the wind changes directions."

"Pray for rain," Mattie said.

"I will." Ben jogged to the barn. *Lord, please lead me. I'm* nett *sure which cutoff trail Mitch was talking about, but You know where she is. And please send rain to put the fire out.*

He made his way to the horse stalls and shooed the horses into the pasture. He propped the gate open for the pigs and tried to herd them outside. The goats were already outside grazing along the fence line. The dog barked as Ben exited the barn. He raced around to the back side of the barn to the red hound with long ears. He launched up on his hind legs as Ben approached.

"Easy, boy." Ben reached for the chain. The hound jumped up, landing his dirty front paws on Ben's shoulders. Ben flinched as sharp, stabbing pain shot through his arm. He sucked in a breath, and as the dog licked his face, he unhooked his collar. Ben wiped the wetness from his face using his shirtsleeve. "How are you at tracking?"

The hound's ears perked. He took off running toward the house, but quickly changed directions when he noticed Ben wasn't with him. The dog ran to the edge of the woods and barked. That wasn't the footpath they had taken when they were searching for Mitch.

"*Nett* that way. *Kumm* on."

The dog looked at Ben, barked, then darted into the woods.

Lord, I hope this is right. Ben headed in the direction of the fire. He entered the woods with the dog running ahead. A moment later the hound returned carrying a stick and dropped it at his feet. "You're *nett* a tracking dog." And he was crazy to follow him into a burning forest on an unknown path. Ben turned and jogged a few feet before a heavy force launched itself against his back and knocked him down. Ben spit a mouthful of dirt. The hundred-pound dog panted over him a moment, then barked. "I should've left you chained up." He clambered to his feet.

The dog picked up the stick and pushed it into Ben's hand.

Ben growled under his breath. He tried to grab the stick and the dog not only wouldn't release it, but he pulled Ben a couple of steps. Ben let go of the stick, but once again, the dog tried to give him the stick, then tugged him into the woods. This time Red dropped the stick, and when Ben glanced down, he spotted a shiny nail. He picked it up and rolled it over in his hand. It was the same type of nail he'd used for Grace's shoe. Ben smiled. God had given him a sign. "*Danki*, God. And *danki*, Red."

A chunk of bread landed in Grace's lap as she was sitting on the ground with her back against a log.

"That's all you're going to get for a few hours," Jack said. "I suggest you eat it."

She stared at the bread and knew she wouldn't be able to choke down anything, not with her stomach in knots. The wet ground had soaked through her dress and she silently thanked God for the rain they'd had over the last few days. Maybe the fire wouldn't consume the woods after all.

Grace squinted at Jack as he went down to the river, then glanced at Gordon sitting beside her, turning the knobs on the radio. He hadn't been given much to eat either. She offered her portion to him. "Would you like this? I can't eat it."

"Really? You want to give me yours?" His eyes lit, staring at the piece of bread.

Grace nodded.

He frowned. "Gordon's not allowed." He shook his head. "No sharing allowed. Stay in your seat. Eat your own food. Those are the rules." He rocked back and forth. "Rules are good for us. They are."

"You follow all the rules?"

"Rules are good."

She forced herself to smile even though it hurt. How did this man get involved with Jack? "I think rules are *gut* also." She looked at the bread. It would be a shame to feed it to the birds when Gordon was hungry. "Have you ever been on a picnic where people sit outside?"

He shook his head.

"Everyone shares their food on a picnic."

"We're outside. Is this a picnic?"

"If you want it to be."

He nodded but quickly frowned again. "But I don't have nothing to share." He set the radio down long enough to hold up his dirty palms with his fingers spread. "See."

"It's okay," she said, holding out the piece of bread. "Next time you can share with me."

He looked at her, the bread, then back at her.

She nodded.

Gordon snatched the bread from her, then hunched over as if guarding it and the radio.

She glanced at the balsam wood nailed to her shoe, then over to the hot bed of embers. With Jack down by the river and Gordon eating, maybe she could toss a few pieces of wood into the campfire without them seeing. She wiggled the wood, but the nails held it tight. She had to think of something else. She focused on the shovel. If she grabbed the shovel, would she be able to swing it? Grace sighed. She didn't believe in violence. Besides, she wasn't even sure which way she should run—and she would have to run.

Birch trees clustered close to the riverbank. A few oak saplings were green with buds. Without being close enough to the river to judge the depth, she couldn't be certain how far downriver they were. Still wiggling the wood from her shoe, she caught a glimpse of Jack climbing up the river embankment in her peripheral vision. She lay down, placed the prayer *kapp* over her face, and pretended to be asleep. The cloth was no longer cold, but she wasn't concerned as much about reducing the swelling as she was about avoiding eye contact with Jack. His face had a leathery, sun-beaten look, and his cold, penetrating eyes made her insides shudder.

"Turn that radio off," Jack barked at Gordon, then nudged her leg with the tip of his boot. "Get up. We're leaving."

Grace removed the wet *kapp* from her face, set it on the ground beside her, and pushed to her feet, her hair falling in front of her face.

Gordon stood, clutching the radio, blaring static. "Where are we going now?"

"You tell me," Jack said, handing Gordon the basket. "It's your treasure we've come to find. Where is it?"

Gordon shrugged.

Jack jerked the radio from Gordon's hands. "Think hard."

He jumped, trying to reach the radio.

"Where's the treasure?" Jack stormed over to the riverbank and tossed the radio, deadening the static din. "If you don't tell me where the treasure is, I'll take you back to the Behavioral Unit."

"No!" Gordon rubbed his upper arm. "No more shots. Shots hurt. No-no-no-no more."

"Settle down." Jack tapped his shirt pocket. "Or I'll give you one now."

Gordon shook his head and fixed his eyes on her. "Gordon will be good."

"I believe you," Grace whispered.

"Quiet." Jack motioned for Grace and Gordon to get down, then crept a few feet over to a large beech tree. He crouched down behind it.

Grace's pulse quickened. Had Mitch followed them? Knocked unconscious, she couldn't be certain how much time had passed since she had seen him last. The sun wasn't helpful either; the smoke and storm clouds had it hidden.

"What do you see, Jack?" Gordon asked.

"Hush and bring me the rifle."

Chapter Twenty-Four

Ben focused on the carpet of pine needles, searching for more nails as he trudged through the woods. Red, the name he'd given his floppy-eared companion, darted from one side of the path to the other, chasing squirrels up the hemlock trees. The dog had as much pent-up energy as a hooked worm.

"Where is she, Red? Where's Grace?"

The dog looked at Ben with his head cocked, ears perked, and tongue dangling from the side of his mouth. For a moment it looked as if the dog understood what he'd said, but a fuzzy, gray rabbit hopped over the path and diverted Red's attention. The dog leaped over a fallen log and disappeared into a thicket.

"You're about as loyal as Toby," Ben called out. He kicked at a rock on the path, wishing he could cast thoughts of his friend's betrayal aside too. How could he have been so blind—so stupid? His friend was a coward. Had Toby said something—or even thrown a punch at Ben after he kissed Neva—things would be different. Toby wouldn't have rejected her, Neva never would have been drunk on the beach that night, and Ben would still have his father's respect. Toby shouldn't have assumed Neva had fallen for Ben—Toby should have asked Ben straight up what had happened.

The past no longer mattered. Grace mattered. She hadn't asked him to stay, but something in her eyes beseeched him. When the time came to board the bus—he couldn't leave. Her sullen expression, when he tried to convince the kidnappers to take him instead, flashed before his eyes. She must have thought it cruel of him to point out her limp. But he could think of nothing else to say to make them leave her.

The woods came alive to the musical sound of rain falling on the ferns. God had answered part of his prayer. Danki, *Lord*. Nau, *please guide me to Grace*. Ben whistled for Red, but the dog wasn't anywhere in sight. The hound would have to find his way home. Ben wasn't about to wait. While trying to skirt the fire area, he'd gotten off the main path. The deer trail wound through some thick and thorny bushes, which scratched his face and tugged on his shirt and pant legs.

Ben came upon a black, mucky creek. He placed one foot on a moss-covered log and tested his weight. He started slow, teetered for balance, then increased the length of his stride as the foul scent of rotten eggs leached from the loam below.

He'd made it three-quarters of the way across when he heard a splash. If this were Florida, he would assume it was a gator. Ben made the mistake of glancing behind him and his foot slipped on the mossy log. Suddenly he was straddling the log, tilting sideways, his face inches from the putrid, black pit. Wrenched in pain and breathing raggedly, he didn't want to move.

Red lumbered through chest-deep muck to reach him. The dog licked his face.

Ben clawed at the bark to right himself, but at the cost of stepping in the muck. His foot sank into the soft ground. The clinging substance made a sucking noise when he pulled it out. Afraid his wet boot would cause him to slip, Ben crawled the remaining feet to dry land.

Red sprang out of the mud and shook, spraying Ben and the ferns around them with the rotten stench. Ben surveyed the area. He didn't want to get tangled back up in the thornbushes if he could avoid it. He followed what looked like deer prints on the soft ground. The hound sprinted in the opposite direction, this time barking as he chased after something. Ben wasn't disappointed. He stank, but nothing like Red, who had bathed in the muck.

Swampy water squished out from his boots, making sloshing sounds as he walked. After pressing through another thorny patch, he found a more traveled pine-needle path. The side of his face stung from having been scraped by the thorns. He wiped what he thought was sweat from his brow and found blood on his shirtsleeve.

He hadn't gone far on the path when he discovered more nails— several were dispersed over the ground in the same area. He picked one up and squeezed it in his hand. "Hold on, Grace. I'm going to find you."

☙

"Don't shoot!" Grace charged Jack. She couldn't cower in fear while Jack aimed the gun at someone or something. She pushed against him, her feet losing traction on the wet ground.

He shoved her aside with one hand. Grace landed several feet away, facedown in the dirt. "Shut her up, Gordon."

Grace pushed herself up to her knees only to be struck down by Gordon's heavy foot. The sole of his boot pressed against her back with such force she wouldn't be surprised if it left tread marks.

Grace lifted her face from the dank soil. "Please, I can't . . . breathe."

Gordon released some of the force.

"You made me lose my shot." Jack lowered the gun. "Haul her up and let's go."

Gordon lifted his boot. "What was it, Jack?"

"That rabid fox." He wiped rainwater from his forehead with his shirtsleeve. "I'll shoot it yet—all of you."

Once free from Gordon's foothold, Grace scrambled to her feet unassisted. Trying to save the fox was foolish. But it could have been Mitch—or Ben.

Jack grasped her neck, adding enough pressure on her windpipe that she wheezed for air. He pulled her up against him, and she dangled like a rag doll off the ground. Leveling her nose to nose, he hissed, "The next time you pull a stunt like that, I'll bury you alive. You got that?"

Unable to talk, unable to nod, she blinked.

He released his hold and she tumbled to the ground, gasping for air.

Jack bent at the waist. "Get up."

Her arms quivered with weakness as she pushed her torso off the ground. Unable to hold her weight, her arms buckled and she collapsed. "What do you want from me?" She started to sob.

"Security." Jack stormed a few feet away over to the clearing and surveyed the grassy meadow.

Her cheek resting on the cool soil, she lay still, pleading silently for God to rescue her.

Gordon had covered his ears and was pacing, uttering something indecipherable.

"Stop it," Jack snapped.

Gordon's eyes closed. He rambled faster. Louder. Words without meaning. Seemingly able to separate himself from this place and from Jack's harsh tone, he shuffled his feet through the sandy soil.

She'd never seen someone in a trancelike state. Gordon's actions had a more calming effect over her than she dared to admit, and that frightened her even more. She started mumbling herself. "Yea, though I walk through the valley of the shadow of death, I will fear no evil. For thou art with me . . ." She finished the Twenty-Third Psalm, then repeated it over and over until Jack stormed back from the clearing.

"Stop it, both of you."

Grace did, but not Gordon. He walked closer to Jack, chanting defiantly.

Jack knocked Gordon in the shoulder with the heel of his hand. "I said stop it!"

His chanting stopped and Gordon opened his glassy eyes. His

gaze drifted over his surroundings slowly, as if his mind were numb. Then, without acknowledging Jack, Gordon walked over to Grace and reached for her hand.

She jerked her hand away and stood without his assistance. She waited until neither of them was looking, then dropped the prayer *kapp* on the ground.

Directed by Jack, she skirted the riverbank. Acid rose to the back of her throat as she heard the rushing water off to her side. *Please don't make me cross the river.*

Showered in rain, her hair matted in front of her face. She stopped and gathered it into a ponytail, holding it with her hand to keep it out of her eyes.

"Keep moving." Jack shoved her from behind.

She stumbled over a rut and landed hard on her knees. A wave of mallet vibrations thrummed her spine.

"Get up," Jack said, jabbing her with the end of the gun.

Her joints locked, freezing her in position. *Nay!* Her muscles couldn't betray her now. "I can't." Her hope spent, she bent over, lowered her forehead on the ground, and closed her eyes. "Go ahead. Shoot me."

Jack sneered and cocked the gun.

The steel barrel was cold against the back of her neck. "Lord, please forgive *mei* iniquities—the wrongs—I've committed—the jealousy I've harbored . . ." As she prayed in Pennsylvania *Deitsch*, her words ran together.

"No!" Gordon shouted.

"Maybe we don't need her," Jack hissed.

Thwack!

Jack grunted.

The gun discharged—a deafening blast rang in her ears.

❦

Ben jolted at the sound of a gunshot. He spun around, looking all directions as the echoing blast faded in the distance.

"Lord . . ." His throat tightened. "Don't let me be too late." He sprinted in what he hoped was the right direction, jumping over fallen logs and dodging low-hanging branches. The rain fell harder, making the pine-needle path more slippery than normal, but at least the fire would no longer be a threat. Deep in the woods, he was sheltered, but that wasn't the case once he reached a meadow. He bolted across the grassy wetland, his soaked pant legs clinging to his skin and weighing him down.

His lungs burned and his muscles grew weary from running, but he pushed himself to keep going. The sun had disappeared behind a widespread haze of storm clouds. It would get dark soon. Too soon. His stomach clenched at the thought of her being alone with those two men. He couldn't let that happen.

Ben reached the edge of the meadow and slowed his pace as he reached the river. He looked over the edge of the embankment at the frothy water swirling below. With no sign of Grace or her captors, he followed the river downstream. Ben remembered the day the current swept him away and how every so often he would flip and see Grace running along the riverbank, following him. The water had been so cold that his legs went numb almost immediately and he was certain he'd never feel his legs again. Ben didn't want to think what Jack would do if Grace couldn't keep up with them.

"Please, Lord, keep her safe from those wicked men."

Ben reached the edge of the embankment and started down the sandy hill. He lost his footing and slid to the bottom, landing with a thud on the sandy shoreline. Ben spotted a set of footprints leading away from the river and followed them. His eye caught a glimpse of a white cloth. A numbing sensation washed over him as he bent to pick it up. A prayer *kapp*.

Chapter Twenty-Five

Grace had lost her sense of direction hours ago when the deer trail they'd been following took them into a dense cedar swamp. Her feet were swollen and the area above her ankle had turned raw from constantly rubbing against her leather shoes.

Gordon had paid a high price for tackling Jack to save her. The bullet hit a tree, but Jack pulped Gordon with his fist until poor Gordon vomited blood. Grace hated to see him suffer, but the hope that someone might have heard the gunshot and would know their direction lifted her spirit.

Gordon, staying a few steps ahead of Jack, trailed alongside of her. "Hey, lady," he said, after they had been walking awhile. "Did you hurt your leg?"

"No," she said, "I was born this way."

"Me too."

She glanced sideways at him but said nothing. The man wasn't limping.

"You and me are both special," he said, sporting a wide smile.

She forced a smile in return. "*Jah*, I suppose you're right."

Jack came up between them. "You two stop yapping and walk faster."

Grace clamped her mouth closed. She hoped Gordon did the same.

A few minutes of silence went by when Gordon stopped, tossed the shovel on the ground, and sat. "I'm tired of walking."

Grace would have joined him had Jack not grabbed her arm before she sat.

"You and I aren't stopping," Jack said.

Grace inwardly cringed. She wasn't sure of Gordon's state of mind, but the thought of being anywhere alone with Jack made her stomach curdle like week-old milk left in the sun.

"Pick up the shovel and let's go."

Grace bent down and grabbed the shovel, silently willing Gordon to get up. But he made no attempt to join them, and Jack pushed her forward. She had no choice but to follow his orders. She took a few steps and looked back at Gordon still sitting in the same spot. "Aren't you worried he'll get lost in the woods?"

"He might. But I'm not waiting."

They walked several minutes. She looked back once but Gordon was no longer in sight. "Isn't Gordon the one who knows where the treasure is?"

"What all did he tell you?" He jabbed the gun barrel against her spine when she didn't answer immediately.

"Nothing." She gripped the handle of the shovel tighter.

Branches snapped.

Jack pushed her behind a tree. He leaned toward the sound of snapping branches and slowly lifted the gun.

Gordon strolled into view.

Jack lowered the gun. He grabbed her by the wrist and moved out from behind the tree. "It's about time you caught up to us."

"Gordon doesn't like to be alone."

"Then I suggest you keep up. It'll be dark in a matter of a few hours and you need to show me where that cabin is."

Lord, where are You? Tears streamed down her cheeks. Her legs felt like she was dragging sandbags just to walk and Jack wasn't about to let anyone rest. She took small steps, shuffling as she went. Pushed by Jack from behind, she fell.

"Get up."

Even if he aimed the gun at her head, she couldn't move. Spasms caused her muscles to constrict. She searched her mind for a reason to continue, but nothing gave her strength to press on.

"I said get up!"

Gordon walked past them a few feet and froze. "That's it." He pointed to his right.

Jack reached down, snatched Grace's arm, and jerked her up.

Her shoulder socket popped and Grace cried out. He didn't ease his grip until she started to move. Grace whispered scriptures mixed with prayers for strength with every step she took. The fifty or so feet felt more like miles before they reached Gordon.

Once they passed the towering pines, she spotted what Gordon had found. Only all that remained of the cabin was its burned-out shell and the stone chimney.

Grace swallowed hard. Her brothers had talked about this cabin—the cabin set on fire by an unbalanced son.

Gordon stared at the structure. He lifted his hands and covered his ears.

Jack came up beside him and clapped Gordon's shoulder. "Good job. Now, go gather some sticks to make a fire."

Gordon kept his hands covering his ears.

"Did you hear me, Gordon?" Jack spoke louder. "You found it."

Gordon faced Jack with a haunted gaze that seemed to look through Jack. Gordon nodded, but Grace wasn't so sure Gordon was aware of his action. He ambled away.

Grace turned to follow Gordon, but Jack grabbed her arm. "Where do you think you're going?"

"I was . . . going to . . ." Fear stole her voice. She looked away from his probing eyes.

"You're staying with me," he sneered.

Prickly sensations traveled along her arm like thousands of spiders crawling all over her. She didn't want to be alone with him for even a second.

His grip on her arm tightened. "You're going to be a good girl tonight, aren't you?"

She stared at him hard and unblinking.

"Doesn't it say something in that Bible of yours about a woman being submissive?"

A shiver snaked through her. She was running tonight even if he killed her.

❧

The downpour had gradually reduced to a drizzle. The scent of burning wood was still strong, but only a trace of smoke curled over the trees. Ben held the prayer *kapp* and closed his eyes. "God, there's a part in the Bible where Joshua prayed for the sun to stand still so that he could defeat his enemy. I need that same favor *nau*. I don't know my way in the woods, and once the sun goes down I won't be able to find her."

The eyes of the Lord are on the righteous . . . His ears are open to their prayers.

Ben dropped to his knees. "I'm far from being righteous, God, but I beg of You to hear *mei* prayer. Grace needs You—I need You."

When he opened his eyes, a fox was standing before him. Ben froze. Everything he'd ever heard or read about wild animals said they feared humans. But this fox not only wasn't running away, it didn't seem fearful at all.

Ben gulped.

Matted with mud, the animal's body was slender, its reddish-orange fur dull. His small black eyes stared at Ben. Perhaps the animal was sick or hungry. Ben had heard about a raccoon that showed up at one of the local parks. When someone stopped to feed part of his sandwich to the raccoon, it bit him. Later, the park officials issued a warning about not approaching nocturnal animals that appeared friendly during daylight since they had a high likelihood of carrying rabies.

Ben wasn't that curious about a fox. He wasn't about to get close enough to be bitten. But that meant waiting for the fox to move away from the path.

The fox lifted its nose and sniffed. Then, taking long, sleek strides with its tail lowered, it crept closer to Ben.

Ben held his breath and froze, afraid to breathe, to move. He should be searching for Grace, but instead he was trying to hold still while a fox sniffed his pant legs.

Don't bite . . . Oh, God, I need help here.

The fox looked up at Ben, then turned and walked away.

Ben blew out a breath. "*Danki*, God." Now he needed help to find Grace. But the human footprints he found in the dirt were traveling in the same direction the fox had gone.

ℜ

Grace took shallow breaths, keenly aware that Jack's wandering eyes were canvassing every inch of her. He leaned the gun against a nearby tree, then removed a flask from his shirt pocket and took a long drink. He licked his lips.

Grace looked away. Being alone with Jack curdled her stomach. Where was Gordon? He'd gone into the woods to collect sticks to start a fire and still hadn't returned.

Jack stalked toward her.

Stay calm. Grace tightened her hold on the shovel and backed up.

"What are you going to do, hit me with that?" He took another drink from the canister, then placed it in his pocket. Laughing, he reached for the shovel.

She jerked it away, which seemed to provoke his determination.

He grabbed the handle, but instead of snatching it from her, he leveraged it between them, backing her up against a tree. He leaned closer, touching his lips against her ear as he spoke. "We have all night."

The stench of alcohol wrenched her stomach. *God, help me.*

Jack released his hold and reached for the flask.

Grace waited until he took a drink before she whirled the shovel with all the strength she could muster. *Thwack.* Jack held his head, staggered a few short steps, then dropped to his knees.

"*Ach*, God. Please help me. Please." She ran, cutting through the woods toward the sound of the river. Her dress snagged on a thorny bush and tore when she pulled it free.

"Woman!" Jack bellowed.

She should have hit him again while he was stunned.

Brushwood snapped under his heavy steps. Her heart hammered as she broke through the buckthorn. The droning sound of her blood pulsating in her ears made the trout stream, babbling over a shallow bed of rocks, barely audible.

Jack grunted, closing in behind her. She looked back, caught a glimpse of him, then her feet went out from under her. A shrill cry escaped her mouth as she hit the rocky riverbank with a thud.

He pounced on her, clamping her mouth closed with a calloused hand, the weight of him stealing the air from her lungs. "Did you really think you could run away?" Licking his lips, he bent down, buried his bristly face in her neck, and slathered her neck with wet kisses.

She tightened her lips when his mouth moved over hers.

He lifted his mouth slightly. "Cat got your tongue?" His breath sour—wet—his lips touching hers as he spoke. "Fight me." Jack took her mouth again, this time with more force.

She caught his lip between her teeth and latched on. He weakened momentarily, giving her enough wiggle room to free her hands. She reached for his neck and gouged her nails into his flesh.

He pulled her against his body and logrolled her into the cold stream. Her head slammed against a rock. She cried out, releasing his bottom lip in the process. He buried her scream underwater. The image of his face—his bloody lip—distorted. Black spots filled her vision before he yanked her out of the water by her hair. She gasped for air seconds before being immersed again.

"Jack! Stop it!" Even muffled underwater, Gordon's shout rang out.

It wasn't until Gordon added "please" that Jack jerked her to the surface.

"Don't you see we want to be alone?" Jack growled between clenched teeth. "Go back to camp."

"Ah . . . what are you doing?"

"Help—" She wheezed as Jack pressed his thumb against her throat, cutting off her air.

"I'm going to help her bathe." He turned his head and wiped his bloody lip on his shirtsleeve. "Now give us some privacy."

She wiggled, was able to squeak, "*Nay!*" but her desperate cry didn't reach past her mouth. The pressure against her throat increased and she fell limp in Jack's arms.

"Jack!" Gordon's voice deepened. "What did you do to her?"

"She passed out—that's all." He hoisted her into his arms and stood. "Don't worry, she'll be fine."

The night air chilled her to the bone, but she fought the urge to shiver and clamped her teeth together so they wouldn't chatter.

"Are you sure she's not dead?"

"Not yet," he mumbled under his breath.

Chapter Twenty-Six

Nothing felt worse than being cradled in Jack's arms. With her eyes closed and her face pinned against his shirt pocket, which held his flask, she let her body go limp. If he suspected she was conscious—even alert—she would be in great danger.

Lord, danki *for sending Gordon when You did. You saved me from Jack's evil intent.* Her throat tightened. *I'm scared. I don't want to be alone with him . . . It's dark, God. What will he do to me when Gordon is asleep? I need a miracle.*

In the same moment she finished the silent prayer, she heard the familiar scripture play over in her spirit. *My grace is sufficient for you, for My strength is made perfect in your weakness.* An image of Jesus flashed in her mind. She envisioned herself resting against His shoulder, safe in her Savior's arms. Tension drained from her body. Her eyelids grew heavy and peace washed over her.

Sometime later, something stiff jabbed her in the ribs.

"Wake up." Jack poked her side with the toe of his boot.

It took a moment for her eyes to focus. When they did, a shadowy form stood between her and the campfire. She closed her eyes. Maybe if she concentrated, she could pretend she was somewhere else. But she was toed in the ribs again, this time harder.

"She's awake," Jack said.

So much for pretending. He wasn't going to let her forget she was under his control. Something minty wafted to her senses. When she opened her eyes, Gordon had sat down beside her.

He handed her a strip of dried jerky, a chunk of sourdough bread, and a cup of minty tea. She sipped the tea. Strong. He must have boiled it too long. It tasted bitter, but she wouldn't complain. Not after Jack held her underwater in the frigid river. Her dress was still wet despite lying close to the fire.

Grace took a bite of bread. After not eating since breakfast, the sourdough tasted like candy. So did the jerky. She finished the crusty heel of the loaf and the smoked meat, wishing she had more. Though she would rather starve than ask Jack for more food. He hadn't stopped staring at her—the snake. Pure evil ran through his veins. She lost her appetite.

Gordon scooted closer to Grace. "You talk in your sleep," he said.

"Oh?" She should probably be concerned. After all, a man shouldn't know her sleeping habits. But as odd as it was, she appreciated him watching over her as she slept—protecting her from Jack as darkness settled in. Over the past several hours, she'd developed an unusual sense of trust in Gordon. He had intervened for her twice, when Jack held the gun to her head and then at the river.

"You were talking about God's grace being suffic"—Gordon looked at Jack—"what word did she say?"

"How would I know?" Jack grunted and tore another bite of meat off with his teeth.

"Sufficient," Grace said, giving Gordon her full attention. "It's a Bible verse I often quote."

"I heard it before." Gordon nodded and pointed to his head. "I have a weak mind. But my mom said I have God's power. Like David had against Goliath."

"God's power, really?" Jack huffed. "You don't even know what that means."

"My mom said." Gordon's voice rose.

"She's right, Gordon," Grace said. "Your mom's right."

Gordon nodded.

"*Mei mamm* used to quote the Bible because of *mei* weak leg. 'My grace is sufficient for you, for My strength is made perfect in weakness.'"

Gordon smiled. "We're both weak."

"Yeah, you are," Jack interjected.

Grace leaned closer to Gordon. "We're both strong. Don't forget that." She needed to heed her own advice. "Your mother is a wise woman."

"She's dead." Jack stood and tossed another log on the fire.

Tiny red embers squiggled to the sky.

Gordon stared at the flames.

"*Mei mamm* has passed away too," she said softly.

"But I bet you didn't kill her," Jack said, poking the burning log with a stick. "Gordon got rid of his family." He motioned over his shoulder to where the stone chimney stood several feet away. "He torched the place with them in it."

Oh, God, the rumors are true. The hairs on Grace's arms stood on end. Her throat dry, she took a large gulp of tea. Now that the tea had become tepid, the bitterness seemed more pronounced. Her tongue tingled. Grace tipped the cup. Tea leaves. Mattie's words replayed in her mind.

Don't drink the tea.

❧

A wolf howled in the distance and Ben froze midstep. He had run hard, trying to make it as far as he could before the sun went down, but now he couldn't see his hand in front of his face, let alone his surroundings. He stumbled over a root and fell facedown.

"You must want me on *mei* knees, God." He lifted his hands up in the air and tilted his face toward the blackened sky. "Well, here I am!"

he shouted. "Broken." He dropped his arms and buried his face in his hands. "I'm like a blind man. How will I find Grace now?" His thoughts reeled. How he'd failed Grace, his father, everyone in his life. How he had dodged responsibility . . . dodged baptism and joining the church. Ben rubbed his eyes. This wasn't the time to let his emotions run amuck, he tried to tell himself. But as he dropped to the ground, inhaling the earthy scent of the soil, he realized his spirit had been heavy for a while. "I am clay, oh God, and You are the potter. Please forgive me. Mold me into the man You've made me to be."

You fool. You can't barter with God, he chided himself. But as he lay quietly before the Lord, searching his heart, a greater power rose up within him. "Search *mei* heart, God. I want to be made new. A new creature through Jesus Christ, *mei* Savior."

Something touched his hand and he opened his eyes, startled. In front of him, the fox lay down and placed his head on Ben's hand. But what was even more amazing was how the sky flickered with light. Streams of greens and yellows bouncing across the sky stole his breath.

He scrambled to his feet and turned in a complete circle, mesmerized by the changing hues. He stood in awe of the work of God's hand, too dumbfounded to move, to speak.

Ben glanced down at the fox, sitting patiently at his feet.

"I suppose this isn't new for you, is it?"

The fox stood, turned around, and walked a few feet down the lit path.

Ben made another circle, admiring the vibrant colors. "Praise Your holy name, Jesus."

Captured by the tranquility, Ben sighed. He wished he could have shared this moment with Grace.

Grace! He could find her now. As he headed down the path, he caught sight of the fox sitting on the carpet of pine needles. It hadn't dawned on him until now how God had used a raven to bring Elijah food. Perhaps the fox was sent to lead him.

❧

It wasn't long after Grace ingested the tea that her vision blurred and she became light-headed. Her heart was beating in an irregular way, skipping beats, then coupling a few in a row. She wiped her moist brow. What was in that tea?

Grace glanced at Gordon. He looked confused, staring at something. She followed his line of vision upward and her jaw dropped open. Brilliant lights—flickering greens morphed into yellows and stretched across the sky. She had seen the northern lights plenty of times, but they had never been this spectacular. Maybe she was hallucinating. Even the old stone chimney that was once part of the burned-out cabin seemed to glow.

Jack took a long drink from his flask, then set it on the ground and stood. He walked around the fire pit and stopped before her.

Her surroundings waved like heat off a paved surface. His face went in and out of focus. She would never be able to fight him off.

"Grab the shovel and follow me," Jack said.

She glanced at Gordon, dazed and staring at the sky. *Please, Gordon, pay attention. Don't leave me alone with him.*

"Do as you're told." Jack reached for her arm and jerked her up off the ground.

One whiff of his alcohol-laced breath and her stomach roiled. Acid gurgled to the back of her throat. She swallowed, but instead of diluting the burning sensation, it made her cough. She almost lost what stomach contents remained. The back of her throat flamed even more.

"Gordon!" Jack waited until he had Gordon's attention. "Watch her." He stormed toward the river. Once he was gone, Gordon redirected his attention to the flickering lights in the sky.

An inner prompting told her to run, but Grace's brain couldn't convince her muscles to move. She plopped down. Her eyelids felt heavy, as if her lashes had glue on them, because every time she blinked they wanted to stick. She closed her eyes and saw the same beams of greens and yellows.

"Who said you could go back to sleep? Get up." Jack nudged her arm with his wet boot.

She had difficulty prying her eyes open and when she did, they closed again. Whatever was in the tea, it made her sleepy.

Jack grabbed her arm and forced her to stand. "Gordon, grab the shovel."

"But . . . it's nighttime." Gordon crinkled his brows in confusion. "Isn't it?"

"What have you been smoking?" Jack motioned to the shovel leaning against the tree. "Pick that up. While it's light enough to see, you two might as well be digging."

Grace moved as Jack prodded. She followed Gordon, who had the task of finding the spot to dig.

Gordon roamed aimlessly around the stone fireplace, touching the river rock more in a sentimental gesture than in search of something. The corners of his mouth turned down and tears glazed his eyes, obviously affected by seeing what remained of his old homestead. Grace wanted to reach out to him, but Jack trailed Gordon's every move.

"Was it behind one of these rocks?" Jack asked.

Gordon ignored the question. If purposefully or because he was deep in a trance, Grace wasn't certain.

Jack shuffled his feet. "Gordon, you said the treasure was buried." "I did?"

Jack blew out a breath, growling. "Just use your head and think."

"Gordon has a weak mind." He ran his hand over the large stones. "Gordon's simple."

"We talked about finding your treasure all winter," Jack said. "Gordon's treasure. Remember?"

Gordon continued to study the chimney. A tear slipped down his face.

"I might as well take you back to the behavior ward."

"No."

"Yep. That's what I'm going to do. I'll tell Nurse Phyllis that you went wild—that you stabbed the nurse at the hospital."

Gordon shook his head. "But I didn't. You did."

"Who are they going to believe?"

Gordon paced the old cement foundation.

Jack paced beside Gordon. "They'll put you right back into a chemical straitjacket. You didn't like that, did you?"

"No." He covered his hands over his ears and shook his head.

Jack tried to move Gordon's hands, but he fought back, arms flailing. Jack pinned him in a headlock.

Grace winced. "Don't hurt him." Her words slurred. *Lord, I need Your power to work through me . . . I need to think straight.*

"It's by a tree," he said, trying to wiggle out of Jack's hold.

Jack released him. "Now you're thinking."

Gordon shied away from Jack and walked a few feet away, adjusting his shirt collar.

Jack picked up the shovel and handed it to Gordon. "Let's find that tree."

Grace didn't want to be the bearer of bad news, but from what she'd heard, when the cabin caught fire over twenty years ago, the fire spread over several acres. None of these trees looked older than that. The pines were huge, but they were also fast-growing; they would have sprouted after the fire.

Gordon wandered from tree to tree. He finally picked one. Although she believed it was purely a random choice, it didn't matter. Jack wasn't thinking about manhandling her, and she would dig holes all night if it meant him not having his way with her.

Gordon sank the shovel into the soft ground and tossed the dirt to one side. In a matter of minutes, he had a waist-deep hole dug and was moving to a new location.

Jack tipped the flask and drained it, then tossed the container on the ground. "Make yourself useful, woman. Make me something to drink."

Gladly. Mint tea coming up. It ought to be potent now that it had steeped so long. Danki, *Lord, for increasing his thirst.* She ambled back to the fire pit, added more tea leaves to the already boiled ones, and placed the pot on the cinders. The steam alone caused her eyes to water.

She carried the tin mug back to where they were digging. "I tried not to make it too hot," she said. Although she couldn't have cared less if he burned his tongue, she also wanted him to drink it quickly.

He grunted something that might have sounded like a thank you and drank.

She moved over to the other side of the mound of dirt. While she fought to stay standing and keep her eyes open, Gordon acted as though he'd been given a shot of energy. He was on his third hole. She stole a glance at Jack drinking the tea and she smiled.

Jack grinned. "What are you smiling about?"

She shook her head. "Nothing."

He eyed her hard, head to toe, as he moved boldly toward her.

"How's the tea? Do you want me to make you more?" Her words running together only made him smile.

He stopped in front of her and tipped his mug. "I have plenty. In fact, I want . . . to share it . . . with you."

"No thanks." She took a step backward. He sounded intoxicated. Whatever plant those tea leaves came from, they didn't mix well with the alcohol he'd consumed earlier.

He pushed the cup toward her. "Drink it."

He'd consumed most of it, but there was still more than a sip left. She pretended to take a drink, then passed it back to him. "Thank you."

"Drink it all."

She straightened her shoulders. "I'm *nett* thirsty."

"I don't care. Drink it." His eyes narrowed. "You did something to it—didn't you!" He placed his hand on the small of her back and jerked her up against him. "Do you want me to spoon-feed you?"

A shudder went down her spine. She was still feeling the effects of the last cup. What would more do to her?

She took the mug from him, her hands shaking. She slowly lifted it to her mouth, drank some, and gagged on the bitterness.

"Keep drinking."

"It's hot. Maybe if I put some river water in it—"

He tightened his hold, burying his fingers into her ribs. "Do you need a lesson in obedience?" His hand roamed over her backside.

She shook her head and drank more. She'd rather die from poison than be his victim. By the time she finished the drink, the warm liquid had numbed the back of her throat. Her heart pounded erratically. She was vaguely aware of Jack walking her backward, pinning her against a tree, and moistening her neck with his traveling mouth.

"I found it!" Gordon shouted.

Jack pushed away from her and staggered over to the hole. "Let's see it."

Sporting a wide smile, Gordon lifted a quart-sized canning jar, which looked empty from her view.

Jack snatched it from Gordon's hand and headed back to the campfire.

Gordon shot out of the hole and trailed Jack while Grace walked gingerly over what she perceived as shifting ground.

Jack emptied the contents on the ground, then examined them using the fire for light. He rubbed his eyes and brought the piece up closer. "Tell me these aren't just rocks."

"Gordon's treasure." He patted his chest. "David's stones to fight giants."

"Rocks?" Jack's voice grew louder. He lunged toward Gordon and had him by the collar.

"Stop!" Grace shouted. "There is a treasure around here."

Jack pushed Gordon aside and grasped her arms. "Where is it?" He swayed, used her for support, then shook her hard. "Where?"

Dizzy and unable to focus on anything that wasn't spinning, she felt vomit rise to the back of her throat.

"Answer me!"

"I've heard people talk . . . there's gold or silver . . . maybe copper."

"Copper cave," Gordon said. "Long tunnel. Dark. Too dark."

"Where, Gordon?"

He shook his head. "Too dark. Too, too, too dark."

Jack released her and took hold of Gordon, who shrank. "Where is it! Tell me or I'll dump your body in the river!" Suddenly, Jack grasped his abdomen and doubled over.

Gordon squatted down beside him. "What's wrong, Jack?"

He moaned.

Gordon peered up at Grace. "Something's wrong with Jack."

Guilt replaced any thoughts of celebrating his incapacitation. She took the mug down to the river, rinsed it, and filled it with water. She hurried back and sat down next to Jack. "Drink this."

"Why should I trust . . . you?"

"You shouldn't." She drank it herself, and surprisingly, she was thirsty. Grace handed the mug to Gordon. "Fill it with more river water."

"I'll . . . get you . . . for this." His body convulsed.

She believed him. *Let the poison take me first.*

Gordon returned with the water, and as he helped hold the mug to Jack's lips, Grace moved to the other side of the campfire not feeling so well herself.

Something crept into the firelight.

Her vision was cloudy, but that wasn't a tree stump. It looked a little bit like . . . a fox?

Chapter Twenty-Seven

The fox had kept Ben company on the trail over the past several hours, then suddenly shot ahead and disappeared. It took awhile to warm up to the idea of a wild creature tagging along, but now that he was alone, Ben sort of missed it. The woods made an array of eerie sounds at night. Nothing the fox showed concern over—and nothing Ben cared to investigate.

A strange light in the distance caught his eye. Ben paused a moment, then continued in a slow crouch. He spotted the glow of a campfire through the trees. He went up on his tiptoes and craned his neck. The trees were blocking his view. He couldn't see Grace, or anyone for that matter. He edged closer.

"Lord, where is she?"

Would they have left the fire burning if they had decided to move on? Not likely. Then again, he found it strange that they started one at all and risked someone finding them. He moved a little closer and hid behind another large tree.

Suddenly Ben spied Jack, the man who roughed him up and pushed him into the cellar. Jack was lying on the ground near the campfire while Gordon sat beside him. But where was Grace? What had they done with her?

The gunshot he had heard earlier came to mind. *Don't think it . . . Grace is . . .* He struggled to push the thought aside. God was in this.

All he had to do was look at the neon sky. He had to think positive. *Walk in faith. Oh, Lord, where is she?*

Ben went closer still. That's when he spotted her long, wheat-colored hair. He eased out the breath he wasn't aware he had been holding.

"*Danki*, Lord," he whispered.

He had to rein in his thoughts of rushing into the middle of their camp. He needed a plan. A distraction. Maybe he could create a diversion. But what? A low, growling sound answered that question. The fox had already gained everyone's attention.

✺

Grace blinked. Her eyes were playing tricks on her. She wasn't truly seeing a fox. But shortly after she noticed the fox move, Gordon announced he saw it, too, then jumped into a patch of ferns and hid.

Jack scrambled to his feet and staggered a few steps. Apparently, his vision was askew and the ground was moving for him too.

She could hardly stand to keep her eyes open. Even the brightness of the flames was making it harder to focus.

The wild animal growled when Jack tried to come near it. Obviously, Jack was after the gun. But where the fox had stationed itself, Jack had to pass the fox to get it. Jack made another sloppy attempt, but the fox stood its ground. It even backed Jack up several feet with rabid assertiveness.

The bushes rustled and a form stepped out from the darkness. Grace's breath caught in her throat. She followed the newcomer with her eyes as he entered the camp. *Ben?* Light from the fire illuminated his face. Her heart jumped a beat.

"Ben!"

Jack charged Ben, tackling him at the waist and wrestling him inches from the fire.

God, help him!

Ben kneed Jack in the chest, who wavered, gasping raspy breaths. Ben struck him again. And again. He pushed off Jack and stood. Jack staggered toward him, but just as he swung at Ben, the fox leaped in between them. The snarling animal foamed at the mouth.

Don't move, Ben. But he didn't heed her silent plea. Ben sidestepped the fox.

She covered her hands over her face and squeezed her eyes closed, unable to watch. "Protect him, Lord. *Please.*" Grace opened her eyes and peeked between her spread fingers as Ben snatched the gun leaning against the tree.

Grace pushed off the ground too fast and a wave of dizziness dropped her to her knees. She took a deep breath and willed her muscles to move.

Ben reached for her hand and helped her to stand.

She'd never been happier than when she saw his smile. Tears sprang to her eyes and she couldn't wipe them away fast enough.

Ben touched her swollen cheek with his thumb and growled under his breath.

"Shoot it!" Jack shouted.

Ben's expression hardened. "I'd shoot you first." He turned his attention back to her, the lines by his eyes softening. "Are you ready to go home?" he asked, taking her by the hand.

She didn't have to answer that, nor did he give her a chance. With a firm grasp on her hand, Ben whisked her into the woods.

❧

Ben wanted to get Grace as far away from the men as possible before they stopped running, but she tugged on his arm to stop.

"I need . . . to catch . . . *mei* breath," she said between gasps.

"I'm sorry. I should have been more thoughtful."

She leaned her back against a tree, held her hand to her chest, and sucked air like she'd swum up from the bottom of the ocean.

He scanned the area and when he looked at her again, she was hunched over.

"Are you okay?"

She nodded.

He bent down and cocked his head to one side to get a better view of her face. "Would you tell me if something was wrong?"

"*Jah*," she squeaked.

"Hey, are you crying?" He tipped her chin with his hand. "It's over, Grace. You're safe." Without uttering a word, she wrapped her arms around him and buried her face in his neck. This wasn't like her at all. He wasn't sure how to respond. He sure didn't want to break the embrace to put the rifle down. Besides, she had him in such a tight bear hug it was obvious something was wrong.

Under different circumstances, he would have held her all night, but they had to get to a safer place. He pulled back. "We should—"

She stole his words with a needy kiss.

It didn't take longer than half a second for her soft lips to infuse desire through his veins. He lifted his free hand, furrowed his fingers through her hair to the back of her neck, and reined her in. Why did he have to be holding a gun?

Ben broke from the kiss having never been breathless like this before. "Grace," he said, his voice hoarse, "I have a loaded rifle in *mei* hand."

Her eyes widened. "I don't know what got into me. I just . . . I mean . . . I've never—"

"Tell me you'll do it again sometime."

She covered her hand over her mouth, staring wide-eyed and stunned.

"Okay," he said, intent on staying optimistic. "We'll talk about it later."

She cracked a smile. "You're awfully confident."

"Hmm . . . You fueled *mei* ego." He motioned to the path and she followed. This time he started at a slower pace. "I've never seen it this bright at *nacht*," he said after a period of silence.

"I thought I was hallucinating when the colors appeared. Mattie said not to drink the tea as she handed me the basket, and I did without thinking."

He reeled around to face her. "How much?"

"A cup and a half. I started to sweat and thought I might pass out." She lifted her hand to her neck. "*Mei* pulse is still skipping beats."

He stopped. "Why didn't you say something sooner?" He reached for her hand and placed three fingers on her wrist. Weak. He searched her neck for her pulse, and she flinched.

"Do you think I'll be all right?"

"*Nay* talking." He counted the beats awhile longer, then lowered his hand. "There are long intervals between your heartbeats and they're erratic. Whatever it was you ingested, you have to get it out of your system."

"I drank water thinking I could dilute it."

He shook his head. "That's *nett* enough. Stick your fingers down your throat."

She attempted, but apparently didn't get her fingers far enough to stimulate the gag reflex before she pulled them out.

"Try it again."

"I can't."

Ben set the gun on the ground. He snapped a small branch off the oak tree. "Open your mouth."

"What? *Nay*."

"It's either this or *mei* fingers." He inspected his fingers. "I've been in the swamp muck today." The way her face paled, she might vomit at the thought. When she didn't, he moved closer. "Are you going to do it or am I?"

She turned her back to him and bent at the waist. This time she managed to make herself vomit copious amounts of dark liquid. She brushed her hair away from her face. "You happy?"

"Do it again."

"I already feel light-headed."

"I'll carry you when you're done." She didn't understand the seriousness. Not all herbs were safe. "*Kumm* on. If you did it once, you can do it again."

She stared at him.

Ben reached down and picked up the gun. "*Kumm* with me." He went in the opposite direction, listened for the sound of the river, and cut through the alder brush to reach the water. Ben set the gun down away from the water and out of the sand, then glanced at her silhouetted form standing on the bank. "You want to get a drink and wash your hands and mouth, don't you?"

She hesitated a moment, then joined him at the water's edge. Grace went down to her knees, washed her hands, then cupped some water and drank.

He knelt beside her and did the same.

She gulped another handful of water and sighed.

"Okay, do it again."

"*Nay*, Ben, please. Let's just go home. Mattie will know what to do."

"You have to get it all out. Besides, it's going to take several hours to get home." He inspected his hands for cleanliness, then lifted his palms and wiggled his fingers as though playing a piano midair. "*Mei* hands are clean. I'll do it if you can't."

She hesitated.

"*Kumm* on, you can do it." He pulled a stick of gum from his pocket and waved it before her. "I'll give you this."

"Once more, but that's it." She hunched over and gagged before her fingers made it into her mouth. She rinsed out the foul taste with river water, then stretched out her hand. "The gum."

237

Ben peeled off the wrapper and handed her the stick, then popped another one in his mouth.

She chewed the gum, its mint flavor making her gag again. She bent over to vomit, only this time nothing came up. The dry heaves made her ribs ache. Her shoulders shook and she began sobbing. Exhaustion was taking its toll. "I just want to go home," she said, crying harder.

"Okay, but only after you drink more water. You need to dilute whatever's left."

"Ben . . . ," she pleaded.

"Tough love, Gracie—start drinking." His words were stern, but his heart was as soft as cookies fresh out of the oven.

She spit her gum into the bushes, then cupped her hands and drank more water. Color was returning to her face.

Ben swept her hair away from her eyes and hooked the long strands behind her ears. "Better?"

She nodded.

"Promise you'll tell me if you start experiencing any strange side effects."

"Okay."

Ben rose, reached for her hand, helped her up, then pulled another stick of gum from his pocket and handed it to her.

"*Danki*," she said so softly he had to strain to hear. She looked up at the sky. "I heard Alaska has nights when it never gets dark, but I've never seen it like this in Michigan."

"I'm claiming it as an answer to prayer. I prayed God would make the sun stand still so I could find you."

"I was praying for a miracle too."

Ben bent down and retrieved the rifle. "Are you ready?"

She lumbered a few steps and stopped.

"What's wrong?"

"We have to go back for Gordon."

Chapter Twenty-Eight

Absolutely *nett*."

Grace flinched at Ben's furrowed brow.

"Why on earth would you want to go back?"

She had asked herself that too. "I can't leave Gordon alone with Jack."

Ben took a few steps down the trail, then spun around and marched back to her. "That tea must have messed up your mind. You don't even know what you're saying—what you're doing. You're acting . . . out of character. You're acting delusional."

She lowered her head. Her actions were certainly out of character. Kissing him was *narrisch*. "I was wrong."

"You got that right."

"I shouldn't have kissed you." She bowed her head, unable to look him in the eye. As much as she wanted to erase the memory of Jack kissing her, it was still wrong to involve Ben the way she had. "I'm sorry. Will you forgive me?"

He withheld his response, making the moment unbearable.

"Please."

He smiled, although it was much too wide to be natural. "There's nothing to forgive." His smile disappeared. "Are you ready to go home?"

"I was serious about going back for Gordon."

"You've got to be kidding. Why?"

She blinked at the harshness in his tone. "The treasure they were searching for turned out to be river rocks. Jack was disoriented by the tea, but when he's sober, he will go into a rage."

"So? Those two are partners. Let them kill each other."

"Ben," she snapped. "Gordon saved *mei* life. He's *nett* a bad person."

"Grace, he's unbalanced. Those people can flip in a moment."

Ben had a point. Gordon had set fire to his family's cabin, taking the lives of his own parents. Still, Jack was a monster; he wouldn't think twice about hurting Gordon. Grace squared her shoulders. "I'm going back. I understand if you don't want to *kumm*." She motioned to the rifle resting against his shoulder. "Can I take the gun?"

He shifted his weight to his other foot and looked at her hard. "Can you really shoot someone? *Kill* someone?"

She was raised to adhere to the Ten Commandments. The *Ordnung* forbade members to join the armed services because of her people's belief in the Commandments. She had already acted in violence when she hit Jack with the shovel. At that particular moment, she hadn't cared if he lived or died. She had fallen to Jack's level. Even knowing something was wrong with the herbal concoction, she'd made him a strong cup. Her shoulders dropped and she hung her head in shame.

"I didn't think so." He motioned to the trail. "I'm sure everyone's worried about you. We need to go home."

She nodded. But as they hiked along the trail following the riverbank, she couldn't push aside her thoughts of rescuing Gordon.

Something slapped the river.

Ben stopped.

"Sounded like a trout jumping," she said.

"*Shh.*" He lifted his index finger over his mouth.

The alder bushes rustled.

Grace had dismissed the sound as coming from an animal. Apparently Ben wasn't convinced. He took her by the elbow and motioned with his head for her to follow him off the trail. Her heart rate ratcheted up a notch. The farther away from the river they were, the hillier the terrain became. One incline wasn't even steep but it left her breathless.

"How's your leg?"

"I'm managing." She wished she could manage her thoughts as well. Gordon's voice echoed in her mind. Weak-minded and simple—the way God had made him. Gordon accepted his lot in life better than she had her own.

Grace dug her heels into the ground going down the slope, but the downward momentum got away from her and she tripped over her dress hem. She logrolled several feet before coming to a stop.

Ben galloped down the hill. "Are you hurt?"

"*Nay.*" She pushed up into a sitting position. "I think going uphill was easier."

Ben set the gun on the ground and lent her his hand. Once she was standing, he brushed the dead leaves off her dress. "I know the trail following the river would be easier, but I'm sure that's where they'd look first for us."

"Is that what you think the noise was?"

"It was probably an animal." He looked over his shoulder, then from side to side. "Stay here a minute." He picked up the gun and tucked the butt of it between his waist and elbow, placed one hand on the steel barrel and the other on the trigger, then proceeded to the right with slow, steady steps.

Grace watched him until he disappeared into the darkness. She closed her eyes. *Lord, please keep him safe. Watch over him, and please, Lord, don't let anything bad happen.* She sat quietly with her eyes closed, then said into the darkness, "Lord, show mercy to Gordon, and . . ." She exhaled loudly. She couldn't add Jack's name to her prayer. She couldn't pray for something she didn't have in her heart. "And help me understand Your grace. Gordon seems to grasp Your grace being sufficient in his life, but why is it so difficult for me?"

Footsteps tromped over sticks. When she opened her eyes, Ben was coming toward her.

"I found a cave opening. Do you want to see it?"

She stood. "That must be the one *mei bruders* talked about." She went with him, but the closer they came to the entrance, the more she began to have second thoughts. Had he already checked it for bears?

Ben stopped at the mouth of the cave. "If this comes out at those sinkholes, I'll know how to get to the main road. Are you feeling adventurous?"

She gulped.

Grace peered into the cave. Dank. Musty. Dark. *Gordon don't like dark. Gordon afraid.*

Ben came up beside her. "I think we'll be safer."

Safer? Grace spun around. "We have to help Gordon. He's a victim."

"Grace, we've gone over this."

"But Gordon saved me. Jack would have . . ." Tears burned her eyes. "I couldn't . . . fight." Noticing Ben's Adam's apple move down his throat, she couldn't continue. Grace turned her back to him and lowered her head.

He stepped in front of her. "I know this has been hard on you, but don't feel guilty about leaving Gordon with Jack."

She lifted her head. "He's a victim."

Ben shuffled his feet. "You're *nett* going to let this go, are you?"

"I can't."

He touched a ringlet of hair that had fallen loose from behind her ear, and for a moment, staring at the lock of hair, he seemed to be lost in thought. He lifted his gaze to hers, his eyes searching, his chest rising and falling. For a minute, she thought he might kiss her.

He released the lock of hair. "Do you think Gordon will leave?"

"*Jah,*" she said with a shaky voice.

Ben cupped her elbow. "Okay, I'll go get him." He led her into the mouth of the cave. "But you stay in here where it's safe."

"He won't go with you."

He shuffled his feet impatiently. "You just said he would."

"With me."

"Either I go alone," he said firmly, "or we leave him with Jack."

Something sounding like a slow-dripping faucet filled the silence. The thought of being alone in the cave was unnerving. She reached for his forearm in the darkness, and his muscles tightened under her grasp. "Gordon doesn't know you. He trusts me."

"I'm *nett* backing down on this. It's dangerous and we could be on the run again and your legs—"

"*Mei* legs will what?"

"You're tired. I am too."

She narrowed her eyes even though he couldn't see them in the darkness. "But you don't have a disability."

"Don't make it about that." His sharp tone echoed against the walls. "I'm trying to keep you safe." He reached for her hand, giving it a gentle squeeze. "Will you pray for me while I'm gone?"

"*Jah*, of course."

"If something happens to me . . ."

"Don't, Ben, please." Tears pricked her eyes.

"Go through the cave. You remember how to get to the main road, right?"

Alone?

⁂

Ben hiked through the woods at a steady clip. Going after Gordon was crazy, and if it wasn't for wanting more than anything to please Grace, he wouldn't take the risk. The woman had a good, but stubborn, heart.

Even exhausted, she refused to back down from her conviction, a trait he admired.

He wished she shared the same fervor toward him, but instead, she sent him mixed signals. She had responded to his kiss—melted into his arms—the afternoon he found her in the bishop's barn. She claimed it'd never happen again. Then tonight, she kissed him. The moment he responded, she ended it, saying she was wrong. He was beginning to wonder if all women were like this. Neva had thrown herself at him. Had he been as drunk as her, things would have gotten out of hand— they nearly did anyway. She was on the rebound and because they had been on *rumschpringe*, he mistakenly believed the man she rambled on about was an *Englischer*. He never dreamed it'd been Toby.

As Ben reached the footpath near the river, the sound of branches snapping stopped him in his tracks. He clicked the gun's safety mechanism and raised the rifle.

Chapter Twenty-Nine

Ben recognized the heavy breathing and lowered the gun before Grace entered his line of vision. He groaned. What was she trying to prove, that she had an independent streak? She'd made that clear the day he arrived in Badger Creek.

He charged across the path, a mixture of frustration and relief coursing through his veins. "What are you doing here? You almost got shot."

"I forgot. They know about the cave."

The whimper in her voice pulled at his heart. He wanted to reach out and take her into his arms, but instead, he clicked the gun's safety.

"Let me go with you," she pleaded.

Her teary eyes were difficult to avoid, and no matter how hard he tried to redirect his gaze, he couldn't. "Grace," he said, moving a strand of hair away from her face. "I see the bruises he left."

Her shoulders rounded and she diverted her gaze to the ground.

"I don't want him near you again." His throat dried as anger rose up inside him. The man wouldn't lay his hand on her again.

She lifted her head, her eyes pleading with his. "I'm afraid to be alone."

Behind her quiet whisper was a spirit of determination. She would follow him. He rubbed the back of his neck. "You're hard to say *nay* to."

She smiled.

"I hope your humanitarian efforts don't get us into trouble."

Her jaw dropped.

Ben turned as she squared her shoulders. He didn't have time to listen to her defend her reasoning for going back for Gordon. He took a few steps and looked over his shoulder. She hadn't moved an inch. "If you're coming with me, let's go."

Grace rushed to his side, then walked quietly for several minutes. "Is that how you viewed rescuing me? A humanitarian effort?"

"*Nay.*" It was much more than an *effort.* He would have died for her. Something he wasn't prepared to do for the man who took her hostage to begin with.

"Just *nay?* That's all you're going to say?"

"We're *nett* too far from their camp. We shouldn't be talking." His thoughts were as tangled as an unspooled reel of fishing line. Maybe once this was over he'd have his thoughts sorted out.

It wasn't long before she stopped and pointed off to the right. "Is that . . . ?"

He bent slightly to get her perspective. "*Jah.*" Campfire flickered in the distance. He glanced sideways at Grace rubbing her arms. "*Kalt?*" he whispered.

"*Mei* skin is crawling." She cringed.

Cold feet. Good. They were far enough away that they could still turn around without anyone noticing. "Let's *nett* do this," he said.

"*Nay,* please. I . . . ." She looked down.

He'd heard before it was good to face your fears, but not like this. "Grace, you don't owe him anything. They *both* took you. They're in this together."

Her bottom lip trembled and she wrapped herself in a tight hug and closed her eyes.

"Grace," he said, placing his arm around her shoulder. "Let's go home."

Her muscles stiffened and she wiggled out from under his arm. "Gordon is as helpless as a child." Blowing out a breath, she turned and marched down the path, arms swinging.

"Okay," he said, joining her. "But you can't just charge into their camp spouting demands."

"We'll figure out something."

That was all he needed—to follow a woman with no common sense. Although if he'd had any sense, he never would have agreed to return. But right or wrong, that decision had been made and they weren't far from the camp now. He needed to figure out how to keep her out of his way.

Once they neared the camp, Ben stretched out his arm and stopped Grace. He guided her to an area behind a stand of birch trees and turned to face her. "Stay here. If there's a problem, don't wait for me. Run."

She craned her neck to look around his shoulder.

Ben repositioned himself in her direct line of vision. "You must listen . . . or you might get us both killed."

The corners of her mouth turned down and the lines across her forehead deepened. If she started crying now, she would give them away.

Ben leaned closer. "Do what you must to hold it together."

Grace covered her hand over her mouth. As she closed her eyes, tears seeped out and rolled down her cheeks.

He hated to walk away, but if he stayed any longer, he might lose the opportunity of surprise. Ben took a few steps, whispering a short prayer for protection as he went. He crept forward trying not to think about the irony of praying for protection while clutching a rifle at the same time.

Ben reached the campsite perimeter and ducked behind a tree. He drew a deep breath and released it slowly. His heart was thumping so hard he found it difficult to distinguish other sounds from the *whoosh* vibrating his inner ear. He glanced back at Grace, standing in the same place with her hand still over her mouth. At least she hadn't followed him.

Ben leaned around the tree and spied Gordon, pacing next to the fire, mumbling to himself, and raking his fingers through his hair. His mental instability was unpredictable and risky. Ben could outfight him. But could he keep Grace from coming between them? And Jack, where was he? Ben wasn't about to go any closer unless he had Jack in his sight. Scanning the area, Ben spotted Jack lying curled in a fetal position not far from where the fox had cornered him. Ben stood for what seemed like hours, staring at Jack, but the man showed no signs of movement.

Against his better judgment, Ben eased out from the shelter of the tree. As he walked into the firelight, it became more apparent that Gordon was discombobulated, muttering about himself in third person, his words running together.

"Gordon don't like dark places. Darkness bad." Wringing his hands together, Gordon paced a few feet, then pivoted. Shuffling sand as he moved, he repeated the same steps in a trancelike state.

Ben stepped into Gordon's path.

Gordon stopped less than an arm's length away. As his gaze traveled from Ben's boots up to his face, Gordon's complexion turned ashen. Gordon began to sway from side to side, nostrils flared, and an active facial tic caused his cheek to twitch.

"Gordon." Ben glanced at Jack to see if his whispering had awakened him. "Do you want to go with me and Grace?" When Gordon stared at him blankly, Ben added, "Grace will make you some cookies." If cookies didn't entice him, probably nothing would. He stole another glimpse at Jack, who still hadn't moved.

Gordon lurched sideways, eyes searching beyond Ben. His cheek twitched again, and he lifted his shoulder and rubbed it against his face.

Futile. What was I thinking letting Grace convince me of this? Ben waited a moment longer, then turned.

"Gordon likes cookies."

Grace had counted to one hundred twice, and Ben still wasn't back. There hadn't been any commotion, so what was taking them so long? She resumed counting, *one, two, three*—she couldn't wait any longer. Grace tiptoed toward the camp. She spotted Ben and Gordon first, then Jack several feet away, huddled into a ball.

She came up behind Ben as he was talking about cookies. She hadn't meant to startle him, but he jumped and in a split second had the gun aimed at her.

His brows furrowed as he lowered the gun. "You told me you were going to wait."

She broke eye contact with Ben and smiled at Gordon. "Gordon, we want you to go home with—"

"Jack," Gordon called in a high pitch. "She came back." As Gordon stepped toward her, Ben cut him off. Gordon narrowed his eyes, then looked over his shoulder to where Jack was lying. "Jack!"

Grace shook her head. "Don't wake him, he's—"

Jack groaned and lifted his head slowly. "You!"

As Jack slurred profanity, Ben wheeled her around and nudged her lower back. "Run!"

Grace didn't need to be told twice. She ran into the woods, pushing pine-needle branches out of her way, vaguely aware of Ben behind her and unsure if Gordon was following, too, or not.

Keep going. Don't stop.

Her lungs burned.

Breathe.

Grace jumped over a fallen tree, but her dress snagged on one of its branches. She sprang backward, lost her footing, and fell.

Ben reached for her arm and helped her to her feet, but the moment she put weight on her foot, pain shot through her ankle. She took a small step and bit back a yelp.

"Hold this." He handed her the gun, then scooped her into his arms. "Don't shoot yourself."

"Okay," she whimpered, slipping her finger off the trigger. "Where's Gordon?"

"He stayed. And don't ask to go back."

Ben broke a new trail through the woods and came out near the river where he eased her to her feet. Holding her waist with one arm, he reached for the rifle with his free hand. "Can you walk a few steps over to the embankment?"

"I think so." She didn't put all her weight on her left foot, but enough to maintain her balance with his assistance. He helped her to sit on the edge of the embankment. She blew out a breath. Rest was exactly what she needed.

Ben lowered himself next to her but didn't stay. He pushed off the side and slid down the sandy ridge. Once at the bottom, he set the gun down, then climbed partway up the hillside and waved his hand, motioning her to come down.

She hesitated half a second, but hearing crunching noises coming from the bushes moved her to action. She pushed off the side with enough force that she plowed into Ben and they both cascaded to the bottom, coated in sand and tangled in each other's arms. For a moment, she just lay there, her head resting against Ben's chest, and counting the *lub-dub* of his heart beating steady and strong.

She lifted her head for a second before he pushed her back against his chest. This time, his hand cupped her jaw, his thumb pressed against her lips. "*Shh*," he whispered next to her ear.

He didn't have to explain. Over his ragged breathing, she could make out the muffled voices of Jack and Gordon.

Chapter Thirty

Tucked safely in Ben's arms, Grace let her body go limp. *Lord, why are Jack and Gordon still on the cliff above us? Do You see that we are weary?* A shudder of remorse seeped through her pores. She shouldn't have convinced Ben to go back for Gordon. Her foolishness would have serious repercussions if Jack found them.

Shelter us from the wiles of evil, Lord, I pray.

The northern lights vanished. As if God had extinguished His guiding lamp, suddenly the sky was black.

Jack and Gordon's voices trailed off.

A whip-poor-will's call droned out the crickets and frogs. Had she not prayed, Grace might have let the eerie sounds of the night overwhelm her, but lying in Ben's arms, she was surrounded with peace. Danki, *God.* For a long moment, neither of them moved. The once chaotic rise and fall of his chest fell into a rhythmic lull.

Several minutes after Jack and Gordon's voices faded, he tipped her face toward his and brushed his sandy hand over her cheek. "I think they're gone," he whispered.

A thick cloud uncovered the moon, shedding a faint light that flickered in his eyes. Grace swallowed hard. She had no way of gauging the rush of heat spreading over her body. Even Philemon had never generated these sensations.

Ben released his hold. "We need to go."

Grace pushed up to her feet, smothering a screech when she put weight on her ankle. She squinted at the incline, but with limited light, it was impossible to see the best place to start climbing. "I'm *nett* sure I can make it to the top."

Ben picked up the gun. The chamber clicked and the shiny bullets caught in the moonlight as they fell to the ground. "We're *nett* going up," he said, kicking dirt over the bullets with the toe of his boot. "Stay here a minute."

He walked off, leaving her teetering for balance. She hobbled in his direction, but she didn't make it more than a few paces before he returned.

"We can't stay here. They'll find us," she said.

"I know." He looped his arm around her waist, picked her up, and headed to the edge of the water.

"Wh-what are you thinking?" Panic laced her words.

"I think you talk too much."

"Why are you . . . taking me . . . into . . . th-the water?"

"Well, I'm *nett* going to baptize you." Water splashed as he stepped into the river.

She craned her neck and wiggled to get a better look, but she wasn't able to see well enough to judge the depth.

"Why are you squirming so much? Surely you're *nett* afraid of the water."

"*Jah*, I-I-I am."

"Hmm . . . Didn't you say the fly rod in the shed was yours?" He took another step and they sank deeper.

The drag of the current tugged at her dress. Her legs totally submerged in the cold stream, she shivered. The river was getting deeper and memories flooded her mind of when she'd been swept downstream as a child. Grace clung tighter, burying her face in the crook of his neck.

"Grace," he rasped. "You're choking me."

"Sorry." She loosened her death grip, but the moment his foot slipped on the rocky bottom, she scrambled to reestablish her hold. They dipped farther down, the icy water so numbing she could no longer feel her toes. "Oh, Lord!"

"God didn't bring us this far to leave us," Ben said. "But you are going to have to switch to a different position."

"*Nay.*" Instead of loosening her grip, she wrapped her arms tighter around his neck. She would crawl into his skin if she could. The river was too deep—too strong for him to let her go now.

"Grace . . ." His muscles tensed, battered by the chest-high current. "You have to get on *mei* back." His voice sounded strained. "Where's your faith?" His tone was stern.

Tears pricked her eyes. Her faith might as well have been on the bottom of the river, it amounted to mere words—not action. She pressed her face against his neck, feeling his Adam's apple move when he swallowed. This was where she wanted to be.

"You'll be all right," he said, peeling her arms from around his neck. "I promise."

She shook her head. "Don't let me go."

Behind them, something heavy splashed into the water. Jack surfaced, cursing and plowing through the water in their direction. Her breath caught in her throat. Even though Jack looked to be staggering, he wasn't more than a few feet away.

Ben shifted her without warning, and she found herself facing his back, clawing at his shirt, then latching onto his suspenders just as they went under. She came up sputtering, having taken in a mouthful of river water. She sucked in a quick breath before they sank once more. Ben swam hard, but the current kept them from making much progress.

Something rubbed against her leg. In the blink of an eye, Jack had wrapped his arm around Ben's neck and was forcing him under. Still holding on to Ben's suspenders, she went under as well. When she finally managed to get her head up, they were all three whirling downstream. Only Ben and Jack were fully engaged in a war with legs kicking and arms batting.

Something hit her foot, and she kicked feverishly. A hand moved along her leg and snatched hold of her ankle. Feeling herself torn from Ben, she kicked her free foot in a wild frenzy, landing the heel of her shoe on Jack's face. He caught her other leg and pulled her under. She struggled, but to no avail. She held her breath and lost her fight fast.

Surrounded in blackness, she heard garbled voices. Or maybe that was the water. Her body hit something hard. She couldn't think—couldn't react—when someone's arms came around her waist.

Thrust to the surface, she gasped a lungful of cold air, vaguely aware of someone holding her up in the process. It took a moment to get her bearings and realize the movement inside her head wasn't because she was adrift on the river. She was bent over a fallen tree limb, inhaling the loamy scent of moss.

"He's gone, Grace. You're safe." Ben's voice was like balm to her soul. He gently rubbed her back. "Are you okay?"

She was now, but she lacked the strength to say more than a weak "Uh-huh."

The rotting limb groaned. Ben peeled her away from the tree.

"*Nay*, please . . ."

"I'll keep you safe. I promise," Ben said. "Get on *mei* back and hold on."

She did, but only because he'd pushed them away from the log and the current was threatening to carry her away.

Too exhausted to fret, she wrapped her arms around his chest and rested her head against his shoulder. Ben took even strokes with the steadiness of a trout swimming upstream. A few minutes later, they reached the shallow area where Ben could stand once again.

"See," he said, exhaling laboriously. "I told you . . . I'd . . . keep you safe."

Ben crawled up onshore and collapsed against the cold sand, his muscles throbbing. Grace flopped over beside him, her chest rising and falling in deep pants. He mustered a weak smile knowing they were safe. His conscience pricked him and he promptly closed his eyes. *Forgive me, Father. I didn't bring her safely across. You brought us both to safety. You rescued us from the hand of our enemy. You are my rock and fortress . . . I take refuge in You . . .* Peace washed over him.

He heard her teeth chattering and opened his eyes. Spasms wracked her body. He reached his arm around her waist and pulled her into an embrace. The chilly night air would have made him shake, too, if his muscles weren't refusing. But the longer she lay folded in his arms, warmth dispersed through his veins. He buried his nose in her hair and took in the mineral scent of the river. *You've been through so much,* mei *Gracie . . .*

Several minutes passed before her shivering stopped and she started to stir. Ben rose to his elbow, leaving his other arm still around her. "Next time we go swimming in the moonlight, I hope it's summer."

Her body went rigid.

He tipped her chin. "What's the matter?"

"Where's Jack?"

"He plowed into a boulder headfirst and the current swept him away."

She vaulted into a sitting position and faced him, pointing a shaky index finger. "Why did you bring us over here?" She immediately broke into a sob. "We'll just have to cross the river again."

He wrapped her in a tight hug, stroking her hair until she released her pent-up emotions. Crossing the river at night had obviously frightened her—and with reason. Before Jack jumped him, Ben had been reminding himself that Michigan didn't have alligators roaming the river.

Grace sniffled. "Why this side, Ben?"

"This side was closer, and quite frankly, I was tired. I didn't think we could make it to the other side." He paused, took a deep, calming breath, and exhaled slowly. "Let's get off this wet sand." He pushed off the ground and reached for her hand to help her up.

She lowered her head. "I'm sorry."

He tipped her chin with his thumb so that she would look him in the eye. "We'll find an easier place to cross *kumm* morning," he said, softening his voice to a whisper. Seeing the way her eyes glistened in the moonlight tugged at his heart. *Please don't cry.* Ben cocked his head sideways and grinned. "Are you doubting *mei* ability to swim again, or are you worried about being alone with me all *nacht*?"

"I know you can swim." A smile pulled at the corners of her mouth. "Should I be worried about being alone with you?"

"Uh-huh."

Her eyes widened. "What?"

He shrugged. "I assume you'll want to kiss me again. After all, I brought you safely across the river. And"—he paused for effect—"you did kiss me the last time I rescued you from Jack."

Her lips formed a tight, straight line. "I don't know what got into me."

"Me either, but I liked it." He turned his face and pointed to his cheek. "Right there will be fine."

"You, Ben Eicher," she said, poking her index finger into his chest and pressing deeper with each tap like she was sending her message via Morse code, "assumed wrong."

He grabbed her hand and pressed it firmly against his chest, then leaned toward her, his lips almost touching hers. The warmth from her shallow breaths teased his craving to steal a kiss. He jerked back, then chuckled nervously to diffuse the way she'd affected him. "Then I suppose you're safe." He turned. "But I don't know how you'll get across the river tomorrow," he said over his shoulder while taking a few steps away.

"Don't you dare leave me." She gathered her dress skirt and toddled toward him. "I kissed you," she said, "because . . ."

"Because I'm irresistible."

"*Nay.*" Her brows bent. "Because . . ."

His grinning only seemed to fluster her more.

"Oh, it doesn't matter. It was just a kiss." She walked ahead of him, kicking up sand with every step she took.

A glutton for more punishment, he pursued her. "That certainly wasn't *just* a kiss. If you remember, I had to remind you that I had a gun in *mei* hand."

Something between a hiccup and a gasp escaped her mouth.

"Admit it." He jutted his jaw, oozing with confidence and enjoying every second of watching her seethe. She glared at him, probably tallying the reasons why he irked her.

"Jack had kissed me," she blurted. "I wanted to somehow erase those ugly memories. I wanted his . . . scent off me and the taste of his cigarette . . . out of *mei* mouth." She blinked, batting tears off her lashes.

Ben ushered her into his arms. He stroked the back of her wet hair as she cried against his chest. Pressing Grace even tighter, he vowed that Jack would never touch her again, that is, if the man was even still alive. Ben wanted Jack dead, and that thought frightened him. *Love your enemies . . . Father, Your Word says that vengeance is Yours. Please forgive me.*

Grace lifted her head. "I hope you don't think badly of me for . . . kissing you."

He brushed his palm over her cheek. "I wish you would have told me at the time."

"Why?" Her eyes searched his.

"I would've put the gun down."

Her crooked smile was enough to overpower what reserve he'd managed to contain. He leaned closer, drawn by the vulnerability in her moonlit eyes. She didn't pull away nor did she stop her trembling lips from parting or her eyes from closing. He lowered his mouth fully over hers, kissing her deeply. If she was going to have memories of anyone, he wanted them to be of him. He lingered, savoring the softness of her lips. "*Mei* Gracie," he said, trailing kisses across her jaw to the lobe of her ear. He nibbled on her lobe until a soft moan escaped her lips, summoning him back to her mouth. This time, she met his kiss with matching passion. His control slipping, he melded completely with her, something he'd never done. A frightful shudder sounded the alarm in his conscience.

He broke from the kiss, faltering back a few steps, exhaling ragged breaths, and for the first time, he was at an utter loss for words. Sorry didn't seem right, but his conscience pulsated with a slew of reasons why he should be sorry—all of which regarded the hours left until daybreak, their lack of a chaperone, and the fact that she wasn't safe— not at the moment—not with him. *Lord, help me!*

"We probably should . . ." He stopped from adding, "*wait until we are married.*" *Where did that come from?* He scratched his bristled jaw. It must be the fatigue. "We have a few hours before it gets light," he said, refocusing his thoughts. "Let's find a tree to sit under. Maybe we can get some sleep." After she'd awakened every fiber in his body, he wasn't sure he could sleep. But the Lord knew he needed to.

"Okay," she muttered. Her eyes sorrowful and avoiding, she tilted her face to the sky and closed her eyes.

Please don't regret what we just shared. He gave her half a second, then cleared his throat. "Let's check out the trees over there." He traipsed through the meadow, his wet boots squishing water as he walked.

Her big, brown eyes—the vulnerable gaze she'd given him— flashed in his mind, unleashing a tidal wave of guilt that washed over him like acid. He should have controlled his craving. She wasn't the type of woman who gave anything away freely—not like Neva.

Ben glanced over his shoulder at Grace. Her limp more pronounced, she wasn't just lagging behind to avoid him. He stopped. "I'm sorry. I didn't even ask how your ankle was."

"I think the cold river water took away the swelling. It's fine," she said, offering a tenuous smile.

"I don't believe you." He scooped her up.

"Ben, I'm more than capable of walking," she said, her tone growing more agitated.

"Can you allow me the privilege of carrying you just once without complaining?"

She crossed her arms.

"You look rather cute when you pout."

The line between her eyes deepened and she let out a low growl that he fought silencing with a kiss. He stopped under a large oak and let her down, then sat down beside her, leaning his back against the tree.

She shifted in several positions.

"Do you want to find another tree with a smoother bark? There is probably a beech nearby."

"*Nay*, I'll be fine."

Clearly she wasn't fine; she wiggled miserably. Ben slipped his arm around her, moving his shoulder so she could rest her head against him.

"Do you think this is wise?" she asked while yawning.

"*Nett* at all." He smiled. "*Nau* close your eyes and go to sleep." *And dream of me.*

❧

If Grace yielded to her own sage advice, she would insist that Ben not hold her so close. But wet and shivering, she wilted into his arms, absorbing his warmth. When he pressed her closer into his cocoon, she didn't resist. She peered up at him, taking in his brawny jaw and the lips that ravaged hers so completely that they still pulsed.

Ben grinned. "Grace, aren't you tired?"

Heat climbed her neck and dispersed over her face. She shut her eyes.

He brushed strands of hair away from her face, threading his fingers through her hair and gently caressing her temple with the pad of his thumb. Within a short time, he'd lulled her into sleepiness. She was sure he'd called her Gracie—something only Philemon had called her—and she didn't know how she felt about that.

Chapter Thirty-One

The kiss Ben and Grace shared stole his breath, his heart, and his mind all at the same time. Now, as she slept in perfect peace, cozy in his arms and practically purring, he wrestled with notions of waking her just to kiss her again. Never had a woman affected him so completely, nor had someone awakened his conscience to this degree. He should pray. Ben squeezed his eyes closed. Except for before meals, he had never been one to pray much—especially like he had over the last several hours, but he couldn't deny the peace he felt when he had. As if this experience had confirmed that the true hope of salvation could only be found in Jesus. Ben trembled at the thought that God's grace had extended to him despite his lukewarm attitude toward fully embracing his faith, becoming baptized, even joining the church.

Ben gazed upward as the morning light filtered through the oak branches above them. Working on a fishing boat in Florida, he'd seen plenty of beautiful sunrises, but none as breathtaking as today. Golden rays of light illuminated Grace's face in an almost angelic glow. A heavenly reminder to keep his hands off her. But what harm could come from letting her sleep awhile longer so he could hold her?

Grace moaned softly, then without waking, she turned her face into the crutch of his arm and lifted her hand to his chest. His heart hammered with unrestrained force. As if she knew the effect she had on him, her lips curled into a smile. Then her eyes fluttered open. She blinked several times before steadying her gaze on him.

"*Gudder mariye*, Gracie." He lifted his hand to his chest and placed it over hers. "Sleep well?"

Her eyes widened and she jerked her hand out from under his. "How long have you been awake?"

He shrugged. "I heard you talking in your sleep." He shouldn't tease her so early in the morning, but he was fond of the rosy shade of pink her face was turning. "I hope those dreams were of me."

She shot up, lashes shuttering.

His arms empty, a chill settled over the place where she'd been. He chuckled nervously. "Don't you want to know what you said?"

"Yes—no! Never mind." She shook her head and took a few steps backward. "I don't want to know."

He stood and, kinked up after sitting so long, stretched his muscles. She turned her gaze away, but not before he saw the deep crimson hue her face had turned. She'd only mumbled a few words during the night, nothing that he could decipher, but oh, how he loved getting under her skin. "Oh, I think you would want to know what secrets you shared, Gracie." He grinned with inflated confidence and moved toward her.

A rosy shade of pink still colored her cheeks.

Hands covering her face, she spun around. "Why do you call me Gracie?"

He placed his hand on her shoulder and kept it there despite her flinch. "It's a term of endearment," he said, turning her to face him. His gaze drifted to her lips and the moment she licked them, he couldn't shift his focus. He cupped his hand over the back of her neck and brought her closer to him. "Don't you like it?"

Hearing her raspy breaths made fighting the urge to kiss her nearly impossible, but as he leaned closer, her words cut him off. "Do you call many women that?"

"*Nay*," he said. "The only other Grace I know is *mei mamm's* age."
He moved back into position.

His lips had barely brushed against hers when she pulled back.
"You know what I mean, Ben."

He dropped his hand to his side, then raised it to rub the back of
his neck.

"I thought so," she hissed. "You're *nett* adding me to the lot."

He'd wanted to be honest with her about his past, but her self-
righteousness ignited a fire he couldn't squelch. "Yes, I've flirted
with women—several. If you're waiting for someone pure like yourself . . . it's *nett* me."

She stiffened, stared at him blankly, then closed her eyes and
dropped her head in disgrace.

"Grace." Ben's mouth dried and he swallowed. "*Mei* feelings for
you are real . . ." Until this moment, he hadn't realized the fullness of
what he'd felt toward her, but he would never question his love for her
now. If she would have him. "Most of *mei* flirting with *maedels* has
been innocent." He shouldn't have said that. Her jaw tightened. "But
one person . . . Neva. *Mei* flirting was . . . misunderstood and, well,
she was drunk and . . . we ended up staying out all night on the beach."

Grace bristled. "Spare me the sordid details."

"Will you just hear me out before you cast me to the devil?"

Her eyes narrowed. "I'm *nett* God. I don't need to listen to your
confessions."

"And I bet you're stingy with forgiveness too." He nodded, fuel-
ing himself. "You're all balled up in self-righteousness. You've judged
me since the moment we met." Ben snorted. *A gentle answer turns away
wrath, but a harsh word stirs up anger.* Ben blew out a breath as the verse
from Proverbs spoke to his spirit. *Apologize.* Ben grimaced. "I'm sorry.
I shouldn't have said that."

"You shouldn't have said what? That you slept with someone, who
apparently you cast aside to come to Michigan—or what?"

A gentle answer turns away wrath . . . gentle answer. Gentle. "I shouldn't have called you self-righteous. And the time Neva and I stayed out all *nacht*, I was trying to sober her up."

Her glare never faltered.

Either she was stone deaf suddenly or she'd disregarded everything he'd said. The back of his neck prickled defensively. He should let it go . . . but he couldn't. "You're stingy with forgiveness."

She squared her shoulders and tipped her chin smugly.

Ben crossed his arms. "But you're *nett* stingy with your kisses." He smiled, wide and gloating.

❧

The air left Grace's lungs in a whoosh and she spun around as her eyes burned with tears. Ben was right, she hadn't been stingy. She'd even kissed him in her dream during the night, only in her dream, they were married. He probably knew that, too, because he teased her about talking in her sleep. Grace batted away the tears as they collected on her lashes. Once she moved to Ohio, things would return to normal.

She heard Ben approach from behind before he spoke.

"Gracie, please don't hate me."

"I don't," she said, avoiding his rueful gaze. "I just want to go home." She collected her hair, her fingers fumbling to braid it.

"Can we talk about——?"

"*Nay.*" She didn't need any more pleas of forgiveness and she didn't need more memories to infest her dreams. But what she did need was to contain this tangled mess of hair. A simple braid shouldn't be this difficult.

Ben sighed. He reached into his pocket and pulled out her prayer *kapp*.

Her hands froze. Had he had her prayer *kapp* all this time? Perhaps if he'd returned it earlier she wouldn't have been so forward. *I'm sorry, God. I shouldn't need to depend on a* kapp *to remind me to pray or to avoid temptation . . .*

"I found it when I was searching for you. I went half mad when I found it next to the river. *Jah*, I was really worried." He nodded as if amazed by the realization.

"Only half mad? Why doesn't that surprise me? Is the other half of your worry still in Florida with . . . Neva, was it?"

He furrowed his brow. "Are you going to criticize everything I say from *nau* on? I went *completely* mad—I even prayed for a miracle." He mumbled something under his breath, turned a sharp circle, and came at her with fire in his eyes. "You know," he said, pointing his index finger close to her nose, "had God *nett* answered *mei* prayer—I wouldn't have found you." He inched closer to her still. "Or maybe I would've arrived too late. Maybe Jack would've done more than kiss you. Would you have asked me to erase those memories as well?"

Every fiber within her ignited. She narrowed her eyes.

He took a step back, lifting his hands in surrender. "All right, I shouldn't have said that."

"I hit Jack with the shovel, so you might not want to . . . to get me riled."

He grinned. "You're *nett* riled yet?"

Ben ignited more than her temper, but she wouldn't give him the satisfaction of knowing. She resumed braiding her hair. He would probably hold it over her forever that she had initiated a kiss. Thankfully, he didn't know what effect it'd had on her. Nothing so wrong had ever felt that right. *Lord, forgive me.*

The sound of branches snapping and dead leaves rustling underfoot startled Grace. Ben heard it too. He stood in front of her, spreading his arm out protectively.

Her breath stilled in her lungs. She peeked around Ben's shoulder as the figure emerged from the thicket, and then, recognizing

Philemon, she let her tension drain with a breathy exhale. Ben shot a glimpse at her over his shoulder, but kept his arm locked in place.

Philemon charged toward them. His clothes wet and clinging to his body, he appeared as weary as they did.

"It's okay." She gave Ben's shoulder a pat and stepped out from behind him.

"Gracie!" Philemon rushed to her, surprising her with a bear hug that lifted her off the ground and into his lumberman arms. She giggled as he whirled her around, then gently lowered her to the ground. He eyed her over, head to foot, as heat prickled to the surface of her face. A look of shock spread over his face and he lifted his hand to her cheek. "You're black-and-blue. What have they done to you?"

"I'm all right *nau*."

Ben approached, smiling buoyantly. "You must be one of Grace's *bruders*." He thrust his hand toward Philemon. "I'm Ben Eicher."

With Philemon's hand still capping her shoulder, he extended his other hand to Ben. "I'm Philemon Troyer. But I'm *nett* Gracie's *bruder*. We've been very close friends for . . ." He gazed at her with a gleam in his eyes. If she didn't know his plans to propose to Becky, her heart might have been fooled by the affection in his tone. Even so, it felt good to be missed.

Ben cleared his throat. "I think he's asking you, Grace."

"*Ach*." She exchanged smiles with Philemon. "Feels like . . . forever," she and Philemon said in unison, then laughed. She glanced at Ben. His smile had faded and his slightly narrowed eyes were aimed at her. "*Ach*, Philemon, this is Ben Eicher."

Ben's jaw twitched.

"Ah . . . I meant to say, Ben is from Florida."

"*Jah*, so I've heard. Bishop Yoder says you've been staying with them," Philemon said, adding, "I know I've been giving Gracie all the attention, but everyone has been worried about you, too, Ben."

Ben lowered his head sheepishly.

Philemon clapped his shoulder. "*Danki* for taking care of her. She's a very special woman."

Philemon had spoken highly of her and always with a hint of pride that fed her false belief that one day she would become his wife. Her thoughts adrift, she hadn't even noticed Philemon staring at Ben until she followed his line of sight and noticed her prayer *kapp* in Ben's hand. She stifled a short gasp.

"*Jah*, she is special." Ben handed her the prayer *kapp* without lifting his gaze.

Her stomach pitted with a heaviness she wasn't expecting as a mix of relief and regret fought to dominate her thoughts. She was anxious to get home and relieved that the nightmare had ended, but she regretted having ever kissed Ben.

Ben masked his somber mood with a smile when Philemon made the comment about how he and Grace must be starved. Ben's stomach stopped growling hours ago, but his physical hunger—the craving, which burned in his gut whenever he held Grace—could never be satisfied.

"Well, should we get started?" The lines that cornered Philemon's eyes softened as he looked to his side at Grace. "I know where there's a safe place to cross the river."

She offered a weak smile. "I'm afraid I gave Ben a fit when we crossed it last *nacht*." She glanced over her shoulder at Ben. "Isn't that right?"

"We were in a dogfight with Jack," he replied dryly.

Her nose scrunched as if she didn't like his snippy answer and she redirected her attention to Philemon. "It was awful. I thought I was going to drown. Jack held me under . . ." She wiped her eyes with her dress sleeve.

Philemon certainly had more willpower than Ben, not taking her into his arms at the first sign of a tear. It wasn't Ben's place now to console her. He'd done enough of that last night.

Philemon merely offered her a crumpled hankie, damp from the river. "The police found him washed up downstream."

"Dead?" Ben asked.

Philemon nodded. "*Jah.*"

Ben couldn't help but notice Grace's back stiffen. He would have expected some sort of elation, but when she glanced at him, all that showed was hooded despondence. She lifted the hankie to her nose and blew.

Another man met them on the trail. It didn't take long listening to the conversation to know that he was Mattie's husband, Andy. Grace introduced him once again as "Ben from Florida." Not as the man she'd passionately kissed—or who'd held her in his arms all night. Not even the man who had rescued her from Jack.

"Ben?" Grace lifted her brows. "Philemon asked what brought you to Michigan."

"*Mei* rebel tendency got me into trouble," he said, fixing his gaze on Grace. "I was on the first bus out of town."

She peered at him just as he expected—with disgust—then jutted her chin in that self-righteous snub and looked away. It would be easier if she despised him, he decided.

"Mattie's been worried sick about you," Andy said. "She told me how the man had threatened to take her first . . . I don't know that she would have been strong enough to . . ."

"God makes the weak strong." Grace cast a furtive glance at Ben.

Ben turned to Andy. "What about the fire? How far did it spread?"

"By the time we crossed the river, the millhouse was gone. The heavy downpour of rain kept the fire from spreading past the meadow. *Danki* God, *nay* homes were lost."

Ben nodded. "A miracle for sure," he said, remembering Erma saying they needed to pray for rain.

They reached the river and stopped. It didn't appear that much safer. *Don't look at her. Avoid her.* He stole a glance anyway. Hugging herself in a tight embrace, her face had turned as white as a capped ocean wave.

Philemon nudged her with his elbow. "Remember when your fishing waders filled with water?"

"Do you have to remind me of that *nau*?" She glowered. "You were so busy reeling in a fish upstream, you almost didn't see I was about to drown."

"Oh, I remember. I lost a *gut* pole that day." His eyes flickered with playfulness.

Andy laughed. "You two should get married."

Grace and Philemon exchanged a glance that soured Ben's stomach. He'd seen that same look between his sister and her intended just before the bishop announced their upcoming plans to wed.

"Well," Ben said, moving to the edge of the river. "I'll meet you on the other side." He plunged into the frigid water. Without Grace's arms wrapped around his neck, cutting off his breath, he didn't have any trouble paddling to the other side. He should have let the current carry him downstream so he could walk the remainder of the way alone. But concerned for her safety, his conscience wouldn't let him. Ben plopped down on the sand. Philemon seemed to have more experience than Ben carrying Grace across. Except for her dress hem, she didn't even get wet. She also never panicked as she had with Ben.

Red bounded out of the stand of cattails. The hound's muddy coat was the same as when Ben had seen him last. He jumped on Ben and lapped him with kisses. "Okay, okay, that's enough, Red." Ben pushed off the ground and swept what sand he could off his pants.

Philemon helped Grace reach the top of the embankment. She didn't need Ben's help anymore. Emptiness washed over him. He plugged along behind the others, eager to get back to the bishop's house and change into something dry. Then he remembered his duffel bag was at Grace's house and cringed.

Two more men who had been out searching greeted them. The older one had tears in his eyes when he touched Grace's bruised face, and the younger one, who Ben discovered was her older brother, Emery, appeared genuinely relieved to see Grace, but neither of her family members picked her up and whirled her around as Philemon had.

"I'm Reuben, Grace's father. You must be Ben." He pulled a hankie from his pocket and wiped his eyes with it. "*Danki* for saving *mei dochder.*"

"God kept us both safe in His hands," Ben said.

"He sure did, praise God!" Reuben turned to Grace. "You look exhausted, *dochder.* How are you holding up?"

"I'm better *nau.*"

"And your legs, have they given you more problems?"

She flicked a scowl toward Ben before turning back to her father with a pasted smile. "*Daed,*" she said, smiling at a few more members who walked up. She leaned closer and whispered, "Can I answer tomorrow? I haven't even had time to take *mei* shoes off yet."

"Fair enough." He turned to Ben. "How is *mei dochder?* Has she been in much pain?"

She crossed her arms and aimed her narrowed eyes at him.

Ben smiled. "Your *dochder* is too stubborn to admit anything's wrong. *Nett* to me anyway." His comment elicited an under-the-breath growl from Grace. Ben faced her. "Is that your stomach growling, Grace?"

"Ben," the bishop said, weaving through the crowd. "I can't tell you how pleased I was to hear you had decided to stay." He glanced upward. "God has a way of supplying for us before we're even aware we have a need. I don't know what Grace's family would have done without you. By the time LeAnn reached our *haus,* the fire was encroaching and we were blocked in. I felt much better knowing you hadn't left town, but were there with Grace and Erma."

Ben smiled. "Apparently God had different plans for me because I had a ticket in *mei* hand." *And no reason to stay.*

"I know," the bishop said. He looked around at the men who had gathered after the search. "If I could have everyone's attention," he said. "Those of you who haven't met Ben Eicher, he's a young man from Florida and will be staying with us." Several of the men nodded and welcomed him to Badger Creek, including Toby's uncle, Alvin. Ben spied Grace whispering something to her father, then followed her with his eyes as she walked toward LeAnn and Erma, who were rushing to greet her with open arms.

The bishop continued. "*Nau*, I think we should let him rest. We can visit with him after service on Sunday." He turned to Ben. "I know we had service last week; however, we always gather the first week the men are home regardless. And this year we have much to give thanks for." He glanced at Reuben. "I'll be sure to inform the search team that Grace and Ben are home safe. I know the police were canvassing the area where they found the men."

The members dispersed, leaving Ben with Grace's father, brothers, and Philemon. Even the bishop bid them good-bye once he realized Ben had to go back to the Waglers' house to retrieve his duffel bag.

A gust of wind swept through the trees, sending a chill to Ben's bones. He couldn't keep his teeth from chattering. Philemon, purple-lipped and shivering, walked a little faster. Ben had spent enough time submerged in the river since his arrival that he almost felt at one with it. As they made their way to the house, the men talked mostly about trees that needed debarking and plots of land to be planted and timbered, and Ben thought about fishing. Only thoughts of Grace invaded his dreams of hooking a great northern catch. Her banter earlier with Philemon about her fishing waders filling with water and him losing a pole over it in the process might have been an interesting story, but watching their ease of interaction left an aching void in Ben.

"I heard this wasn't your first river crossing, Ben," Grace's brother Peter said. "*Mei fraa* said you caught a *kalt* when you tried to cross the time Mitch went missing."

"I don't think I've ever been that *kalt*, but Grace fixed me up with . . ." Seeing Reuben glance at his sons, then Philemon, Ben quickly added, "Mattie's herbal brew was exactly what I needed to get on *mei* feet again." He pointed to his boots. "Emery, I think these are yours. Grace let me borrow them, but I'll be sure to return them."

"You can keep them. I have another pair. We're all grateful you were here."

The others agreed.

Ben bowed his head. "I was glad to help. But the next time I fight that current, I'd like to have a fishing pole in *mei* hand."

The men smiled and nodded in agreement and the conversation shifted when Philemon said, "I caught some prize steelhead last summer."

"And your fish grow an inch every time you tell that story," Emery teased.

"You're just sore you haven't caught a legal-size trout in a decade." Philemon elbowed Ben. "I'll show you *mei* spot upstream. You'll catch one large enough to brag about back home. By the way, what do you do in Florida?"

"Landscaping mainly, and before that I worked for a commercial fishing boat."

Emery laughed. "A commercial fisherman, hmm . . . Philemon, you've met your match."

"Sorry to disappoint you, but I didn't have much opportunity to fish while I was on duty. I worked for a charter service and *mei* job was to help passengers bait their hooks, untangle lines, and reel in their catch."

Philemon chuckled. "So, you fished for them."

"*Jah*, I guess so." Ben smiled. "And most of them were tourists who only wanted to take home a photo of them standing next to the fish, *nett* the fish."

"That's crazy." Philemon motioned to another path branching off the one they were on. "It was nice meeting you, Ben. Anytime you want to go fishing, let me know." Philemon tapped Reuben's back. "About that matter I wanted to discuss with you, is tomorrow all right?"

Reuben nodded. "*Nau* that Grace is safely home, we have time tonight if you want to have a bowl of chili with us. We can talk after supper."

"*Nay*, it's been a long day for everyone. We can talk tomorrow."

It sounded as though Grace's *bu* wanted to ask for her hand in marriage. Ben silently rebuked the heaviness growing in his chest. Maybe Toby was right when he had accused Ben of wanting women he couldn't have.

Chapter Thirty-Two

Ben had fidgeted all night waiting for the sun to rise. Now that it had, he still couldn't get Grace's kiss out of his mind. He was out to the barn to do chores at dawn. He had fed and watered the livestock before the bishop entered the barn.

Bishop Yoder filled the milking bucket with sudsy water. "Couldn't sleep?"

Ben shook his head.

He dropped a rag into the bucket. "Anything in particular bothering you, *sohn*?"

"*Nay*." Nothing he could talk about with the bishop. He was already feeling bad about his involvement with Grace. He didn't need someone else telling him how wrong it was to kiss her.

Bishop Yoder set the bucket aside, then started filling another one.

"I'll get started on the milking." Ben reached for the handle and picked up the bucket. He carried it into the milking area where the cows were already fastened in the stalls and chewing on their cud. Ben doused his hands with sanitizer, then sat on the stool and washed the cow's udders. He leaned his forehead against the cow's side and began milking. Once he'd mastered the rhythmic technique, spraying milk into a galvanized pail sounded musical.

"It didn't take you long to become a farmer." Bishop Yoder entered the station next to Ben. "Any interest in becoming a lumberman?"

"Sure," he said, then quickly added, "Today?"

"*Nay, sohn,* the men still need to bring the cut logs across the river. They were in the process of transporting them when they noticed smoke from the watermill fire. Besides, you need time to relax. Monday will be soon enough to start working."

"Okay." Ben eased into a lulling cadence milking, his mind reliving the moment when Grace's kiss had sent him stumbling backward, tongue-tied and breathless. He'd never experienced anything like it. Women walked away from him dazed and touching their lips, not vice versa. It was just a kiss, nothing he wouldn't share with another woman. But that wasn't the truth. No other woman would bring his every fiber to a boil like she had.

"Do you have anything else you want me to do?" Ben asked after they had finished the milking. "I just remembered we left Reuben Wagler's rifle by the river last night. I should get it before it rains and return it to him."

"I'm glad you remembered. You run along. I'll put the cows out to pasture. Should I tell Mary you'll be home by supper?"

"I wouldn't miss it." Ben hurried out of the barn. The cloudless, blue sky didn't hold any immediate threat of rain, but he wanted a reason to see Grace.

∽

"You've got to help me convince *mei* father to let me go to Ohio, *Aenti.* I don't want to stay here any longer." Grace rubbed her leg. The strain on her muscles while on the run had taken a toll. She went to bed with her legs elevated and lathered with liniment, but the medicated ointment didn't bring down the swelling or stop them from throbbing.

Aenti stretched her hand across the table and patted Grace's arm. "Are your legs hurting more?"

"Enough so that I'm ready to see a specialist. If there's a cure

275

available . . ." She closed her eyes. Muscular dystrophy was incurable. But leaving Badger Creek would cure her broken heart. She would make sure of that.

Aenti Erma stirred a spoonful of honey into her tea. "You haven't said much about what happened when those men took you."

"I know. I was so tired when I got home, I just wanted to put those medicated rags on *mei* legs and go to bed." Grace touched her cheek. The swelling had gone down some and it didn't smart as it had at first.

"We should ask Mattie if she has anything for those bruises."

"It'll heal in time." Her heart, too, she hoped.

"Maybe so, but you should have stayed in bed longer today."

Grace smiled. Her aunt had coddled her since she was a child. Yesterday afternoon Grace had barely walked through the door and *Aenti* was fussing over her. *Aenti* shuttled her to the bathroom where she insisted Grace soak in a warm tub and wash her hair.

"Do I look that haggard?" she had asked jokingly. *Aenti* Erma shook her head, but Grace saw through that fib. Once she'd washed her face and removed the mud, *Aenti's* face turned pale.

Aenti gasped. "What did he do, hit you?"

Deadpanning her expression, Grace shook her head. "*Nay*, I think this happened when we were skipping rope."

"Grace Elizabeth Wagler, are you trying to give your ol' *aenti* an ulcer?"

"I'm sorry," she said. "I just want to forget about everything that happened." *Including how wonderful Ben's kiss made me feel.*

Footsteps interrupted Grace's memories.

LeAnn yawned as she entered the kitchen. "I didn't expect to see you up this early, Grace." She made her way to the cabinet next to the stove and removed a coffee cup.

Grace cleared her throat. "Ben told me about seeing you at the bus station."

LeAnn's face paled.

"What do you have to say for yourself—frolicking with an *Englischer?*"

LeAnn's back stiffened. "I'm old enough to make *mei* own decisions."

"Father will have something to say about that."

"And I'm sure his oldest daughter—his self-righteous mole—will tell him everything. Or have you changed since you spent the *nacht* in the woods alone with a man?"

Grace's jaw dropped.

"*Nett* so pure anymore?"

"That's enough!" *Aenti* Erma scowled at LeAnn. "Your father *will* have something to say about this behavior and about you carrying on with an outsider." She swiped the egg basket from the counter and thrust it at LeAnn. "Go pick the eggs, and when you finish with that, you can gather the dirty clothes for washing."

LeAnn took the basket and left the room.

Aenti blew out a breath. "That *maedel* is going to give your father many sleepless *nachts*, I'm afraid."

"And once he hears about the *Englischer*, he'll expect me to spy on her—to be his mole, as LeAnn put it. Oh, *Aenti*, he won't ever give me his blessing to go to Ohio."

"It wouldn't hurt if we make him his favorite meal," *Aenti* said. "Once his belly is full, I think we can convince him."

Grace nodded, but her mind reeled with LeAnn's accusations about her changing since being alone all night with Ben.

"I'll make peanut-butter cookies," *Aenti* said as someone knocked on the door. Her aunt toddled out of the kitchen, and a few moments later, Philemon asked if Grace's father was home.

❦

Ben couldn't remember leaving the gun this far downstream. He glanced up the grassy incline. This wasn't the place. The embankment had been sandy and much steeper. Ben smiled, recalling how Grace had slid into him and how they'd tumbled down to the shore as one. With her warm breath fanning his cheek, he hadn't wanted to let her go.

Focus, he scolded. Pining for a woman he could never have was more painful than having all four wisdom teeth pulled out with tongs. Overhead, an eagle glided down to the surface of the water and snatched a fish from the river. Ben walked along the edge of the water, amazed by the tranquility. He spotted a heron wading in a shallow section, its long neck making a backward *S*. The bird speared a fish with its long, sharp bill, then ingested it whole. As Ben approached, it let out a warning croak, then spread its wings and relocated farther downstream. He'd seen plenty of cranes on the fishing pier in Florida, panhandling scraps as the fish were cleaned on the dock, but watching them forage fish and frogs seemed different.

Ben almost missed the footprints in the sand where he and Grace entered the water. He located the gun where he had stashed it, then clamored up the river embankment and sat on the edge. As terrifying as the night had been, once they were safely across the river, he'd wished their time together wouldn't have to end. But it did. Why hadn't Grace told him she had a *bu*? Ben rubbed his jaw. It must be true that extreme stress allows you to detach from reality, see and hear things differently. He was certainly delusional when it came to her. She had a way of leaving him unbalanced after he kissed her, and those memories were real. Was she as haunted? He had to find out.

Ben pushed off the ground. He caught sight of something shiny in the grass and reached for the Mason jar filled with stones. Ben removed the five smooth stones, perfect for skipping across the water. He returned them to the jar. Gordon's treasure wasn't anything more than ordinary stones. Now a token of the time he'd spent with Grace.

Ben took the wooded path to Grace's house, and Erma answered the door. The moment he stepped inside, he smelled cookies baking.

Erma motioned to the gun. "Have you been hunting?"

"Oh *nay*. This is Reuben's gun. I wanted to . . ." His gaze roamed the sitting room.

"She's *nett* here."

Ben crinkled his brows. Was he that obvious?

"Grace went for a walk."

After everything she'd gone through yesterday, she was taking a walk? But before he opened his mouth to ask which direction she had gone, Erma cut him off.

"She won't be long." Erma led him into the kitchen. "Would you like a cup of *kaffi*?"

What he'd like was to find Grace so they could have a few minutes alone, but he replied, "Sure," and followed her like a golden retriever.

Erma served him a mug of coffee that looked as thick as mud, and even doctoring it with cream and sugar didn't mask the bitterness.

She peeked inside the oven, then removed the cookie sheet and placed it on a cooling rack. "You're just in time to sample the first batch."

"They smell great." His mouth watered, watching her place the cookies on a plate.

She set the dish on the table. "You might want to give them a minute to cool," she said with a chuckle as he reached for one. Erma pulled the chair out from under the table opposite him and sat. "So, tell me how you found Grace. I was worried sick about you two."

"Do you believe in miracles?"

"Of course I do."

"Just as it was getting dark, the entire sky lit up in color. It was a miracle."

Erma patted his hand. "That was the northern lights. I'm sure living in Florida you've never seen them. Although, in all *mei* years, I've never seen them so bright that they lit the sky like it was daylight."

"A miracle," he said, reaching for a cookie. "I prayed for the sun to stand still. I wouldn't have found Grace had God *nett* provided the light."

"That reminds me of the verse in Psalms, 'Your word is a lamp to my feet and a light to my path.'"

He took a bite of the soft, warm cookie and chewed it slowly. He had read that scripture many times—even prayed for God's Spirit to light his path spiritually—but he'd made so many mistakes in the past, he'd stumbled off the path. Maybe the biggest miracle was that God heard and answered his prayer. Although God would have done that for Grace, not necessarily for him. His sins went too deep.

"I'm worried about Grace," Erma said.

Ben pulled the cookie away from his mouth. "Why? Is she sick?"

"Something is . . . different. She's *nett* herself."

"She was traumatized. I'm sure in time . . ." In time what? She would forget what happened that night? He didn't want her to. *Narrisch* fool.

Erma picked up a cookie and inspected it. "How long were you and Grace together last *nacht*?"

Ben choked on his cookie and took a swig of his coffee.

The door opened and laughter flooded into the room. "We're back, *Aenti*. I smell your cookies." Grace rounded the corner of the kitchen, Philemon behind her.

Ben took another sip of coffee.

"*Ach*, I didn't know we had company," she said, then looked at Philemon. "Are you staying for *kaffi*?"

"If you're offering a cookie to go with it." He pulled out the chair at the head of the table and sat. "So, how are you doing, Ben? Are you as exhausted as Gracie?"

"Nope. I slept like a *boppli* last *nacht*." Ben eyed Grace at the stove. "Couldn't you sleep, Grace?" *Up all night, wondering why you never said anything to me about your* bu? No wonder she'd asked Ben why he'd called her Gracie. She should have told him about Philemon.

Coffee spilled over the rim of the mug, and she sucked in a gasp. She mopped up the spill with a rag, then brought it to the table and gave it to Philemon.

Ben waited until she sat before lifting his mug. "Can I get a refill?"

She motioned to the stove. "There's some left in the pot. Help yourself."

Erma started to stand, and Ben stopped her. "Let me." He pushed off the chair. "A minute ago she referred to me as company. If I pour *mei* own *kaffi*, does that make me like . . . a distant cousin?" A kissing cousin twice removed. He enjoyed watching Grace shift uneasily in her chair.

"You're family to me." Erma beamed.

He finished refilling his mug. "Would you like another cup, *Aenti*?"

"*Nay, danki.*"

Ben returned to his chair. "You two aren't cousins by chance, are you?"

"*Nay*, just friends," Philemon said, smiling at Grace.

Thwack! Ben rubbed his shin, twisting slightly in his seat to peek under the table. Grace tapped her shoe against the floor. He looked across the table at her and grinned.

Grace glared. "Doesn't the bishop have work for you today?"

"Ben brought your father's gun back," Erma interjected.

Grace's eyes widened. "You went and got it? *Danki.*"

He nodded. "There's a lot of wildlife down by the river. I've never seen an eagle close up before. He swooped down and snatched a fish right in front of me."

Grace stared pensively at her mug.

"I've seen a bear in the river before." Philemon took a long drink, emptying his mug. "I don't have anything to do today. Would you like to go fishing, Ben?"

"Sure." Ben looked at Grace. "Did you want to go with us?"

"*Nay.*"

"Then do you mind if I use your pole?"

Grace gathered her and Philemon's mugs from the table. "Make sure you put it back."

"I have to run home and grab *mei* tackle box and pole. I'll meet you at the river in a few minutes," Philemon said over his shoulder as he left the kitchen.

Ben crossed the kitchen to where Grace was running water in the sink. He leaned against the counter. "I found this down by the river," he said, lifting the Mason jar.

"That was Gordon's." She dried her hands on a dish towel. "May I?"

He handed her the jar.

"I haven't been able to stop thinking about Gordon. Do you think he's all right?"

Ben nodded. But he wasn't concerned about Gordon. Ben wanted to know if she had been thinking about him.

❧

The farther upstream Ben and Philemon went, the rockier the terrain became. Ben edged along the side of the river, his back against the slick slab of limestone as the footpath narrowed.

"*Nett* many people know about this spot," Philemon said.

"*Jah*, I think I know why." The six-foot drop onto boulders below would detract most. Ben studied his footing, grateful that Jack took Grace downstream and they were spared this trek in the middle of the night.

Philemon descended. Ben was anxious to get into the stream and drop his line, but he paced himself, moving cautiously in the awkward rubber waders. "I see why Grace doesn't fish with you anymore if this is where you brought her," Ben said, landing on the rocky shore.

"She was boiling mad at me that day." Philemon set the tackle box on the ground. "She has a temper."

"Don't doubt that." Ben unraveled several feet of line. He swiped his index finger along the side of his nose, then slipped the line between his thumb and index finger, using the oily residue to coat the line.

"Here's some beeswax." Philemon tossed the caked wax to Ben. "That pole hasn't been used in a while."

"Since her boots filled with water?"

Philemon nodded. "And she wasn't going to drown, as she likes to tell the story."

"Her fear of the water seemed real to me." Ben greased the line. *Very real,* he thought, remembering her death grip around his neck.

"When she was eight, a group of us were cooling off in the river one summer. Her foot got pinned between a rock and she panicked. I think she did come close to drowning that day." He cast his line. "She had gone fishing with me before, but after her waders filled with water, she refused." He motioned to the pole in Ben's hand. "She threatened to snap that rod in half." He pulled his line back and recast. "She put it in time-out instead and it hasn't been used since."

Ben entered the river. He brought the pole back, the pang in his shoulder muscle as he snapped the line forward reminding him of Grace. The line sailed across the water and floated on the surface. He wished he could cast his care for Grace so easily. *Cast all your care upon God, for He cares for you.*

"Yep, Gracie's a handful," Philemon said.

Ben retrieved his line and sent it sailing through the air again.

"You two seem to get along well." Philemon tugged on his line.

He must not have noticed when Grace kicked him under the table or the glare she'd given him. "I suppose people . . . bond easier in stressful situations."

"I've never seen her with her hair down. Well, other than when she was a young *maedel.*"

Beads of sweat collected at the back of Ben's neck, and he pulled his collarless shirt away from his skin. "I think her prayer *kapp* was ripped off her head. I found it by the river."

Philemon looked off his shoulder at Ben for a long moment. "That's what she told me too."

Ben released more line from the reel and moved farther into the water. He didn't think they would catch many fish midday, but he wasn't expecting to catch flack either. If Philemon had questions about last night, he should interrogate Grace.

After several minutes of silence, Philemon asked, "So, how long do you intend on staying in Michigan?"

"I haven't made any plans." Ben studied Philemon's profile. His jaw remained set, and if he wasn't pleased with Ben's answer, it didn't show.

"You don't have a *maedel* at home?"

"*Nay*."

"Have you been baptized?"

Ben hesitated. He wasn't sure where this line of questioning was going, and he wasn't sure how many more questions he would answer. He sighed. "*Nay*, I haven't made that decision."

Philemon looked at Ben with a scrutinizing gaze. "You're still on *rumschpringe*? I would have thought you were old enough to have made that decision already."

"Then why did you ask?"

Philemon shrugged. "Just curious."

The man was starting to sound as self-righteous as Grace. Ben tightened his grip on the pole. Those two deserved each other. "*Mei* character is flawed, if that's what you're curious about."

"We're all sinners."

The muscle in Ben's jaw twitched. "Some more than others."

"True. But nothing so great that God cannot forgive."

Philemon apparently never had a large laundry list to confess. Ben was so wretched, the dirt would be difficult to scrub off. He doubted baptism would cleanse him of the stench. He tugged his line, let it go slack, then tugged it again. He moved slowly, giving his full attention to the end of his line.

They continued casting and reeling in their lines, neither one catching a fish. Too much talking. Ben and Toby used to fish all day together and barely say a word to each other, and even then, it was a whisper.

"Well, I suppose we should start heading back," Philemon said. "I don't think we're going to catch anything."

"Doesn't look like it." Ben glanced at the sky. In another hour or two, the fish would be jumping for insects. If he were alone, he would stay. But he'd rather clean out the bishop's barn than go through another hour of Philemon's questioning. "I think I'll take the river back. Maybe fish along the way."

"Give me a minute to grab *mei* tackle box." Philemon waded through the water, a wake following his stride. He snatched the tackle box from the shore and made his way back to Ben. "I suppose you figured out there's about three unmarried women to each unmarried man."

"I met several of the men last *nacht* when we crossed the river, but I didn't count."

Philemon smiled. "There's a singing tomorrow evening. I'm sure you'll have a chance to meet everyone there."

"Sounds like fun." Ben headed downriver. Every so often he would spot a mottled green-and-brown brookie that would hover near the bottom of the river, but he didn't stop to fish. He'd promised the bishop he would be back for supper, and he didn't want to disappoint him by showing up late.

Ben had tossed in bed for hours. Finally, through with wrestling his thoughts, he climbed out of bed and slipped on his pants. Grace had some explaining to do and he wasn't waiting until morning.

He finished dressing and tiptoed out of the house, grabbing the pole leaning against the side of the house on his way. The moon shed enough light to stay on the path and it didn't take long to reach Grace's house. He collected a few pebbles from the driveway and lobbed them one at a time at her window. After pinging the plate glass several times, she opened the window. "Are you *narrisch?*" she whispered.

"Probably. *Kumm* out here."

"*Nay.* It's late."

He tossed the remaining stones in the air and caught them. "There's a whole driveway filled with pebbles to throw."

"You are *narrisch.*"

"*Kumm* out here. I want to talk to you."

She closed the window, disappeared from view, and a few moments later appeared on the porch. Grasping her cloak tight at the neck, she limped toward him. Without wearing shoes, her legs' unevenness was much more pronounced. "What's so important?"

"I couldn't sleep."

"Ben." She said his name with a hint of disgust. "You woke me up to tell me that?"

"I didn't think you were sleeping." He grinned. "I thought you were lying in bed thinking of me too."

She stiffened. "You were wrong. What did you really *kumm* here for?"

"I wanted to return your fishing pole." He motioned to the shed. "I put it away."

"Ben, go back to the bishop's. It's late and we have church in the morning."

"Why didn't you tell me about Philemon?"

"We're friends."

"He calls you Gracie."

"It's a term of endearment," she said smugly. "*Nau,* I'm going back into the *haus,* and I'm going to sleep. Like a *boppli.* I suggest you do that as well."

"Grace, we kissed. What are you going to tell Philemon?"

She narrowed her eyes. "Those kisses were a mistake. They shouldn't have happened."

"But they did. And *nau* you have me half crazy."

She grinned. "Only half?"

"Well, I can fix that right *nau*." He pulled her into his arms, tipped her slightly, and kissed her firmly on the lips. Even when she pressed her hands against his chest in resistance, he refused to yield. She was his the moment a soft moan escaped her mouth and the tension drained from her body. He broke from the kiss and stepped out of the embrace. Scratching his jaw, he smiled. "*Nau* you've got me totally out of *mei* mind."

"*Gut*," she hissed.

"Either you tell Philemon tomorrow or I will."

She glared, nostrils flaring and deep grooves separating her brows. Moonlight glistened in her watery eyes. She opened her mouth but only released a squeak before clamping her lips tight and sprinting to the house.

Ben tunneled his fingers through his hair. He'd heaped a shovelful of coals on himself, and now he had more sins to confess.

Chapter Thirty-Three

Ben had to work hard not to nod off during the three-hour church service. Seated on the opposite side of the room, Gracie's head bobbed, too, which garnered more than a few looks from Erma, seated beside her.

Bishop Yoder read a passage from First John. "'If we confess our sins, He is faithful and just to forgive us our sins and to cleanse us from all unrighteousness.'"

Ben glanced at Grace. She needed to hear this. The bishop repeated the verse, and this time the words sank deeper. Ben sat up straighter. Did the bishop know he'd snuck out last night? He was looking at Ben, only Ben didn't sense condemnation from the man as he had with his father over the years. He sensed love and compassion for the weak. The words of the verse rolled around in his mind. *Cleansed from all unrighteousness. All.* He bowed his head. *Is it true, God? I've done so many things wrong. I know I'm a disappointment to my father, but I also disappoint myself. I want to be the man of God that You created me to be. But I don't know how. Please forgive me. Make me whole. I want to walk from this day forward in fellowship with You.*

The service closed as Ben whispered, "Amen," to his own prayer. Numb and totally at peace with himself, he sat with his elbows resting on his knees and looking down at the plank floors in the bishop's sitting room. God had forgiven him. Now he needed to make amends with Grace. He'd stolen her kisses and tried to steal her heart.

The bishop asked for everyone's attention. "Before we dismiss for the fellowship meal, I wish to make an announcement. Philemon Troyer, would you join me?"

Ben's blood went cold.

"Philemon has asked for a young *maedel's* hand in marriage."

Ben craned his neck to get a better view of Grace, who was staring straight ahead and smiling wide.

"Becky Lapp, will you join us, please?" the bishop said.

The remainder of the bishop's announcement blurred into the background as Ben focused on Grace. Her smile never faltered. Not once. It looked genuine, too, not pasted on as Ben had seen her do before.

The congregation was standing, moving around the couple. Grace slipped through the crowd and dashed into the kitchen.

Ben stood. He made it a few steps, then the bishop caught his arm.

"I'd like to introduce you to the men."

"Uh . . ." Ben glanced at the kitchen. More women were meandering in that direction. He redirected his attention to the bishop. "Okay."

Ben shook hands with several men. He answered a few questions about the size of his district in Florida, but his thoughts were consumed with Grace.

"Ben's going to start working in the lumber mill tomorrow," the bishop said.

Grace's father stepped forward. "He and Grace are supposed to go to the police station in the morning and fill out a report. The police drove out to the *haus* yesterday, but Grace had gone grocery shopping, and I wasn't sure where Ben was."

"I went fishing." Ben's mind whirled. Having to give an account for everything that happened would be difficult for Grace to relive. "Did you tell Grace?"

"I plan to this evening."

"Ben could tell her at the singing tonight," Philemon said. "You're still planning to go, aren't you?"

"I, uh . . ." Ben turned to Bishop Yoder. "May I have a word with you outside? I have a few things to get off *mei* chest."

❧

"Grace, you look sapped. How are you handling Philemon and Becky's engagement announcement?" Mattie popped the seal on the lid to the jar of butter pickles.

"I'm at peace." Now if she could only find peace about Ben. After last night's kiss, her nerves had coiled tighter than a skein of wool.

Mattie frowned. "Are you sure you're okay?"

"I haven't slept *gut*. *Mei* muscles are weak."

"You have to give your legs time to heal. Once the swelling goes down—"

"It's *nett* just *mei* legs. It's *mei* arms, *mei* hands . . ." She fisted her hand and released it. Her fingers tingled, something new. "*Mei mamm* started out like this." Her throat tightened. "The *doktah* said *Mamm's* condition was triggered by stress."

Mattie's forehead crinkled, and she chewed the corner of her lip. "I'll make a tonic. Something that will calm your nerves."

If only one of Mattie's tea concoctions would work for Grace's ailment. As it was, Mattie had her soaking rags in liniment and sleeping with them wrapped around her legs. Several of the women entered the kitchen and clustered around the counter, preparing the dishes. Little Jonas broke from her sister-in-law's hand and ran to Grace.

"*Aenti*," he said, throwing his arms around her legs. "I *lieb* you. Did you see the fire?"

"I love you, too, Jonas. And *nay*, I didn't see the fire."

Susan came up beside them. "How are you? I meant to stop by

290

yesterday to see you, but your *bruder* and I had a long conversation about Mitch's punishment for starting the fire and time got away from me."

"I understand. Maybe soon we can have a big family supper." Grace wanted to spend time with everyone together before she and Erma left for Ohio.

"*Jah*, let's plan something before *Aenti* Erma leaves." Susan motioned to the door. "I have a three-bean dish in the buggy I need to get."

"I'll get it," Grace offered. Once Susan walked away, Grace tugged on Mattie's dress sleeve. "I want to tell you something in private," she said. "*Kumm* with me to get the dish."

❧

The bishop stopped next to the equipment shed and faced Ben. "What did you wish to speak with me about, *sohn*?"

"I, um . . . Is it true anyone can be cleansed from their sins?"

"*Jah*, that's the promise God gives us in First John. 'If we confess our sins, He is faithful and just to forgive us our sins and to cleanse us from all unrighteousness.'"

Ben nudged a stone with the toe of his boot. "I've heard that scripture before, but I've never . . . I never believed it applied to me. I've done so many things that have disappointed *mei* family. *Mei* father sent me up here."

"I know. He sent me a letter."

"Then you know how badly I've disappointed him. I couldn't face him. That's why I changed *mei* mind about going home."

Bishop Yoder clapped his shoulder. "Are you familiar with the parable of the prodigal *sohn*?"

Ben nodded.

"The father waits for his *sohn* to return because more than anything, he wants his *sohn* to have a change of heart . . . and turn from whatever it was that drove him away. The father in the story is God. He's waiting for you to *kumm* back to Him. He doesn't want you wandering in darkness. He wants you on the path He's chosen, the one where He has provided His light to lead the way."

"I want that, Bishop Yoder. I want to be cleansed from *mei* unrighteousness so that I can walk wherever God leads me."

"Have you prayed about baptism and joining the church?"

Ben nodded. "How soon can I?"

The bishop chuckled. "You need some instruction first." His voice grew serious. "Is there something else troubling you?"

Ben shrugged. "I was hoping I could be baptized today. I have this . . . heaviness, and . . . I don't want to carry it any longer."

"The moment you confess your sins to God, He washes you clean. Baptism and joining the church are your commitment to Him." He paused a moment. "I noticed the fishing pole you left against the *haus* was missing this morning. Does this heaviness you're feeling have something to do with seeing Grace Wagler last *nacht*?"

⚭

Grace hadn't reached the bottom porch step when Mattie said, "I'm all ears, spill. I want to hear all the gossip about him."

Grace shook her head. "It isn't about Ben. I'm going back to Ohio with *Aenti* Erma. I almost have *mei daed* convinced."

"Oh, I don't want to hear that news." Mattie waved her hand with disregard. "I want to hear about you and Ben. He stared at you during most of the service. The man's smitten."

"Ben Eicher is a flirt. He's smitten over everyone. Besides, I have to know if I have muscular dystrophy like *mei* mother. *Mei daed* has told me the weakness is from one leg having to overcompensate for the shortness of the other, but it's more. *Mei* arms, even *mei* hands are weak."

Mattie frowned. "Stay and try one of *mei* concoctions first, please."

Grace smiled. Her friend peddled herbs like the vagabonds in the last century peddled snake-oil remedies. "Those tea leaves you packed in the basket did awful things to me."

"*Ach!* I told you *nett* to drink it. Didn't you hear me? Oh, Grace, I'm surprised it didn't kill you."

"It probably would have if Ben hadn't made me vomit so many times. What was it?"

"Foxglove. Several of the women had asked for some of the seeds I had harvested last fall. The flowers are purple and trumpet-shaped. I thought you had asked for seeds too."

Grace shrugged. "I don't usually plant flowers."

"That's the plant that helps keep the deer out of *mei* garden."

Grace nodded. "I remember *nau*."

"I slipped them into the tea I'd given you for muscle relaxation before packing it in the basket. I thought it might help you get away. Oh, Grace, I would have never forgiven myself if something had happened to you."

"You're always trying to help and I appreciate it." She looped her arm with Mattie's and gave hers a pat. "It didn't hurt me," she said. "I thought I was seeing things. First a neon sky, which I realized were the northern lights, then a fox, then Ben. Ben was real. I might have been hallucinating about the fox."

"That is one of the side effects."

"Is viewing everything in slow motion one too? Even . . ." Her thoughts drifted to how mesmerizing Ben's kiss was and how it made her rise to her toes. Had that been real?

"Even what?" Mattie's brow quirked.

"Ben," she whispered. Then, as if slapped with a wet rag, her eyes widened and she looked around to see if anyone was within earshot. "Don't you repeat that."

"You haven't told me anything yet. But by the sound of your warning, there's a lot to tell."

"There you are," Andy said, stepping off the porch. He came up beside his wife and placed his hand on her back. "Did *mei fraa* share our *gut* news? We're going to have a *boppli*."

"I'm so happy for both of you," Grace said, admiring how over-joyed Andy was.

He turned to his wife. "Should you be outside without your cloak?"

"Probably *nett*. I'll be in shortly," Mattie said, then, looking beyond him, she smiled and nudged her husband. "You're right. We need to go inside."

Grace glanced sideways and noticed Ben walking toward her. She started to follow Mattie and Andy to the porch when Ben called her name.

He jogged over to her. "Will you take a walk with me?"

She had to safeguard her heart, and being alone with him wasn't the answer. She shook her head. "I'm needed inside to help with the meal."

"Can't you give me just a minute or two? I want to talk with you about something." He bowed his head sheepishly, then lifted his eyes and smiled.

She faced him. "I have a few things to say to you, Benjamin Eicher, but *nett* here."

"At the singing then?"

She hesitated. "Maybe I'll meet you there." She should feel guilty giving him false hope, but the prospect seemed to appease him.

"Can I walk you home afterward?"

"You shouldn't assume the talk will go well." She turned, but Ben shot in front of her.

"I'm sorry about last *nacht*."

She looked around the yard but didn't see anyone other than her nephew and a few of the other boys playing tag. She lowered her voice. "I told you, I don't want to talk here."

He nodded. "I'm sorry."

The intensity in his eyes unsettled her nerves. She headed up the porch steps, her heart racing ahead of her.

❧

Seated at the supper table, Grace flitted her attention from her father, as he took a bite of the warm peach cobbler, to *Aenti* Erma, who was supposed to bring up the topic of moving to Ohio—again. Grace had used the excuse of her legs hurting as the reason she didn't go to the singing, and with Emery having supper with his girlfriend's family and LeAnn at the singing, this was the perfect time to speak with him privately.

"Reuben," *Aenti* said, fiddling with the corner of her napkin. "You know how much I'd like Grace to *kumm* to Ohio and stay for a little while, *jah*?"

He nodded.

"Grace and I have discussed . . ."

He glanced at Grace, then tossed his fork on the plate, abandoning his half-eaten dessert. "You two have discussed what?"

"I want to go to Ohio," she blurted. "I want to find out what's wrong with me. If there's a chance to be normal—I want it."

"Grace," he said softly. "Please wait in the other room. Erma and I need to talk about a few things."

Grace stood. She glimpsed Erma's sullen expression and left the room, stopping on the other side of the wall to eavesdrop on their conversation.

"Erma," he started. "I appreciate everything you've done for *mei* family, but I'm asking you to stay out of this matter."

"She's twenty-two and she needs to know, Reuben."

"Why? God is in control and she needs to rely on Him."

A kitchen chair scraped against the wooden floor. Grace peeked around the corner as *Aenti* stood. "Have *you*, Reuben? I don't think you've accepted God's will about Eleanor or Grace either."

"Woman," he said harshly. "You don't know what you're talking about." Dishes rattled as he shoved away from the table. He met Erma at the sink. "Things changed after Eleanor found out . . . Learning the disease was incurable, she became depressed." His voice quivered. "I don't want that for Grace."

"I know. But, Reuben, you cannot protect her forever. Her life has stalled because she doesn't know."

His expression turned pained, and he rubbed his forehead.

"Your life has stalled, too, since Eleanor passed away."

He nodded. "I've tried to move forward . . . It's difficult."

Barely able to hear, Grace inched closer into the entry.

Her father placed his hand on *Aenti's* cheek. "You mean a lot to me, Erma."

"But you've avoided me since . . ."

"I know." He dropped his hand and scratched the back of his neck. "I wasn't ready for . . . what I was feeling."

Standing at the kitchen entrance, Grace gasped, then slapped her hand over her mouth to smother the noise.

Daed looked her direction and tightened his mouth. He stormed over to Grace. "I told you to wait in the other room."

She dropped her hand, vaguely aware her mouth still hung open.

Her father pushed past her, grabbing his hat from the hook as he went to the door.

The door closed hard, jolting *Aenti*.

Grace stepped farther into the room. "I'm sorry I interrupted you two."

"You don't have to apologize." She added soap to the dishwater and waved her hand underwater to create bubbles. She plastered on a tight smile. "I'm sure once he thinks about it, he's going to give you his blessing to go back with me." She nodded. "He will."

"*Aenti*, do you feel the same way about him?" Hope surged within Grace.

"Your father and I go back a long ways, and long-standing friend-ships can be . . . mistaken for more." She scrubbed the plate with vigor, then handed it to Grace to rinse. "Did your father tell you that the police want you and Ben to give a statement tomorrow?"

"*Nay.*"

"Ben was going to tell you tonight at the singing."

"*Daed* made that arrangement?"

Erma cringed as she nodded. "Reuben also arranged for Philemon to take him fishing . . . to find out Ben's motives concerning you."

Heat clawed the back of Grace's neck. It was final. She was going to Ohio with or without her father's blessing.

❧

Grace punched her pillow and flipped to her other side. She closed her eyes as something pinged against the window. After hearing it again, she climbed out of bed and peeked out the window. Ben. She grabbed her robe from the back of the chair and sped outside barefoot.

"What are you doing here?"

"We were supposed to talk, remember?"

"I already know about having to give a report to the police."

He stepped closer. "Did you know about Philemon's engagement?"

She lowered her head and nodded.

"He means a lot to you, doesn't he?"

"*Jah.*"

"I'm sorry . . . Well, *nett* really," he said, pushing gravel into a pile with the tip of his boot.

She snorted. "At least you're honest."

"I thought Philemon asked to speak with your father to ask for your hand in marriage. I wasn't expecting the bishop to call another *maedel's* name."

She winced. "Philemon and *mei* father plan to harvest a field together . . . He came over the other day to speak with him about the crop."

"And when you two went for a walk?"

Grace recalled Philemon questioning her about Ben. After trying hard to change the subject, she finally admitted to having feelings for Ben. At the time, she had no idea her father had put Philemon up to probing her for answers. She would have diluted her feelings for Ben much more had she known. It didn't matter; she was leaving for Ohio and that was final.

Ben's voice softened. "He wanted to break the news before you heard it from the bishop."

"Philemon told me before he left for camp," she said. Then, seeing his eyes glimmer with pity, she stiffened her resolve. "You don't have to feel sorry for me. I'm going to Ohio with *mei aenti*."

He exhaled loudly, scratched his jaw, then moved his hand to the back of his neck. "When?"

"Soon."

"You're running away because he's getting married?"

"I'm *nett* running away." She was, but for other reasons. Letting go of Philemon wasn't as difficult as letting go of Ben.

"Then stay."

She shook her head. A cool breeze swept through the trees and she shivered. "I need to go back inside. If anyone sees me out here standing in a robe, I'd be mortified." She turned. "Good night, Ben."

Chapter Thirty-Four

Grace added a large spoonful of lard to the fry pan and chased it around, coating the pan as it melted. *Aenti* Erma handed Grace a plate of potatoes she'd diced to be fried. *Aenti* hadn't said much; Grace figured *Daed* was the reason.

Her father sat at the table sipping coffee and pretending to read the newspaper. He probably wished he hadn't finished the morning milking so early. Emery had risen early, made a roast beef sandwich out of last night's leftovers, and was out the door saying he wanted to get to the mill early. But everyone suspected it had more to do with Rachel Raber, whom he'd had supper with last evening.

LeAnn was the only one whose chatter erupted sporadically. But she often talked a lot when she was hiding something. No doubt her mood had something to do with the *Englischer* she was seeing.

Grace flipped the potatoes over in the pan. She hadn't heard anything but grease splattering, so catching a glimpse of Ben in her peripheral vision caught her by surprise.

"*Gudder mariye,*" he said, removing his hat as he entered the kitchen.

"Have a seat." *Daed* motioned to the chair. "Grace, will you get Ben a mug of *kaffi*, please?"

"Sure." She set the spatula on the counter and moved over to the cupboard to remove a mug as Erma slipped into her spot at the stove. Grace filled the mug and handed it to Ben.

"*Danki*," he said, looking at her only briefly.

"You're *welkom*." She walked back to the counter, picked up a bowl of eggs *Aenti* had already cracked, and began whisking them together.

"You didn't stay long last *nacht*, Ben," LeAnn said. "Where did you go?"

"I had a . . . stop to make."

"Mmm . . . ," her father said behind the paper.

Grace spied Ben from across the room. His leg bounced despite him rubbing his hand along his thigh.

Daed folded the newspaper and set it on the table. "Have you eaten breakfast, Ben?"

"*Jah*, I was up early." He glanced at Grace as he lifted the coffee mug to his mouth.

She half-expected him to say he slept like a baby or make a comment about the dark circles under her eyes.

LeAnn placed the biscuits and butter on the table along with the jar of honey. Grace came behind her with the fried potatoes and *Aenti* Erma with the dish of scrambled eggs. Grace took her place at the table, bowed her head, and silently blessed the food they were about to eat. She looked up to find Ben staring at her, a blank expression on his face.

"What does your father do in Florida?" *Daed* asked Ben.

"He's a shoe repairman."

The plank floor vibrated and *Daed's* brows creased. His gaze drifted to the floor on Ben's side of the table.

Ben slipped his hand under the table and the vibrations stopped.

"Is that what you did in Florida, repair shoes?"

"For a time."

Daed held his fork suspended in midair.

"I worked on a fishing boat, and more recently, as a landscaper."

Her father continued eating, and except for the sound of forks scraping the plates, the room was silent.

"What does your father think about you coming to Michigan?"

Ben shot a feeble glance at Grace. "He bought *mei* ticket."

Her father's lips twisted as they often did when he mulled something over. "How old are you?"

"Twenty-three." Ben lifted his mug, but he eyed his trembling hand and set it back down.

"Baptized?"

"*Nett* yet." He cleared his throat. "I've spoken with Bishop Yoder about making *mei* commitment."

Grace ate faster. Another time she might have enjoyed watching Ben squirm, but this sounded too much like *Daed* was interviewing him as a potential son-in-law, and that wasn't going to happen. She set her fork down. "I can't eat another bite. Are you ready to go into town, Ben?"

"*Jah*." He pushed his chair back and shot out of his seat.

"Sit down." *Daed* eyed Ben and motioned to the chair he'd just vacated. "Please."

Ben eased onto the seat and wiped his palms on his pant legs.

Grace looked at *Aenti* Erma, who shrugged slightly, then over to LeAnn, whose eyes were darting between Ben and *Daed*.

Daed's eyes hooded when he studied Ben. "Do you know how to drive a buggy?"

Ben shook his head.

"Grace," *Daed* said, turning his full attention to her. "Did you get enough sleep last *nacht* to feel comfortable driving into town? Or should I take you two?"

He'd never questioned her driving into town before. She nodded. "I feel fine."

"Okay, be careful."

She cleared her throat. "Can we go?"

He nodded.

She and Ben both scrambled to their feet.

"One more thing." *Daed's* words stopped them at the kitchen entrance.

"*Jah,*" she replied.

Daed turned in his chair, facing Ben. "If you want to see *mei dochder* in the middle of the *nacht,* you knock on the door."

"Yes, sir."

Grace's breath seized in the back of her throat.

"Better yet," her father said, standing face-to-face with Ben. "You want to court *mei dochder,* you come at a respectable hour."

"I will." Ben nodded.

Grace wanted to object, but this wasn't the time.

He eyed Grace. "Are you sure you don't want me to drive you two into town?"

"*Nay.*" That came out too fast.

LeAnn's snicker caught *Daed's* attention. He dismissed Grace and Ben, then turned to LeAnn. "I understand you have some things to tell me."

Grace grabbed her cloak from the wall hook as her father fired off questions about the company LeAnn had been keeping in town. Under different circumstances, Grace would have wanted to hear the conversation, but she knew when to leave. Besides, she didn't want to answer questions about being outside with Ben in the middle of the night. Her father probably saw them kiss too. She shot out the door, Ben on her heels. "See what you did, coming over in the middle of the *nacht?*" she snapped.

"*Jah!*" He chuckled. "I got your father's approval to court you."

All police stations, Ben decided, smelled the same. Old sweat, stale coffee, and an odd mix of some lingering air freshener that failed to mask any other scent in the place. His eyes scanned the room, past the patrons seated on the plastic chairs, to the gray-haired officer seated behind the thick wall of glass. He led Grace to the window with a sign dangling from a set of small chains, and swaying from the vent located above it, marked Information.

The uniformed officer looked over his reading glasses. "May I help you?"

Ben leaned down to speak into the metal vent opening. "Hi, I'm Ben Eicher and this is Grace Wagler. We're here to speak with Detective Kline."

"Have a seat and I'll let him know you're here."

Ben turned. One seat open, center row, and stationed between two men, one burly and the other in a questionable state of consciousness. "Let's stand by the pay phone," he whispered.

Grace nodded, and when they stopped, her shoulder touched his. "I've never been in a police station," she said under her breath.

"Just keep your eyes open and don't stare at anyone directly."

"You've been inside a police station before?"

He leaned closer. "*Nett* in the lobby."

Her eyes steadied on his. "What does that mean?"

"*Shh.*" He motioned to the opposite side of the room. "You might wake that drunk that's slumped over in the corner."

"Don't change the subject."

Their names were called over the loudspeaker. Ben reached for her elbow and he guided her back to the information window.

"Step through the door when it buzzes." The man pressed a red button and admitted them into a long hallway of glass offices.

A lanky man in a white shirt, black tie, and jeans came out from the second office. "Hi, I'm Detective Kline. Thanks for coming in." He motioned toward a small, windowless office, then directed them to take a seat in the two chairs positioned before a metal desk.

Grace sat board-straight. She swept the wrinkles from her dress, then wrung her hands.

Detective Kline picked up a legal pad and a pen. "This shouldn't take long. I need to get your account of the events." He glanced at the pad. "I've already spoken with an Erma Milner and a Mattie Diener." The detective recapped the information Erma had provided during the time she was alone with Gordon. Then Ben described the events from his and Grace's arrival to the point when Jack shoved him down the cellar steps.

The detective made notes of Ben's account, then looked at Grace. "Is that accurate to the best of your knowledge?"

"*Jah*," Grace said.

The detective asked Grace if she wanted to add anything, and when she didn't, Detective Kline asked her to continue from the point after Jack and Gordon had forced her to go with them.

She was strong until she reached the part where Jack held her underwater. Her voice trembled and she looked at Ben. "If Gordon hadn't stopped him, Jack would have killed me."

Ben reached for her hand, intertwining his fingers with hers. "Do you want me to finish?"

Grace nodded, wiping tears from her eyes.

"Jack came after us in the river. He and I fought and he tried to drown Grace. He hit a boulder and the current took him under. It was dark. I assumed he was swept downstream." He paused as the detective finished making his notes. "We heard Jack was found dead, but we haven't heard anything about Gordon. What's going to happen to him?"

"He has a list of charges that will put him behind bars for several years. You won't have to worry about him."

Ben glanced at Grace's downturned mouth, then turned to the detective. "What type of charges?"

"The list is extensive. Grand-theft auto, robbing a convenience store, assaulting the emergency-room nurse, and kidnapping Miss Wagler are enough to put him away for years."

"But what you said isn't all true." Grace leaned forward in her chair. "Jack attacked the nurse. I heard him and Gordon talking. It wasn't Gordon."

"Are you sure?"

"Positive."

The detective jotted down the information. "I'm making a note."

"Can I say something else?" Something came alive in her. Ben had seen it before when she was adamant about going back for Gordon.

"Yes, please."

"Gordon doesn't seem . . . well, he's simpleminded."

"Yes, I'm aware of that."

"I think Gordon was forced to go, the same as I was. Jack was cruel and bullied him. I know when Gordon was younger, he killed his parents, but I don't think he's the same person."

"His parents died in a fire. He didn't kill them."

"Wasn't he the one who set the fire?"

The detective shook his head. "Not according to his case file. The fire was caused by faulty wiring."

Grace sank into the chair. "Someone needs to tell him." She chewed the side of her lip. "I don't believe he stole a vehicle. He's *nett* even capable of driving. Will you make sure you note that also?"

"Yes, thank you, miss. Is there anything else you'd like to add?"

She shook her head.

Detective Kline stepped away from his desk. "If you think of anything else, please be sure to contact me." The detective handed them each one of his business cards and walked them to the door.

"Sir," Grace said. "Do you think it would be possible to visit Gordon? I have something to return of his."

"And what is that?"

"It's a jar of stones. I think they're important to him."

The detective shook his head. "Glass items and stones wouldn't be allowed. I'm sure after his sentencing you can arrange to visit him though."

Grace lowered her head and nodded. "Thank you." She walked out of the building in silence.

"I'm proud of you, Grace," Ben said after they were inside the buggy. "I think your testimony will help Gordon."

"I hope so. I'm glad it's over." She clicked her tongue and Jasper went forward.

Ben chuckled. "The detective's questions were less intimidating than your father's were this morning."

"I'm really sorry he put you on the spot."

"I think your *daed* likes me."

"But does he know you've been arrested before?"

Ben frowned. "Technically I wasn't arrested. *Nett* charged anyway." She eased onto the street. "What did you do?"

"Trespassing on private property. After working all day in the heat, I went swimming in a hotel pool . . . which happened to be closed for renovations."

She pulled back the reins and stopped Jasper at the stop sign, then waited for a car to pass through the intersection.

"The hotel owner dropped the charges," he said defensively. "But *mei daed* still held me accountable for being defiant, irresponsible, and disrespectful. The following day, I was on a bus heading up here and I don't think he's forgiven me yet."

"Weren't you going back home when Toby left?"

He shook his head. "I couldn't face *mei* father. I had planned on changing *mei* ticket for Indiana where *mei* sisters live, but found out— Will you find a place to pull over?"

"Ben, I don't think that's a *gut* idea."

"I just want to talk. Please, Grace?"

After what seemed like forever, she turned down a dirt road and stopped the buggy.

Give me the right words, please, Lord. Ben shifted on the bench so that he was facing her. He reached for her hand. "I'm *nett* proud of *mei* past. I did get into trouble with the law and I'm a huge disappointment to *mei* father. I've gotten drunk before and maybe keeping Neva out all *nacht* was wrong. But she seemed to need someone to talk to and I didn't want to take her home drunk." *Not that it mattered in the end once the accusations started flying.* "I told her I would marry her. I told her parents—*mei* parents . . ."

"Ben, you don't have to tell me this."

"*Jah*, I do. If you're going to judge me, I'd like you to know all the facts." He continued. "I had known her for years. Several of us hung out together, and we used to flirt with each other—harmless flirting. Then one day Neva and I were caught inside a shed during a hailstorm . . . I stole a kiss and she slapped me."

Grace mumbled something under her breath.

"A week or two later, I was getting off the boat from work and she was on the dock with an opened bottle of tequila and talking nonsense about her life being ruined. I couldn't make heads or tails out of her rambling." He paused, putting the pieces together in his mind.

"Is that it?"

"*Nay.* We sat on the beach under the dock. She was upset and drinking hard and I was upset with *mei* father who wanted me to quit *mei* job on the boat and go to work for him repairing shoes . . . It didn't take too many more shots of tequila for her to . . ."

"Succumb to your advances."

He huffed and shook his head. He would never win her respect. Just like he would never earn his father's respect. "She was drunk. I should have hog-tied her hands . . ." He glanced at Grace. Her lashes shuttered. She started to reach for the reins, but he caught her wrist. "To keep her from drinking and losing her . . ."

"Virginity?"

"*Nay*, she already—*nett* with me." This conversation was heading the wrong direction.

"Losing her . . . ?" Grace stiffened. "*Boppli?*"

He nodded. "Once I found out, I couldn't let her keep drinking."

Grace's stony gaze held his for a long, agonizing moment. "You said you proposed, so why aren't you married?"

"We woke up the next morning at high tide. There was a big meeting between her parents and mine and I agreed to marry her." He shrugged. "I quit *mei* job on the boat and went to work for *mei* father. A few weeks later, she was gone. Her parents refused to share her whereabouts and *mei* father treated me like I wasn't his *sohn*." He drew a deep breath and let it out slowly. "I waited almost a year to hear something from her—or about her. I still would have married her. She needed someone, and I foolishly thought if I settled down it would mend things between me and *mei* father."

"Why are you telling me all of this?"

"Because I've never loved anyone . . . but you."

"Ben." Her eyes glazed.

Say it. Say that you love me.

She grabbed the reins and as she reached for the buggy's brake lever, Ben stopped her. "Grace, you know there's something between us. It's real and you can't deny it."

"Ben, you just said you would still marry her."

His throat dried. "She's never contacted me. I found out the other day that she lives in Indiana and Toby has been writing letters to her. They were secretly courting at the time I kissed her."

Grace gasped.

"I didn't know." He exhaled. "Apparently, Toby accused her of having feelings for me . . . I didn't know any of this until the other day when Toby left some letters for me to read."

Grace's mouth fell slack.

"I'm ashamed of *mei* actions . . . I hope you can forgive—"

"Ben, it doesn't matter what I think."

"But it does. I love you."

She shook her head. "I'm moving to Ohio. *Mei* plans are already set."

He moved closer. "I prayed for a miracle and God answered *mei* prayer. The bright lights, the fox—all God."

"The fox was real? I thought I was hallucinating from that tea."

"It was real. And God sent him."

"Even so, it was a miracle for that moment. God led you to me for that purpose. Nothing more."

Ben scooted closer to her on the bench. "God brought us together, Grace, for more than just a *nacht*. I believe that in *mei* heart."

Grace peered at him with uncertainty, then she reached for the reins. "We should get back. Did you want to be dropped off at the lumber mill or at the bishop's?"

Ben sighed. "The lumber mill."

Without looking at him, she tapped the reins and the buggy lurched forward. They traveled in silence. Grace stared straight ahead, coaxing the horse to go faster, and Ben studied her solemn expression. Were his sins unforgivable in her eyes? An hour later, they reached the lumberyard. Grace stopped the buggy.

"I'm going to pray for another miracle," he said. "Promise me you'll pray also."

She fidgeted with the reins. "God doesn't always answer *mei* prayers."

"If you're referring to Philemon, I'm glad you didn't get the answer you wanted. Because you and I are meant to be together, and if you pray about it, God will reveal that to you." He waited a moment for her to speak, and when she didn't, he opened the buggy door.

"Ben?"

"*Jah.*"

"*Danki* for rescuing me and . . . holding *mei* hand at the police station. I'm grateful you were at *mei* side through all of this. I'm glad it's over."

It's nett *over, Gracie. I don't plan to ever leave your side.* Ben smiled. "Will you go for a walk with me tonight?"

She shook her head. "*Nett* tonight."

He lost his nerve to ask about tomorrow night. Instead, he touched the brim of his hat and climbed out of the buggy. Then, standing next to the barn, he watched her pull away with his heart.

Philemon walked up beside him. "I wondered when the slacker would get here." He nodded at Grace's buggy bouncing over the ruts in the road. "I should have known a *maedel* held you up."

Ben smiled. "Did you think I was fishing?"

"Well," Philemon said. "I did show you *mei* best spot on the river."

Ben reminded him they hadn't caught anything in his spot and the bantering continued as they headed into the sawmill.

❧

The moment Ben was outside of the buggy, Grace whispered, "I love you, too, Ben Eicher," then sobbed the entire ride home. *God brought us together, Grace, for more than just a* nacht. *I believe that in* mei *heart.* Ben's words stung. She, too, had allowed the time they'd shared to linger in her thoughts—take root in her heart—wanting to believe God had something more in store. But her sore muscles and stiff joints reminded her why that couldn't be possible. When Ben said he loved her, she had steeled her will not to respond. After everything he told her about Neva, how could he discard his past so easily?

She parked next to the lean-to and took a minute before climbing off the bench to wipe her eyes. She hitched in a ragged breath. Her lungs tightened as if the air were solid. More tears pricked her eyes. Her heart was in pieces—not broken from rejection, but just the opposite. Ben loved her and she him. But he had other obligations with Neva now that he knew where she lived. And Grace needed to move to Ohio.

Grace removed Jasper's harness and fed, watered, and curried the horse, removing his thick winter coat, a sure sign of spring. After putting up the tack, she lumbered to the house. When she walked into the kitchen, *Aenti* Erma, her father, and LeAnn were seated at the table.

"You may be excused, LeAnn," *Daed* said sternly.

LeAnn rose from the chair. Her face red and eyes puffy, she stared at Grace as she hurried out of the room.

"I'll give you two some time to talk." Grace turned. Her father wasn't in a pleasant mood, not after a long morning interrogating LeAnn. This wasn't a good time to bring up Ohio.

"Grace, sit down," *Daed* said.

She glanced at her *aenti*, but her expression held no clues. Grace sat next to *Aenti* Erma and folded her hands in her lap.

"How did it go at the police station?" he asked.

"The detective took our statements. He said Gordon wouldn't be a threat. He had other charges besides kidnapping."

"I'm glad Ben was with you and you didn't have to go through it alone. Erma tells me he's a nice young man."

Grace nodded. "He is."

His brows lifted. "And respectful of you?"

She lowered her head and nodded. His question probably stemmed from seeing them in the yard kissing last night. She didn't want to explain that. Ben held her rather firmly until she surrendered, but her father would be more curious as to why her hands went from pushing against his chest to going around his neck, encouraging his embrace. Her face heated at the memory of furrowing her fingers through his thick, golden locks. Ben had a way of putting a static charge on every fiber within her. Even just thinking of him made her arms pucker with bumps and the hairs stand on end.

"Erma and I have talked," he said, clearing his throat.

A shot of hope infused Grace's body.

"We've decided to send LeAnn back to Ohio with Erma."

"Oh . . ." Grace slumped in her chair.

"I know you want to find out about your condition." He rubbed the bridge of his nose. "I'm *nett* sure that's a *gut* idea. And I'm *nett* convinced you've thought it through."

She sank further into despair. Her throat swelled, preventing her from agreeing or disagreeing, and that was probably for the best. She would only be lying if she agreed. She had thought through the decision to see a specialist for several months.

"But Erma has practically become your mother since your *mamm* passed away, so . . . in this situation, I believe she should have a say in the family matters. After all, Erma is . . . part of our family."

Grace sat taller in the chair.

"She believes you're old enough to make your own decisions. I only ask that you pray for God's guidance and you accept His will."

"*Jah*, I will."

He sighed. "This *haus* is going to be lonely this summer with all you women gone." His gaze shot beyond Grace, and his eyes lit.

"Yes, well, we will . . ." *Aenti* Erma stammered. "We'll be sure to bake peanut-butter cookies before we leave and mail you care packages while we're away."

"I hope you send brownies too."

Grace pushed her chair away from the table and stood. "I think I'll just . . ." Neither one of them seemed aware she was leaving the room. Grace went outside for a breath of fresh air. She had so many things to do—to pack. It would take the better part of the week to catch up on her father and brother's dirty laundry and get the house in order. They hadn't had a chance to finish the spring-cleaning. She inspected the windows. The ones in the sitting room and kitchen were spotless, but the bedrooms still needed cleaning. She glanced at the ground outside her window and spotted the pebbles Ben had thrown. Grace squatted down and collected them. Rolling them over in her hand, she walked back into the kitchen. But finding *Aenti* in her father's arms, Grace halted in her steps. She spun around, but not before *Aenti* gasped.

"Did you need something?" her father asked.

Grace swiped Gordon's Mason jar off the counter. "I'm leaving."

"What do you have there?"

She turned around, a wide smile on her face. "Pebbles. Would you like some to throw at *Aenti's* window tonight?"

His eyes widened, but that wasn't as startling as seeing her father's face turn the shade of hot embers. "Grace Elizabeth." He pointed to the kitchen entrance. "Go."

She rushed out of the room and shot down the hallway. Once inside her bedroom, Grace opened the Mason jar and removed the river rocks. Gordon's words echoed in her mind. *I have a weak mind . . . but I have God's power, like David had against Goliath.* Grace turned the five stones over in her hand. Did they represent the same number of stones David had used?

Grace returned the stones to the jar, adding with them the pebbles from outside her window. God had used her infirmity to form a bond with Gordon in the woods, which was probably why Gordon had come to her rescue with Jack. Her thoughts sobered. For the first time since Grace had discovered she was different, she was thankful for her condition.

Was it wrong to want to be normal? Tears trickled down her cheek. Gordon had accepted the way God had made him—why was it so difficult for her?

Chapter Thirty-Five

Fishing passed the time, but the solitude in the river did nothing to diffuse Ben's thoughts of Grace. Every evening that week he had stopped by her house hoping she would go for a walk or sit on the swing with him, but she'd refused. If he wasn't so determined to capture her heart, he might have developed a complex, receiving so many rejections.

But tonight would be different once he presented her with his first catch of the season—a nice ten-inch steelhead at that. Ben trekked across her yard, fish in tow. His waders left wet footprints on the porch steps and a puddle next to her doorstep as he waited for someone to answer his knock.

"Ben?" Grace's forehead puckered either with surprise or at his fishy scent.

"I wanted you to have *mei* first catch. A token of appreciation for letting me use your pole."

"*Danki.*" She opened the screen door wide enough for her hand to pass through and reluctantly accepted the catch chain holding the lone fish.

"I've never tasted river trout before." *Please, invite me to supper.*

"We've already eaten. But I'll put it in the *icehaus* for another time. If you give me a minute, I'll be right back with your chain." The screen door snapped and she disappeared. A few minutes later, she handed him the empty chain.

"I'll walk to the *icehaus* with you," he said.

"That isn't necessary. I have to clean and wrap it yet. *Danki* again."

A sigh dragged out and he hung his head like a whipped dog. The woman was impossible. That fish was a prize catch she barely acknowledged. He plodded back to the bishop's place, removed his waders, and hung them on the hook inside the shed, then ambled toward the house. A lantern was aglow in the sitting room and Bishop Yoder looked up from reading the Bible as Ben entered.

"Did you catch many?"

"One. I gave it to Grace."

Bishop Yoder closed the Bible. "I used to pick flowers in *mei mamm's* garden to give to Mary." Bishop Yoder cracked a smile. "They smell better—and there's probably more of a chance you'd get invited inside if you didn't smell like a fish."

"I haven't seen any flowers in bloom."

"Soon."

Ben nodded. But *nett* soon enough.

"You received a letter today." Bishop Yoder reached over to the lamp stand, then handed Ben the envelope. "I also received a letter from your father."

Ben glanced at the handwriting on the envelope. His mother's. "I suppose *mei* father told you I'm a lousy *sohn* for *nett* writing. Worrying *mei mamm*."

"Him as well."

Ben snorted, then tried to cover it up with a cough.

"Would you like to talk about what's bothering you?"

Ben had already confessed to the indiscretions with Neva and the bishop had led him in prayer, asking for Jesus' forgiveness for his sins. "I don't feel like a new creature, as it says in the Bible."

"Perhaps you're harboring unforgiveness in your heart."

"If you're referring to *mei* father, it's him who can't forgive. I'm sure the letter he sent prior to *mei* arrival spelled it out. I'm his wayward offspring that's brought nothing but heartache and disappointment."

Bishop Yoder stood. He ambled over to the desk at the far side of the room, opened the top drawer, and removed an envelope. "I think you need to read this."

Ben noticed his father's handwriting the moment he removed the sheet of paper. He read the first paragraph and looked up. "He wants me to reach *mei* full potential—to become the man God called me to be?"

Bishop Yoder nodded.

Ben continued reading. Honest, loyal, kindhearted . . . the traits his father listed about him brought tears to Ben's eyes. "He's never told me any of this. I assumed his letter was about the things I've done that embarrassed and disappointed him."

"He loves you and wants you to be a God-fearing man who serves the Lord."

"I should tell him I've decided to be baptized and join the church. According to the letter, that has been his prayer."

Bishop Yoder patted him on the back. "He's given me his work number. If you'd like to call him, I'll be happy to take you to an *Englisch* friend's *haus* to use their phone."

"*Jah*, I would like that."

After saying good night, Ben retreated to his bedroom to read the letter from his mother. His thoughts drifted to Grace. When he called his *daed*, he'd ask him to send shoe-making supplies. Perhaps Ben would become a shoemaker after all.

Ben drove the wood planer down the side of the log. Debarking logs was strenuous, but even more taxing was wrestling with his feelings for Grace. He hadn't seen her all week, despite the nightly fish offerings he'd brought. His courting method was wrong, but the tulips, which Mrs. Yoder said were the first flowers of the season, hadn't bloomed. He glanced at the cedar shavings on the floor and remembered her dog beds.

Later that evening, Ben stood on Grace's porch with a bagful of cedar clippings in one hand and a large package of flayed brookies in the other. He quit fishing with Philemon early so he'd have time to clean the fish, wash up, and change his clothes. He hoped Grace would notice the effort. The door opened and Grace's father smiled.

"You certainly have a knack for catching fish," Reuben said, eyeing the package in Ben's hand.

"I'd rather catch your *dochder's* heart—" His thoughts slipped off his tongue, causing his face to flame.

Reuben smiled. "I know what you mean." He stepped outside. "I'll walk with you to the *icehaus*."

Ben's heart rate hiked. Did Reuben think Ben had pestered Grace too much?

"It seems Grace is determined to live with her *aenti* in Ohio." Reuben sighed. "I've delayed the trip as long as I could, but she's leaving on Thursday."

"In two days?" The air left Ben's lungs.

Reuben yanked the *icehaus* door open. "I'm afraid so. I don't like the idea either."

Ben tossed the brown-paper packages on the shelf next to the others. *God, please . . . I don't know what else I can do.*

"I'm *nett* sure what all she's told you about her . . . condition."

"Her limp? That's nothing a *gut* pair of shoes won't fix." Ben's *daed* was shipping supplies. "Can't you delay her another week? Just one more week?"

"It's *nett* about one leg being shorter than the other. Her mother died of complications from muscular dystrophy. Grace hasn't been diagnosed, but she shows all the same delayed motor functions and muscle fatigue as her *mamm* had at her age. She's determined to see a specialist."

"Can't she be cured in Michigan?"

Reuben's eyes swelled with tears. "There is *nay* cure."

"She never told me," he whispered.

"She watched her mother suffer, especially at the end. Eleanor spent the last few years of her life wheelchair-bound and spoon-fed."

Ben swallowed hard. "I'm sorry."

"I just thought you should know." Reuben swept his hand over his face. "I don't think delaying her trip will do any *gut*."

"Maybe *nett*. But I'm in love with your *dochder* and I've been pray-ing—feels like every waking minute—and I haven't lost faith that God will provide a miracle."

❧

Grace tossed a handful of clothes into the crate she planned to take to Ohio. Leaving her friends and family would prove more difficult than she expected. Even her nephew Jonas had cried when the entire fam-ily gathered for supper tonight. Grace had tried to reassure him she wouldn't be gone long, but the five-year-old had no concept of time. Now Grace was starting to believe it'd feel like forever. But she blamed Ben for those feelings. Not seeing him—even to reject his invitation to sit on the swing—would leave a hollow space in her heart.

Something pinged against the window. Grace strode across the room as Ben lobbed another pebble at the window. She hoisted up the window. "What are you doing? You know you're *nett* supposed to be here this late."

"We have to talk."

"Ben, it's late."

"I'm *nett* leaving." His voice rose to a pitch that woke Rusty, who started barking.

"You're going to wake everyone up."

He lifted his arms, then slapped his hands against the sides of his pants. "You don't like *mei* fish, maybe you'll like *mei* singing." He belted out a few out-of-tune notes of a song she'd never heard before, causing Rusty to howl.

She shut the window, rattling the pane glass, and stormed outside to quiet him. "What's gotten into you?"

"Don't you like *mei* song either? I made it up for you."

She figured it hadn't come from the *Ausbund* when he sang, "Woman, you've broken my heart." She crossed her arms. "It's lovely, and I'm sure everyone within the settlement has heard you."

Ben cuffed his hands on her upper arms and stepped closer. "Grace, don't go to Ohio. I love you. I want to marry you."

A lump formed in her throat. She forced herself to look away from his penetrating gaze.

"You love me too. Don't deny it," he said in a deep, husky whisper.

She tried to step back, but he tightened his hold. "You love me."

She shook her head. "I won't—I refuse to love you." Her resolve was faltering. "Ben, you said Neva was pregnant. Maybe you didn't know where she was sent, but you know *nau*. You need to honor your commitment to marry her. Take care of your *boppli*."

"Is that why you've been avoiding me? You-you think I'm the father?" He shifted his feet. "We've never." His face turned red as he shook his head. "We've never had that type of-of relations."

He muttered something under his breath about Toby being responsible, and the color drained from his face. He seemed mortified by the thought, something she admired.

Ben rubbed his jaw sheepishly. "Oh, wow. I must be the scum of the earth in your eyes."

"*Nett* quite," she said, toying playfully. "After all, you did rescue me and you kept your promise about getting me across the river safely."

A smile tugged at his lips. "*Gut*, because I promise to always love you and to treasure you. I'll be the best husband—"

"Ben." She lifted her hand.

His Adam's apple glided down his neck as his eyes searched hers.

"I can't marry you." *Stand strong. This is the way it has to be.*

"I know about your condition. I know you might live your last days in a wheelchair. I want to share your *gut* days and your bad."

Her lungs tightened, stealing her air. She spun around, unable to bear his tender gaze. "You don't know what you're saying—you don't know what you would be sacrificing."

He circled in front of her. "Love is a sacrifice. But love also bears all things, believes all things, hopes in all things, endures all things. That's how God designed love. When one is weak, the other one will bear their burdens." He cupped her face and dragged his thumbs over her cheeks, wiping her tears. "Tomorrow doesn't matter as long as we're together. I promise never to leave your side. I love you, Gracie. I always will."

She batted tears off her lashes and her heart fluttered when he kissed them from her cheek.

"Please, marry me." His kisses traveled over her jaw, to her ear. "Say it." He kissed her earlobe. "You love me." His ragged breaths fanned her ears, stimulating every nerve in her body to respond.

"I love you," she whispered, betraying herself. Then she pulled away. "I love you enough to say *nay*." Before she lost her nerve, she ran to the house. Grace collapsed on the bed and buried her sobs in her pillow.

The following morning, Grace arose and dressed at dawn's first light. Not wanting to wake anyone, she grabbed the jar of rocks off her dresser and tiptoed to the door. Before she left for the bus station, she had something to do. She eased outside, making her way down the porch steps and over to her bedroom window. Bending down, she collected the pebbles Ben had thrown.

"What are you doing?"

Ben smiled when she jolted.

She clutched the jar of stones. "Wh-what are you doing here?"

"I slept on the porch." He rubbed his arms. "I could use a cup of *kaffi*. That is, if you've finished gathering your *keepsake* pebbles."

"These aren't . . ."

He removed the jar from her hand, inspected it, then handed it back to her. "You've already started a collection, I see. The ones I tossed the other *nacht*."

"I don't want a bunch of pebbles in *mei* flower bed."

He cocked his head sideways and smiled. "You're in love with me—you said so last *nacht*." If he had to kiss another confession out of her, he would.

"You're like the hound, Ben Eicher. One day Rusty showed up on the porch step, hungry and lost. I gave him some attention and he never left."

Ben's brows formed a straight line. "I'm just a poor, lost stray to you?" He moved closer, his eyes fixed on hers. "You showed me some attention and *nau* you think I'm going to hang out on your porch?"

"Where did you sleep last *nacht*?"

Her words cut to the core. His shoulders dropped and he hung his head. He'd spent the night praying he would be able to convince her to stay—and at the same time he prayed for God's will and the ability to accept her decision. His stomach knotted. How would he accept this? Technically he wasn't a stray any longer. He could go home. He and his father had patched things up. Maybe in time his heart would mend. Was this God's way of turning him into a prayer warrior? *God, You're going to have to see me through this.*

Ben straightened his shoulders. "Maybe it is time for me to go home."

Epilogue

Grace stepped onto the bus platform and drew in a deep lungful of crisp October air. She had missed Badger Creek more than she cared to admit. So did *Aenti* Erma, judging by the smile on her face when she stepped off the bus. *Aenti* held that same smile every time she received another letter from Grace's father.

Ben's letters stopped shortly after Grace arrived in Ohio. Maybe he'd heard about her test results and found another *maedel,* or maybe he went back to Florida. Either way, she was returning home for *Aenti's* and her father's sakes. *Daed* had mentioned wanting to spend time with Erma before he left for camp, and Grace wasn't about to spoil their reunion.

"It's so *gut* to be back, isn't it?" *Aenti* stretched her neck to gaze over the crowded platform.

"*Jah*, I'm excited to see Mattie's *boppli*." Her friend had sent a letter telling how baby Nathan had been born in the middle of the night and had taken her by surprise, arriving almost three weeks early. Grace smiled recalling Mattie's letter—"This new *mamm*," as she referred to herself, "was never more exhausted or thrilled to become a mother for the first time. I have two *buwes* to take care of *nau*." Mattie wrote that Andy hadn't completely recovered from his bout with German measles. "But I have everything I want, and I know you will, too, Grace."

322

Everything I want . . . Grace was happy for her friend, but she couldn't dislodge the niggle of jealousy that marriage and motherhood were something Grace would never experience. Even LeAnn had seemed to find her calling. Her sister had taken a teaching position in Ohio and had moved in with Erma's cousin. Grace had prayed her sister would find contentment with the Amish way, and it seemed moving to Ohio had given her sister a second chance.

The station worker opened the hatch to the baggage compartment on the side of the bus and began unloading the luggage onto the platform. Grace was suddenly excited about being home. She wanted to unpack the baby quilt she'd made for little Nathan and spend some time with Mattie right away. But even trying purposefully not to think of Ben, she did.

Her *daed's* voice boomed behind her as he greeted *Aenti* Erma. Grace glanced over her shoulder at the two of them exchanging smiles. Together, they strolled over to where Grace was waiting for their belongings.

"*Dochder*, I've missed you." He reached for Grace's hand and gave it a gentle squeeze. "How are you feeling?"

"Rested." After months of struggling to understand, and spending time praying and fasting, she had finally surrendered her life to the Lord. Once she allowed God's power to work through her weakness, she found peace and rest for her weary bones. His grace had been sufficient all along.

"Reuben, I think those are our boxes being unloaded *nau*." *Aenti* pointed to the stacked baggage and *Daed* went to retrieve their belongings. "He's concerned for you, Grace."

"I know. But I don't want to be constantly hovered over. That's *nay* life."

Her father picked up the boxes and paused next to her and *Aenti*. "I hope you don't mind, Grace. I've arranged for another ride home for you. I'd like to talk with Erma privately."

Grace stole a glance at Erma smiling ear to ear. "I think that's a *gut*—" Her concentration broke as Ben stepped into her peripheral vision. A shudder cascaded down her spine at simply seeing his smile.

"Hello, Grace."

Emotions she thought she'd buried suddenly sprang to life as a mixture of anticipation and trepidation flooded her soul. "Ben," she said, barely above a whisper. Disarmed by the depth of his stare, her mouth fell agape.

"It's *gut* to see you again."

"You . . . too." Why did her knees have to wobble? And why was she disappointed he didn't call her Gracie?

"Are you ready to go?"

She scanned the area for her father and aunt.

"They've already left." Ben placed his hand on her shoulder and turned her toward the exit. "You don't have to be nervous."

"I'm just . . ." *Trying not to fall apart.*

Ben smiled. "The first time we met, you were as nervous as a mouse cornered by a cat. You wouldn't look me in the eye then either."

She glanced his way only to redirect her eyes to the automated doors opening.

Once in the parking lot, Ben motioned to the buggy parked under the lamppost. "I learned to drive while you were gone."

"Jasper!" She hurried across the lot and threw her arms around the horse's neck.

Ben untied the reins from the post. "Even the horse gets a better greeting than me," he grumbled.

Grace withdrew her arms from around Jasper's neck. Still smiling, she climbed into the buggy, taking the driver's side.

Ben cocked his head sideways. "Slide over."

"Jasper's *mei*—"

"I've fed and watered this animal for the last six months, and he's been staying at the bishop's *haus* with me."

"Well, I'm back *nau*."

"Are you?"

She narrowed her eyes. "Ben Eicher, you can't steal *mei* horse."

He sat on the edge of the seat and nudged her over, then, taking the reins in his hands, clicked his tongue.

She crossed her arms. "I thought you didn't like horses."

"We've *kumm* to an understanding, and he no longer nips."

"Hmm . . ." She studied his profile. Oh, how she'd missed him.

"And you and I will *kumm* to an understanding too." He smiled, staring straight ahead. "That is, if you want to borrow *mei* horse."

"*Your* horse!"

"I need a horse to court *mei* girl."

The air caught in her throat as jealousy stormed her thoughts. "You've been courting women in *mei* buggy?"

Ben ignored her and continued to stare at the road ahead.

She sank against the seat.

"I hope you're *nett* going to sulk all day." He turned off the pavement and onto a dirt road.

"Where are we going? *Mei daed* is expecting me."

"He knows I don't plan to bring you straight home."

"Ben," she said firmly. "It's already late afternoon. I promised Mattie I would stop by as soon as I got back home."

"Well, you're *nett* back yet." He paused, then, with less edge in his tone, continued. "Can't I have a few minutes of your time?" He veered Jasper into a deserted roadside parking lot and stopped the buggy. "I missed you."

If he missed her, he wouldn't have said he was using her buggy to court his girl. "You wrote me three letters. Three. In six months."

"That was two more than I received." He slid closer on the bench. "You apologized for calling me a stray and gave me rubbish about being friends."

She focused on the wrinkles in her dress and pressed them flat with her hand. "Can't we be?"

"*Nay.*"

Her head shot up. "*Nay?*"

"We need to talk, Grace. A lot has changed in the last few months."

His sobered—almost humbled—demeanor took her by surprise. No longer the overly confident flirt, he wrung his hands as if he had more to say, but wasn't sure where to begin. Her mind whirled. Philemon had been the same way. When he first broke the news of his plans to marry Becky, Philemon had even started the conversation with how much things had changed. Her mouth dried and a lump like cotton quilt batting lodged in her throat.

"You've fallen in love with someone?" She steeled herself for his answer.

"*Jah.*"

A sharp gasp caught in her lungs and burned. Tears welled in her eyes and she turned to look out the side window. Only she couldn't see anything through blurred vision.

"I fell in love with Jesus," he said, a hint of nervousness in his voice. "I never really knew Him before and . . . while you were gone, I talked a lot with the bishop. I've been reading the Bible every day."

She cleared her throat. "That's *wunderbaar*, Ben." Her voice screeched as hot tears streamed down her cheeks.

"I'm getting baptized and joining the church on Sunday." His arm came around her shoulder and he turned her to face him. "Why are you crying?"

"I'm happy—"

He stole her words when he kissed her cheek. "Hmm . . . salty." He trailed feathering kisses along her jaw.

"Ben, I don't think—" *Oh, Lord, I can't breathe.*

His mouth captured hers with a light, airy kiss that lifted her off the bench and summoned her heart to flutter. "You're mine, Gracie." His voice rasped. Then, taking his kiss deeper with an even greater need for possession, he placed his hand on her lower back and pressed her closer. "I love you."

Grace pushed him back. "We can't be . . . doing this."

"Marry me."

She shook her head. "I can't."

His eyes bored into hers. "Why?"

"*Mei* tests came back positive. I have muscular dystrophy. I wouldn't make a *gut fraa*."

"Your *daed* wouldn't say that about your *mamm*."

"That's different."

He shook his head. "*Nay*, it isn't. I had a long talk with your *daed*. Your mother's condition didn't change his love for her."

Grace wiped her tears with her dress sleeve. "She didn't find out about her condition until after they were married. Had they known . . ."

"What are you saying?"

"Maybe they wouldn't have gotten married knowing what was ahead of them. She passed this disease to me without knowing . . . don't you see? *Nau* that I know, I wouldn't want to risk having children. Besides, I'll start to decline. You wouldn't want to spend your days—"

"Hold your thought." He jumped out of the buggy, removed a brown-paper bag from the back, then opened the door to her side of the buggy. "Okay, I'm listening," he said, reaching for her leg.

"How can I finish *mei* thought when you're unlacing *mei* shoes?"

He removed a pair of black leather shoes from the bag. "I made these for you."

Tears pricked her eyes as she turned the shoe over. He'd made the left heel higher than the right. "You're a shoemaker *nau*?"

"Fifth generation." He guided her foot into the comfortable shoe. "*Nau* you're ready for a journey. And I'm going to walk that path with you."

"Ben . . ." Words wouldn't come. She wiped her tears with the palms of her hands.

He climbed back into the buggy and slid across the bench. "Grace, I want to spend *mei* days with you." He drew her into his arms. "I know what I'm getting into and I *willingly* want to walk with you on the path where God leads us."

"Ben . . ."

"I'm sure, Grace."

He pulled her into a tighter hug. "Say that you'll marry me." Before she could answer, he kissed her, stopping only to whisper, "I love you." Then, with a growing intensity that left her breathless, he deepened his kiss. "Do you have an answer for me?" She hadn't even caught her breath before he took her mouth once more.

"Yes," she rasped.

"Yes?"

She nodded. "I love you, Ben Eicher. I'll marry you."

"I love you, too, Gracie." He gave a quick peck on the cheek. "*Nau*, let's go fishing." He motioned to the back of the buggy. "I brought the poles."

"Fishing? It's going to be dark soon." But despite her protest, he was already unloading the poles and tackle. She followed him along the pine-needle path that ended at the river.

"I'll be leaving with the men for camp in a few months. We need to get some fishing in while we can." He clasped her hand and intertwined his fingers with hers. "I plan to marry you the minute we get back, so don't fall in love with any strays that show up on your porch while I'm gone."

Grace smiled. Last year, when the men left for camp, she'd been heartbroken by Philemon's engagement decision, and this year, she would count down the days with great expectation of becoming Mrs. Benjamin Eicher. They reached the water and sat along the riverbank.

Ben hooked a worm, then handed her the pole.

"Grasshoppers usually work better—"

He frowned. "Are you going to talk so much that you scare the fish?"

She squared her shoulders. "And if I do?"

"I have ways of quieting you." He baited his hook, tossed the line, then leaned toward her and kissed her. "That's one way."

"What other ways do you have?"

He waggled his brows. "You'll find that out as soon as you're Mrs. Eicher."

Her cheeks warmed. The end of her line tugged. "I think the fish like the sound of *mei* voice." She stood and reeled in her catch with Ben's help.

Ben tapped her shoulder and motioned with his head toward the path.

Grace spotted the fox and gasped.

"He won't hurt you," Ben said as the fox approached. "He led me to you that *nacht*."

The creature sniffed the bottom of her dress and Ben's pant legs, then slowly walked away. He stopped at the foot of the path and turned to look at them. A moment later, the fox disappeared.

"Ben." Grace's voice shook. "Do you think God sent him?"

"I know He did that *nacht* in the woods." Ben wrapped his arms around her waist. "If God can make Balaam's donkey talk and order ravens to feed Elijah, He can use a fox to perform a woodland miracle for us." Ben kissed Grace's forehead. "God is with us. And I believe He has many more miracles in store."

Discussion Questions

1. Ashamed of his past, Ben felt as if he would never regain his father's respect. Do you think those feelings contributed to his getting into trouble with the law?

2. Do you agree with Grace's thoughts about her nephew Mitch's faith being based on someone else's words? How much easier is it to believe in God's power when you've already experienced it in your own life? Once you experienced God's faithfulness, how did it change your faith?

3. Although it was a constant struggle for Grace to accept the increasing weakness of her limbs, how did she finally come to understand the meaning behind 2 Corinthians 12:9?

4. How did Grace's limp help form a bond between her and Gordon?

5. Gordon accepted his lot in life with seemingly more understanding than Grace. Do you think his childlike mental state played a role? If so, how was his acceptance different than Grace's?

6. In the Bible, God used a raven to bring the prophet Elijah food. What role did the fox play in helping Ben?

7. Gordon seemed to cling to earthly treasures, but what significance did the buried treasure have once it was found? What value did it have?

8. Wanting to protect his daughter, Grace's father didn't want her to

see a specialist about her muscle weakness. Was his apprehension of her moving to Ohio justified?

9. Ben lost his father's respect after keeping Neva out all night. He worked to earn his father's forgiveness but always felt as though he fell short. Do you think those feelings could have contributed to his doubts about God's ability to forgive so easily?

10. Grace was so self-conscience of her infirmity that she nearly missed out on finding love. What did Ben say love was (1 Corinthians 13:7)?

Acknowledgments

A simple thank-you isn't enough to truly acknowledge all the support, prayers, and encouragement I received while writing this book. My family is the best. Dan, you had the patience of a saint—even though I know you're not always listening to me ramble. Lexie, I'm so proud of you going to UF and still finding time to help me with my computer issues. Danny, I hope this book doesn't disappoint you. A bear does not eat the main character. But thank you for that brainstorming suggestion. Sarah, your sweet prayers have seen another book to completion. Thank you for always believing!

I'm truly blessed to have such supportive parents, Ella Roberts and Paul and Kathy Droste. You've all helped so much in promoting my books and I am so encouraged by your continuous love and support. I would also like to thank Joy and Gary Elwell for explaining the process of how to extract and boil sap in order to make maple syrup. Yours is by far the best I've tasted.

I'd like to thank my critique partners for their prayers and input. Having other authors to bounce questions off and to give honest feedback makes writing much more fun. Jennifer Uhlarik, G.E. Hamlin, Sarah Hamaker, Susanne Dietze, and Colleen Scott, we've critiqued each other's work for several years now and I treasure the friendships we've formed.

This book wouldn't be possible without the expertise of my agent,

Mary Sue Seymour, and the publishing team at HarperCollins. It means so much that Daisy Hutton, Vice President and Publisher, would take a chance on me. I'm still awestruck. I owe a huge amount of gratitude to my editors, Becky Philpott and Natalie Hanemann. I am so blessed to have your guiding knowledge. I adore working with both of you. Jodi Hughes, you do a wonderful job proofing and typesetting the pages. Thanks for making it easy to turn in my corrections. I don't want to forget Laura Dickerson and Katie Bond, whose wisdom for marketing is outstanding. I'm in awe of your promoting abilities.

I'd like to give a special thank-you to my Amish friend who has read all of my books to date. Your feedback is so valuable and I appreciate the time you've spent reading the ever-changing drafts.

To God be the glory above all! Lord, it's through Your power that I can finish a book, and I thank you and praise YOUR HOLY name! Let it always be about You.

About the Author

AUTHOR PHOTO BY LEXIE REID

Ruth Reid is a full-time pharmacist who lives in Florida with her husband and three children. When attending the Ferris State University College of Pharmacy in Big Rapids, Michigan, she lived on the outskirts of an Amish community and had several occasions to visit the Amish farms. Her interest grew into love as she saw the beauty in living a simple life.

Visit Ruth online at ruthreid.com
Facebook: Author Ruth Reid
Twitter: @authorruthreid

Don't miss Ruth Reid's brand-new series
full of sweet romance, thought-provoking
questions, and captivating mystery!

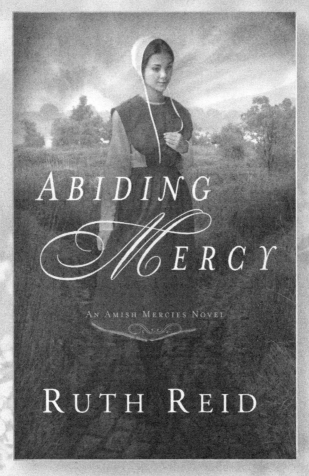

ABIDING
Mercy

AN AMISH MERCIES NOVEL

RUTH REID

AVAILABLE JULY 2017

THOMAS NELSON
Since 1798

"Ruth Reid is skillful in portraying the Amish way of life as well as weaving together miracles with the everyday."

—Beth Wiseman, bestselling author of the Daughters of the Promise series